Copyright © 2024 Clifton Brown

IN THE GHOST'S SHADOW
The Shadow Core Saga #1
by Clifton Brown

Copyright © Clifton Brown 2024

Design Layout: WSP

All rights reserved. This book or any portion thereof may not be reproduced or used in any manner whatsoever without the express written permission of the publisher except for the purpose of brief quotations in a book review.

First printing, 2024

ISBN:
Paperback: 978-81-972310-4-9
Digital: 978-81-972310-2-5

Published by:
Wicked Shadow Press
Wicked Shadow Press is an imprint of
Induswords Books 11/1, Khanpur Road,
Kolkata 700047
West Bengal, India

DEDICATION

First of all, I'd like to thank Jay Chakravarti and Parth Sarathi Chakraborty of Wicked Shadow Press for taking a chance on me and my debut novel, In The Ghost's Shadow.

Without them, this journey would have taken a considerably different track.

I want to give a huge thanks to my wife, Becky, for putting up with my late nights while I was on this novel journey—pun intended.

I must include one of my editors, Dibyasree Nandy, an accomplished author and poet. Thank you for your advice and insight as you perused my story, guiding me down the right path.

Now for the ones who set me on track to becoming a true author and not a simple writer. The ladies in my very first critique group raked me over the coals, and rightly so. They showed me the path to becoming, at the very least, a decent writer and how to continue to improve in the craft. E.M. Swift-Hook is a published author and wrote the dark space opera series, Fortunes' Fools, among many other works, and co-author of the Dai and Julia Mysteries. The other two women who helped guide my journey in the writing craft were Melanie and Kathryn.

Thank you for all of the hard lessons. I would not have made it this far without you.

Okay, everyone, you can stop snoring now. It's time to get on with it. Hopefully, my tale will keep you awake for much longer than you should be, especially if you, like me, have to work in the morning.

In the Ghost's Shadow lies the truth of its passing. In the Ghost's Shadow lies the path it has trod. Could the Ghost's Shadow hide the lie everlasting? Could the Ghost's Shadow hide the power of a god?

- FROM THE CHARRED REMAINS OF A JOURNAL FLINT REDSTONE RECOVERED WHILE ESCAPING FROM A SECRET LAB

CHAPTER 1: PROJECT

Tish despised him, and for some reason, Brick was all about her. He'd arrived on campus early for the slim chance of snagging a seat near her. Why was he still enamored with Tish when they'd never had so much as a thrilling conversation? Was it hope, habit, or obsession? Because the answer remained a mystery, Brick settled for the sophomoric rebuttal, 'just because.'

Regardless of how Tish treated him, she had been the first person in a long time to capture his heart. Perhaps he was a borderline masochist? Maybe he wanted someone unattainable, so they remained safe, unlike Fritz and Kaylen?

Two weeks ago, a rebel faction in Myanmar killed Fritz before Brick could reach him, despite his supernormal abilities. During winter break, his father ordered him to assist his ex-lover in taking down a rebel base and eliminating the leader. Exterminating the Russian general had been far too simple, but something troubling had occurred after that, which disturbed him even now.

When Brick engaged his powers, the energy was normally warm and full of light, and he remained calm and emotionless through the altercation. However, after Fritz's death, boundless wrath filled him, and he vented that rage on the general and his elite protectors. That energy had been cold, dark, and limitless as it fed on his emotions. Instead of dissipating after the battle, the wrath had invited or, perhaps, created a dark seed in his body, which had taken up residence behind his solar plexus.

It lay dormant for the time being. but during his trip back to the United States, he'd touched it with his mind and discovered an orb smaller than a needlepoint, possessing infinite power within. The energy's dark affinity initially concerned him, yet it emitted neither evil nor good, only a limitless reserve of power. So, like the other skill he'd hidden from his family, he kept it to himself.

An internet search yielded no results regarding the seed, but this did not surprise him. His predicament was unique. Hell, his mere existence defied belief, so why wouldn't he manifest an anomaly that also eluded explanation? It's too bad his birth didn't come with an instruction manual.

Perhaps he should give up on Tish before she became a victim of his family's vendetta. Like Fritz. Like Kaylen.

Brick stared at his reflection in the science hall doors' mirrored surfaces, his nose puffing wisps of steam as each breath failed to thaw the frigid winter air. He had no idea when he'd arrived at the door or how long he'd been staring at himself.

It was fortunate that he arrived early so that no one might witness his psychosis. Though, to be fair, other people's opinions had never mattered to him. It may improve his image as the wimpy, pacifist nerd-freak and possibly earn him the title of weirdo extraordinaire. It was a poor cover like Clark Kent's glasses, and the reason for their secrecy was almost nonexistent.

Hiding was pointless after Brick's family made their stand in Colorado Springs. Their enemies knew where they were, but they had not made a move in nearly four years. He hoped the nameless organization would show up since they owed him a bucket of blood for everything they'd done. Without thinking, he clenched his fists firmly enough to force blood from his palms.

Let them come, Brick thought. *Let them discover me, the culmination of their grand experiment, and I'll make them pay for what they've done to my family.*

Brick opened his eyes, having no recollection of closing them. The image peering back at him had just a passing similarity to what he considered normal. The fading traces of wrath had stiffened the medium-brown skin on his face and neck, and anguish had stolen the light once present in his dark brown eyes.

He wasn't handsome, but he wasn't hideous either. He was neither short, nor tall, at 188 centimeters, and he concealed his lean muscles beneath layers of oversized clothing to preserve his disguise, minus the Clark Kent glasses. For Brick, that would have been a bridge too far.

He closed his eyes again and sighed, trying to dispel his foul mood lest it awakened the dark seed. When he forced his fingers to wrap around the door handle, the cold hurt the bleeding crescents his fingernails had gouged into his palm.

Despite his feelings for Tish, he had to let her go. Of course, he'd never had her in the first place. Still, he needed to move on, but what would that do to him? Would he, like his father, retreat from the world? No. Mara wouldn't let him. She'd kick his ass if he tried. The thought brought a smile to his face. He'd be fine as long as he had his sister. Mara gave him the courage to walk through the doors and into his Combined Sciences 401 class to begin his final semester of college.

When Brick entered the amphitheater-like auditorium, Tish and her entourage of soul-sucking sycophants had already claimed their seats, building a near-impenetrable wall around her. He struggled to maintain his smile as she turned her head and said hello to him, but it did shrink to a reasonable replica of a smirk without the power of sarcasm to back it up.

Her followers swiveled their heads his way, as if they were a single entity, staring at him with the soulless, blank eyes of androids. At least, that's what he imagined. He sat towards the center of the room, four rows above and almost directly behind

Tish. The buffer of space and people should be sufficient to keep him from falling off the wagon during the first step of his version of the AA, the After-Tish Anonymous twelve-step program, assembly of one.

Tish rose and walked to the central aisle, then up the stairs. She stopped at the end of Brick's row and approached him. He was too stunned to do anything but stare as she perused him with her cinnamon-colored eyes. She gazed, not glared, and offered him a smile for good measure. Searching for malice, he couldn't find any. It was truly bizarre.

Except a memory sprang to mind. She'd been almost cordial during the final couple of weeks of the semester before winter break. Her eyes hadn't ridiculed him, and her words hadn't been tainted by disdain when she'd talked to him. He'd dismissed it as holiday spirit.

A 165-centimeter-tall gymnast stood before him, dressed in an alluring yet casual ensemble of dark blue distressed jeans and a basic, purple, form-fitting long-sleeved tee. Tish was a handsome woman. While her looks narrowly evaded classic beauty, her intelligence, charisma, and scathing wit set her apart from other women. Her thick, waist-length, wavy black hair and medium-brown skin tone represented a blend of her African and South Asian heritages.

"Too late again, Brick. I tried to make room, but the others rushed in and surrounded me. Sorry."

"You've never been sorry before. What's different now?" Brick regretted that he hadn't managed to exorcise the sarcasm from his tone. A few gasps from the peanut gallery floated upward, disturbing the silence.

Either Tish didn't catch it, or she chose to ignore his snark because she didn't react to it. "I wanted to speak to you before class. I was hoping you'd call me back before the semester started."

"Call you back?" Curiosity drove Brick's eyebrows toward the bridge of his nose. Her sycophants began murmuring among themselves. He filtered out their banter.

Tish cocked her head to the side. "Yah. I called and left messages."

Brick's eyebrow raised against his will. "Messages? Plural?"

"Yah."

Searching for irony in her reaction, Brick found none. He retrieved his phone from his book bag and examined it for the first time since returning from Myanmar. She had indeed called him several times and left messages. Then the internal whys and the hopes and desires followed, which he shoved to the side with great difficulty.

Brick restrained his emotions and responded, determined to stay the course. "Oh. Sorry about that, Tish. I was unreachable. I spent the holidays in the wilderness."

At the very least, it wasn't a lie. He despised lying and had advanced to grandmaster level in truth-stretching. Of course, the philosophy did not apply when he was on mission. Everything was on the table in the field.

Tish exposed more cuteness by raising her eyebrows. "Oh. No service?"

Brick struggled to maintain a flat tone. "Not even close."

"Didn't you check your messages when you got back?" Tish asked. She glanced at a student descending the stairs and nodded at him.

"No reason. You have to have friends and family to get messages, and the only ones I have live in the same house as I do." Brick glared at the guy who leered at Tish's rear end as he passed.

Despite his best efforts, Brick felt himself tumbling from the AA wagon. How did she manage to disarm him without even trying?

The earth must have begun tilting off its axis because her eyes expressed sympathy. "I had no idea. Sorry."

Brick's brain had a hard time accepting what his senses told him. *What in the hell is going on?*

"Not your problem. What can I do for you, Tish?"

She was like a bottle of vodka sitting before an alcoholic. Brick stopped himself. No. She was more like a fine vintage cognac or a well-aged single-malt scotch.

He pondered. *Did I just call her an old woman? Well, it's better than reducing her to outdated male stereotypes like eyes, lips, hair, and breasts. Isn't it? Maybe?*

"We don't have time to go into it right now, Brick, but please keep an open mind about me. Please? Yes, I've been a bitch to you, but if you give me a chance, I'd like to try and make up for it."

Though he squinted his eyes, inside his heart leaped. "I don't know."

What in the world is going on? Is she from Htrae, Superman's alternate reality Bizarro World? Is this some Bizarro-Tish I'm dealing with?

"Trust is difficult for both of us, Brick, but with time, perhaps we can find a way. What do you say?"

"I'll think about it, Tish. It's too abrupt, and I'm not sure I understand your motives."

Brick anticipated anger from his remark, but he found reason.

"I'd expect nothing less from the second-biggest brain in the school." The corner of her mouth tilted up.

She was joking with him. Tish was *joking* with *him*?"

"Gotta visit the Rink, Brick. Bye for now."

Now I know the script done flipped up in here. Or it hasn't, and she's trying to punk me.

As she made her way back to the steps, disaster struck. Tish began to fall. Perhaps her foot hooked one of the seat mounts. Brick wouldn't allow her to hurt herself, even if it meant revealing his abilities. He shifted into hyper mode. This boosted his senses and reaction time so much that Tish's plummet became an ultra-slow-motion cut scene, no music, though. He examined the entire classroom. No one was looking their way, so he took a chance.

From his perspective, Brick stood, strolled over to Tish, climbed over the seats until he was directly in front of her, fell to one knee, and positioned himself to catch her. The droids forming her shield rotated their heads, their mouths open and eyes wide.

Martial arts and gymnastics training had taught her how to fall, and she had already started twisting to make contact with her shoulder rather than face-planting or risking a broken arm to catch herself.

Despite her excellent physical condition, he didn't want to risk dislocating her shoulder by grasping her arm from behind. Disengaging hyper once he was in position, she fell into his waiting arms. as her startled squeal pierced his ears.

"What the hell?" Tish attracted the full attention of her group.

A light breeze ruffled her hair, but Brick didn't think she noticed. Even though his abilities violated the principles of physics, some components of science refused to be denied.

Smiling, he focused on Tish's face. "Are you all right? Seems as though the chair jumped out and tripped you."

"Wait. How did you? But you were... What the hell, Brick?"

"You made me think of the Rink, so I was behind you. I guess you didn't see me." Again, not a falsehood, but stretching the truth to its technical limit.

"But... But... Oh, forget it. Thank you, Brick. That would have been a bad fall."

Tish lay in his arms, her back resting on his knee. She looked up at him, wrapping her arms around his neck, smiling.

One side of her mouth curled upward. "Well, you could lift me up… or something."

With the last two words, her broad smile turned predatory yet seductive, destroying any residual thoughts of giving up on her.

Gasps echoed around the room from the twenty, or so students now populating the space. Brick struggled to remember exactly when they'd shown up. Had they witnessed his heroics? Was his cover blown now? He found he didn't care. Tish was in his arms.

"And if I choose the *or something*?"

"It could be wild and wonderful; I might draw blood or maybe both. You willing to take the risk, Brick?"

Now, this was more like his Tish, minus the claws. Her reaction was mild in comparison: stranger and curiouser.

Brick, the operative, would not hesitate and wear the consequences as badges of honor, but the nerd would not, so he stood up and helped her back to her feet.

Her smile vanished, replaced by an expression he couldn't place, but it appeared to be disappointment. There was no way to tell for sure because they seldom hung out. Despite being able to read strangers in the field in less than a minute, he had no idea how to read her. He'd either built up mental blinders when it came to the woman before him, or she had some serious mojo.

Tish's shoulders drooped. "That's too bad. I wish I knew what I would have done."

Brick's ears warmed and the flush ran down the back of his neck. "Wait. You didn't know?"

Having lost interest in them, the gallery's chatter lowered to a normal level.

"It would have depended on how good you were. Well, I'm off to the rink. Coming?"

Brick shook his head, wondering why she was so focused on him. "Nope, changed my mind." It couldn't be because he'd sav—.

Tish darted in and kissed him on the cheek before flying up the stairs, yelling over her shoulder, "Thanks again!"

As Brick swept his fingertips across the place of contact, he discovered a little moisture from her lips remained. Forcing the grin from his face, he dried his fingers on his jeans.

◆ ◆ ◆

Everyone dubbed the restrooms in the Phinegan T. Jarvis science hall, *The Rink*, when a group of kids, who had much too much time and creativity, executed a stunt three years ago. Earlier in the semester, they completed a fluid dynamics segment and a chemistry session on theoretical refrigerant formulas and decided to put theory into practice.

Someone who shall not be named spent a sleepless night testing a solution that came to him in a dream and solicited the assistance of two other genius students. They flooded the co-ed restrooms and sprayed the water with the freezing solution invented by the unknown student. In less than a minute, it froze into an almost undetectable, ultra-slippery barrier. Classes started around a half-hour later. After three hours and various hilarious mishaps, the ice dissolved into a swiftly dispersing cloud of steam, leaving a fine crystalline powder on the floor that easily washed down the drain.

No one ever discovered any evidence revealing the identity of the perpetrators, and nobody claimed responsibility. Campus security dropped the case because no students or faculty were seriously injured. So far, stories of the epic stunt have survived three years and may become an urban legend of the science building. At the very least, the unnamed one hoped so.

Brick sighed again as he sank back in his chair. Wasn't it his luck that just as he was about to let Tish go, she up and dumped a block of C4 in his lap and shoved a deadman's detonator into his hand?

Though deep in meditation about recent occurrences, he kept a subconscious awareness of his surroundings for his safety. While it had little effect on his stream of thought, Brick noticed when Tish returned, his classmates filled the room, and the professor, Dr. Sandra Brennan, called the class to order.

The same part of Brick acknowledged that the professor had announced the class project she'd revealed to him the night before. However, the majority of his intellect was still engaged in solving the puzzle of Tish's abrupt evolution.

After his senses noted an uncharacteristic reduction in sound within the classroom, he retreated from his cerebral meanderings and entered an aural vacuum where a pin drop would have sounded like a thunderclap. He brought the rest of his thoughts back into the world, only to discover that all the students in the classroom were staring at him... every single one of them.

Brick's nerves pinged like a Geiger counter as he scanned from left to right. "What? What did I do?"

Of course, the pout had to look so blasted adorable on Tish. "You completely ignored me, Mason Redstone. I chose you as my project partner, and you just sat there staring at the wall."

The silence was unsettling, like everyone held their breath, waiting for word from him to exhale. Brick was not used to, nor did he want that type of attention. Despite everything, there he was, the center of the enclosed universe of the classroom. The weight of their collective gaze weighed on him. Two pairs of eyes bored into him. One pair hovered over perfect lips smiling from the front of the classroom. The other beneath furrowed brows, from a few rows below.

Brick only addressed the closest pair as his emotions pulled up the right side of his mouth, just a little. "Why me, Tish? We're not friends."

Her brows relaxed. "Maybe not, but I believe we'd work well together."

"Seems like the last three years and more have told a different story."

A set of wrinkles formed over the bridge of Tish's nose. "You really want to go down this road right now?"

"You started it."

"In front of all these people, Brick?"

Everyone, including the still smiling Professor Brennan, followed the exchange with their eyes as if they watched a Ping Pong tournament. Several of them uttered verbal reactions to the jabs Tish and Brick traded.

Suppressing the dark seed that threatened to awaken, Brick allowed a little irritation to show. "They're just collateral damage. Let's get it all out… or you could back off."

If darts could fly from her eyes, they would at this moment. "If you had answered your damn phone, I wouldn't have to start anything."

Brick dragged his brows down to the bridge of his nose, stretched his lips thin across clenched teeth, and answered in a rumbling growl as he stood up slowly. "I was busy. I'm not one of your sycophants, so I'm not privy to your every whim, princess."

Tish leaped from her seat. "Don't call me princess, Brick." Tish spat his nickname as if it were a curse.

They exchanged stares across what appeared to be an unbridgeable chasm. When their argument reached its ultimate crescendo, the classroom fell deathly silent.

Why was he doing this? At any other time, he would have jumped for joy at the prospect of working with Tish. But it wasn't any other time, was it? Still, he should reserve his rage for those who deserved it. She didn't.

Brick reined in the anger; afraid it would fully awaken the dark seed. He relaxed the muscles in his face, offering a neutral expression. As reason returned, he wondered why Sandra, or rather, Professor Brennan, hadn't stopped them. One quick look and her familiar half-smile explained everything. She was enjoying their exchange.

Brick apologized, placing his hands together as if praying. "I'm sorry, Tish; I guess we both struck a nerve."

Softening her expression, she exhaled sharply, as if astonished at how long she'd held her breath. "I'm sorry too. Look, we've had our disagreements, mostly my fault, but I think we'd make a great team. Your skills complement mine, and we both need the extra credit to graduate summa. If we work together, I believe we can win."

The winning team of Professor Brennan's project would pass the class and receive extra credit for their overall grade for the semester. Additionally, if the judges determined the winner's presentation to be viable, the university would provide them with a research and development grant and a partial scholarship for a graduate degree. Brick would be a fool to decline Tish's offer. And she was right. Their skills did complement each other, and Brick would love to work with Tish in close quarters.

Oh, she's not done talking yet.

Brick cringed at that last thought since not too long ago, his Lit. professor had slapped him across the face with the metaphorical gauntlet over the difference between the words done and finish. Despite the situation, his voice echoed in Brick's mind, *"People finish while things are done. Remember that Brick."*

Filled with snark, Tish's next words spilled forth. "I figured you'd jump at the chance to be close to the woman you love."

Brick would have leaped to his feet if he hadn't already been standing. "Aw hell naw." His temper flared for the second time and his eyebrows returned to their position on the bridge of his nose.

Despite his clenched teeth, his response was crystal clear. "If we do this, and that's a big frigging if, you will NOT use my feelings against me. Is that understood?"

Tish stood there, jaws agape and eyes wide.

That must be her look of astonishment.

Brick searched faces and found similar expressions throughout the classroom as light banter tickled his ears and not in a good way. His actions were out of character. He didn't stand up for himself, and he didn't show emotion. Everyone called him the wimpy, pacifist nerd-freak, which was precisely how he wanted it. With a bit of luck, one anomalous episode wouldn't strip away his cloak of invisibility.

"Is that clear, Tish?"

"Um, yah, Brick. Sorry. I just... I mean..." Her next words were a near-whisper. "Is it true, Brick?"

He sighed. Perhaps they shouldn't have done this in front of everyone, but it's not like they didn't already know. He never had to face it in public because only a few people talked to him on the daily. Still, he never disputed it on those rare occasions when someone did.

"Depends on whether you believed my ex-bestie when she outed me, Tish."

Contrition was not something he expected from Tish, but

there it was. "Well, I'm asking you, and who better to ask than the source?"

The way she gazed at him after her query made Brick question everything he deemed indisputable. Tish wore another of those looks he couldn't place, but if he had to guess, it was somewhere between curiosity and what? Wonder? Concern? Interest? He closed his eyes and took a deep breath. "Why? Why do you need to know?"

Dead silence reigned in the classroom once again. Every student, and the Professor, remained focused on their every word.

"I don't *need* to, and I can't explain why, Brick. I'd just like to know... If you want to tell me, that is... It's fine if you don't."

Searching for malice in her eyes and body language, he found none. Tish remained a mystery to him. In the field, he had little trouble reading people. Hell, it was necessary for his success and survival. Did his feelings affect him that much? Maybe, making it, and her, a severe liability, but would he pass up a chance to work with the woman of his dreams? His heart told him no, and his subsequent words confirmed his rebellion against the family philosophy of the head before the heart.

Focusing on her face, Brick conveyed his answer. "Yes, it's true."

"Oh." Her expression softened into a half-smile. "I really hope you'll work with me on this project. Will you?"

After a moment's hesitation, Brick surrendered to his heart. "Sure. Why not?"

Tish's next transformation confirmed he'd made the right choice. Joy spilled from her every word. "I'm glad you'll be my partner. Or... or rather, that you'll partner with me, Brick. Thanks"

The room exploded with applause, and nearly everyone stood up cheering. A nearby student, Brick couldn't remember his name, clapped him on the back and congratulated him for finally standing up for himself. Others said their dialogue was better than the last play, and another was upset that they hadn't recorded the entire thing because it would have gone viral.

Professor Brennan chimed in once the uproar subsided, her Irish burr slightly thicker than usual. "Well, that was quite the show, you two. Let's hope your project will at least be half as stimulating as this little tiff we witnessed."

A few snickers rang around the classroom.

Brick began apologizing, but the Professor motioned him to stop. "No need to apologize, Mr. Redstone. Yours was a thoroughly enjoyable exchange... enjoyable and revealing."

She flashed him *that* smile. The one that fueled Brick's fantasies when Professor Brennan tutored him and what came after the lessons concluded.

Tish narrowed her eyes and flicked her gaze between him and the professor, but Sandra's following words broke the spell.

Professor Brennan waved her arms as if dismissing the two of them. "Because you two spoke up first, you may leave. I'll be seeing the both of you two Mondays from now."

Brick's jaw dropped, and Tish's mouth also hung open. The classroom exploded again, this time with catcalls, complaints, and a few congratulations tossed in. Hands immediately shot up, likely hoping that the next set of partners would get at least half the deal they had received. Professor Brennan prodded them to leave, so Brick grabbed his belongings and headed for the exit with Tish a step or two ahead of him.

CHAPTER 2: TISH

Part 1

Tish contemplated Brick's confession as she made the unusually long journey up the stairs to the classroom exit. It was one thing to suspect when his ex-bestie outed him and quite another for him to confirm it. When Katrina approached her about a month before winter break, she didn't want to believe it. How could a man she'd mistreated for three years still be in love with her? It made no sense. Or did it? Processing the whole thing would take some time.

Why do the front doors seem so far away? She wondered.

Strange emotions flooded her as she thought of Brick being in love with her. She'd never been in love, and no one had ever confessed their love to her, except for meaningless admissions made in the heat of passion. Her previous relationships had all been about prestige, power, and/or sex. Tish felt an emptiness inside her after seeing love from the periphery through her parents but never falling in love herself. Could she even feel love? Or was she broken?

Then there was Brick. An enigma. She'd only ever known him as the brilliant but wimpy pacifist nerd-freak. Her off-at-the-moment boyfriend and his posse frequently roughed up Brick for sport, but *that* Brick didn't match the one she'd seen in class. And he had confirmed his feelings for her. How did that make her feel? Had this happened a few months ago, Tish would have had a fit and sent Bran after him. Now, a part of her welcomed it, maybe even craved it. How would it be to interact with someone who was in love with her? She would very much like to find out and she would soon get her chance.

I guess processing it didn't take as long as I thought. At the very least, the front doors to the classroom stopped racing away from me.

Tish glanced behind her to see if Brick had followed. He was most likely staring at her butt. Guys said that was her second-best feature, after her legs. Though aware that she was no beauty queen, she was not unattractive, but lovely in a plain, girl-next-door way. Tish stayed in peak condition despite being on the hefty side because of a strict gymnastics and self-defense training regimen. Her father was a retired Force Recon Marine; thus, fitness was never optional for her. She'd loved flowing through the forms and despised the fighting at first, but after her father had to hire a martial arts master to instruct her after she had bested him multiple times, she'd grown to enjoy it.

Brick dismantled the wall of silence between them just as they entered a parking lot awash with a sea of vehicles. "So, where and when do we meet to start planning this whole thing?"

Despite the late morning hour, not much traffic passed on the nearby street.

She wondered why he asked such an obvious question. "Let's go to my house and start planning right now." Plumes of steam flowed from her lips and vanished in the cold, dry air of the Colorado winter.

His face scrunched up in the oddest way. He looked cute. "Your place? It'll take me two hours to get there by bus, and then I gotta find a way home. Why don't we set a time and place for tomorrow?"

"Brick, I'll drive us to my place and then drive you home, you goof. If we're gonna do this, we might as well get used to being around each other."

"You're okay if people see me ride with you?"

"Yah. Brick, I'm not the same person I used to be. Someone helped me find a new perspective on life before winter break. I've decided to take a different path from the one I've been on for the past three years. It's only been a short time, but I already feel better about myself and the new direction I've chosen. Let's jet."

Tish dashed across the vast parking lot toward her car, and Brick followed her as he had through the hallways. She reasoned that he was most likely following the sway of her hips. She wasn't sure how she felt about it, but it didn't creep her out for some reason. Neither of them spoke until they were near her car.

Brick's voice sounded wistful. "Gods, what a view."

Tish stiffened, and irritation crept into her voice. "Excuse me?"

When she looked at him, Brick was staring at Pikes Peak. "Yeah. We caught it at the right time. Have you been to Pikes Peak recently?"

"Oh. You meant the... I thought... " Tish shook her head and turned to face him.

"Thought what?" With eyes wide and round, Brick's brows rose at least an inch.

So, he was staring at my butt. Not a total geek, after all.

The thought occurred to her far too naturally.

Has my opinion of him changed so dramatically in such a short time?

Tish set it aside for later. She'd have to mull it over before she found an answer, and now wasn't the time. She spun away to face The Peak again.

"Ah, forget it. I went before the season ended last year..." Tish sighed, rapt in the beauty of the snow-crested mount. "I love this. The air is clear, there's hardly any wind, and the sun is at just the right angle. The mountains look so close."

Brick's voice relapsed into wistfulness. "That's what I call the lensing effect. You feel like you can reach out and touch The Peak."

"And Garden of the Gods, too." Tish tossed him a glance, one brow bouncing off her hairline. "Is that lensing thing a scientific term, math boy?"

"Nope. My very own creation."

"So, you do have an imagination." Tish used a bit of snark to lift one side of her mouth.

"It's kind of a prerequisite for most role-playing games, and stop smiling. It wasn't that funny."

"Yah it was. You smiled too."

When Tish approached the driver's side door of her electric vehicle, she turned, placed a hand on her right hip, bent her left knee, and stared at him, letting instinct rather than logic guide her actions.

Brick has bedroom eyes. Never noticed before. Huh. Never had the opportunity to see. He's no pretty boy, but he is cute.

Was that her thoughts or her emotions? And did Brick's feelings for her have anything to do with it? Tish wanted to know. She had to figure out whether or not it was a good thing.

A group of students passed them, heading toward a car in the nearby handicapped parking spot.

"We need to make a deal, Brick."

Her words snapped him out of his puppy-dog-eyed trance. "Deal? What kind of deal? What do you mean?"

"We need to be able to trust each other, and I know it will take time for you to trust me, but I also need to be able to trust you. We set some ground rules, okay?"

"Okay, I guess your half of the deal is not to use my feelings against me. So, what's my half?"

Tish took a pause before responding. Her palm gripped her chin, and her index finger pounded an arrhythmic beat on her cheek. "You can't objectify me."

"Define objectify."

"Seriously? Do I have to spell it out for you? I thought nerds were supposed to be smart?"

"Being a nerd means that I pretty much don't have a lot of experience with women, right? Besides, your concept of objectification may differ from mine, so clarity is essential."

"Yah, you're right. Let me think about it."

Still maintaining her pose, Tish raised her left hand to her mouth. One brow dipped towards the bridge of her nose, while the other arched high above it. She paused for a few seconds before responding.

A semi that was not supposed to be driving on that stretch of highway caused her to pause extra-long. She wanted to be sure her project partner heard every word.

"Okay. No brushing against me, no looking down my blouse, no innuendos of any kind, no offer to massage my shoulders or any other part of my body, and no staring at me with those damn puppy dog eyes you had a second ago. That sort of thing. Deal?"

Brick extended his hand to shake, struggling to keep a straight face. "Deal."

"Uh-uh. You know I seal serious deals with a kiss. Everybody knows."

Though he should be delighted at the prospect of kissing her, Brick's mouth had other ideas "Why would you want to kiss someone you hate?"

She couldn't stop the sigh from passing through her lips. "I'd hoped we were past this, Brick. I don't hate you. I just don't like the way you represent."

His face assumed a look that could only be called ponderous. "Not following."

The smell of diesel exhaust reached her but despite the discomfort, she persisted.

"You're a pacifist." Tish counted off the reasons with her fingers. "You run from trouble. You don't defend yourself or fight back. How can anyone expect you to stand up for them if you can't stand up for yourself?"

"I just stood up for myself in class against you a few minutes ago."

"Yah. Once in, how long?"

"Still happened. Look, just because I don't use violence at school doesn't make me a pacifist. Maybe I'm a different type of warrior, and just so you know, I do stand up for and protect those I care about whenever I can."

"Really? When?" Tish folded her arms across her chest.

"Many times, and before winter break, you were there when it happened."

A crew of goons led by Brantley, Tish's on-again/off-again boyfriend, had been trolling the Quad for a victim and had found one in a science geek. Tish had been sitting on a nearby bench, talking to a friend because she and Bran were having an off-again period. Brick happened to be crossing the Quad at the moment and noticed the goons single out one of his gaming buddies. He veered off course and 'accidentally' stumbled into Bran, who turned his attention to his all-time favorite punching bag. Brick gave his friend a nod, and the guy bolted.

"Wait. You did it on purpose? Why?"

"Because I knew I could handle whatever the thugs dished out, but the guy they bullied couldn't. Those guys can't hurt me. Hell, my sister punches harder than they do."

Despite the obvious question of why his sister would hit him,

Tish took a different tack. "Huh. I never would have guessed. So, how are you a warrior?"

"Caught that, did you?"

"I advise you to remember it, Brick. Go ahead."

More students flowed past them. A few of them waved, though none of them were part of her entourage.

"I know I'm paraphrasing Sun Tzu, but a successful warrior wins first, then goes to battle, whereas an unsuccessful warrior goes to battle first, then tries to win. I was the victorious warrior when I took my buddy's place."

"How?"

"My plan was to divert their attention away from my buddy. I succeeded in mine while they failed in theirs."

Tish repositioned her crossed arms to just beneath her bosom. "Which was?"

"To instill fear, pain, and panic. I took it away by becoming their target because I'm not afraid of them and they can't really hurt me. Sure, they get in a lucky shot every now and then, but nothing serious. Like I said, my sister hits harder."

"Huh. It just looked like you stumbled into him."

"That's the way it was supposed to look, Tish."

She wanted to lower her arms but regretted not wearing pants with pockets. Her jacket remained in her car which she started with her fob to warm it up. "Don't you care what other people think about you?"

"The only opinions that matter to me are those of my family and a few people I associate with. They're aware of who I am and what I stand for. Everyone else? Irrelevant."

Mixed emotions ran through her. "Doesn't my opinion matter to you?"

Brick shrugged his shoulders. "Why would it? Despite my feelings, we've had zero relationship till now."

A few more cars passed by on the road and in the parking lot.

"I... I didn't think about it that way."

Brick's matter-of-fact demeanor set her at ease. "No reason you should."

Still, Tish was taken aback at his lack of anger or bitterness. Why he bore no ill will towards her remained a puzzle, considering most guys in his position would.

"You're very different from what I imagined. You're way cooler than most of the guys I hang with."

The man exuded peace and acceptance. "Conversation creates more understanding than condemnation"

She joked with him again, feeling more at ease by the second. "Still a geek, though."

Brick tilted his nose up. "And proud of it."

Wondering from where the new feelings originated, she dreaded the answer to her next question. "So. Do we seal the deal or look for new partners?"

Brick's gaze filled Tish with feelings she didn't recognize, and none were hostile. She tried her hardest to keep them at bay but had less success than expected. *What is going on?*

"I vote for the deal, Tish. You?"

How did the power shift so abruptly? Tish had held all of the power up to that point. She and Brick now owned equal shares. Was it her choice, or had he stolen it from her somehow? Yet another thing to figure out when she had the time.

There was more to this man than what appeared on the surface, and she promised herself she would never underestimate him again. After Brick came a step closer, she answered in kind. One more step each and they would be close enough to seal the deal. Her heart pounded, and she noticed the artery in Brick's neck pulsating rapidly as well. Everything around her faded into a blur as the world receded, plunging them into a universe all their own.

Elated that he wanted to move forward, she made the final move, or, perhaps, the first one. "Yah. Let's seal it."

Brick lowered his face to hers but paused just before their lips met. She bridged the gap and slipped her arms around his neck, while his encircled her waist, drawing her close.

Tish's tongue teased his upper lip. Brick responded, offering her additional access, which she gladly accepted. She retained complete control over how far the kiss went, and Brick responded precisely how she wanted him to as if they were in sync. He tightened his arms to take up the slack as she crushed her body into his. The kiss lasted far longer than she had anticipated, and she wouldn't have cared if they had extended it a little more.

Before she ended the kiss, she wished they hadn't been in such a public place. What a turnabout. Hell, what a kiss! It made her feel a little breathless, flushed, and to be honest, turned on.

Brick never gave the impression of lust during their embrace. She'd sensed it from other partners and didn't enjoy it. That lust felt selfish and demeaning. Brick's aura emitted longing and desire. It felt nobler than lust. She'd never felt desired before, and while they stood there, foreheads pressed together, she basked in the unfamiliar yet delicious sensation.

As the world began to intrude, Brick broke the comforting silence. "I think that seals it for me. And how about you?"

"Yah, Brick. Our deal is sealed. I think. No, I *know* I can rely on you. I hope I made an impression that puts a dent in how you think of me."

"Well, I think our kiss made more than a dent. Pretty sure it bent the frickin' frame."

Tish grinned as she hesitated before pulling away from him. Despite temperatures in the twenties, she wasn't the least bit cold.

Part 2

As they drove away, Brick asked for a favor.

"I'd appreciate it if you could call Brantley and discuss the kiss with him. A few people noticed us, and you can bet it'll get back to him. I've already got a public beatdown coming for partnering with you, but I'd prefer to limit the chances for a second."

"Yah, sure, but me and Bran are on the outs right now, maybe for good. I'm not sure if it really matters."

His voice lilted upward. "Does he know that?"

"I don't know. He should." Tish wasn't as certain as she would like to be.

And Brick sealed it for her. "We are talking about Brantley."

"I'll send him a text."

"Thanks. Preciate' cha."

Traffic was light and they made good time despite hitting every other light.

Tish fired a strong opening shot as their conversation progressed. "That wasn't your first kiss, was it, Brick?"

If it was, and we kiss again under different circumstances, I might be in some real danger. She paused. *Or on the path to some serious pleasure.* The thought quirked her lips up.

He snorted. "No. I'm not a twenty-year-old virgin."

"I wouldn't know. What was your best kiss before this one?"

Brick remained silent. His brows descended, almost concealing his eyes. His entire body tried to collapse into itself, and he squeezed his lips together so tightly that they all but disappeared.

Wrong question. Think I struck a nerve, and a huge one at that.

"I don't want to talk about it." She hadn't expected her question would elicit such a clipped tone.

With an almost visible effort, he shook off the cloud that threatened to prolong his gloomy mood. Sitting up straight, he cast a glance in her direction. "Sorry. I thought I was over it, but it hit me like a ton of bricks, pardon the pun."

He shook his head. The gesture lay somewhere between a denial and a decision. "No, I'm not gonna talk about it. I've only told my ex-bestie the tale, and everyone in school knows how that turned out."

"Alright, Brick. I won't ask."

A short silence followed before Brick filled the gap. "So, what about the kiss? How does it help to earn your trust?"

Tish sighed and inhaled deeply. She had no idea why she was doing it, but despite everything, that was a pretty good kiss, and as a result, she trusted him. Why was this light taking so long to change?

"Remember how, at first, I teased you?"

At least he'd recovered from her question. His tone turned light and humorous. "Not something I'm likely to forget... Ever."

This made Tish smile. "Well, most guys, and girls, take it as permission to go all-in. They grab my boobs or my ass, or both, and begin cleaning my tonsils with their tongue. Total buzzkill."

"And you don't trust them because of the old give 'em an inch, and they'll take a mile thing?"

"Yah."

"So, what was different about the way I kissed?"

Maybe the street lights were getting to her. "Are we gonna play twenty questions, or will you let me finish?"

His contrition sounded sincere. "Sorry. My bad."

Yeah, it was the lights, not him. "Gah, you ask so many

questions."

"It is my nature."

Tish struggled to tamp down on the irritation. Brick wasn't to blame for the damnable lights. "You're not going into the whole scorpion and frog thing, are you?"

"No, but now that you mention it—"

Oh no you don't. "I think we've gotten off topic." *Wait. Did he do that on purpose? Did he sense my aggravation and try to lighten the mood?*

A tiny smile creased his face. "Agreed. My apologies. Please continue."

Tish glanced at him, striving with all her might to prevent a smile from breaking out. *What the hell is going on here? Who is this Brick, and where did he come from?* She took a big breath and sighed, realizing how much she liked this version. *It's also nice to have a cogent conversation that doesn't steer toward sex or sports.*

"Look, I don't make a ton of deals important enough to seal with a kiss. Ours was significant since what we promised would contradict entrenched behaviors, particularly mine."

Brick looked like he was about to jump out of his seat, but he held back whatever question was brewing in his head, so Tish continued. "You were the first person in a long time to respond in the way I wanted. You let me control the kiss and responded without going overboard, but you also didn't hold back. The balance is rare and something you can't teach, Brick."

Well, technically, his response wasn't a question."So, I moved the bar some."

Tish snorted her agreement while simultaneously injecting a 'yah.' She didn't normally snort in front of guys but felt more at ease with him now, knowing he wouldn't be too judgmental. Judging by the way the corners of his lips turned up, he probably thought it was cute.

The conversation flowed effortlessly between them, and Tish discovered they had far more in common than she could have imagined. The most shocking discovery she made was that he enjoyed romantic comedies. They discussed favorite movies such as Roxanne, Something About Mary, and Just Go With It. The best part was that he, like her family, was a huge fan of classic sci-fi. Tish and her parents had a movie night two Fridays a month, where they watched vintage sci-fi films and ate hot dogs and popcorn.

"You are such an enigma, Brick. I thought I knew you, but I honestly don't, do I?"

"An enigma is simply a puzzle that most people don't have the imagination to solve. You don't lack imagination, Tish; curiosity maybe, but not imagination."

"I like that. Did you just come up with it?"

"No. It's..." A cloud crossed Brick's face again, although less intensely than before. It was enough to pique Tish's supposedly remiss curiosity. "It's something I heard from someone once."

"And what do you mean I'm not curious? I ask plenty of questions."

And just like that, he was back to himself. "Asking questions is not the same as seeking answers or the truth. Just so you know, that one's mine."

Brick's reaction took her by surprise. This ostensibly wimpy, pacifist nerd-freak was not only one of the school's brightest minds and skilled engineers, but he was also a philosopher.

Layers upon layers. Maybe he's right. My opinions of him are completely based on rumor and supposition. Perception may be one's reality, yet it is not necessarily the truth, is it?

He'd been correct with his earlier comment about conversation and understanding. The more time Tish spent with him, the more she liked the idea of working alongside him. Professor

Brennan had hinted at the collaboration before winter break, but she hadn't warmed to it right away. Nonetheless, Tish had yielded much sooner than she should have. Maybe a part of her subconscious had always craved this. Maybe that's why she'd treated him so badly. Funny how quickly things could change.

That's when it hit her. The smile the professor shot Brick. She *knew* that smile. She *used* that smile. It concealed a message of some kind. Before her mind could focus on the mystery, she pulled into her driveway, where Brantley Hollister stood leaning on the rear bumper of his Porsche. Neither she nor Brick were able to hold back the expletive.

"Shit!"

Part 3

Tish parked the car on the gravel driveway behind Brantley's vehicle and got out. He approached her, crunching pebbles with each step. Brick exited the car but stayed on the passenger side, behind the front tire.

In the heavily wooded Black Forest near Colorado Springs, it was difficult to see your neighbor's house much less another vehicle or the nearby highway. The pleasant sound of chirping birds acted as a counterbalance to the tension stretching between the two parties.

Wearing his usual scowl, Bran towered over her. "You haven't called me in weeks, and now I find you with the pacifist nerd-freak who has a thing for you. What's up with that, Tish?"

"First and foremost, we're not hanging out like you mean it. He's my lab partner for a science project."

"Right. About the kiss. What's up with that?"

A pulse in her temple began throbbing. "We cut a deal. I don't make fun of Brick's feelings for me. He doesn't feel me up, okay? You know I seal big deals with a kiss."

He swayed from one foot to the other, unable to reamin still. "So why haven't you called?"

Tish rolled her eyes. "I told you I needed a break, Bran, but you keep messin' it up by getting all up in my grill before I'm ready."

Bran's eternal scowl deepened. "Right. I'm supposed to believe you're not steppin' out on me on the down-low."

As her lips pressed into a thin line, Tish's snark thickened. "Right." She barked a quick laugh. "Like you don't. Anyway, Bran, I don't care what you think. I'm sick of all this shit. Just go home. We're done. For good."

Tish skirted past Brantley, ready to escape around the front of her car. Brantley grabbed her arm, swung her around, called her the B-word, and lifted his hand to hit her. Tish lowered her head and raised her arm to block, but surprise slowed her reaction, so she closed her eyes in preparation. The blow never came, but a gentle breeze tousled her hair, just like in class. However, the breeze had not followed the wind's direction. Curious.

When she opened her eyes, Brick, who had been on the opposite side of her car, was now between her and Brantley, his hand clamped around the larger man's wrist. She stepped away from the enthralling scene.

With his scowl transforming into rage, Bran's body shook. "Let me go, you fucking nerd."

From the side, Tish could only see half of his face, but it remained placid. "No prob, Bran. Promise to leave, and I'll let you go."

Taken aback by Brick's calm, controlled, and dominating voice, she could only watch as the conflict unfolded. Brantley, who had nearly eight centimeters and twenty-three kilos on him, failed to wrangle his wrist away from the smaller man's grip. To be fair, he couldn't even move her new project partner's arm, let alone get free.

How is that even possible? How can Brick be so strong?

Sweat flowed down the larger man's face, dripping onto his shirt. "And what if I don't?" Birds continued chirping, oblivious to the conflict brewing in ther midst.

Cool and confident, the immovable Mason Redstone stood firm, leaving Tish wondering how they all had underestimated him. "Your posse ain't here, Bran. It's just you and me, no backup." Brick's voice sank into a low, ominous tone. "You really want to push this while you're all by your lonesome? Do you?"

Brick's voice sounded different—powerful, provocative, assertive. It wasn't the voice of a pacifist, a coward, or a weakling. The last two words contained such power and menace, she felt as though she were in the presence of the most dangerous predator in the world. Still, she felt no fear.

Another layer peeled back from the enigma that is Brick. But does it show more about who he truly is or add another layer to the puzzle?

Though he shivered, Mr. Hollister put on a brave face. "All right, I'll leave. Just remember that your ass is mine later, freak."

The side of his mouth facing her quirked up. "No prob, Bran. I'll see you and your crew after you drink back your courage."

Taking a step to the side, Brick released Brantley's wrist, leaving a garish, white handprint. Staring in awe, Tish watched the color return while Bran shook the hand as if it had gone dead. Her ex-boyfriend stalked to his Porsche, jumped inside, and peeled out.

Brick held his ground as the car's tires pelted him with pebbles. He brushed off his clothes and made his way to her front door. He must have realized she hadn't followed him after a few feet, so he came to a halt and turned his head, peering over his shoulder. "Coming?"

Tish remained in place. She needed answers. "How?"

Turning to face her, his emotionless tone matched his cool, calm, and controlled facial expression.

"Bran's a coward, Tish. Most bullies are. He's a frightened child without his posse to back him up."

"That's only part of it. Again, how?"

He sighed. "Book? Cover?"

"Fine, Mr. Nigma. Why, though?"

"I told you before. When I can, I protect those I care about, and I care about you..." He sounded a little choked up as he trailed off.

Tish caught up with him while he made his way toward the house. Brick said something else, but she couldn't be sure of his exact words. He'd been looking away from her and seemed to be thinking out loud more than anything else, but it sounded like, 'though sometimes I wish I didn't.'

CHAPTER 3: ZINDRIYA

Zindriya stared at the floating vision of her sister Sandra in the holoscreen. She admired every feature of that face, from her strong, dimpled chin to those exquisite Cupid's bow lips. Zindriya loved how Sandra's beautifully sculpted brows arched over almond-shaped green eyes, and she adored her amazing, long, wavy, raven-black hair.

She coveted that face because her identical twin sister lacked the jagged, keloid scar that traveled from the outer corner of her right eye, beneath her own strong and dimpled chin, and stopped at the lobe of her left ear. It was a gift from a dissatisfied client during the brief time she'd had to sell her body to buy food and shelter—a gift paid for with the client's leftover cash, credit cards, and his life.

A year ago, Zindriya didn't know she had a twin sister until a chance encounter at a New York City bodega transformed their lives forever. They knew the moment their two pairs of identical green eyes met, even though she had cut her hair short and colored it bronze.

"So, Sandra, how's the plan progressing?" Zindriya's high tenor voice betrayed no trace of her native Eastern European accent, since she had learned English in the United Kingdom.

"In fact, it worked better than I thought. Latisha asked for Brick all on her own, with little urging from me."

She perused the limited view of her sister's bedroom but hid her disdain. Pink had never been her color. "As you thought she would, Professor. Don't underestimate yourself. You have done well."

"I wanted to be sure of something, sister. I need to be clear about my part of this bargain. May we speak freely?"

"Yes, Sandra, continue."

"You won't be hurtin' Brick too badly, will you? You know I want him after you've finished with him."

"He won't be physically damaged, sister, but he may be broken psychologically. He will be attached to me if my plan succeeds. Putting him back together again will help him fall in love with you, especially if you isolate him."

"I already have a plan, I do," Sandra said.

"Why do you want him so badly? Surely you can find a man with your looks. It's not like Brick is exceedingly handsome, is he? Or is he that good in bed?"

"I haven't slept with him yet, not exactly, though I have let him know it's what I want. I like the looks of him well enough, Driya, and he treats me with dignity and respect. When I'm with Brick, I feel desired, not owned as with others. But what I like most about him is his mind. He will be the most brilliant innovator in the field of Quantum Physics the world has ever seen."

"How do you know this?" Zindriya sat up in her chair, her curiosity piqued. She ignored the nauseous sound of classical music drifting from the other side of the holoscreen.

Professor Sandra Brennan had tutored Brick during her Quantum Mechanics class since he had struggled at the start of the previous semester. He had mastered the curriculum in just six days of teaching. Subsequently, he outperformed every other student in the class. It was like busting a logjam. Once it was gone, his mind flew into hyperdrive.

Within three weeks, he had equaled, then surpassed her knowledge. She began feeding him unsolvable equations and untested theorems disguised as typical school testing fodder.

One by one, Brick solved the majority of them with stunning ease. The only issue was that she had trouble understanding the math he employed. Sandra was a talented mathematician, but Brick's solutions were on a scale that Sandra had only heard rumors of in high-level think tanks.

Average, everyday math employs a base of ten; logical since we have ten fingers. Binary math is based on the number two. When solving problems in an infinite multiverse or a subatomic microverse where macro-physical rules do not apply, it is essential to employ math with alternative bases and then frame the solution in a way that others may understand, if not decipher. Brick had used a pencil, paper, and a Smart calculator to solve equations that had frozen the most up-to-date Quantum Computers.

"Have you ever heard of the Akashic Field or Zero-point Energy?"

"No to the Field, Sandra, and yes to ZPE." It sounded more like metaphysical BS than anything else.

"To put it in layman's terms, the Akashic Field is similar to that connective energy from Star Wars. It is believed to be the source from which everything in the universe was created and by which it is still connected. Brick has the potential to discover how to access the Field. Once he does, he will be able to control the forces of creation and chaos. If he can pierce the veil to the that source, he could alter reality itself."

To Zindriya, controlling or influencing reality sounded like a fool's errand. It would also take decades, if not centuries. She required something less time-consuming. Something that would put her in the lap of luxury soon enough for her to enjoy it.

"Could he also crack the Zero-Point Energy problem, Sandra?"

"I believe he can access the Akashic Field, Zindriya, and the multiverse will be his playground. By comparison, ZPE is child's play. We've already discussed workable theories after he solved some equations others considered unsolvable."

"Then he is truly valuable. Hmm. Don't worry, sister; I'll not damage him, and he will be yours after I retrieve the information I need."

Sandra was confident in her capacity to develop ZPE into a marketable product. Zindriya could leave her perilous profession years earlier than intended if Sandra could only hold on to the younger man, something she found difficult to believe even though she was a desirable woman.

"I can make it easier for you to get what you need from Brick." She liked the eagerness in her sister's voice because it represented leverage.

Zindriya pressed for more information. Sandra and Brick had arranged to spend his graduation night together because they could finally reveal their relationship without repercussions from the university. She could get whatever information Zindriya needed from him without kidnapping him. She may also steer his search for the ever-elusive, near-mythic Akashic Field.

"You care for him, don't you?" The scarred twin leaned forward.

"I do, Driya. I've never met a man quite like him."

Zindriya reminded Sandra that Brick would spend a lot of time with Latisha, a woman he apparently loved. With her in the picture, the fifteen-year age gap between Sandra and the young man might make all the difference. Her sister objected, sure of her hold on the younger man. Her unscarred twin revealed that he had devised his own method of keeping their affair alive and secret.

They met frequently and intimately in an Augmented Reality system he had created. Sandra wouldn't risk her tenure by having an open relationship with an undergrad, but a virtual romance with Brick's closed system was untraceable—except for someone with Zindriya's resources. It was always useful to have some leverage, just in case Sandra became problematic regarding the young man.

Zindriya had no emotional attachment or love for her sister. When she was two, their parents sold Sandra to an Irish couple to support their drug habit, or so her mother told her before she died. Zindriya looked into the couple and discovered that they were loaded. Sandra had the best of everything, whereas Zindriya had spent her entire life struggling to survive. Her sister was merely a tool, a conduit to Brick. That unexpected meeting had been a convenient way in without revealing herself or her agents to her quarry. No need to infiltrate the campus when she already had a spy in place. The fact that Sandra had developed an intimate relationship with her target was an additional boon. The circumstances could not have been more favorable.

For the time being, she decided to let her sister cling to her fantasy. However, Zindriya had a plan that could yield results sooner. Regardless of Sandra's lustful obsession with her target, she had no true desire to wait another four months. Her clients had paid her a large sum of money to apprehend Brick. Still, the more Sandra stayed in touch with him, the better. With his mind divided between the two women, it would keep him off-balance. This might make it easier to capture or influence him. She would have to think about it.

After a few more minutes of conversation, Zindriya ended the holo call because she had scheduled a face-to-face meeting with one of her operatives. Venton Smythe, the head of the gang of mercenaries, or mercies as they ironically called themselves, arrived at her office with a soft rap on the door. She'd contracted them instead of using her own squad to catch Brick since they'd demonstrated great competency in a previous snatch-and-grab operation. Venton, a short, dusky man, sat in a chair on the other side of her desk.

"Report." Zindriya's scowl bolstering the disdain in her voice. Everything about the man; his appearance, behavior, demeanor, voice, and low-brow accent, grated on her nerves. To make matters worse, the Brit was far too arrogant and smelled strongly of garlic and piss. She only hoped he was efficient and effective.

"The boyfriend performed as we wanted, with a bit of a nudge from us about the target's little snog with the girl."

"And?" She steepled her fingers in front of her face.

"The target's definitely a Ghost, mistress. He crossed nearly four meters in a heartbeat and proved stronger than a man larger than him. I've never seen his like. It was as if he disappeared from one spot and reappeared in another."

"Good. I want you to monitor their progress from a distance. I want to give the lovebirds time to get close. Then, slowly ratchet up the pressure on the boyfriend. Get him ready for the coup de grâce, but keep him away until we're ready."

"Already in the works, Mistress."

Zindriya emphasized that Brick was a high-value, highly skilled, highly trained target with genetically enhanced talents and that Venton should bring enough troops to ensure success. Venton assured her he had assembled the perfect team, naming three soldiers and himself. She informed him that if he doubled or tripled that number, he might have a shot. Venton chuckled, claiming Brick was only a child.

She reminded him once more that the young man was a well-trained, experienced operator as well as a Ghost with supernormal abilities. Regardless of his strategy, he was bound to lose some of his troops. She advised him to take it as a warning. If he failed and Brick or the family was harmed, Zindriya would welcome him and any survivors into her dungeon to become her new batch of muses.

"You hired me because I'm a professional Miss Zindriya. I won't fail you."

The woman didn't react. Instead, she fixed her gaze on him for several seconds, like a snake with hooded eyes. Venton fidgeted in his chair. His eyes darted from her to the floor and back. She shifted her gaze to the door, then back to him. He wiped his brow with the back of his wrist, rose, then moved to leave.

"Be sure that you don't, Venton." Though her voice was a hair above a whisper, it must have frightened the man for he picked up his pace in a rush to escape the room. As the door closed, Zindriya smiled. She enjoyed making the supposed tough guys squirm. One sharp look from her had the cowards practically tripping over themselves as they scrambled away.

They would no doubt slink off to some dark corner for comfort or find someone even weaker to torment. Pride demanded they reassure themselves of their place in that absurd pecking order of toxic masculinity they so dearly clung to. She wished he'd taken that smell with him, but it lingered, only slightly diminished despite his rapid retreat.

Zindriya turned her thoughts back to Brick and ZPE. She couldn't care less about the Oshakic or whatever field Sandra had been blathering about. Zero-Point Energy would be an absolute gold mine. That could be her ticket out of her current life. She had millions stashed away in the Caymans, but it wasn't enough to live the life she desired and deserved. Zero-Point Energy was essentially power from nothing, theoretically powerful enough to energize a metropolis for a decade from a suitcase-sized module. It was worth more money than she could imagine, and she had quite the imagination.

She had already decided to turn on the organization that hired her to acquire Brick. They wanted him because of his genetic heritage. He was a Ghost, but they were curious whether he was the *Ghost's Shadow*, a creature infinitely more evolved and lethal than his father and sister combined. Zindriya had secretly installed one of her operatives to infiltrate the ranks of her temporary employers. For such a massive enterprise, their internal security was appalling. Her overseers had no idea how much information she had acquired about Brick and other functions they had going on. She would try to co-opt as many as she could in order to siphon funding away from them.

Initially, she simply wanted to control Brick and his potential powers. However, if her sister was correct, and Zindriya had no doubt that she was, his intellect was infinitely more valuable. Sandra might be an excellent tool for extracting what she needed with negligible risk of physical damage. Her method may be preferable in the long run. Zindriya could be patient if the end result was worth it and if her sister could pull it off, which was a big if. She had a lot on her mind, and nothing helped her think more clearly than consulting her muses.

In the lower levels of her stronghold nestled in the rolling hills east of Colorado Springs and south of Calhan, Zindriya always held a prisoner, whom she called her muse in the ultimate ironic euphemism. She had acquired her new base of operations from the estate of a family who no longer needed it, having died shortly after refusing to sell to her.

The house had been carved into the bedrock on one side of a canyon wall. She expanded the interior to suit her needs. It was now three levels deeper and self-sustaining. She had a direct well to the local aquifer, animals for food roaming the surrounding three hundred acres, and a large hydroponics farm. Adding to that, she had enough solar panels, mini-windmills, and power storage to last for months even if the sun and wind stopped shining and blowing. Not counting a global catastrophe, that section of Colorado got as much sun as Los Angeles, and the wind on those sweeping plains never stopped blowing. When it did, it was time to run for shelter because Mother Nature had something big planned.

Zindriya entered the chamber, where padded leather straps

restrained her muse to a metal-framed bed. The entire area was lined with pristine white tiles and smelled strongly of disinfectant. Anyone would find it difficult to believe what occurred in such a sanitized setting. Every day, she had a crew clean the walls and floors. They knew that if she found so much as a speck of blood or filth anywhere, even in the fine lines of grout, the cleaning crew's foreman would become her next muse. Zindriya smiled in anticipation as she spied her subject's emaciated frame, fed intravenously by dangling bags at the top of the bed filled with dextrose infused with a clotting agent.

"The moon is unzipped and is falling into the flaming pit of the moth-eating gorilla boy." At times, the nonsense her prisoner babbled could be entertaining. He wailed as he strained to take in ragged breaths, staring first at her as she entered, then up and through the ceiling.

"Quite creative, Babel." Zindriya started calling him that after forgetting his name weeks before. Anyone on her payroll or under her control gave up the right to their name. She would call them whatever was easiest for her to remember, and they would accept it.

"The way of the lion becomes the way of the lamb, so who will hunt the lion if the lamb now wears the mane?"

"Spouting worthless prophecies again? No matter. I will release you this night after I finish. I need to think, and you have been the best muse I've had in a very long time."

Despite the torment she'd inflicted on him for several weeks, Babel's physique remained miraculously free of overt damage. Zindriya had mastered the fine art of inflicting pain. Unfortunately, she'd discovered no method to keep them from going insane after a while. She didn't mind as long as they screamed. She liked Babel because of his bizarre ramblings. Some of them made a kind of sense from time to time.

"Let's see, which tool..." She nibbled her bottom lip as she rummaged through the set of sterilized medical instruments on the tray next to the bed, as if deciding which pastry to eat.

Babel closed his eyes as tears streamed down his cheeks. He uttered another stream of words in a dreamy stupor.

"Dreaming is sleeping, but if you die in a dream, do you wake up, and if you do, are you still dreaming when you die, or do dreams keep you awake even after you die?"

Zindriya chose a scalpel and a small hook-like instrument. She bent forward and reopened a two-inch scar on the outside of Babel's elbow that had recently healed, but he didn't so much as flinch. She inserted the hook and slipped it behind the tendon attaching the forearm muscles to the elbow. Then she scraped the hook back and forth along the inside of the tendon.

The technique was incredible: maximum pain with minimal physical trauma or blood loss.

Babel shrieked an opera that cleared her mind and drained the tension from her body. However, the music silenced after a few seconds, and chaos reigned in her mind once more.

Zindriya checked whether he'd passed out or if he'd done the unthinkable and passed away, but Babel's chest continued to rise and fall. His eyes, however, stared through the ceiling and into the beyond, while there had been at least a spark of insane life left in them only seconds before.

"Well, I guess our time is at an end, Babel." She was pissed off that she hadn't had time to clear her mind. Zindriya had no muses left, so she'd have to make do without one. That enraged her even more. She could kidnap one of her employees, but it might cause a stir among the others. She convinced herself it wouldn't be good for morale, so she put it off until one of them failed her.

All of a sudden, Babel heaved upward, every muscle in his body straining against the straps, prompting Zindriya to jump back. His bloodshot eyes appeared to glow as they seared holes into

Zindriya's soul.

"You evil fucking bitch! You whore! You slut! I'll see you in Hell soon, real soon!"

Babel's speech then morphed into a monotone drone, as if he'd entered a trance. Its transformation injected icy needles into Zindriya's spine, chilling her entire body.

"When the lover becomes the liar, the eagle will strike, and your silver tongue will drown you in the Red Sea!"

Rage forced the chill from her body. Zindriya snatched the scalpel and stabbed it into each orifice of Babel's face, shouting a word with every plunge. "Never. Ever. Call. Me. A. Bitch, Arsehole." She buried the scalpel in the back of his throat.

"Now you have a silver tongue, fucker."

She stalked out of the torture chamber, covered in crimson.

CHAPTER 4: ANDRA

Tish walked past Brick as they climbed the stairs to the front doors of the expansive Owusu mansion.

They are seriously loaded, Brick thought, *or in some serious debt.*

He had no idea, and to be clear, it wasn't his business. He was aware that Mr. Owusu was an independent contractor for the Department of Defense. Tish's mother was a Human Resources consultant with a vibrant, lucrative lecture circuit.

Tish's amazing, big, beautiful body drew Brick's eye again as she entered her code into the keyless entrance lock on the hand-carved ebony wood front door. Recalling the agreement they had sealed with a kiss, he averted his gaze. He would not forget their kiss anytime soon, mainly because he might never receive another. She had faith in him, and he had to earn that trust by fulfilling his end of the bargain.

Tish finished entering the code but didn't open the door. Instead, she turned to him with squinted eyes, hunched shoulders, and clenched fists at her sides. "Someday, I'm gonna want an explanation of how you got around the car so fast, okay?"

Brick hadn't expected her to let it go, so he'd planned a suitable response—he hoped. At the very least, it wasn't an outright lie. He didn't want to lie to Tish. He'd lie to everyone on mission, but he needed to keep it real with her. At least as much as he could.

While his response was not a lie, it was a significant evasion. "Maybe I saw what was coming. Maybe you and Bran were so focused on each other that you didn't see me inching closer. Maybe I was close enough to step in by the time it happened. Did you think about that?"

"No, I didn't, but I suppose it's possible. You saying that's what happened?"

"So, you'd prefer to think I had superspeed rather than face the possibility that I could foresee your angry, violent, asshole ex-boyfriend hitting you? If it helps my image in your mind, maybe you should go with it. Anything to give me a shot at earning your affection." Brick hoped he had inserted the proper amount of snark to press his point.

"Earning my... You're for real, aren't you? You want to earn, not win my affection."

"Well, yeah. You're no trophy to be fought over and won. You're an incredible woman, and anyone who respects you should be willing to work hard to earn your respect and affection."

The flash of indecision on her face told Brick that he'd caught Tish off guard, but, true to form, she activated her level 100, Legendary Class, Scathing Wit ability and lobbed one hell of a grenade at him.

"Would you tell me if I offered to sleep with you?"

Now, that threw Brick off guard, but he recovered quickly. He was growing accustomed to Tish's attempts at keeping him off balance.

"I doubt you'd do it."

"Why? I might be into you enough to give it a try. You did save me from Bran, and I'm feeling grateful."

"Okay, then I wouldn't do it, especially not for that reason."

Tish cocked her head to the side, her brows pressed together.

"Why not? I thought that's what you wanted from me."

"Only a fool would want only sex from you, Tish. You have so much more to offer those of us who are able and willing to see.

My love for you has more to do with your intelligence, quick, abrasive wit, and how you interact with your real friends rather than your looks or your body."

"And he actually says the L-word. And you were right. I wouldn't. Not because I'm not into you, but because it would degrade both of us. Respect is important, and I believe we would lose that if we jumped into a physical relationship right now."

Saying the L-word had been second nature; he'd blurted it out without thinking. And she'd reacted to it with acceptance rather than disdain. Did he miss the asteroid knocking the world off its axis? Where was this coming from? Who talked to her before winter break because the one-eighty was throwing him off-balance. Brick cranked up a corner of his mouth and the opposing brow, needing to shift the conversation to something less earth-shattering.

"Even if I had superpowers?"

Tish exhaled as her shoulders relaxed and her eyes softened into what appeared to be a thank you.

"I guess you're right. You" A superhero?" She snorted. "Not very likely, right? Oh, and about the sex thing?" She placed a hand on his arm. "To be clear, I'm not saying no, math-boy, just not before we've completed our project. We'll see how things turn out." Tish beamed the second broadest smile she'd ever given him. "Okay?"

Brick couldn't respond since his throat chose to seize at that moment. Tish turned to the door, unlocked it again, entered the house, and shouted that she was home with a guest. Recent events drew a silent exhale from his lungs. Not only had he succeeded in the evasion of the century with a woman who should have caught him in the act, but the same woman first insinuated, then flat out told him he had a chance with her after the project.

The Brantley incident had to have rattled her something fierce, or time had stopped, or they had slipped into an alternate reality.

Or she's setting a trap for me because Tish is one of the most astute observers I've ever seen. Working together, I'll either have to tell her what I am and risk losing her because of it, or take the chance that she'll trick it out of me and lose her forever. This life is full of nothing but bad choices, and I was born into it with zero opportunity to say no.

Shoving the negative thoughts back into a mental niche, Brick followed her into the house's foyer, a room roughly the size of his family's living room but more elegantly decorated in an art nouveau design with whites, grays, and blacks dominating the scenery and thin strips of dark-stained maple surrounding the windows and doors.

As they passed through the foyer into the house proper, it was clear the same theme spread throughout the entire mansion. A faint hint of lilac caressed his nostrils and made him wonder how they could suffuse such a large area with the precise amount of aroma to tickle the senses yet not overwhelm them.

The foyer emptied into what Brick would call an oval-shaped lobby or hall, large enough to cause an echo if he were brave enough to pierce the silence with a shout. An enormous crystal chandelier hung overhead, casting small rainbow arcs across the walls and floor.

The lobby ended in matching double stairways curving to the left and right up to a second-floor balcony. A set of open, wooden doors to his immediate left was inlaid with what appeared to be crystal panels.

Tish's mother and father sat on a wide, plush, dark gray, L-shaped sectional with a chaise on one end. *At least they're smiling,* Brick mused. To his right was another set of identical double doors that concealed the room beyond.

To his surprise and dismay, after Tish barked a greeting to her parents, she bolted up the flight of stairs to the right, shouting over her shoulder something about wanting to get comfy. Issuing a silent groan, Brick kept his shoulders straight, stretched his mouth into as genuine a smile as he could muster, and walked toward Mr. and Mrs. Owusu, trying not to trip on a crack as he traversed the increasingly long distance of tiled flooring.

His worst nightmare almost came true when his toe snagged on the transition from the tiled lobby to the carpeted living room. He caught it in time and, he hoped, corrected the mistake without Tish's parents noticing.

Brick approached the imposing broad-shouldered figure of Amaye Owusu, a six-foot three-inch-tall Eritrean immigrant. His family immigrated to the United States when he was very young. He had served as an officer in a Force Recon unit, a special forces branch of the United States Marines. He'd been deployed to Afghanistan and Iraq and earned the Silver Star Medal and the Purple Heart—a real-life war hero.

"Mr. Owusu, my name is Mason Redstone, but people call me Brick. It is such a pleasure to meet you."

Tish's father smiled as Brick extended his hand, striving to keep it steady. Brick relaxed slightly as he accepted the hand and shook it firmly but not forcefully.

"It is a pleasure, Brick," Amaye said, his deep baritone rumbling. "Well done, and I'd expect no less from Flint Redstone's son. I met him once, long ago."

"Cool. I didn't know you knew my father."

"I wouldn't say I knew him, but we did meet once. You know, most of Latisha's boyfriends aren't brave enough to introduce themselves. I'm impressed already."

"Oh, I'm not her boyfriend, sir, just her lab partner."

"I see-e-e-e-e."

Ignoring the insinuation hiding in Mr. Owusu's smile, Brick turned his full attention to Mrs. Owusu and introduced himself. He noticed the similarities between the five-foot-four-inch-tall, stockily built, mixed-heritage Indian-American Hiral Biswas Owusu and Latisha. Brick saw the light in her eyes as she took his hand in a firm grip of her own.

"Are you sure about that?" Hiral asked.

"I'm sorry, ma'am. Sure about what?"

"That you're not her new boyfriend?"

"Oh, I'm positive about that." Brick chuckled.

Mrs. Owusu had the same wrinkles as Tish atop her nose. "Why?"

"Because she hates me, or at least, used to."

Their scrunched-up expressions were almost comical. Mr. Owusu opened his mouth, possibly to say something, as Tish entered.

"Yah, but Brick's in love with me." Tish strolled into the room wearing a coral-colored, form-fitting workout suit with a white stripe trailing down the outside of the sleeves and legs. Brick did a double-take before regaining self-control.

Despite the situation, Brick had to restrain his laughter as the parents' faces morphed from scrunched to round-eyed, open-mouthed visages. Their focus shifted to Tish, then back to him, then back again, almost like they were watching a tennis match.

"So-o-o-o, Brick. Could you clear this up for us? You admit to being in love with Latisha even though she hates you?"

"Yes, sir. Everyone at school knows, so I own it. That way, no one can use it against me."

"So, how can you two work together?" Hiral still wore the cute wrinkles above the bridge of her nose.

"Because our skill sets complement each other perfectly, Mom, and we cut a deal so our feelings don't get in the way of our work."

"A deal you sealed with a kiss, I imagine." The tone of Mr. Owusu's voice spoke volumes.

"Of course, Dad. It was definitely important enough."

"I see-e-e-e." A smirk that lightened his eyes and lifted a corner of his mouth replaced Amaye's shocked expression.

Yeah, he sounds convinced, thought Brick.

"Oh God, Dad. Seriously?" Tish exhaled loudly, raised her arms to shoulder height, and let them flop down to her sides. Her mother said nothing but covered her mouth to conceal the smile behind her hand. Brick caught a glimpse of it before it vanished.

Tish put one hand on her hip. Brick was fascinated by the entire exchange, wondering if this was how a typical family functioned. He never had an ordinary family, thus he had no frame of reference.

"You know, whatever. Think what you want, Dad. Anyway, are you gonna be using your workshop any time soon?"

As it turned out, Mr. Owusu didn't need his shop and consented to let them use it for their project. He pushed a gentle elbow into Brick's side and whispered that the workshop was an engineer's paradise. He wondered how Mr. Owusu knew his field of expertise but chose not to ask.

As she moved to leave and guide him away from her parents, Tish brushed her hand across the crook of Brick's elbow. The contact sent a wave of pleasure through him. As he turned to leave, Mrs. Owusu winked and mouthed the words 'good luck,' which plastered a grin on his face.

Tish led him through the large, labyrinthine mansion to what he assumed was the back door. Though she called out room after room as they passed, Brick was so overwhelmed by the sheer size of the place that he had trouble remembering much. There was no way he would find the path to the front of the house without going around the outside. The place was a maze.

They emerged from the back door into nearly two acres of paradise. A small flower garden flowed down the side of the house to the left, or what remained of it, given that it was winter. To the right, a gazebo covered in what appeared to be leafless grapevines housed an oversized, covered hot tub. Wisps of steam curled into the cool midday air from one side of the cover, only to vanish shortly thereafter.

The large pond with lily pads floating along its edges about a hundred feet ahead was the best part of the vast, grass-covered plain. How the grass was still green and the lily pads blooming in the dead of winter remained a mystery for Brick to solve another time. Across the pond was a house.

When he asked who lived there, Tish told him it was a guest house. The three-bedroom cottage was larger than his own family's home. A stable and an arena stood fifty yards to the left of the guest house.

She turned right and walked past the gazebo to a building squatting behind the five-car garage. She punched in a code on the keyless entry lock and showed Brick the numbers so he had access as well. Mr. Owusu had been correct. He was in an engineer's paradise. Brick touched his chin to make sure he wasn't drooling.

Just about every instrument and piece of equipment needed to make whatever you needed, from micro to macro devices, littered the room in a masterfully organized state of chaos. Open storage and cupboards flanked the walls, while several tables of various sizes carpeted the floor, leaving aisles large enough to walk through.

Everything he saw revealed exactly what Mr. Owusu did for the Department of Defense: he designed and built custom triggers and detonators for all kinds of explosive devices, from conventional to nuclear to antimatter-type weapons.

Implosion grenades, too freaking cool, thought Brick.

Fortunately, no magnetic bottles capable of holding antimatter lay anywhere in sight. They might have tempted Brick to play. The faint aromas of machine oil, ozone, and the acrid tinge of C-4 tickled his nostrils. "Ho-ly-shit!"

Tish beamed at him. "I thought you'd like this."

Brick couldn't tell Tish what he knew because it would shatter his cover. He'd already exposed himself when he saved her from Bran. He wasn't even sure if she believed his attempt at evasion, but he hoped she did. "The word *like* is not strong enough. This place is like Underland to me."

Tish followed him around the shop. "Don't you mean Wonderland?"

"Tomato, tomaato."

"Whatever, Brick, so who's gonna be in charge?"

"You, of course."

"I think I should... wait. What?"

"You're a lot better at multitasking, and your organizing skills are off the hook. Depending on what we decide to build, it will likely have a lot of mini-projects that will merge into the whole. You have the best skill sets to manage something on that scale."

Brick classified the look on Tish's face as contemplative. "Huh. I didn't see that coming."

"That's what you get for hanging out with guys who suffer from toxic masculinity syndrome and OD on testosterone and steroids, turning their brains into testicles in a gourd. I'm not at all threatened by strong women. In fact, I'm quite attracted to them, to women like you."

"Don't you mean women like Professor Brennan?"

Brick scrunched his face, wanting to appear more curious than disturbed by her observation. "Huh? What do you mean?"

"Uh-huh," Tish responded, "I saw the smile she threw you as we left. I know that smile, Brick. I *use* that smile. What's up with you two? Are you sleeping with her?"

Pretending not to care, Brick continued his impromptu tour of the workshop. "Don't know what you're smoking, but you need to share."

He was sure she could see him blushing. His face was burning, and he was certain the blood coursing through his cheeks would expose him. Despite the clear and present danger Tish represented, Brick's mind wandered back to the last official day Professor Sandra Brennan tutored him weeks before winter break.

◆ ◆ ◆

All the blinds were closed, and the curtains had been drawn in her office when he entered. Brick thought it had been odd but ignored it. She closed the door behind him, and he heard a clicking sound like she had engaged the deadbolt. Brick turned as she approached to congratulate him on doing so well. Professor Brennan usually smelled of seaspray and lavender, but something was different that day. The scent of raw, unfiltered honey overlaid her base scent, making his head spin.

He extended his hand to thank her for all of her help. She took Brick's hand, told him she would miss their time together and didn't want it to end, and pulled him closer. Brick had never dared to dream about what would happen next. She slid his hand under her blouse, then kissed him softly and slowly as his hand caressed her bare breast.

"Sandra, I..." Words failed Brick; it wasn't every day that a fantasy came true for guys like him.

"I want to be with you, Brick, but the University..."

Finding it hard to breathe, Brick struggled to think clearly. "Then how does this work?"

Sandra's hands roamed across his body, finding every sensitive spot she could. "I wanted, no, I needed to show you how much I want you, hoping it would be enough."

Even though distracted, his hands were also busy. "Enough?"

"For you to wait for me."

She could be with him without risk after he graduated in a few months if he could wait for her despite his feelings for Latisha. At the time, Tish was unattainable, and the beautiful, brilliant professor with multiple PhDs wanted him. Hell, he wanted her too because, aside from Tish, Sandra was the only other woman who stimulated him on emotional, intellectual, and sensual levels.

Brick's attraction to the older woman was strong, and unlike Tish, Sandra was available. "Does our age difference worry you, m'love?"

Brick's yearning for Sandra was only heightened by her deepening Irish burr. "Fifteen years? Pssshh, Please." Brick snorted. "Back in the day, men used to go off and earn their fortunes. Then, when they were settled, they looked for a bride ten to twenty years their junior to marry and bear children. We're over four decades into the twenty-first century. Why shouldn't women do the same?"

His professor responded with a broad, beaming, beautiful smile tinged with a hint of oh-so-delicious snark. "So ye'd be willin' to bear me children, would ye?" Arousal further thickened Sandra's accent.

The more she talked, the stronger Brick's desire. "Perhaps, if it were possible."

Closed eyes and a sudden intake of breath urged Brick on as he softly massaged her nipple between his thumb and forefinger.

"It has been so long since I've desired someone as I do you, Brick. I really want to be with you.

He breathed hard as Sandra slid her hand past his belt and

wrapped her strong, talented fingers around him.

"But Sandra." Brick managed to murmur between gasps as her fingers worked their magic. His hand delved under her skirt, then between her parted thighs. Her breath quickened, and she squeezed him tighter.

"Oh God, that feels so good." Sandra voiced her surrender. "Right now, love, I don't care."

"I have a way, Sandra..." Her insistent manipulations forced him to pause. "A way for us to be together."

"But... I want you now."

Brick swallowed hard, smelling her desire for him as though raw honey oozed from every pore of her body. With each passing moment, rejecting her pheromones and very skilled fingers grew more difficult. "Wait, Sandra."

Gasping for air, she found a modicum of control. "Ye want to stop?"

"Hell no, but if they found out..."

Sandra followed Brick's lead and withdrew her hands after one last squeeze. "Ye're a strong one, love. Moreso than I." She kissed him again. "What is it ye have to be givin' the both of us what we're wantin'?"

Her accent held enormous power over him, but he remained firm. As Brick explained his alternative, she gloriously distracted him with kisses to the side of his neck, just under the earlobe, driving him insane and causing him to shiver each time her lips and tongue caressed his skin.

"I've built an Augmented Reality device... with direct neural stimulation."

This piqued Sandra's attention, and, much to Brick's chagrin, she stopped driving him crazy. Brick cursed himself for being so damned sensible.

He'd cobbled together parts for the device from wherever he

could find them. In addition, he designed the cranial contacts from scratch after reading every word of peer-reviewed medical articles on neural stimulation, or so he told Sandra.

Brick couldn't tell her, but he had access to research conducted by the OSRD, the Office of Science, Research, and Development, and DARPA, the Defense Advanced Research Projects Agency, thanks to his father's contacts in the DOD.

He had impressed some higher-ups in both organizations by assisting them in overcoming obstacles with a couple of their projects, including the Gravity Surfing technology. So, they allowed him access to even more classified and discontinued research since then. At the same time, they worked through a mountain of red tape to grant him a higher clearance level.

The basic design for the neural stims came from a failed attempt at direct neural control for piloting bomber drones, which resulted in an 'enhanced interrogation' tool called the Neurovex. It made the unfortunate recipient believe every nerve was on fire but caused no physical damage. It had resulted in several deaths due to improperly designed failsafe mechanisms that detected neither the potential for heart failure nor persistent psychological repercussions.

The higher-ups also wanted Brick to fix the torture tool as well. He copied the schematics without notifying the hierarchy, but he refused to assist them in repairing the abomination since he would not sanction such devices. However, he modified it to serve as the foundation for the direct neural stimulation aspect of his AR machine.

"I knew you were a master mechanical engineer, but I had no idea you were so advanced, love. Does it work?"

When Sandra looked at him with stars in her eyes, he would do anything for her. "As far as I can tell, it does; I need to tweak it a bit, and I need a partner to test the two-way neural transmi—"

"I'm all in." Sandra cut him off before he could finish. "Until then, this moment will have to fuel my battery-operated fantasies."

"Yours and mine both, Sandra."

"Call me Andra in private, Brick."

After a few days, he delivered the compact AR module to his new assistant and demonstrated how to use it.

His Augmented Reality system did not use the Internet or Cloud technology, therefore it was safe from scrutiny since his direct-connect invention was virtually unhackable. It used a section of the electromagnetic spectrum generally reserved for deep earth resonance mapping.

Less than two months later, their virtual affair flourished under the guise of continued tutoring. One of their planned rendezvous was that night, which was the reason for the smile Tish had seen. He'd have to tell Andra about it so they could be more cautious. He had five hours to get home and prepare, but what would he do about Tish?

◆ ◆ ◆

"Dude, seriously? You did *not* just fade out on me. Did you, Brick?"

Tish crossed her arms and raised an eyebrow. "I'm waiting for your answer. Are you sleeping with the professor?"

She stood there, her foot tapping a beat, her eyes blazing. She had caught him so flat-footed that he could only think of one word for the second time that day.

Shit!

CHAPTER 5: MESSY

Brick did the only thing he could think of when Tish caught him off guard. He coughed violently as if choking, to redirect her attention. She asked if he was okay. Brick nodded and thrust out his hand, keeping her at a safe distance. Then he hacked and sputtered while spraying the concrete floor with gobbets of spittle, bending over and placing his hands on his knees.

After a while, he took a few ragged breaths and choked out an answer. He told her that something went down the wrong way. It was another half-truth that flirted with disingenuity. He pretended to clear his throat after coughing for a few more minutes. Tish brought him a glass of water from the workshop's kitchenette.

He received it with feigned appreciation and sipped at leisure. "Thanks for the water. It helped."

At the tone of her voice, a warning flared in Brick's soul. "Are you okay?"

"Yeah. Yeah, I'm fine."

Her gaze spelled danger. "Good. So? Did you?"

"Did I what?" She was persistent. He had to give her that.

"You know, Professor Brennan?"

Unsure if evasion would work once more, Brick also remained firm. "Back to that again?"

"Yah."

Feeling an oppressive silence from the well-insulated

workshop, he pressed on. "Persistent much?"

"Not working, Brick. I let you evade before. But not this time."

"Why does it matter so much?"

Tish shrugged a shoulder. "I don't know. I'm going with my gut. Now, fess up."

"Why would you think she'd sleep with me?"

She leaned forward. "Why you dodgin'? Got something to hide?"

"Everyone has something to hide. I'm sure you do, too."

Tish crossed her arms again. He wondered whether he should have commented at all on her lack of curiosity. He was now dealing with the consequences of his admonition. Tish seemed determined to extract the truth from him. Still, he couldn't be disappointed with her ability to adapt. He was all about her, after all.

Brick realized he couldn't avoid answering, so he told Tish the literal, if not figurative, truth with a skosh of evasion on the side. But, of course, he and Andra had worked out their stories in case someone grew suspicious. When in doubt, answer a troubling question with some that promote even more.

"Do you really think I'd turn her down if she offered? That would be insane. Anyway, why would she be interested in a geek like me? I was too stupid to pass her class without tutoring. Also, there are plenty of pretty boy grad students for her to choose from. Why in the hell would the professor choose the wimpy pacifist nerd-freak undergrad and risk her tenure?"

"It's not always about looks, Brick. Sometimes, it's about the way they make you feel. I'd take a guy who made me feel special over good looks any day." Tish's voice softened slightly, and the searing glare she had previously directed at him dissolved as her eyes slowly turned away.

To steer the conversation even further away, Brick inserted a double-edged diversion that also served to satisfy his curiosity.

"Is that what Brantley did for you?"

"What? Oh God, no! No one has done it for me until recently..." Her gaze floated back up to him. "... anyway, that's why I broke up with Bran. Look, let's forget the whole thing, alright? Sorry, I brought it up."

Tish set her shoulders and strode toward an office-style desk framed by file cabinets in the corner of the workshop. She motioned for Brick to follow and plopped into a chair behind the desk.

Another crisis averted, Brick reasoned. *Don't know how long I can keep up the campaign of evasion. She's way too savvy and will eventually put things together. Maybe it's not such a good idea for us to partner up. Tish will probably figure out the thing with Andra, not to mention who I really am.*

Brick knew deep down that the chances of him passing up this one chance to earn Tish's love were slimmer than the chances of a micro-singularity growing inside his brain. So, he pulled up a stool, and they got down to business.

They needed to figure out what they were going to build. For an hour, they bantered ideas back and forth before Brick told her about a personal project he'd been working on. He'd been looking for a technique to use molten metal in a 3D printer but had run into a problem controlling the temperature at the printing nodes. He needed to write an algorithm to sense and adjust the temperature to the hundredth of a degree Celsius at millisecond intervals, which remained beyond Brick's programming skills. Tish, on the other hand, specialized in coding.

She inquired as to whether he had created a prototype yet. Brick had, but it didn't work properly due to the temperature regulation issue. Nonetheless, he had designed all of the other modules required, including a compact power supply based on specs acquired from the government, using a process known as Aneutronics. It was a type of nuclear reaction that produced neither heat nor harmful radiation, but only pure energy that was easily convertible to electricity. However, he could never reveal its origins to Tish. He pulled up his design specs and notes on her dad's computer at her request.

It took a few more hours, but by the time they finished, they had a functional plan for a device based on Brick's original idea but expanded to a design marketable to the general public. If they could make it work, the device would melt down undesired metal goods like tools or jewelry and print them into something new. The full name would be The Metal Recycling 3D Printer. They abbreviated it to the more marketable Re-D Printer.

Brick checked his watch after they finished the preliminary work. It was already seven in the evening, and he was late for his date with Andra.

"So I have an idea on how we should start, Brick."

Tish's eyes sparkled as she sat erect in her chair, leaned forward, and locked her gaze on him.

"Tish, I really need to go. I'm already late for dinner."

It was the truth, sort of. If everyone was in town, his family usually sat down for dinner at 6 pm. His father, however, was not around at the moment, and his sister was out on a date with her latest love interest, Katja Anderson. When it came to his sister's proclivities, perhaps 'love interest' was a bit of a stretch. 'Sex toy' might be more appropriate. Long-term partnerships were not Mara's forté.

Brick had never known what it meant to appear deflated until that moment. Tish's face, shoulders, and entire body sagged. Even the chair she was sitting in seemed to have lowered five centimeters. He had effed this one up, big time.

"Oh. All right, Brick. I guess I'll take you home." She sounded like someone shot her dog.

Tish stood up in slow motion. The air seemed heavy, and the

temperature felt as though it had dropped ten degrees. Why would she be sad at getting rid of him? Perplexed by Tish's mixed signals, Brick furrowed his brow. Despite everything his sister had taught him, he'd always been a bit slow on the uptake when it came to women. While he didn't understand Tish's answer, he felt it was directly related to his desire to leave.

What are you doing, Brick? The mini-hims had been asleep ever since Myanmar, but now, they awoke.

It was frustrating, but he could never tell who was speaking: the one with the horns or the one with the halo. This time was no exception. It was yet another aftereffect of the experiments to which his family had been exposed by the damned organization.

Ignoring the internal irritations, he forged forward. "Tish, you know..."

But Andra! They shouted.

He filtered them out. "... I'm already late."

Dude, seriously? It's ANDRA.

Brick wished they would shut the hell up. "I guess..."

This is gonna get messy, Brick!

As he formed a trap in his mind for them, he continued. "...another hour or two won't matter."

Yeah, real friggin messy, asshole.

And there it was. The mini-Bricks finished with his least favorite title. Why did so many people call him that? And into the trap, they go. Jerks.

When Tish's whole body transformed, Brick discovered what turning the frown upside-down meant. The smile she beamed warmed practically every part of him, except the section of his mind trying to figure out how to explain what had occurred to Andra. Or was it time to call it quits with the professor?

Working with Tish could lead to something; if she found out about the professor, it would destroy any chance he had with her.

"You mean it, Brick? You'll stay?"

The internal silence was Heaven. "Sure, why not? What's this idea you have?"

The majority of what Tish discussed was procedural, an orderly progression of micro-projects and how they would fit into the larger picture. Before she began in earnest, Brick informed her that he needed to send a text to explain why he was running late. He didn't tell her who he was texting; thankfully, she never asked. Technically, it kept him from actually lying to her.

It could have been due to his overabundance of caution, but Brick had rebuilt numerous burner phones for his supermodel scientist, making their communications at least somewhat difficult to track. He texted that he'd gotten hung up discussing details of the project with Tish, but should finish in a couple of hours. He also told her what they had planned for a project in the hopes that the professor would not think of him abandoning her for the first time since they began their virtual romance. Andra was disappointed, but she understood. She'd remain awake until ten o'clock, but if he hadn't contacted her by then, she'd go to sleep. They could reschedule for the next day. She appeared to understand, but it was difficult to tell how she truly felt via text message.

Despite having a productive chat with Tish about how to proceed with the project, Brick kept looking at his watch, but only when Tish wasn't looking at him.

She'd been very excited the entire time about what they might accomplish. She discussed a patent application, going into business together, and inventing more marketable products. In just a few hours, their relationship had progressed from a tenuous, fleeting one-project stand to what may be a long-term, permanent partnership. Maybe a friendship, perhaps even more. Then Brick's thoughts returned to Sandra Brennan and how he'd completely fallen off the wagon regarding Tish. He needed to break up with Andra.

Tish, the main driver of their conversation, began to wind down around 8:30 pm. Brick didn't have much else to say, and by 8:45, Tish admitted she was ready to call it a night. Brick gathered his belongings and acted the gentleman by opening the workshop door for Tish. He scanned the local area and the perimeter as they approached her car, just in case Bran tried something stupid. But nothing seemed out of the ordinary. He still led Tish to her side of the car and opened the door for her so he could check the backseat for anyone hiding on the floor. *No one's ever died from an overabundance of caution.* Brick's sister had instilled it in him from the very start of his training. Tish didn't notice what he was doing and thanked him for being such a gentleman. *Nothing like scoring points while being safe.*

She spent the thirty-minute drive home telling Brick about her life and hopes for the future. Tish wanted him to know who she was and what she stood for because they would be working closely together. However, she never revealed the identity of the person who had changed her view of him before winter break. Deciding that he didn't care, Brick let it go.

Once she finished, Tish informed him that his turn to bare his soul would come the next day. After classes, they would list the required equipment and the best places to find it all so their day would be shorter. Tish told Brick that when they finished, she would take him out for dinner before driving him home. He didn't seem to have a choice in the matter. He found that he was okay with it.

After so many years of longing, loneliness, and pain, Brick was less than thrilled with the fact that he was pretty much stuck between his dream woman and the woman of his dreams. He never in a million years dared to imagine they would be two different women. "Good night, Tish. Thanks for the ride. See you tomorrow, 10 am, right?"

"Right. Night Brick. Thanks for what you did with Bran today. I owe you."

"No, you don't."

"Yah, I do. It meant a lot to me. You let me peek behind the curtain, and you didn't have to. So I owe you, okay."

After unlocking the door, an overwhelming urge to kiss Tish struck him, but he fought it. They had come a long way in a short time, and he would do nothing to jeopardize their progress. The strange thing about the sensation was that it had not originated from within him, and the dark seed lay dormant for the time being. Perhaps it had come from Tish herself. But it still wasn't worth the risk.

"Okay. Later." Brick shrugged nonchalantly, closed the door, and watched for a few seconds as she drove down the street and rounded the corner.

Brick needed to talk to his sister, but he knew what she'd say. She'd laugh her head off at the predicament he'd gotten himself into. Then she'd give him a ration of shit for getting involved with not one, but two women, and then even more because both women knew each other. She would only give him advice after that. The advice would be to follow his head. Use logic to determine the best course of action. Find the path with the least resistance, the greatest gain, and the highest likelihood of bringing down the organization that had caused their situation. Everything was always about the organization.

Brick's training and upbringing had never included the adage of following your heart. Both his dad and sister considered emotional attachment a weakness. Anything that clouded the mind hindered their plans to eradicate the damned organization. The question was how damned they would be if and when they succeeded. Nobody talked about the after, only the now. It sucked the entire notion of a future into a black hole, just like the one inside him, literally and figuratively. He was sick of the darkness at the end of the tunnel because it most likely cloaked a silent train careening toward them at full speed with a busted headlight.

Brick was torn between his family's obsession and his desire to chart his own course. He wasn't so sure that their counsel about never following the heart was correct. Sure, he would work with his father and sister to bring down the organization, but he would do it because they had taken his mother away from him before he had even known her. He only had one memory of her, and it was so ingrained in his mind that he would never forget it. His mother smelled of raspberries. Brick believed that losing her was a matter of the heart, not the mind, and that his heart would continue to drive him to that end. He turned to walk up the little path to his house but didn't quite make it.

A familiar voice pierced the darkness behind him. "Where you going, freak?"

Shit. Some covert operative I am, letting a bunch of idiots catch me off guard.

Now that his abilities were functioning again, he smelled Brantley and his five posse members as they emerged from the bushes on the opposite side of the street and walked toward him. They reeked of alcohol and held a variety of blunt weapons. He could see exceptionally well in the dark and noted how the posse carried their cudgels as if they had no idea how to use them. They moved as though their feet were slogging through molasses. Brick looked to his left and right, scanning the street. No one was in sight, so none would witness what was about to happen. He cracked a smile that didn't reach his eyes.

"Bran. I see you couldn't wait. Kind of cold out here to be hidin' in the bushes, ain't it? I must've really pissed you off." Sweet sarcasm dripped from his lips.

"Yeah, and now we're gonna piss on you, fucking nerd-freak."

Brick had to try, albeit a poor attempt. "Not tonight, Bran. Walk away, and none of you get hurt."

The six of them laughed and then Bran showed how little money improved one's class. "Whatcha gonna do, call the cops? Cry for your mommy? Oh, that's right, your mom's fucking dead!"

They all laughed again, then formed a semi-circle about a meter and a half from Brick. His fury aroused the dark seed, but he suppressed both, grateful that he remained in control. There was no real danger—only the need to dispense some much-delayed justice.

Three seconds later, the five members of Bran's posse rolled on the ground, bleating like sheared sheep before falling silent and still.

I guess their pain threshold is really low. Cockless wonders.

Brick stood practically nose-to-nose with the wide-eyed and whimpering Brantley-fucking-Hollister.

"Wh-what the fuck just happened? What the hell are you?"

The vile odor of Bran's breath nearly choked him. "Talk about my mother again, and I'll shove my foot so far up your ass you'll be clipping my toenails with your fucking teeth."

Brick's fist traveled no more than six inches before burying itself in the bully's abdomen. He then stepped back three paces for what came next. As he leaned forward, stale alcohol and stomach acid stung his nostrils.

"Bran, It's a damn shame you won't remember what happened tonight, but maybe this will imprint on your subconscious. If you come near Tish or me again, you'll find out exactly what I am and what I can do."

Brick fired a low-power back fist into Brantley's jaw. He

dropped to the ground, his head landing face down in the lap of one of his associates. Brick took out his phone, snapped a photo, and then turned to his sister, standing a few paces behind him. He'd heard her approach after dealing with the posse.

"Neat, clean, relatively silent, and you barely used your hyper-speed. You have done well, Padawan Asshole." She scanned the group. "Friends of yours, Lil bro?"

"You could say that. You bring the Rohypnol? And I got your Padawan, you frigging hag."

Marble 'Mara' Redstone chuckled. Her white teeth gleamed in contrast to her light brown complexion and short, black curly hair. She flexed her well-defined muscles as she planted her fists on her shapely hips. Mara was an attractive thirty-something woman who resembled her brother in many ways and enjoyed showing off her long, muscular legs in shorts. Despite the frigid temperatures in Colorado, she wore a tiny, tight t-shirt that showcased her medium-sized bust.

The faint aroma assaulting Brick's nostrils revealed just what she had been up to that evening. He wondered if Katja was still in the house. "Of course, though, I laced it with a little Lasix just to give them an extra kick in the head for the morning. Hell, they might even piss themselves. This have to do with your girlfriend?"

"She's not my girlfriend, Mara. At best, my chances with her are slim," Brick stated, more to dampen his enthusiasm at recent events than anything else.

"Yeah, Lil bro. You keep telling yourself that. Someday, you might believe it. Bring the five-ton around before somebody sticks their head out and sees this mess."

"You got it, sis."

"And I got yer hag, Lil punkass negro."

Brick grinned at her and stuck out his tongue before trotting around the side of the house to retrieve the surprisingly quiet electric truck. He'd already decided where to dump Bran and his entourage, but he'd leave it up to Mara to choose whether to leave their clothing on or arrange them in compromising positions.

CHAPTER 6: WE NEED TO TALK

Part 1

We need to talk.

This phrase nearly always followed a breakup on television, and it turned out to be no different in real life for Dr. Sandra Brennan. Brick's words scorched a path of anger into her mind, and she had no one to blame but herself.

She'd been happy to see him when he appeared on her front porch. Their virtual sessions were satisfying, but they only went so far before she felt him slipping away. He wasn't in love with her any more than she was with him. Still, Sandra was sure they could at least have been happy together, especially when it came to sex.

They would have been a power couple in the scientific community. They could have accomplished great things together with Brick's skills and her connections. The two of them could have changed the course of the world. History teemed with those who remained together for the power and influence they wielded. She was confident that Brick would have unlocked the keys to the universe someday with her as his guide. She'd discovered and awakened his potential; he owed it to her to be there when he finally realized it, dammit. It would now be up to Latisha Owusu.

Sandra had decided to transition their relationship from virtual to physical to build a more solid bond and to hell with the consequences at the university. With Zindriya as her backup plan, she could leave the misogynistic dunderheads behind and forge a new path forward with Brick. Of course, there was no guarantee it would work, but it would have been worthwhile nonetheless. Brick's decision had made it all moot, though. She had tuned out nearly everything else he said as irrelevant when he didn't call her Andra. It's funny how one single letter could speak volumes.

With him working in such close quarters with Latisha, she always knew there was a chance she'd lose him, but she had hoped. She let out a snort. It never occurred to her that he would break up with her less than a week after they started working together.

Sandra initially believed the girl had finally given it up to Brick, using her plan against her, but she hadn't. He simply wanted to let her down before she could become more invested in him.

Fucking noble bastard.

Still, Sandra couldn't stay mad at him. Most guys would have led her on, having sex with her for as long as they could, then slink away into the night. At least Brick had the courage to face her, unlike many before him who had either dumped her by text or ghosting. Even the reason he'd dumped her had been, well, noble, and as much as it hurt, she could accept his reasons if not the outcome.

Most men walked away from her because they couldn't contend with her strength and intelligence. This was not an assumption on her part because some of the bolder men told her why they dumped her—generally via text.

Weak-minded assholes.

Since she and Brick were over, she could only access him and his beautiful mind through Zindriya. It was better to cut ties with the university immediately so she could better manage his treatment at the hands of her less-cultured sibling. As much as she could, anyway.

Sandra sat in front of her holoscreen, entered a secure access code, and dialed her sister's direct line. The scarred face of her twin appeared in the holo tank, sporting a raised eyebrow tugging up the corner of her mouth, as if she'd been expecting the call.

She did her best to paste a neutral expression on her face. "You were right. He chose her over me."

Zindriya's smirk was almost nonexistent—almost. "For what it's worth, dear sister, I am sorry."

She wondered why her sister's office, or at least the part she could see, was all white, no highlights. Cream would make for a warmer atmosphere. "I really did care for him, Driya."

The scarred twin flashed a smile that never neared her eyes. "So we're back to Plan B."

Pressed lips were Sandra's response to her sister's mirthless smile. "Right. What do you need from me?"

"Glad to have you on board. Tell me everything about your virtual encounters."

"You know about that? Brick said it was unhackable."

There goes Driya's damned smirk again. "It is unless you have access to one of the modules. I planted a cloning device on yours weeks ago."

"You were spying on us..." Sandra furrowed her brows, attempting to restrain her anger. "No, you were spying on me. You wanted leverage in case I refused to help you with Brick."

The predatory smile returned to Zindriya's face. "Of course. I needed to ensure you wouldn't run off with my prize asset. I suspected something when he missed the last few engagements with you."

"You're a real...."

"Watch it, sister. Remember never to call me the B-word."

"I was going to say *manky cailín*, Driya." It was as if a dark cloud descended on her soul. "I want her dead."

Raising an eyebrow, the scarred twin smirked again. "Who?"

"You know who the fuck I'm talking about. Kill her for me."

"Such language, and from a college professor no less."

"Yeah, well, we're people too."

"No. Latisha must live for now. If my strategy fails, I will have to use her as leverage since your effectiveness in that area has suffered a significant decrease."

Scowling at the answer, Sandra struggled to restore her mask of neutrality.

Part 2

Seeing her sister's beautiful face contorted into the mask of wrath filled Zindriya with a foreign emotion. It was affection. Perhaps filled was an overstatement. To say that she felt a pang of affection would be more accurate. Emotions were a liability to the scarred twin. Nonetheless, it was the first time she felt she had shared something with Sandra. She found it fitting that it was the thing that had fueled Zindriya most of her own life... rage.

Holding back a scowl at the horrid cream-colored walls in Sandra's bedroom, she leaned forward. "Will this be a problem, sister?"

"No. Not as long as I get him after you're finished, Driya. That was our agreement."

"Yes, it was, and once he is in your arms, I will kill her. It will make it easier for you to make him yours, Sandra."

Zindriya observed her sister's expression go from pinched, contorted wrath to forced complacency. She knew Sandra would be a problem regardless of her answer. Sister or not, with Brick preferring the girl over her, the good professor had outlived her usefulness. If problems arose, Zindriya would have to eliminate the problem, familial affection aside. It's not as if she loved Sandra. She'd never loved anyone, so why start now?

Suddenly experiencing the need to disengage, she ended the call with Sandra and sent for Venton Smythe.

When the mercie strolled in, his scruffy, half-bearded chin leading the way, Zindriya's face transformed into a sneer. At 170 centimeters, he was too short for his fourteen-and-a-quarter stone. His big face, broad physique, and shaggy, unkempt black hair reminded her of one of the seven dwarves named Quee from the 1912 Snow White Broadway play. She believed the moniker suited him because she felt a bit queasy whenever he was near. Zindriya wondered how many people were aware that the dwarves had no names in the original 1812 Grimm fairy tale and had remained unnamed until the Broadway production, and then renamed in the outlandish and juvenile Disney revision.

"You called Mistress."

What made it worse was his nasally, upper baritone voice. He sounded more like a talking French horn than a human. Zindriya clamped down on the urge to end the creature before her. He still had his uses, at least for the moment, despite the garlic and piss smell.

"Get the boyfriend ready and deploy him when Brick attends the Owusu family sci-fi night. I do not want anyone harmed, and you must take the boy alive. Is that understood?"

"Yes, Mistress. You can count on me."

Zindriya leaned back in her chair, elbows on armrests, hands steepled in front of her emotionless face. "I hope so, Venton. My lower dungeon is currently empty. I'm sure you wouldn't want me to, um, *hire* you for the vacant position, yes?"

She lifted a corner of her mouth. Venton looked as though he might pee his pants. The odor of stale garlic intensified as he shifted in his chair. She wondered if he wore cloves around his neck to ward her off, as though she were a vampire.

"Understood, Mistress."

"Dismissed, Quee."

"Mistress?"

"Get out!"

Venton flew from the chair and out the door, leaving Zindriya with a parting whiff of garlic and stale urine. She pulled a can of air freshener from her drawer and chased away the foul scent.

She summoned one of her regular soldiers. Bruno was the name she had given him, not bothering to remember his real name. They all worked for her, so she could call them whatever she wished. He entered and stood at attention. Bruno, she liked. He was tall, bald, big-boned, and in good shape. He was also hung like a donkey and didn't mind mixing a little pain with pleasure. He wasn't the prettiest thing to look at, but neither was she, and he had satisfied her needs on several occasions. A few healing bites and scratches from their last encounter remained as a reminder of their coupling. And for all the looks of a brute, he was quite intelligent, skilled, and efficient.

"We shall have a guest soon, Bruno, perhaps two, maybe even three. Is everything prepared?"

"Yes, Zindriya. I've prepared everything according to your specifications in both the upper and lower chambers. About the possible third—upper or lower chambers?"

"Lower, I think. Prepare one of both just to be sure."

"As you wish."

Bruno didn't cringe in her presence. She liked that he didn't fear her as much as the others in her crew but still respected her.

Zindriya was energized by the end of her wait. She would have Brick in her clutches in a little over a week, and she could start programming him with pain, then pleasure. Bruno would supply the pain, and she would ease his pains with pleasure. She'd used the technique before and had been quite successful, where full-on brutality and torture yielded nothing but garbage intel. When you tormented someone, they only told you whatever was necessary to stop the suffering, regardless of what you saw in the movies.

Zindriya recalled Babel and his final, blood-chilling prophecy. It hadn't sounded like his typical ramblings. Maybe she should have written it down because, at the moment, the exact words escaped her.

"Anything else you need, Zindriya?"

She had forgotten Bruno was still there and dismissed him. After he left, her mind drifted back to the moment before she ended Babel. The prophecy went something like this: *when the lover becomes the liar, the eagle will strike, and your silver tongue will drown you in the Red Sea.*

Zindriya scribbled it down on her notepad. Chills ran up and down her spine as she wrote the words into her memory. No matter how much she told herself they were just the ramblings of an insane man who teetered on the ragged edge of death, her blood still ran cold. Something about it felt far too real. She took a bottle of Gin from a drawer and poured two fingers into a glass before downing it. Not many people shot Gin, but she relished the burn as it passed down her throat. Two more fingers chased the jitters away so she could focus on running her organization.

Part 3

After the holocall ended, some part of Sandra knew her twin would cut her out of the whole deal with Brick. It could be time for her to make her own arrangements. But where would she start? She didn't have Zindriya's underground ties, nor did she think the same way. Her genius leaned toward science rather than criminality. On the other hand, her ability to navigate a world dominated by fragile men with eggshell-thin egos had honed skills that could come in handy.

How would she go about creating her own syndicate? Would she require one? Could she wield the same kind of power that her sister did, or should she rely on her cunning to stay relevant in Zindriya's eyes? The second option would suit her better because raw power had never been her forte.

Zindriya was all about fury, power, fear, and dominance. On the other hand, Sandra's strength rested in her brilliance, cunning, and, yes, a smidgeon of manipulation, especially when exploiting her looks to persuade love-starved science types to see things her way. She despised such techniques and used them as little as possible, but they may become her greatest assets in the coming days. Her lifestyle would change in any case, and whether it would be better or worse would rely on her capacity to adapt.

The only other option was to stay out of it all and wait for Brick to outlast his usefulness to Zindriya, assuming he ever did. Sandra had to accept that she still had feelings for the younger man. On her part, her connection to him ran more deeply than it had for anyone in a long time. Love was far from what she felt, but it would suffice.

So much for clinical objectivity. Brick had proven to be a generous and inventive partner, and she had thoroughly enjoyed all of their sexual encounters, even if virtual. His generosity and respect influenced her feelings, but it was his mind that had always captivated her. Brick had a unique perspective on both the macro and micro universes, mathematics and technology-related challenges, and, most significantly, the Quantum Field. He could see past obstacles like no one she'd ever met.

Take, for example, the 'unsolvable' equations she gave him during their tutoring sessions. Nobody had ever taught him such advanced math. It had been pure intuition, as natural to him as flying is to a bird. At least that's how he'd explained it when she asked him where he'd learned his skills. It simply made sense to him that the math should flow as it did. Sandra had read about savants before but had never met one until Brick.

Arthur C. Clarke's third law told us that if technology were advanced enough, everyone would confuse it with magic. It was the reason Sandra was certain Brick would someday unlock the mysteries of the cosmos and prove to everyone that magic truly existed in the form of science and technology. Because of the first two laws, she had begun introducing the unsolvable equations to Brick. First, scientists were supposed to make the impossible possible, and second, they were not to be obstructed by walls erected by others.

Walls, Sandra thought.

The answer to her problem was to find a way past the wall that Zindriya and her cohorts represented.

Or be the keystone, ready to either support the wall or bring it down around her ears.

With Brick, her sister was the keystone, and her minions were the bricks forming the wall. Sandra would join her sister's syndicate, become an indispensable part of the wall, replace Zindriya as the keystone, and if her twin tried to betray her, the whole damn thing would collapse squarely on her dear sister's head. Brick would be hers even if she had to take down her sister to get him.

Professor Brennan chuckled. Despite growing up in completely different surroundings, she and Driya shared many of the same traits. In this instance, genetics played a substantial role in a person's development, contrary to the Nature versus Nurture argument. The similarities between the women proved it, especially one attribute in particular. Her birth parents selling her to support their drug habit proved that ruthlessness most definitely ran in the family.

CHAPTER 7: CONFLICTED

Part 1

Tish took a break from writing code for the master control program on their nearly finished project. She flexed her fingers and arched her back, and several vertebrae sounded off like firecrackers. She looked to her left, hoping to catch Brick admiring her breasts as they rose magnificently, but he toiled slavishly at their creation.

He'd kept his end of the bargain for the entire two and a half months since their first kiss. Dammit. This was the first time Tish ever wished for someone to break a deal with her, but, Gods bless him, he didn't. How could she be disappointed when Brick kept his word? It was illogical yet true at the same time.

She was still unsure about her feelings for him. He'd turned out to be a very different person than she had initially imagined. Tish had always known he was a brilliant, skilled engineer, but she had no idea how imaginative and innovative he was. He had created every piece of hardware required to melt the metal for the initial stage of the Re-D Printer. He did all of this literally from spare parts, and in the short time they had worked on their concept.

How could she not like a man who showed that much

dedication. It made her wonder how much more he would give to someone he loved. Then again, maybe that was why he was so determined. Brick was in love with her and wanted to earn her respect. *And my love,* Tish thought.

For the first time in a long while, she took a good look at herself using his eyes as a lens. What did he see in her? Why did he love her when she struggled to love herself? Then she found it. A spark of light she'd buried when she became a member of the popular clique. Next to that spark was another, though it was barely the size of a pinhead. It was small, but it radiated a warmth that belied its size. When she looked closer, she recognized what it was, and it rocked her to the core.

That infinitesimal speck of warmth was the beginning of an emotion she didn't know she could feel. There was hope for her, and it lay in the man she worked with. Unbidden, the muscles in her face quirked her lips upward ever so slightly.

Their first kiss had awakened a chain of emotions, and the links grew in size and number as they spent more time together. Since they had begun their project, the two of them had spent at least four hours working on it every day after school. On weekends, they worked eight to ten hours a day, and Brick spent most of those nights in the guest house. Her parents treated him as if he were a member of the family, and after six weeks, Brick even started calling them Mom and Pops. No matter how hard she fought against it, Tish's feelings for him grew.

When they began sparring, she could no longer deny it. The person she had always thought of as a wimpy, pacifist nerd-freak was just a front. He was so much more. To top it all, he was also an incredible fighter.

Tish discovered his skills ten days ago while in a playful mood. When she snuck up behind him, Brick appeared to be fully absorbed in creating one of the acceleration nodes for the first melting stage. She intended to tickle him. She had no idea if he was ticklish, but that didn't matter. She only wanted to goof off.

Brick moved with blinding speed as soon as she touched him. His right hand blurred as it snatched hers from his ribs and twisted it into a wrist-lock.

He rose and turned to face her, an apology in his eyes. Despite her shock, she countered his move by spinning toward the twist, grabbing his wrist, and trying to bend his arm behind his back. Brick used his index and middle fingers to strike what must have been a nerve in between her second and third metacarpals. The shock ran up her arm, weakening her grip, and he slipped free.

She thrust the same hand forward, the heel of her palm out, to catch him off guard. Again, moving faster than anyone she'd seen, Brick spun to the side, evaded the strike, seized her wrist, and turned it, forcing her to spin with it or risk dislocating her shoulder. Tish didn't fight the maneuver but continued the spin, causing him to follow her or lose his grip.

Once more in control, she fired a knee at his exposed rib cage, but Brick blocked it with his free hand, twisted her arm again, and drew her toward him as he backed away. The maneuver forced her into another spin, but his backstep pulled her off balance. He stopped when she was bent backward, her arm over her head, teetering on the edge of falling and entirely under his control.

"Tapping out Brick! You got me."

Brick placed his free arm under Tish and helped her stand up straight. "I expected an overhead or reverse butterfly kick, followed by a back somersault. You've got the flexibility and the skill."

"Wouldn't have done any good. You'd've countered it. This wasn't a life-or-death sitch, so I figured it'd just be a waste of time and energy."

"Good point. You got some serious skills, Tish. You move a lot faster than anyone would expect."

Tish smiled at the compliment. Brick admired her physique. He was one of those guys who liked thick women.

"And you don't react like a pacifist, wimpy nerd-freak, Brick. You can fight. Show me the hand strike. I didn't know there was a nerve there."

"I just got lucky. I don't know what you're talking about, Tish."

"I think that's the first time you straight-up lied to me. Don't bullshit me, Brick. I know you a lot better than I used to. You've evaded my questions in the past, and I let it slide, but you've never outright lied. I hate lies with a passion because they destroy trust. If there's something you don't want to talk about, fine, tell me. But don't lie to me, okay?" She fixed his gaze on him. "This is important, Brick. Like relationship-ending important."

Brick sighed and slumped his shoulders. Shortly after, he shook his head as if he'd decided something important. Undergoing an exciting transformation, he stood up straight, shoulders back, nearly at attention. Strength and confidence radiated from him as if an aura encircled him.

Holy shit. I might have resisted the other guy, but him? Not a fucking chance, Tish thought, surprised that the possibility no longer bothered her.

For the first time, the real Mason Redstone stood before her. He hadn't shed all his layers, but today marked a significant step forward. Much like the Grinch's evolution, that pinpoint of warmth inside her grew.

"This is one reason I don't get close to people. I'm an open book to anyone who knows me." Brick exhaled. "Yes, I can fight."

"Who taught you?"

"My father, until I surpassed him, then I spent some time in a monastery in the Sierra Nevadas called Nil Parity, and afterward, my sister taught me how to win."

With a hand on her chin, a finger tapped a beat on her lips. "That explains it."

"What?"

"Why you've always said your sister hits harder than Bran and his posse. I think I've always sensed the real you hiding beneath the surface, Brick."

"I'm not surprised. Your intuition is off the hook, Tish. I'm actually shocked it took you this long."

In the face of new evidence, she looked at him in a new light. "It's because you found a great balance between deception and reality. You've kept everyone off-guard with brief displays of strength and agility cloaked as oafishness and incompetence."

"Years of practice."

"Why, Brick?"

"There may... False. There *will* come a day when I tell you, but it's not today, alright?"

"Finally, a man who listens." A grin stretched her face. "I gotchu. I can live with that. Come on."

Tish was curious to see how good he was. Her father had also trained her, and when she'd gotten too good for him, he'd hired Krav Maga masters to continue her training. She'd also trained in the Brazilian martial art, Capoeira, and acrobatics. Tish practically dragged Brick to the five-car garage, which included a gym with a padded blue floor and various fitness equipment for strength, martial arts, and flexibility training. All of it was in the last two car stalls. The place smelled like sweat mixed with motor oil and a dash of hydraulic fluid, so she turned on an exhaust fan to clear some of the stink. Tish told him there was a shooting range underneath the garage as well.

Brick was much better than she was, and Tish suspected he was holding back. Why would he let a bunch of jackasses beat him up when he had such advanced combat skills? He could be running the damn school. No one would dare challenge him. Everyone would know who he was, and the ladies would be all over him. Tish caught herself there because she would likely have been one of those ladies. She didn't understand, so she asked him after they finished sparring.

"Because it's not who I am, Tish. I don't need adoration and don't want the attention it would bring. I like staying as far under the radar as possible."

"Did you ever think... I'm not trying to break our deal, but I have to know."

"Of course, I thought about how it would change the way you felt about me, Tish, but I'm not that guy. I won't *be* that guy to impress someone. Even someone for whom I have feelings."

"Don't you mean..."

"Love? Yes, Tish, I'm still in love with you."

She'd noticed how they'd started finishing each other's sentences or answering half-asked inquiries as he'd just done. Was this thing between them getting serious?

And so what if it is? Her unbidden thought failed to surprise her.

"You're making it really hard not to like you, Brick."

"Don't worry. Wait till you get to know me. I can be quite the asshole. Ask my sister. She raised me, and I pretty much grew up thinking Asshole was my middle name."

Tish wasn't sure if he was joking or not because he said it with such a straight face, but she chuckled anyway, just in case.

Afterward, they sparred at least twice a week, generally three times. Brick proved to be a better instructor than the ones her father had hired. Over time, her skills developed at the same rate as her feelings for the man she once despised. He peeled back additional layers, revealing more of his true personality, but Tish wasn't sure she'd ever know everything about him. It always seemed as though he held back.

Every time their conversation turned to the company his father and sister owned, Brick would clam up or change the topic. She decided to try to get him to open up about another issue she'd been curious about. So one day, after a somewhat intimate sparring session in which they worked on grappling maneuvers, she felt comfortable and aroused enough to ask. "Are you ready to tell me who she was?"

Brick's entire body stiffened. "What "she" are you talking about?"

Still a little out of breath, and not because of the grappling, she forged forward. "Your last good kiss."

"Damn, woman. Do you have elephant blood?"

His body relaxed, but only slightly. Brick's brows nearly touched as he glared at her, and his face stretched thin over his skull as if he'd spent a month in the desert.

What am I seeing? Is it guilt, maybe?

She wasn't sure, but perhaps she was onto something. He turned away and spoke.

"I guess there must be something to that *knowing someone if you fight them* thing."

"Or kiss them?" Tish wasn't sure why she'd brought it up. *Yes, you do, girl. Quit denying it.*

Brick's gaze briefly met hers, but the curvature of his lips never approached a smile.

"Yeah, that too."

His voice was different. He sounded tired. No, not tired. He sounded weary and sad, almost tortured. He collapsed onto the training room's padded floor. Tish sat directly in front of him. Both crossed their legs, Native American style, and Brick began his brief but tragic story.

Part 2

He'd been in love with a girl named Kaylen in high school in another city where his family had lived. He had offered her a promise ring a few days before their summer break. She didn't say no but acknowledged it was a big decision. She wanted time to think about it, and she'd let him know after she and her family returned from their vacation. Brick had misinterpreted it as a rejection. He'd been jealous after seeing his girlfriend laughing and joking with another guy later in the day. Instead of talking to her about his feelings, he retaliated against the imaginary wrong she'd done him.

Kaylen always informed him when she returned from a vacation. She would come over to his house for some alone time to, ahem, renew their relationship.

Hannah, Brick's stunningly beautiful cousin, happened to be in town at the time. They were incredibly close, and both admitted that they would be a couple if they weren't first cousins. He invited Hannah over for a visit, and they snuggled up on the front porch swing.

Kaylen had never met his cousin before and discovered them entangled on the swing. Brick knew he had effed up as soon as he saw the agony in Kaylen's eyes and his promise ring on her finger. Kaylen dashed back to her car and sped off. She lost control of the vehicle a block from her house. Hundred-year-old oak trees were unforgiving. Hannah never forgave him for using her. So in one day, he lost the two people he loved most in the world. In his mind, though, he hadn't *lost* anyone. He'd murdered Kaylen and had driven Hannah away.

Part 3

"God, Brick. I'm so sorry."

"Thanks. That's the other reason I don't get close to people."

By only a hair did she resist reaching out to him. "What do you mean?"

"I've been in love twice before, and I killed them both with decisions I made with my head instead of listening to my heart."

Taken aback by his confession, Tish chose silence over a verbal gaffe. She extended a hand to console him, but Brick moved out of reach. Her heart ached for him as the guilt and shame drew lines across his forehead and at the corners of his squinting, tear-filled eyes.

"Told you once you got to know me, you'd see how much of an asshole I really am."

Brick rose in one smooth motion and exited the garage.

When he left the training room two weeks before, Tish wasn't sure she'd see him again. The chasm it opened in her soul shocked her. Her heart pounded, threatening to burst from her chest.

The next day, she found him waiting at her car. Brick had skipped school, and his red-rimmed eyes told the story of the last twenty hours. He apologized for walking out on her and then slid in through the passenger door.

Tish resisted the urge to leap into his arms when she first saw him. The pressure encircling her heart vanished, and her stomach stopped its hours-long gymnastics routine. She had no idea such powerful feelings could sneak up on you like that. Tish had never been in love before, and she hadn't been sure she could feel deep emotions for anyone but her family. No one else had stirred such feelings in her. Upon seeing him, all doubt fled her mind and heart. She needed Brick to be in her life at the very least; at most, she was in love with him.

Tish took the wheel, and they drove home in comfortable silence. Home? Brick might not live with them, but when they were together, she felt at home. Maybe she was in love with him. The idea didn't bother her in the least. She felt no urge to strike up a conversation, and as it turned out, neither did he.

She spied Brick watching her, a half-smile on his lips. Warmth spread through her body, and somehow, she knew they'd be okay. When they arrived at the workshop, They returned to work and never spoke of it again.

Their relationship settled into a new normal. There they were, still working together on their grand project, as Tish's feelings for Brick exacerbated her confusion. They would finish their device in a few weeks, two months at most. Then, their partnership would be over. It looked as though their machine would be marketable. They could be business partners, but it wouldn't be enough for her... not anymore.

Tish asked him about his last, best kiss because she was curious about the competition she faced. Little did she know that she would be up against two ghosts and an Olympus Mons of guilt, the emotion she had not recognized in his face until after he finished his story.

The other, and most important, reason was that their grappling session had been intense, intimate, and erotic. She'd finally gotten the better of Brick, ending up on top, hands on his shoulders, pinned to the floor, face inches from his. She'd felt his arousal as it pressed against her own. A part of her wondered whether he could feel her throbbing down there or if he noticed her nipples stretching the thin fabric of her training gear. She'd been out of breath, and it wasn't just because of the spar. She'd wanted to kiss him but instead stood up and extended a hand to assist him. She probably would have jumped his bones if she hadn't asked about the kiss. Part of her wished she had.

That was a watershed moment for both of them. Brick grew closer to her as the days passed, and she to him. He'd previously declined every invitation to her family's sci-fi movie night, but had finally accepted the one coming up the following Friday. Tish was happy, despite the fact that it presented a dilemma.

Should she tell him about her growing feelings for him, or would he interpret it as exploiting his emotions against him and breaking their deal? Would he believe her? What would he do if he didn't? Would he walk away or give her a chance to explain? It was easy to figure out most guys, but Brick was the most complex person she'd ever known, and it was all at once incomprehensible, infuriating, intoxicating, and, frankly, irresistible. She remembered how she had teased him when he had used four 'I' words to describe his feelings for her. It brought a wan smile to her face.

Doubt and confusion surged through her mind, clouding her judgment. So she chose the safe route, keeping things as they were. Once they finished the project and fulfilled the deal, she could safely talk to Brick about how she felt. Until then, she would show her feelings for him subtly, non-threateningly so it wouldn't break their deal or drive him away, hoping he would notice.

Tish hadn't realized she'd been staring at Brick the entire time her mind had strolled through the past. He looked up from his work, stretched, turned around, and caught her staring. She didn't look away this time.

He beamed broadly at her. "What? Was I snoring or something? Do I have a booger hangin' out of my nose?"

"No, nothing like that, silly." She chuckled at the dumb joke.

And there goes that cute smirk of his. "Then what, or do I want to know? Planning on the best way to slide a dagger between my ribs since I've shown you where to strike?"

Damning the blasted deal, she softened her voice, trying to help him understand how she felt. "Brick, I would never do anything to hurt you. I've gotten to know you better, and hurting you is the farthest thing from my mind."

"Whoa. It almost sounds like you actually like me."

Tish gave him what she thought was a sarcastic smile

but realized she didn't have enough snark to pull it off convincingly. *And maybe that's okay,* she thought. *This might be an excellent time to toss some hints his way.*

"Stranger things have happened, Brick. Time heals all wounds."

"True, but distance makes the heart grow fonder, and we've spent a grip of time together lately."

"Absence."

His brows flew up. "Huh?"

"Absence, not distance, and not all of the old proverbs fit every situation, Brick."

Tish rolled her head from left to right, grunting as a minor ache in her neck bothered her.

"Would you mind massaging my neck and shoulders for me, please?"

More familiar with him now, she noticed a hint of reluctance. "Uh, isn't that against our deal?"

"Only if *you* ask *me*. I'm the one doing the asking. So. Will you?"

And there's the smile she sought more of from him. "Of course."

Of course, her mouth took precedence over her feelings this time. "Don't let your hands 'accidentally' slip. I don't need a breast exam, all right?"

"No problem, Tish. I'm not gonna mess up what we have."

Did I hear what I thought I heard, or is it wishful thinking? Does he sense my feelings for him changing, or is he letting me know his haven't changed?

She closed her eyes and bit her bottom lip to stifle a moan as Brick's hands gently but firmly eased the tension from her neck and shoulder muscles.

Oh, God. Such amazing hands; gentle, yet strong and firm. It feels so wonderful.

Four minutes into the massage, she was ready to fall into his arms. Tish sat up abruptly, asked him to stop, and thanked him for the incredible massage. He complied. If he hadn't, she probably wouldn't have objected to and may have encouraged that breast exam. She turned her chair around to face him.

"Brick, I wasn't thinking. Does it bother you to touch me like that, feeling the way you do?"

"Are you kidding? It was the bright spot of my entire week." A devilish grin creased Brick's face then vanished. "I'm fine, Tish. I'll provide all of the massages you want on-demand, no problem. I'm good at keeping my emotions in check around you."

Time for a fishing expedition because his behavior early in their project suggested he might have someone on the side. "I mean, neither of us is in a relationship, and you know how it can be when you work closely with someone."

Not a hint of regret shown in his eyes during his confession. "To be honest, I was in a relationship, but I broke up with her shortly after we started this whole thing."

"Oh. You never said anything. Who was she? Did it happen because of our project and all the time we've spent together?"

"It doesn't matter anymore, Tish. I know who I am and who I want to be with, and as amazing as she is, it isn't her. I never hid anything, but she agreed to take a chance on me anyway. She didn't deserve to be hurt, but I thought it was better to call it quits before she became more invested in me. I didn't want…"

Brick trailed off without concluding his sentence.

Tish knew where this was going. "You didn't want her to be in the same situation as you are now with me."

"Right."

"You're not an asshole, Brick," Tish placed her hand on his arm. "We all make bad decisions, but few of us have the wisdom to recognize them, and even fewer have the courage to correct them. You're a good, decent man."

And I should tell him how I feel right this instant, but for all the time I thought he was a coward, I find that I'm the one who's afraid. Of intimacy. Of commitment. Of vulnerability. Of everything I want in a relationship but am too scared to accept because deep down inside, I don't think I deserve it. But Brick does, and he's the first person I've been with who has shown me that I'm more than just an assortment of desirable body parts. I've always known it, but now I'm at the cusp of believing it. When I've crossed that barrier, maybe I can love him like he loves me.

"Let's get back to it." Before she returned to her coding, she lost herself in his eyes, his incredible, thoughtful, solemn eyes that seemed to peer into her soul. "I have a lot of work to do if we're going to make this work."

"It looks like we're heading in the right direction, Tish. Whatever I can do to help, you just let me know."

A tiny smile adorned her face at the double meanings they flung at each other. *He just so gets me like no one ever has.* They would find their path.

"You've already done your part, Brick. The rest is up to me. You'll be the first to know when I'm ready, okay?"

"Looking forward to it."

Tish swung the chair around and pounded out code on the keyboard, punishing it for her weakness but also rushing to finish so she could move forward with the man who was capturing her heart.

CHAPTER 8: THE OR SOMETHING OPTION

More than two months had passed since Brick had broken up with Sandra. Recent events encouraged him to finally accept Tish's open invitation to join the fam for their classic sci-fi movie night. Part of the reason it had taken him so long was the crushing guilt he felt over ending his relationship with Professor Bennett. Brick had developed feelings for Andra, and while they paled in contrast to his love for Tish, they were still there. But being so close to the woman he loved had gradually dimmed his feelings for Andra until they had faded enough to suppress the guilt to the point where it no longer mattered.

Things between him and Tish had improved dramatically since he agreed to attend the Owusu family event. She had a spring in her step, smiled more, cracked on him less, and their conversations became more personal.

Tish talked frankly about her previous relationships, what she loved and hated about the men and women she dated, and what she was looking for in a mate. Brick thought she gave him a map to her heart, but a part of him believed she wasn't ready to give up her position on him totally. However, he suspected that he had caused a few thousand cracks in the ceiling.

Then came the day he had not exactly been dreading but was worried about. While Tish banged away on the keyboard, fleshing out the last hundred or so lines of code, he prepared the setup for a manual test of their creation. All of a sudden, she rushed to her feet and pushed the wheeled office chair across the floor, where it bumped into an unsuspecting Brick from behind, just at knee-level, buckling one of them. As he flailed his arms in an attempt to maintain his balance, Tish darted in and wrapped her arms around him to keep him from falling. She clung to him once he'd regained his equilibrium but spun him around so they were face to face.

Once she finished helping him, to his utter delight, she gazed into his eyes and asked the question. It was awkward, with her body still pressed against his, but he considered it more probative than punitive. "Are you a virgin, Brick?"

Though pleased that Tish felt comfortable asking, he struggled to balance the truth with protecting his cover. "No. You know about both Fritz and Kaylen."

"Yah, but you were pretty young at the time. I was just curious."

Since she still hadn't released him, he allowed his hands to encircle her, and to his surprise, she didn't move away.

"Why, were you going to volunteer to teach me the ways of love?" Brick couldn't stop himself from raising the corner of his mouth.

To his surprise again, she did not seize the opportunity to shut him down but looked thoughtful at the prospect. 'Not yet, but I won't lie to you. It has crossed my mind."

Stunned silence filled the space between them as he struggled to wrap his mind around her confession until his brain jumpstarted his mouth. The craving to caress her cheek, then kiss her, almost overrode his better judgment. Almost. "But not until after the project is complete, right?"

"Right. We have a deal, and I don't want to violate your trust, Brick. I won't ruin what we've built between us, especially with our first sci-fi movie night coming up."

"Tru-dat. We're so close. I can't wait to cross that finish line so we can celebrate our victory."

"We're almost there, Brick, and I promise you, we will embrace our victory wholeheartedly." Tish pulled him closer, laying her head on his chest and squeezing before giving him a gentle shove and a parting smile. "I'd best get back to work."

He had finished constructing the Re-D Printer, which had performed marvelously during their first few manual test runs. So, the technology worked, but the manual controls required the assistance of an engineer. That might win them first prize in the contest, but they also wanted marketability. That part was up to Tish and her coding skills.

Brick watched Tish slave over the control program for the last few weeks. He wished his skill with programming could have been at a fraction of her level, but it wasn't. To pass the time, he fine-tuned the Re-D unit for the umpteenth time, tweaked specs, and sketched designs for additional modules to melt and reprint alternative materials. The whole time, he resisted the increasing desire to put his arms around Tish and hold her tight to relieve her growing exasperation.

Three days before, a severe checksum issue occurred during the initial software trial. Since then, they both had ditched school to focus on their project. It took Tish till today, a few hours before sci-fi night, to narrow the error down to one section of code. She'd been over that section a hundred times looking for her error, but it remained elusive.

Brick watched as her irritation grew exponentially. Four hours before sci-fi night began, Tish grabbed her wireless keyboard and started to wing it across the room, but Brick had been close enough to snag it from her grasp. She glared at him at first, then opened her lips, presumably to tear him a new one, before closing it as her eyes softened and drooped a little.

Irritated Tish was just as attractive as joyful or unhappy Tish. Over the last couple of months, he'd seen about every manifestation of her persona, and he was utterly and hopelessly hooked on all aspects of the woman, good and bad.

"I can't find it, Brick, and I'm tired of looking. Maybe I should take a break until tomorrow before it really drives me crazy." She rolled her head in a circle. Brick heard the vertebrae crack. She turned away from him and pointed at her neck and shoulders. "Would you mind?"

The longer Tish worked on the coding, the more she asked for massages, and Brick had been happy to oblige. Yesterday, she'd leaned into him. It had been a challenge to continue the massage, but there was no way he would urge her to move. "No prob, Tish."

"Thanks, Brick. You have great hands, and your massages are uh-ma-zing." She moved her long hair out of the way, turned the office chair around, straddled it, leaned forward onto the backrest, then rested her head on her forearms. He started working out the kinks in the tight muscles of her neck and shoulder.

"A little lower, please. My middle back is seriously killing me..." Tish sighed. "I know. I know. Don't slouch. I'm trying."

"You know what Yoda said about trying."

"Yah, Yah. You either do it or you don't. No such thing as try."

Brick cringed but managed to maintain control. "Close enough."

Tish had begun wearing baggy shirts and no bra while they were working. Her light blue shirt had a droopy, wide neck that offered him access to a significant amount of skin.

"It's okay to massage under my shirt, Brick. I trust you, and it always feels better when your hands are touching my bod..., uh, my skin."

She pulled the back of her shirt up to her shoulders and tucked the front under her ample bosom. This was the first time Brick had seen so much of her skin at one time, and it was, in a word, exhilarating. Tish exhaled a mixture of sighs and groans that sounded far too similar to another activity in which Brick would love to engage her. As she tilted her head to the side, he noticed a smile spread across the left side of her face.

Everyone had their own distinct scent, but most humans couldn't distinguish it from ambient aromas that assailed the senses at any given moment. Brick, on the other hand, could identify almost anyone by smell due to his mutation. Tish's background aroma was earthy and sweet, like a floral meadow. Even when they sparred, her musk attracted him and reminded Brick of bales of hay stacked in a barn loft. He reminisced about stolen afternoon naps in the hayloft at the Nil Parity monastery.

As he continued to massage Tish, her perfume gradually and discreetly changed to the musky vanilla aroma he'd observed three weeks before during their extremely sensual wrestling match. He leaned in closer, his fingers digging into the base of her spine and tracking up to her shoulders. Tish's breathing became heavier as his hands rose higher.

That musky vanilla aroma became sweeter and more intoxicating, almost irresistible, as he repeatedly caressed her neck with gentle but firm fingers. His breathing grew heavy and he leaned closer, responding to her. His hands now massaged the middle of her back and slowly inched farther toward the front of her well-toned body. Her hand reached for his, guiding it forward and upward until his fingers brushed the bottom swell of her breast. With a husky voice, Tish urged him on. "Brick...I want..."

He glanced at the screen at that moment, and it clicked. He straightened up, shattering the ambiance. His damned, pattern-seeking brain had found what Tish was looking for at precisely the wrong frigging time. "Tish! I think I see what's wrong!"

Tish faltered as though dragging herself out of a trance. "Wha-what? What are you talking about? Nothing wrong."

Brick pulled her shirt down, cursed his brain, and pointed to the code on the screen.

"Right there." Brick pointed at the screen. "That line of code. I'm not even gonna pretend to understand what it does, but patterns come naturally to me. That line is inconsistent with the pattern I see all around it. It's off somehow."

"Holy... Brick, I think you found it!"

She was excited and fully engaged after he pointed out the code.

"I want your hands on me while I fix this." Tish swiveled to the screen, then turned back. "And next time, if I want you to cover me up, I'll tell you, Mr. Redstone."

Brick raised his brows, pursed his lips. "Yes, miss."

While Tish pounded away on the computer, he slid his hands under her shirt and returned to working on her tense-again back muscles. She finished ten minutes later and squeezed his hand as he massaged her neck.

'Thanks, Brick. Let's test it out now."

She ran one of her checksum programs, and it came up clear. She ran it a second and third time just to be sure. No problems. Tish made a sound Brick couldn't even begin to describe, leaped into his arms, wrapped her legs around him, told him he was amazing, and kissed him on the lips, but no teasing this time. Her lips lingered on his for a moment. She quickly hopped back down. He still felt a smile stretch across his face.

She approached their creation. "Let's test it on the Re-D now."

Brick changed the interface modules from manual to automated control, linked it to the computer, and then Tish ran a simulation. The first one finished without an error. The second, however, revealed some minor discrepancies. They found a few simple measurement errors and adjusted specifications, and the next ten simulations worked fine.

The woman almost trembled with excitement. "We can run sims all night and check the results in the morning."

It had been a long time since Brick had seen Tish so energetic, and her exuberance infected him.

"If all goes well, we can try a practical test tomorrow. You're spending the night in the guest house, yah?"

Why can't he stop grinning? "That's the plan. So we can get an early start."

"Cool." Tish looked at her watch. "We have a little over an hour before sci-fi night begins. Wanna grab a bite..." She lay a hand on his arm and brandished one of her peculiar and mysterious smiles. "Or something?"

The smile and the slight hesitation before the 'or something' wasn't wasted on Brick, but he still wasn't sure it was *the* smile. The last time she had offered him an or something option, at the beginning of the semester, her eyebrow cocked at the same angle, and she had threatened to draw blood if he'd accepted the challenge. His heart screamed at him to go for it, damn the fragging torpedoes, but his head advised him to play it safe, even after their close encounter a couple of weeks ago.

No one ever got burned by playing it safe.

The platitude defended his reluctance, and then that infernal inner voice chimed in with their two cents. *Yeah, and if you never get the fire going, you'll never get warm, either.* Brick still didn't know if it was the halo or the horns and would most likely never find out.

He chose the safer path. "I am kinda hungry, but aren't we having hot dogs and popcorn tonight?"

"Yah, but I want a snack. Let's go."

Though Tish's smile was less provocative than it had been a second before, she grabbed his hand and virtually dragged him to the main house kitchen.

Brick mentally slapped himself for not choosing the *or something* option. Once they entered the bastion of white paint, glass-paneled cabinets, honey oak countertops, and hanging stainless steel utensils, he pulled on his big boy pants and forged forward. "What if I had kissed you the first time you offered me that *or something* option?"

"If you had kissed me in the classroom, we never would have had to kiss in the parking lot. And if everything since happened the same way as it has to this point, we'd already be in your bedroom in the guest house."

"Decisions have consequences."

Her index finger tapped the appropriate facial feature. "Right on the nose, math-boy."

Brick felt hopelessly lost when it came to nuance. He was confident in so many areas, but he felt woefully unarmed and inept at deciphering what signals Tish might be sending. When it came to her, well, he was so afraid of making the wrong move that he chose inaction over action. That's what his head told him to do.

His heart, however, told him otherwise. It had told him to take the 'or something' option, but he had listened to his head instead. He guessed that overcoming the programming would be difficult after two decades of propaganda from his father and sister. It would take a conscious effort, and he would make that effort for Tish. "When will it be back on the table?"

"Note to Brick. When I offer you an 'or something' option, take it. The results might be good. They might be bad. But they might also be great."

"Can I get a stat sheet on that, Tish?"

"You're going to have to take your chances and develop your own."

He failed to stop the smile. "So, I'll get enough chances to create my own?"

"I can't tell you when, but I can tell you it's more likely than not that the next time will happen in the very near future."

"That almost sounds like—"

Tish interrupted him with a finger on his lips. "Don't paste a label on it, don't quantify it, don't plug it into an equation, math boy. For once, listen to this..." She placed her hand over his heart. "Instead of this." She traced her fingertip to his forehead. Brick wondered if she could read his mind.

At that moment, Tish's mother, Hiral, swept into the kitchen. Both Brick and Tish greeted her as Mom.

"It seems as though I've interrupted a moment." Hiral smiled at them.

Brick leaned against the counter, and Tish remained within his personal space. When Mom swooped in, she placed her hand back over his heart, nestled against him, and didn't move away.

Hiral's smile grew even broader. "I take it you don't hate Brick anymore."

"I don't think I ever did, Mom. Besides, we've become friends, maybe more."

This was news to Brick, sort of. He'd sensed changes in her, but he'd not assumed their relationship had progressed that far, at least not openly. His woeful ineptitude froze him yet again.

"From what I see, it's more." Mom flashed a grin that brightened her eyes. Tish still didn't move, and her hand remained in place. Brick stayed silent, entranced by the ongoing informational and revelatory conversation.

"So?" Tish's body stiffened.

Uh-oh. There goes the snark. Brick thought.

"You know that your father and I think of Brick as the son we never had. The issue doesn't lie with *us*."

And Mom tossed it right back. Gotta stop volcano time.

As it had before, tension filled the space between mother and daughter. Brick placed his hand over the one Tish held over his heart. She peered into his smiling eyes, and the blaze in hers diminished. He held her gaze. "Mom, what help do you need getting the hot dogs ready?" Tish's eyes conveyed her gratitude to him.

Hiral fired orders as Tish looked into his eyes and lowered her voice. "Too bad Mom's here, cuz that 'or something' option so just popped back up on the table, big time."

Listening to his heart at last, Brick gently placed his hands on her waist and kissed Tish on the forehead. To his surprise, she hooked the fingers of her free hand through one of his belt loops and pressed against him. After a moment, she tilted her head back and opened her eyes. "I gotta go tinkle."

"That was random. Tinkle? You did *not* just say that."

She grinned at him. "Would you rather I say that I gotta go take a piss? I'm not a guy. I'm a lady, and I tinkle. Get over it." She glided from the kitchen.

As she bustled around the kitchen, Hiral spoke to him. "Well played, Brick. I think she's coming around. She's not quite ready to admit it yet, but she's close. Latisha is a lot like her father. They cling to old habits until the tattered shreds leave nothing else to hold onto."

She walked around the central island and hugged him. "And you're more like me. You're all grit and determination. You don't give up easily, even when someone tries to push you away. And we have the same weird sense of humor. You truly are the son I never had, Brick."

"It means a lot, Mom. Thanks."

Brick wrapped his arms around her and squeezed. He had developed genuine feelings for this woman, and she was the next best thing to having a birth mom. Her hugs made him feel all warm and fuzzy inside.

"Okay, enough of that, you lout. Don't try and get out of helping with the hot dogs." Hiral spun Brick around and shoved him in the direction of the appliances. "We're using the indoor grill tonight. No boiling or nuking allowed. You handle the dogs..." Her voice took on a playfully ominous tone. "And I'll warm the buns."

Her demeanor forewarned Brick of what was to come. Hiral grabbed a towel, twisted it around, and snapped him on the backside. Brick grabbed one of his own, balled it up, and threw it at her, and the chase ensued.

The woman was death incarnate with the towel snapping, so he grabbed a ladle from the utensils hanging over the stove to parry her strikes as they played around the kitchen's island.

Tish entered the room. "Oh-my-God! You two are so much alike. I see why you enjoy having him around, Mom. The hot dogs?"

Hiral and Brick, out of breath but giggling, slumped against each other.

"Just having a little fun, Latisha. "Hiral looked up at Brick and hooked a thumb in Tish's direction. "But old stick in the mud is right. It's almost time for the movies."

The stick remark forced a snort from him before he could stop it. He looked at Tish to gauge her reaction, but she just grinned, rolled her eyes, and shook her head.

They finished the hot dogs and arranged the condiments on a table in the family room in time for the first movie. Pops had everything queued up and ready to go. Tish asked which movie it was. He had chosen *At the Earth's Core* with Doug McClure. It was based on Edgar Rice Burroughs' Pellucidar series. Brick tried to stop it, but the groan refused to be denied and forced itself out.

"Oh, you don't like the movie Brick?" Pops swiveled his head in his direction.

"Honestly? It's entertaining, but only a passing representation of Burroughs' vision is all."

"Re-e-a-a-ly. I suppose you have a better suggestion?"

"Sorry, Pops." He threw his hands up in surrender. "It's not my place to question."

"Nonsense, Brick. You're part of this family. You have a say. Spit it out."

He asked them if they had seen the 1968 movie *The Green Slime*, starring Robert Horton and Richard Jaeckel. None of them had, not even Amaye, the classic sci-fi aficionado. Brick gave them a brief synopsis of the film without giving too much away, and they thought it was a good choice. He told them it was his second favorite classic sci-fi film of all time. Second only to, and they all said it in unison, *The Forbidden Planet*, 1956, with an all-star cast led by Leslie Nielsen, Anne Francis, and Walter Pidgeon. Though released long before *The Green Slime*, the visual effects were significantly superior. He might have mentioned it once or twice during their dinner discussions.

"I'm glad you finally joined us, son. Yo-o-u-u are most definitely one of us."

Once he understood that Amaye contracted a mild form of Apraxia of Speech from his service, Brick readily accepted it as the norm. He thanked Pops and used his smartphone to broadcast the film to their local entertainment network.

He sat at one end of the sectional just as Tish moved closer to her parents. "I could sit over here... or something."

He raised his hand. "I'll take the 'or something' option."

"Again, a man who learns from his mistakes, grudgingly at times, but at least you catch on. We'll work through that. I usually snuggle with my teddy or my parents, but you're here now."

Once Brick got comfy, Tish lifted his right arm, half-leaned her back against him, curled her legs up on the cushions, then settled his arm around her midriff, her right hand over the top of his. Her left elbow rested lightly on his thigh. Tish took a big breath and then exhaled slowly, as people do after a long day.

Everything felt perfect, as if it were meant to be. Tish interlaced her fingers with his. Had he finally captured the heart of this remarkable woman? Brick's heart was convinced, and he promised to follow it this time. Mom and Pops sat on the other side of the L-shaped sofa, snuggled up like he and Tish, and smiled at the young couple as the movie began.

CHAPTER 9: REVEALED

The Owusu family clapped and cheered at the end of the film. Mom, Pops, and Tish urged Brick to choose the next film, so he suggested either The Little Shop of Horrors or Way...Way Out. The Owusu family had only ever heard of the 1986 version of LSOH, the musical comedy starring Steve Martin.

They were unaware of the original 1960 Roger Corman black comedy. Brick began to doubt Pops' bona fides regarding classic sci-fi after that. Maybe Mom had a point. He had his faves and always chose the same set of movies repeatedly, stubbornly holding on to the ones he was familiar with.

The second option didn't entice the Fam because it featured Jerry Lewis, despite Brick explaining that it had hit theaters back in 1966. Also, it wasn't one of his slapstick comedy roles, and the film also starred Connie Stevens and Anita Ekberg. He thought those two actresses might sway Pops' opinion because they were Connie-the angel-Stevens, and Anita-whatta body-Ekberg, but it was a no-go. Instead, they chose the original *Little Shop of Horrors*. With the movie choice settled, Mom assigned him and Pops to popcorn duty. They entered the kitchen to prepare more.

Brick and Pops' conversation was firmly entrenched in how much butter to put on popcorn. As a general rule, Pops remained conservative, putting on only enough to give the corn flavor, while Brick was the 'drench it till it floats' type.

They finished with the popcorn and were about to return to the family when Brick grabbed Pops' elbow.

Brick strained to listen. "Stop, Pops. Quiet for a minute."

He held a finger to his lips and bent his head to the side just as Amaye was about to say something. "Shit. It's Brantley, and he's got a gun." A startled cry from both women reached them.

Amaye's eyes widened, and he tried to flee, but Brick's vise grip on his elbow prevented him. Fortunately, the older man's military training kicked in. He stopped struggling and glared at Brick, who drew him away from the gateway and toward the back door. They spoke in a hushed urgency. "We've got to do something, Brick. Our ladies are in danger."

He locked his eyes on the older man's. "You know well enough that if we go charging in there, Brantley's gonna panic, and someone's gonna get hurt. We have to be smart about this."

Pops squinted his eyes and pressed his lips together until they all but disappeared. "This isn't your first rodeo, is it?"

Brick hesitated for a moment and then sighed. "No."

"Fine. If we get out of this alive, Brick, you'll owe me an explanation."

"Once this is over, I'll explain everything to all of you. For now, will you do as I ask?"

Amaye gave the nod. Pops was gone, and the Marine Force Recon emerged. Brick would be the decoy. Amaye balked because he felt he would be better for that, but Brick held firm. Bran didn't see the younger man as a threat because he was the wimpy, pacifist nerd-freak. However, the tall, broad-shouldered, decorated war hero would be a significant threat to the unbalanced, gun-wielding moron.

Amaye would leave through the back door, circle around to the front, and take Bran down from behind. Brick would call 911, then carry the popcorn back to the family room as if nothing was going on and distract the gun-toting idiot.

Brantley's shout urged them to hurry. "Where the FUCK are they?" Amaye bolted through the back door at a dead run. It was a long way around to the front of the house.

Their cover story was that they were low on sodas, and Amaye had ridden his bike to the corner convenience store since he'd had a few beers and didn't want to drive.

Brick closed his eyes, took two deep breaths, exhaled slowly, and put his mind into the right frame for what was to come. He dialed 911, informed them there was an armed intruder in the house, gave them the address, hid the phone behind some kitchen towels, and kept the line open. He proceeded to the family room with the two bowls of popcorn, striding through the open door as if he didn't have a care in the world. When he saw Brantley, he feigned panic, barked a childish screech, and tossed the popcorn into the air.

Bran carried a Glock G17 9mm, a semi-automatic pistol with a cam-lock system akin to the Browning High-Power. It was a popular law enforcement handgun, but in his opinion, not as good as his preferred sidearm, the Sig Sauer P226, 9mm. The action was a hair faster than the Glock's, giving the Sig the ability to fire six rounds in the time it took the Glock to fire five. Understanding the capabilities of your opponent's weapon was critical in designing defensive and offensive tactics.

"Come in, asshole! Stop right there!" Brantley shook with what could either be rage or fear.

Brick walked a fine line, somewhere between panic, manic, and calm. He held his arms in front, palms out. "Whoa, whoa, whoa, man. Don't shoot. It's all good."

The gunman's eyes darted around the room. "Where's Mr. Owusu? Is he still in the kitchen?"

Brantley looked bad. Tremors plagued the hand pointing the gun at Brick. Sweat ran down his cheeks in rivulets, threatening to deplete every drop of liquid from his body. He shifted his weight from one foot to the other as his eyes raced back and forth from him to the women cowering on the couch. Sweat stains in his armpits and down the front of his red t-shirt were practically dripping. His eyes were bloodshot and blurry, as if he hadn't slept in several days. Grime coated his jeans with a crusty, flaking, beige patina. With the miasma of putrid aromas invading the air, he smelled like he'd lived in the sewers, a homeless camp, or both.

When Brick told him their cover story, Bran acted like he believed it. He told Brick to shut and lock the front doors. Brick hoped Amaye had his keys, but then he remembered one crucial piece of information. *The front door is keyless entry, idiot. Get it together, or someone will get hurt.*

Once Brick locked the doors, Bran told him to sit next to Hiral and Tish, but Brick stopped a few paces away from the intruder, between the madman and the ladies, between the Glock and the woman he loved. The first part of his strategy had worked, so now he had to try and talk Bran down before he had to reveal himself, which he would do in an instant to save the Tish and the mother he'd earned.

"I said sit the fuck DOWN!"

"Bran, it's me, dude, the wimpy nerd-freak. I'm no danger, bro. Just tell me what this is all about."

"It's about you and that fucking bitch. She fucking dumped me, and now she's fucking you, fucking asshole."

In a weird turn of thought, Brick found it funny that so many people branded him an asshole. Maybe it really was his middle name. Strange how the mind wandered in times of stress. You never knew where it would take you. "No, she's not Bran. What the fuck would she want with me? I ain't shit. We're just working on this project together."

Bran shook the gun as he spoke. "I saw you all cozy on the couch."

Brick used all of his senses to discern whether Bran was too far gone to be talked down. So far, he still had his finger outside the trigger guard, though the Glock was cocked and ready to fire, but quivering in his shaky hand. Nonetheless, his opponent's heartbeat was rapid but steady. That gave him some breathing room. The scent emanating from Bran was rancid and cloying like stale clove cigarette butts inside a sunbaked car with the windows rolled up. The stench was not from dirty clothes or uncleanliness. It was as though something evil festered inside him.

His arms still extended, Brick tried to defuse the situation. "Tish is buttering me up, so I'll stay and finish the project. You know how she is. She likes to use her looks to get what she wants, right?"

"So you two aren't fucking?"

"Shuh. I wish. She only wants to keep me from walking out on the project before it's finished. She don't give a rat's ass about me beyond that, Bran. She's using me for the grade. Hell, she didn't even know I knew until now. What? You think I'm a tell her not to lay that fine ass body all over me? I'm a lot of things, but I ain't stupid."

Brick couldn't allow himself to care if his words affected Tish. He needed to stay laser-focused on his target. He had to know if and when Bran would make a move.

The barrel of the gun tilted down ever so slightly. "Then why'd she dump me?"

"For real, Dude? You almost hit her before, and now you got a gun in her face, and you ask that? This ain't no way to get her back. You know that, right?"

Bran stroked the side of his head with the pistol.

There's my opportunity, Brick thought, *but I may still be able to talk him down.*

He began shifting from one foot to the other. "Man, I'm so tired and confused. They told me something was going on between you and Tish, but I don't know."

They? Brick thought, who the hell are they? Is he schizophrenic? If he is, I can't take any chances.

"There's too many people telling me too many things. I'm tired. I haven't slept in days. I just want this all to be over."

"It can be Bran." Brick softened his voice, attempting to soothe the gunman.

"I'm just so fucking tired." Brantley appeared to be on the verge of tears. He dropped the pistol to his side. Things started to calm down, but then the front door swung open, and everything went to hell. "Asshole! Trying to trick me? They said you would..."

As Bran raised the pistol, Brick surged into hyper mode. The gun had barely moved an inch by the time Brick covered the roughly four meters separating them. He curled his fingers into a jaguar fist and drove his knuckles into Brantley's trachea just hard enough to stun him. He spun sharply, grabbing Bran's gun hand. Tendons and ligaments popped and crackled, and the weapon began to glide to the floor.

Brick lifted Bran's arm, ducked beneath it, dodging the Glock because it had yet to hit the ground, and finished the action by twisting Bran's arm behind his back. He jammed his knee behind his opponent's, driving him to the floor with no small amount of pain. Plucking the Glock from its long, sluggish descent, he dropped the magazine, ejected the cartridge, and removed the slide so it couldn't be fired.

Only then did Brick drop out of hyper mode, his knee firmly planted in Bran's lower back, pressing on the twisted arm behind him. He took out the paracord bracelet he always kept in his pocket, unbraided it, and hog-tied Brantley, wrists to ankles. Brick leaned over, placed a hand on the floor, and his mouth close to Brantley's ear.

He had not been so enraged since Fritz's murder, and the dark seed pulsed, but he forced it back into dormancy. This was not the time to unleash its energy. Nobody needed to die today. Still, it was good to know he could exercise control over it rather than the other way around.

"If you ever..." He yanked upward on Bran's arms, causing him to scream in agony. "EVER pull a gun on the woman I love again. I...will...end...you. You feel me?" A trickle of saliva fell from his lips and trailed down Brantley's cheek.

When Bran squeaked out a feckless reply, Brick gave his arm a vicious yank. "I said, do you feel me!"

"Yeah, yeah, I get you, man. Please let up on my arm. It hurts."

"Like I give a shit. I'm not done with you yet. Listen up, cowboy. If Daddy buys your way out of jail, I'll come for you. If you try to run, I'll find you. If you ever come near Tish again, it will take decades for them to find what's left of you scattered from coast to coast and border to border. You get me?"

The once tough man began crying. "Alright, I get you."

Maybe, by accident, he allowed a little bit of the darkness out of the seed, but he forced it back before it urged him into doing more. His chosen family had seen him use some of his abilities, and he had to face the fallout and maybe lose them all. Despair threatened to overcome Brick, but he shoved it down.

He rose to his feet, a little unsteady and out of breath. He hadn't used hyper in a long time, and he'd lost a lot of stamina due to spending all of his time with Tish and not training with Mara.

Tish leaped to her feet and stared at him. "What the fuck just happened, Brick?"

Hiral would normally have chastised Tish for her profanity. Her silence was a testament to the intensity of the moment.

"I'd like to know the same thing, son. Answer Tish." Amaye's deep voice boomed.

"Yah. It was like you disappeared from over there..." She pointed to where he'd been standing. "And reappeared where you are now. How's that even possible?"

Brick's shoulders slumped, and his hands shook a little. Part of it was fatigue. But the rest was fear of what would come and what he might lose.

"I'll explain everything, but first, I need to finish with Bran, and I need your help." Brick looked down at Brantley, who was moaning in anguish after the punishment Brick had meted out.

"Bran, I'm gonna do you a solid. What do you think would go over better with your new cellmate and butt-buddy Bubba? That you got taken down by the wimpy, pacifist nerd-freak while you had a gun in his face, or by the decorated war hero who had to take you down from behind? What do you think would be the better story in prison, Bran?"

"Yeah, yeah. The war hero sounds good to me. That's what I'm a tell the police."

"Good choice. And Bran? You've seen what I can do. Twice. I suggest you make it easy and confess because if you don't..." Turning to the Owusu family, he let the threat hang. "This is where I need your help, but first, nighty-night Bran."

Brick punched two knuckles into the nerve bundle beneath and behind the right earlobe and twisted. Bran's eyes closed, and his body relaxed, but Brick checked his pulse and listened to his breathing to ensure he wasn't pretending. He returned his attention to the Owusu family.

Brick wanted Amaye to be the hero of the day instead of him. He needed to stay out of the papers to maintain his cover for the covert work he did for his family business. The look on Tish's face was priceless. It was somewhere between shock and surprise, and *I knew there was something about him*. Her wimpy, pacifist nerd-freak turned out to be a covert operative with superpowers. She and Amaye readily agreed to edit the truth. Hiral was the sole dissenter. Brick stood by Hiral's decision when the other two tried to pressure her.

"You two leave Mom alone. It's her decision, and if she's uncomfortable with it, so am I."

She placed a hand on his arm. "Brick, it's okay—"

"No, Mom, it's not. No one pressures you while I'm around."

Amaye pasted a smirk on his face. "Hun, you sure there's not something I need to know? He's got your spunk, your weird sense of humor, and he protects you like a lion protects his pride."

"I think I'd know if I'd pushed a baby boy out of my vagina a couple of months after Latisha, Amaye. Blood doesn't always make family, though, does it." Hiral put a hand on Brick's cheek. "Blood or not, you are my son, and you just saved our lives. I can do this thing for you."

Brick swept her up in his arms, planted a big kiss on her cheek, and thanked her. Hearing sirens in the distance, he only had about five minutes to tell them his story. That was not enough time. He promised to reveal all after the police left.

The police were quick and efficient and collected information from all of them after cuffing and stuffing Brantley. One officer commended Amaye for his bravery and Brick for his willingness to be the decoy after admonishing them for taking such a chance, war hero or not. It took less than two hours to process the scene, still long enough for Brantley's dad to show up and stir havoc. The officers told him that Brantley had confessed. It was in writing and on bodycam after they read him his rights. They told him to back off, or he'd end up in the holding cell back at the station with his son.

Brick locked eyes with Bran a second before they hauled him off to remind him of what would happen if his daddy did buy him out of jail. Once they were gone, Brick thanked the

Owusus for helping him keep his secret. Hiral disappeared for a few minutes before reappearing with a large pot of what smelled like jasmine tea and several cups. She poured everyone a cuppa.

Brick took a seat on the couch. To his surprise, Tish sat beside him, slid her hand into his, and entwined their fingers. He could feel her shaking, so he let go of her hand, wrapped an arm around her, pulled her close, and kissed her on the forehead. She rested her head on his shoulder. As he began the story, her shakes gradually subsided, and her arms encircled him. He thought he might have lost her, and once she heard the whole story, he still might. For now, though, she still wanted to be with him.

The story he told began in the Antarctic facility where his mom, dad, and sister had been genetically modified against their will. He went on to describe how they destroyed the facility during their escape after discovering his mother, Ruby, was pregnant. The tale continued with their abilities, how and why the whitecoats at the facility had dubbed them Ghosts, and how each of them possessed a unique skill. His father could mold solid stone as if it were clay. His sister could sense ambient energy patterns. This allowed her to detect someone's presence even after they left the area.

The time had come for Brick to reveal his own story. The whitecoats in the organization wanted him because he had been born with the same abilities they had forced on his family. Because of this, they expected him to greatly outperform his family in skills and power. Brick was supposed to be the Ghost's Shadow, a being far more advanced than anyone on Earth, his family included. He decided to show them the unique ability he had yet to share with his sister and father.

After disengaging from Tish for safety, he placed his hand on the couch and took a deep breath. A moment later, he phased his hand down through the couch, wrapped his fingers around an ink pen he found on the floor, dragged it back, and handed it to Tish. With reluctance, she took it from him, tapping on it to verify its existence.

Pointing at a dark patch on the grey couch, Brick explained that the shadow he left after phasing was his guess at why they had predicted he was the Ghost's Shadow. Brick sat up straight, rested his hands on his knees, and waited for them to freak, then kick him out of their lives for good.

CHAPTER 10: CATCH-22

After two hours of exhaustive interrogation, Brick and the Owusu family were ready for bed. Though their discussion had been intense and probing, he'd held nothing back. He would keep no secrets from his chosen family and was relieved when they chose not to evict him from their lives. Tish had not strayed more than five feet away from him except when she reluctantly excused herself to go tinkle.

Hiral hugged him goodnight. "The guest house is ready for you as usual. You know, you are always welcome to move in permanently."

"Thanks, Mom. It's good to know I have options." He kissed her on the cheek. "But I think it's best if I sleep on the couch tonight."

Amaye furrowed his brow. "Do you believe we'll have some trouble?"

"Naw, Pops, but no one ever got hurt by being too safe, right?"

Amaye looked at Hiral, then back to Brick. "Ho-o-o-o-w can two people be so much alike but have never met before, what, three months ago? You two freak me out, but in a good way."

Pops gave him a big hug as Hiral disappeared down the far hallway. "Thanks for saving our family, son. I'll always be in your debt."

"Naw, Pops, no debts with family."

Hiral returned with a sheet, blanket, and pillow, handing them to Brick as she stood on her toes and plopped a motherly kiss on his lips. "Sleep well, my son."

She and Amaye headed to their bedroom up the stairway, and Tish and Brick were left to themselves. She approached him. "Can I thank you for saving my life tonight?"

"Didn't you already do that?"

"Not properly."

Tish took the bedclothes from Brick and set them on the couch. She returned to him, slid her arms under his, hugged him tightly, laid her head on his chest, and sighed. After almost a minute, she pulled back, whispered, "Thank you," and then, lifting herself on her toes, kissed him. His memory of their first kiss must have faded because the current kiss seemed far better. They were no longer strangers, and several barriers had fallen between them after a few intimate moments of sharing.

They teased each other as before, but this time, they fell into a rhythm, pleased with their ballet of tongues. As they detached themselves for a brief pause, Tish smiled, wrapped her arms around his neck, and pulled him down to her lips, hungry for more.

Brick relinquished control, followed her lead, and responded to her signals. Her musky vanilla scent was overpowering, and he almost lost himself in it, ready to give in to all of her desires. She wanted him then and there. Somehow, he resisted because he had to. Was she doing this because of him or because of what had happened? People reacted differently to life-threatening events. The only way to know for sure was to wait.

After an eternity, not tainted by an internal black hole this time, Tish slowly ended the embrace with what felt like a hundred kisses, each decreasing in intensity like a runner slowly cooling down after a marathon. Tish pulled back at long last.

His heart pounded in his chest. "That was the best thank you I've ever gotten."

"You do not disappoint, baby. Two kisses over a couple of months, and both curled my toes. I was beginning to wonder if the first one was a fluke. I'm glad I was wrong."

Brick caressed her cheek. Tish closed her eyes and leaned into it.

"We'd better get some sleep. We have a big day tomorrow," He said.

Tish hesitated for a moment as an unfamiliar look appeared on her face. As quickly as it had emerged, it disappeared. She sighed again. "I guess you're right. Good night, Brick." She kissed him again. Her tongue darted out quickly to caress his before retreating.

"Good night, Tish."

Brick watched her as she exited the family room, crossed the foyer, and glided up the stairs. The 'or something' option had been hidden in her kiss, smile, and scent. He would have accepted the option had it not been for Brantley.

Life sucked, and the three Fates lived to toy with him. The woman he loved finally returned his affection, but was it because of what her ex had done, or was it because Tish was actually into him? Brantley languished in jail, and still, his memory tortured Brick. He arranged the sheet and blanket on the couch, laid down, and slipped into an Alpha Rhythm, his body resting, mind on alert. It was one of the many lessons he'd learned while cloistered at Nil Parity. He used it in case Bran's posse showed up. He didn't believe they would, but as he'd said earlier, you could never be too safe.

At about two in the morning, Brick ended his Alpha State because he noticed Tish's scent and the sound of her feet on the stairs, trying to be silent and doing a decent job of it. It might have worked if he weren't a Ghost. He had expected her because earlier, his enhanced hearing had detected her muffled cries as she'd awakened from a nightmare. When she reached the door to the family room, he greeted her. "Hard time sleeping?"

"Of course, you heard me, superhero. Yah. I kept dreaming about how large the barrel of the gun looked. I've never been so scared in my life."

"I understand, and I'm no hero, Tish. I've done some pretty bad things in pursuit of the thrice-damned organization."

The tone of her voice enhanced the sight of her curvy silhouette. "You're *my* hero. Can I sit with you?"

Like he'd say no. "Absolutely."

Brick sat up to make room for her. She was wearing a silk chemise. He couldn't tell what color, though. His night vision was good but not decent enough to distinguish colors in the darkness of the family room. It was, however, tantalizingly evident that she wore nothing underneath. She snuggled up next to him as she had during the movie. This time though, her elbow rested on the inside of his thigh, and her hand caressed his knee.

Her scent, enhanced by whatever perfume she wore, was beginning to affect him. "Can you hear my heartbeat?"

He traced circles on her arm. "I can. I have your scent, too."

"What's it like?"

"A meadow of wildflowers on a summer afternoon, following a brief, cleansing rain. That's your base scent. Now it's infused with a healthy dose of fresh vanilla."

If she snuggled any closer, she'd be on top of him. "You for real, or are you BS-ing?"

"I'm for real. It's how I interpret it, anyway. Your scent is a pheromone designed to elicit a sensory response, so when I describe yours, it's how I feel when I sense it. Your base scent never changes, but your mood adds to it."

"Like when I'm angry."

"Yes."

"Or horny?"

Brick leaned his head against hers and breathed deeply. "That's the vanilla."

"How often have you sensed it?"

"Do you want the whole list or just the top ten?"

Tish giggled, actually giggled, then spanked his knee. "I'm calling BS on that one. I count three times."

Brick couldn't help but smirk, "You mean I've made you horny three times?"

"Who said it was you all three times?"

"You just implied it was at least once. You gotta give me that."

"All right, I'll give it to you." She squeezed his knee. "It was you all three times, including now."

Their conversation meandered through different topics, then drifted toward martial arts and how much Tish had improved since they began sparring. The time she had pinned him had been the second time he'd noticed the vanilla scent. He'd used hyper because she had gotten so good, but it hadn't mattered. She won anyway. If she could beat him in hyper, she could beat anyone if she trusted her senses.

Technical skill made you a good fighter, but it didn't make you a true martial artist. Using a bit of yourself, like intuition, and innovation, evolved you beyond the technical into the artistry. She had become an artist that day. Tish snuggled even closer to him.

She was curious about various aspects of Brick's skills, exhibiting an inordinate interest in his capabilities. Then she asked him a question for which he had no definite answer. It was a question he'd often asked himself and his family. He'd pored through the notes they had retrieved from the lab, but the whitecoats hadn't considered the question. He had no idea if he would ever find the answer. And on some level, it troubled him.

"Are you still human?"

The darkness of the family room did little to hide his facial expression and seemed to cause her concern. She pulled the arm on her abdomen more closely around her until the top of his hand touched the soft roundness of her breast.

She caressed his knee. "You don't have to answer, Brick. It doesn't matter. It won't change anything between us."

"That's just it, Tish. I don't even know. Genetically, I have both human and viral genomes. They've merged into a new genetic strand, with the human genome dominant and the viral genome in symbiosis. I am truly the only one of my kind."

She leaned her head on his chest. "That sounds lonely."

"Sometimes it is."

"Who was the other one?"

"What do you mean?" He sensed a subject change but needed confirmation.

"Before, you mentioned two people you loved who had died. You told me about one. Would you tell me about the other?"

Brick hesitated for a few seconds, the memories causing him to tense up.

Tish patted his knee. "Brick, you don't have to. Nothing's going to change things. Not now."

"No. I owe it to you." A smirk stretched across his face. "Lord knows you've told me about all your past lovers." Tish slugged his arm. "I can do the same." Brick swallowed hard, then continued. "His name was Fritz, and he was the most beautiful man I have ever known."

Brick told Tish the whole story, all the way to its tumultuous ending. She never interrupted, but she leaned in closer to him. As her hand guided it higher, Brick's palm now cupped Tish's breast.

When he finished, she kissed him behind and below his ear. He shivered. "I didn't know you were Bi, like me."

"I don't know if I am. Fritz is the only man I've ever been attracted to. I'm beginning to believe it was just him. Maybe we were kindred spirits or something."

"My parents have always supported my sexuality. I'm lucky that way."

"My dad didn't care one way or the other. Mara, though, always had my back no matter what."

"You know my parents love the shit out of you, right?"

"Yeah. I got that. Still, I was shocked when Mom offered to let me stay in the guest house permanently. She must really trust me."

"They do, but what they want most is for us to hook up."

"They're that cool about it?"

"Brick, they couldn't stop me any more than their parents could stop them, so they made sure I was safe, well-educated, and protected. They've been waiting for me to bring home someone like you."

"You mean the wimpy, pacifist nerd-freak?"

"No. Someone who truly respects their daughter and would do anything to keep her safe. In a way, I guess that's what I've been looking for too."

"What? You have a daughter?"

Tish giggled again, gently elbowed him in the solar plexus for the stupid joke, then pressed his hand more firmly against her breast. His thumb and forefinger automatically drifted to its sweet spot.

"Mm." She moaned. "This feels right, Brick, doesn't it?"

"It does. No way this one's fake. Still have to check the other one, though, just to be sure."

Tish laughed. "Not my boob, fool. This thing between us."

"Yeah, it does."

Tish stopped talking and leaned her head against his shoulder. The silence between them stretched into minutes, but it wasn't uncomfortable. She held his hand in place on her breast, and the hand on his knee traced some random pattern. She moaned softly and squeezed the hand on her breast. Brick had teased her in just the right way. Soft. Gentle. Sensual. His temperature rose as the scent of vanilla grew more intense.

"Do you still love me, Brick?"

"More than ever."

Tish turned toward him and guided the hand on her breast to her bare bottom. Her elbow lifted from his thigh, and her hand slid across his chest, under his shirt.

"Do you still want me?"

"Desperately, but…" His voice was low and intense.

In a smooth, deft move showing her strength and grace, she straddled him and pressed his hand between her thighs onto her softness as one breast freed itself from the bondage of the chemise. Tish moaned as she kissed him and unbuttoned his pants.

Brick stopped her and gently ended the kiss, turning his head to the side.

"What's wrong, Brick? I know you want me. I can feel your need for me. Make love to me, Brick."

"I can't."

"Why?"

"Mom and Pops are in their bedroom with the door open."

"So?"

"All they have to do is walk out on the balcony, and they'll see us. I won't disrespect them like that, not when they've treated me like family."

"Then let's go to my room or, better yet, the guest house."

Brick opened his mouth, closed it, and dropped his eyes.

"Wait. That's why you're here on the couch, isn't it? The safety crap was all bullshit. Did you expect me to come to you?"

He sensed that Tish was not so much angry as curious, which, oddly, enhanced the scent of her desire for him. She kissed him on the lips, neck, and chest.

"Suspected, not expected, not until I heard you wake from your nightmare."

Her actions continued, and Brick felt his resistance waver. The hand she held against her sex moved almost involuntarily and teased the sensitive bud of flesh at the apex of the labia minora. Tish gasped and nipped his lower lip, drawing a bead of blood. She lapped it up, then inserted her tongue into his mouth immediately afterward. Brick's resolve nearly evaporated.

"So why won't you make love to me, Brick? I need you." She'd undone his zipper and reached inside.

"Catch-22." He managed to gasp as the last of his resistance fled.

In his final, desperate grasp at logic, Brick had been intentionally enigmatic in hopes that his cryptic response would snap them out of their emotional immersion. It worked. She still straddled him and held his hand between her thighs, but her eyes were clear, focused, and drilled into his.

She is magnificent! Brick thought.

Though she slowed her advances, Tish didn't stop. "What do you mean?"

Gathering whatever reserves of resistance he had within, Brick explained, though a part of his mind remained fixated on where she held his hand captive. "Whatever choice I make, there's a good chance you'll end up hating me again."

"I don't get it. Why would I start hating you again?"

People who have had a close brush with death react in different ways. Nearly all of them seek a way to validate life. They need to know if they can ever feel anything but fear. Sex validates life and dispels the fear of death, but it rarely works for long. Brick was concerned about Tish reacting more to her brush with death than her attraction to him. He didn't want her to think he had taken advantage.

The damned cute-as-hell wrinkle manifested above her nose. "So, you think that's what I'm doing now?"

"I don't know if it is or not, Tish, and if it's not, you're going to hate me for rejecting you."

If her desire for him were genuine, she would get over her anger at his rejection in a few days and realize that he had acted in her best interests.

"This is real, Brick. I've wanted to be with you for a while now. I never did anything because of our deal and our project."

"How can I be sure, though? I can't go through it again, especially not so soon after Fritz's death. To have you and then lose you would devastate me, Tish. I have my limits, too."

"So, if Bran hadn't done what he did, we'd be in your bedroom in the guest house right now?"

"In a heartbeat, Tish."

Her gaze softened a little more. "I get it. Don't like it, but I understand. What can I do to convince you this is real?"

She pressed his hand against her sex, threw her head back, closed her eyes, shivered, and then let him go.

"Give me three days. If you still feel the same way." Brick raised the hand to his mouth and tasted her. "I will never, ever turn you down again."

Tish closed her mouth around his index finger and slowly pulled it out, her tongue caressing it. "Sounds like a deal."

Relief pulled a long exhale from him. "What's my half of it?"

Tish placed his hand on the breast that refused to remain sheathed by her chemise. Brick's thumb and forefinger immediately went to work on her erect nipple. Tish leaned in close. Her breath tickled his ear. "On days four and five, we skip school and spend them in the guest house. You'll have to pay for making me wait, Brick, and after I'm finished with you, you won't be able to walk straight."

"And you will?"

"I've been a bit more active than you, lover."

"Ouch, but true." Unperturbed, he held her close.

"Just being real, baby. Do we have a deal?"

"Deal." This was an agreement he could get behind.

Their kiss sealed the deal.

Tish slid off his lap and sat by his side, facing him. Her left leg was folded under, and the right hung over the side of the couch. Her breast, in its act of unadulterated stubbornness, remained unsheathed.

"Can I at least stay down here with you?"

"I'd love it, but there's not much room unless you sleep on the L-shape."

"Uh-uh. I want to sleep in your arms. It's the only way I'll feel safe."

He thought for a moment. "Here, let me lie down and get comfy, and you lie on top of me."

"Be real, Brick. I'm not a small woman."

"Tish, to me, you're as light as a feather."

"You know, you got pretty decent game for a nerd."

"On some of my Ops, I used seduction tactics to get

information."

She pursed her lips. "I did not need to know that, but I deserved it after what I said. Truce?"

"I accept."

After they got situated on the couch, Tish kissed him lightly, and he pushed back a wisp of hair as he caressed her cheek.

"I love you, Tish. I only thought I loved you before. Now, though, I'm sure."

"I know, and it used to bother me. Now, it makes me feel warm, welcome, and wonderful. I'm happy that you love me. I love being with you right now."

Mom was right. She's almost ready to say it, just not yet. We have time. Brick thought.

"Me too. Good night."

"Night, Brick." Tish laid her head on his chest. "I can hear your heartbeat, and you're very comfy. Who said a mattress made of Brick would be too hard to sleep on."

They both chuckled softly.

"So cringe-worthy. You know that, right?"

The feel of her hands roaming across his body felt wonderful. "You still laughed at it."

"True-dat."

Brick kissed her on the forehead and then settled into the sofa cushions. Tish nestled her head under his chin and wrapped her arms around him. She moved farther to the side, partially supported by the cushions on the back of the couch. Her leg lay across his waist, and her foot rested on his knee. His right hand cupped her bare bum.

In a short while, Tish's breathing told him she was almost asleep, so he closed his eyes and slipped back into an Alpha Rhythm.

CHAPTER 11: LOSS

Part 1

As Brick's heartbeat comforted her, Tish considered the guy beneath the mask. The dude, she... what? Was it really down to the 'L' word? She nearly said it back to him. Did she love him? It had never happened to her before. But then, she'd never met anyone quite like him. She was startled at how seamlessly she'd fallen for him. So much so she couldn't remember when it happened. Despite her hesitation to utter the phrase, she was definitely in love with him.

Sure, it prompted her to proposition him, but it wasn't the fear of death that fueled her actions, but rather the idea of living without Brick. What if she died before she could tell him? Why didn't she say something when she had the chance? It was always the same answer: fear. The issue was neither him nor his feelings. Tish had never been in love before, and the intensity of her affection for Brick terrified her while simultaneously exhilarating her. She should have said something and planned to do so in the morning.

Fritz's narrative did not bother Tish in the least; her emotions regarding Brick remained unchanged. He was correct, though. He was no typical do-gooder. Nor was he a no-kill superhero. He was more like Deadpool: dark, menacing, and, at times, utterly brutal, with a dash of comedy tossed in.

Nonetheless, he was identical to her father. As part of Amaye's ongoing PTSD treatment, Tish's father sat them down and revealed what he had done while serving as a Marine Force Recon. His record was also not very clean. Apparently, the old adage was correct. Some daughters did fall for men who resembled their fathers. Tish, stuck on the verge of sleep, replayed the day Fritz died.

Part 2

Brick detested heat and humidity. As if in response to his feelings, the rainforest east of Naypyitaw, Myanmar, attacked him with both.

"Fritz, my cover is blown, dude. We gotta go now." Brick slapped a mosquito on his forearm, observing that his already tanned complexion had darkened by at least one shade after a month under Southeast Asia's blazing sun. Fritz had browned to a smoky bronze. The contrast with his blonde hair made him even more attractive than he had been in high school when they had been together.

The two were unattached, non-official cover agents implanted in a mercenary outfit hired by dissidents. Those would-be rebels threatened to destabilize Myanmar's first democratically elected government in fifty years. Fritz had put in a good word for Brick to become a member. Mercies tended to blame the sponsor rather than the sponsored. But, for some reason, Fritz believed that he would be fine.

Brick's initial impulse was to knock him out and haul him away from the camp before things got out of hand. Though that action would shatter Fritz's confidence, at least he'd be alive. However, his head told him to let it go. Fritz was a grown man and could take care of himself.

"Everything will be all right, Brick. I've been with these guys for a year. They trust me. You should, too."

Brick groaned, lowered his eyes, and kicked a mushroom that

sprang from the rotting tree stump next to him. "I think you're delusional, Fritz. You should escape with me."

Fritz touched Brick's cheek and locked his baby blues onto his browns. "You trusted me in high school. I understand that things have changed between us, but I have not changed. Have faith in me."

Fritz had always known how to placate him. He'd used a similar tactic to seduce Brick back in high school. It still worked. Brick took in a long breath and exhaled with a sigh.

"Fine, but I'm grabbing a Hummer in case we need a quick escape. I'll be hidden in the bush near the lake where you're going to meet your group."

"Just leave. I'll be all right. I don't want them to get hold of you. We may no longer be together, but I still care."

"Do not worry about me, Fritz. You know what I can do. Stay alive." Brick turned to go but paused, about to say something but then decided against it.

He vanished into the dark bush and darted towards the vehicle depot of the massive and well-funded rebel camp. He effortlessly avoided the armed patrols who searched the undergrowth for him.

The rebels may be well-armed, but they're terrible at this. Brick thought.

There was just one guard at the depot, but she was fifteen meters distant on open terrain. *It's time to go hyper.* Brick vanished from the jungle's edge and reappeared behind the oblivious guard in an instant. The sentry made little protest as he clamped his hand over her mouth and inserted his fourteen-inch Maasai Panga between her ribs and into her heart.

Brick drove through the jungle in the cutting-edge all-electric Hummer, which ran quietly. All of a sudden, the skin on the back of his neck stiffened, and an emptiness formed in his gut.

He stomped the accelerator to the floor, praying he wasn't too late.

As Brick approached the lake where Fritz was to meet with his crew, he heard the staccato pattern of automatic weapons fire, followed by a scream. He careened into the clearing just in time to see his friend slump backward, arms flying over his head, blood spurting in the air. Brick slammed on the brakes, his heart in his throat, too astonished to drive, but only for a second. He bared his teeth, grabbed a grenade from his equipment belt, and primed it.

He had created a palm-sized grenade that contained white phosphorus, also called Willy Pete, magnesium granules, and powdered elemental sodium with a C4 catalyst. The mixture made Thermite seem like a guttering tallow candle, and the Geneva Convention prohibited its use against humans. Brick wasn't in the regular military, and these rebels used Willy Pete in their attacks on civilians. Time they got a taste of their own medicine. He set the timer for ten seconds and stood on the throttle as the Hummer approached his friend's prone body. He counted down the seconds.

The armored Hummer easily deflected the rebels' weapons fire as Brick slid to a stop between them and Fritz. With three seconds left on the countdown, he winged the grenade, aiming for the air above the group of twenty rebels. Because of his enhanced strength, his invention covered the forty meters easily. Brick heard the enemy shout a warning about the bomb in flight shortly before it detonated. He was impressed that someone could actually see it.

He checked his ex-lover. Fritz was alive but bled from several bullet wounds. He had to stop the bleeding but realized he needed to leave right now. Lifting Fritz, he carried him to the back of the Hummer, eased him inside, and closed the hatch. Just then, his weapon detonated.

While observing the results of his grenade, Brick experienced mixed emotions because it exceeded his expectations. All but a few rebels were either dead, burning, or both. Since they created their own heat and oxygen, white phosphorous and magnesium would burn until all fuel was consumed. The combustion triangle was no joke. Those who survived the initial blast but were on fire naturally jumped into the lake. When elemental sodium touched water, it violently ignited. The relief the rebels sought in the lake turned into charred flesh and death.

Beyond them, however, Brick noticed an Armored Personnel Carrier careening forward. That model could accommodate up to sixteen troops. He could take them, but Fritz couldn't wait. He dove into the driver's seat and peeled out. With Fritz's life on the line, time was of the essence.

Finally on the road, Brick put the Hummer in auto-drive and climbed into the back to tend to Fritz. When the AI pilot asked for a location, he yelled out the first one that sprang to mind. Brick focused on his ex-lover and tried his best to stop the bleeding, but he knew there was only so much he could do with a simple first aid kit and a few field bandages.

Tampons were ideal for gunshot wounds, but there were none in the container. *Misogynist bastards,* Brick thought. *Women in their crew and no tampons in the kit.* He'd done all he could and had to leave the rest to the Creator. Brick returned to the driver's seat.

He disabled the auto-drive and mashed the Hummer's pedal to the floor. Despite the fact that the road was quite smooth and the Hummer was rushing along at full speed, the APC closed the gap. That APC was acting strangely. At ten tons, even a hovercraft design shouldn't be unable to catch up to an unencumbered Hummer running at full speed. Brick estimated that it would reach them in less than ten minutes. Going off-road could assist, but Fritz would certainly not withstand the punishment caused by the rough terrain.

He dared a glance back at his closest friend and noticed the spreading pool of blood. Brick concentrated on shutting out the noise from the strained electric motor and listened for Fritz's heartbeat, but heard nothing. He re-engaged the auto-drive and searched for the artery in his ex-lover's neck.

Fritz was gone. He'd lost too much blood, and his heart had stopped. Brick wondered whether the troops in the APC could hear his rage-filled scream as he jammed on the brakes and slid the Hummer until it blocked the road. In Brick's mind, his scream was a Klingon death howl, warning those in Sto' Vo' Kor that the great warrior Fritz would soon join them. Klingons did not lament a warrior's death in combat; rather, they praised it. Brick planned to revel in the blood of his foes.

WHUMP, whump.

Pain surged beneath his solar plexus, causing his head to smack onto the steering wheel. It disappeared shortly after. A tremendous negative pressure formed in the same location, threatening to suck his innards to oblivion.

WHUMP, whump.

A second bout of agony erupted in his body, but this time it was more bearable. The pressure manifested a presence in his chest, similar to a piece of candy caught in his esophagus, yet it did not impede his breathing.

WHUMP, whump.

His wrath over Fritz's murder fueled the sensation, infusing his body with energy. A part of Brick's mind shouted at him to reject it, but most of him accepted the boost as a smile curled his lips. He doubted anyone would have recognized it, himself included.

The APC came to a halt around fifteen meters away and vomited ten rebels, including their leader, Leonin Korolev. Brick's grin extended across his face as he prepared his final special grenade, an antimatter implosion. He murmured to Fritz, kissed his forehead, and smoothed out his blonde hair before exiting the Hummer. *You always wanted a Viking funeral, old friend. Until we meet on the other side. A part of me will always love you.* He turned to face his future victims.

"So, we meet at last, Mr. Redstone," Korolev said with a thick Eastern European accent. "It is a shame the conditions could not have been more pleasant. Your combat abilities are admirable."

"I'm surprised you came to see me off, Korolev. I expected you to be a behind-the-scenes leader."

"Does this worrying you, Tovarish?" The dark eyes, short black hair, and little mustache reminded Brick of a tall, slim Adolf Hitler.

Korolev's men split into two phalanxes of five in an open, V-shaped formation, with the leader at the farthest point from Brick. It was an effective tactic for combat against a similarly formidable opponent. No conflicted firing lines meant more killing power with less risk. Perhaps they realized who he was and what he could do.

No matter, it won't do them any good.

"Nope. Not worried at all, but then again, my Russian's a little rusty. Maybe your wife said that you tend to lead with your behind. I'm not sure. I do know she isn't used to men like me. After three orgasms, she starts to slur her words. Then she gets really adventurous." Brick flashed him a wink and a broad grin.

The man's face turned a deep red. *Maybe he should get his blood pressure checked,* Brick thought.

Then Korolev seemed to gain control, growling. "You will die slowly, you capitalist pig."

"To accomplish this, you'll need additional troops. You should have brought more." Brick's mirthless grin spread. "Oh, I almost forgot." The grin evaporated. "They're already dead."

The dark power coursing through Brick made him feel

invincible. It drove him to a whole new level. He lowered his head, glaring through his eyebrows at the general. "Ready to join them?"

Korolev's visage twisted into a squinty, pressed-lipped mask. When he spoke, it sounded as if he pulled his lips apart with sheer force of will, but his clenched teeth refused to cooperate.

"You will die now, Mr. Redstone."

"Can't kill what you can't catch, Leo." Brick wiggled his fingers at his adversary.

Korolev directed his troops to fire, but Brick had already moved. He slid into hyper-mode just as the Hummer flashed into a blinding white flare behind him. He reached the soldier on the far right in an instant, just when his first victim squeezed the trigger on his Kalashnikov. Brick snapped his neck. He flashed into real-time, mowed down three of the other four ahead of him with the rifle, and reentered hyper. The weapon slowly drifted to the ground, catching the light from the Hummer's destruction.

The dark seed drove his speed to all new heights. He could get used to this.

Brick had designed his attack so that the explosion would either distract or blind the soldiers. His tactic succeeded, though, with his newfound speed, he no longer needed it.

Before the others could retaliate, Brick accelerated to the final soldier at the end of the first line. Whipping his Panga from its sheath, he killed the soldier, sped past Korolev, and eliminated the first one in the second phalanx. He dropped out of hyper again for a brief moment, allowing the others to see where he was. He waved at the dumbfounded general and went hyper once more.

The wheezing sound of the implosion grenade as it sucked half of the Hummer into whatever abyss it opened also served to distract the soldiers. In their fear, they fired at him, just as he had intended. The two closest to Brick succumbed to their comrades' friendly fire as Korolev, who was now behind him, dodged out of danger and rolled into a fighting position, pistol in hand. Brick finished off the two men still standing, emerging in real-time alongside Korolev, the Panga dripping crimson.

The rebel leader swung his pistol around. Brick's hand blurred, bending the barrel and batting it away like an unpleasant fly, taking the general's finger with it. Then he grasped the front of the Russian's shirt and lifted Korolev a few inches off the ground. The helpless man struck Brick's hand and wheezed like a ruptured forge bellows. The Russian managed to get out a single word. "How?"

Brick's emotionless brown eyes gazed back at the Korolev as he plunged his Panga through his lower jaw and into his brain, twisting it before yanking the blade out. He lowered the motionless body to the dirt road and shook the blood from his weapon and his arm.

When the Russian died, the energy that infused him retreated to that region behind his solar plexus, transforming into a little nodule of blackness. When he focused on it, he felt a bottomless pit the size of a pinhead but with boundless power. Brick's inner eye tried to peer into it but teetered on the brink of an endless abyss, forcing him to look away. He decided to leave it alone for the time being. He also chose to give it a name: *Dark Seed*.

Brick examined Korolev and the other soldiers for valuable goods and documentation to confirm out who had sponsored the rebel faction. When his father and sister arrived, they could call in a mop-up crew to sterilize the area and recover any operable equipment and evidence from the camp's main tents. He climbed inside the APC to investigate, thinking he had enough time.

Brick's father and sister arrived fifteen minutes later in a hopper he had developed from designs provided by the OSRD, Office of Scientific Research and Development. They handed the schematics to Brick a few years ago so he could solve the problems. Brick poked his head out of the APC. He discovered why it had moved so quickly. After climbing down, he approached his sister.

"When you send up a flare, Lil bro, you send up a flare." Marble grinned at him. She looked around. "That was one hell of a fight, Brick. Not bad. I am fucking impressed." Mara detected latent energy patterns and could profile a scenario if she arrived quickly enough. When she turned to see what was left of the Hummer, her expression sank dramatically. The vehicle had collapsed in on itself as the implosion grenade pulled most of it into what amounted to a black hole. Not even the scientist who invented the bomb understood where the micro-wormhole led. "Oh no, baby bro. Fritz!"

Brick shook his head, then closed his eyes. A solitary tear stained the front of his shirt.

"I'm so sorry, Brick."

"First Kaylen, and now Fritz, Mara. My bad decisions continue to kill the people I love."

"A little sloppy, but darn good job, Brick. Cutting off the head should put an end to the rebellion." Flint Redstone prowled around the scene, oblivious to his children's distress.

Mara frowned at him. "Dad, Fritz is dead."

Flint picked up a little stone to use as a fidget. In his hands, it became malleable, and he sculpted it like clay. "Well, occasionally, there is collateral damage. Part of the business."

If Mara hadn't caught him in an arm lock, Brick would have charged at their father.

"What's with the APC, Brick? Why were you inside?" Mara asked, presumably to redirect Brick's rage. It worked to some extent. His eyes followed his father's movements while his mind crafted multiple ways to bring the old man down. Vengeance had not eased his guilt or anger. However, it was more than ready to find a new target.

"BRICK!" Mara shook him hard enough to rattle him out of his red haze. He took a deep breath and willed the anger from his mind.

"It moved too quickly for a ten-ton pile of armor, sis. I wanted to know why. And I planted a booby. Nobody else will use that thing."

"We could use it."

"Unless you've got a C-5 Galaxy cargo jet in your back pocket, it gets torched, sis."

"Alright. You don't have to get all cantankerous with me. Damn."

Brick snorted. "Seriously? You actually used that word? How long you been saving that one up?"

"There's my Lil' punkass negro."

"Bite me you frigging hag."

Mara grinned at him, possibly because she had successfully diverted his attention away from their father. "So, what's up with it?"

Brick glared at his father again, who had tuned out of their conversation as usual. He prowled the battlefield, looking for anything valuable.

"Brick. Stay focused on me. You know how he is, and he ain't gonna change. It's always been just me and you. What did you find?"

Grudgingly, he turned his attention to Mara. "G.S. tech."

"Gravity surfing? For reals? Nobody but us, DARPA and OSRD, should have that."

"Yeah. Looks like somebody's gettin' rich."

Scientists at the OSRD, which was purportedly abolished in

1947, attempted but failed to develop anti-gravity technology. Some of their hypotheses were innovative, but they lacked the funding and scientific expertise to progress, so they abandoned the project. When DARPA, or the Defense Advanced Research Projects Agency, was established in 1958, it reopened numerous previously closed projects, including anti-gravity research, but made little headway.

Almost ninety years later, an upstart student who was only a sophomore in college stormed into the facility and changed everything. Brick's ideas transformed the way scientists looked at their research. They had taken the wrong approach to developing Anti-Gravity. However, Brick's creative perspective and deep understanding of Quantum Theory assisted them in discovering a mode of propulsion based on fluctuations in the Earth's gravitational field. Gravity Surfing technology was born.

"Dad. Do you hear this?"

"I heard Marble. I sent word to my contact in the Air Force's OSI. She's clean, and she'll find the leak. I think we're done here. We should leave. The clean-up crew will handle the rest of it."

Brick tossed Mara a remote etched with Russian Cyrillic letters. "You do the honors. I know how you like to blow things up. Wait until we're about a mile away, though."

"Awww. You know me so well."

Mara put Brick in a headlock and nuggied his head.

"Get off me, you frigging hag," Brick said, releasing his grip and sticking out his tongue.

"Shut up and get in the hopper, Lil' punkass negro." Mara finished their verbal dance, but instead of laughing back, she wrapped him in a tight hug and murmured, "I gotchu, Lil bro. I'm so sorry about Fritz. I know what he meant to you."

Brick reciprocated her rib-cracking hug, reveling in the unexpected gesture. He breathed in Mara's comforting scent of freshly turned earth spiced with a hint of cinnamon. "Thanks, sis. I love you too."

His entire existence revolved around Mara. Their mother passed away when he was three years old. Since then, she had been his loving mother, strict but fair father, understanding but bothersome big sister, and asshole elder brother. They also shared a freaky, twin-like psychic bond. Mara always knew when he needed her.

The trio climbed into the hopper and surfed gravity while a grinning Marble Redstone activated the detonator, illuminating the rainforest. Perhaps there wouldn't be much for the team to scrub, at least in that location.

Part 3

Tish awoke from her dream when Brick stirred and pressed a finger to her lips.

"We're in trouble."

CHAPTER 12: THE FIELD

Brick's awareness surfaced a few hours after Tish had settled on top of him for the night. Something was wrong, but he couldn't tell what. Field training had taught him never to open his eyes and let an enemy know he was awake.

He needed to remain still, breathing controlled, using his senses to scan his surroundings. He composed himself and turned his focus inwards. This technique improved his heightened senses.

I hear heartbeats—five of them, very close.

Brick tried to roll towards the right to slide Tish off of him, but she woke up.

He pressed a finger to her lips, leaned close to her ear. "We're in trouble. Invaders in the house. I don't know where yet. I'm listening for their heartbeats. Keep your eyes closed and use your senses. If I have to act, stay still because I will use hyper mode. I know you can help, but only as a last resort, my ace in the hole, okay?"

Brick expected her to resist his request, but he had asked her to wait for a reason. Tish had never been in a real fight, and he couldn't afford the risk of her freezing at the wrong moment. That would doom them all. Second, he needed her out of the way when he went hyper.

To his great relief, Tish nodded and remained silent, but he heard her heartbeat race, eyes widening.

Brick continued his roll as Tish helped. Her back was now against the cushions. Their arms and legs were no longer entangled, allowing Brick to maneuver freely. He sensed six sets of heartbeats, two upstairs and four downstairs, approaching slowly. He caught a whiff of their scents. They weren't Brantley's posse as he thought they might be. They moved rather soundlessly. Brick realized they were professionals, but why did they all smell of garlic? And piss? Who were they there for? What did they want? Were they there for him? Did the organization make its move at last? Did they want Pops for his trigger tech? Then he settled on the gist of it all. It didn't matter. These people were there to hurt his family and the woman he loved.

The four downstairs took positions in the four cardinal points around them. Two men and two women were dressed in black, wearing balaclavas. One of the women, from her scent, had her cycle.

Stupid. The idiots can't fire without running the risk of hitting each other. Maybe they aren't as professional as I thought.

Or perhaps they were simply overconfident. Brick readied himself for hyper mode. He heard the unmistakable cough of a tranquilizer gun twice. He assumed they were in Mom's and Pops' bedroom upstairs. Time was up.

First came the intruder to their left, across the coffee table. Brick launched himself from the couch and flew through the air, twisting, just a blur of movement. His scissor kick landed on the bridge of his target's nose, shattered the bone and cartilage, sending shards into her brain. She was literally dead before she knew it. Before she began to fall, Brick snatched her foot-long Bowie knife from its thigh sheath.

One second his time, less than half a second in reality.

He landed in the classic three-point hero stance for an instant, then lunged toward his second target, the one at the L-shaped end of the sectional. Brick held the knife blade down and facing out, its blunt side against his forearm for support. It bit into and through the neck of his next victim, a large man who appeared to be in his forties. He pulled his knees up and used the man's falling body as a springboard to launch towards his third target behind the couch near the balcony.

Two seconds for him, one for them. Brick should have kept up his practice sessions with Mara. According to his usual standards, he was quite slow. The Dark Seed remained silent.

Guess I'm not angry enough yet.

He didn't have enough momentum to reach his next target, so he grabbed the back of the couch, levered himself into a spin, and delivered a devastating roundhouse kick to the left side of number three's chest. The man's heart stopped in mid-beat. He rode the body down to the floor, where he helped himself to the dead man's Glock.

Four seconds to three of theirs. He was seriously out of practice, too damned slow, and there was still one more left at the head of the couch, plus the two upstairs. He heard his father blame him for allowing his heart to guide him.

Brick rolled, then threw the heavy Bowie knife. With its terrible balance, he worried he'd misjudged the proper release point. The knife went almost entirely through the woman's sternum, severing her spine.

Four down in four and a half seconds, three and a half in real-time, and there were still two more upstairs, but half of his stamina was already gone. He should have kept up the practice sessions. Too late to do anything but press on.

Brick spied one man watching the events from upstairs. The attacker drew his Glock in extreme slow motion. Brick wondered if they had cashed in on a special.

Hey, assholes for hire. Get your hot Glocks here for half price. Literally, a buy two, get one free. Buy them in bulk, and we'll throw in an extra magazine and a live human for target practice!

Five seconds.

Seriously, dude? Right now? The mini-him on his shoulder said.

There was no way Brick would make it up the stairs in time. He'd been in hyper for five seconds and was already feeling it. He dropped out of hyper after snatching two leaf-bladed throwing knives from number four. He heard the cough of an air gun but couldn't tell from where.

"One more move, asshole, and that fine piece of ass dies. Bleedin' shame it'd be, yeah."

Tish lay immobile on the couch, and a tranquilizer dart sprouted from the side of her neck. The sixth heartbeat was upstairs with number five, who pointed his pistol at Tish.

"Who are you, and what do you want?"

"Venton Smythe's the name, and we've come for you, asshole..."

Again with the asshole? Don't you people know any other words to use?

Mini-him railed again. *Asshole! Focus!*

Et tu Bricktay?

Not funny, shithead. They must have been pissed at their new name.

"...You killed four of my best. Pray that my employer keeps wanting you alive because the second she don't...."

"Shut the fuck up, lap dog. Tish is the only reason you're alive, and we both know it."

"Actually, I've got her mum and daddy up here too. Wouldn't want anythin' to 'appen to them, would you?"

Number six had been against the wall behind Venton on the balcony. He moved into sight.

"Besides, I have a plan B." Smythe grinned.

Behind him, Brick heard two clicks, then high-pitched whines decreased in level, like power sources on the wind-down. Two heartbeats replaced that sound.

Biometric attenuators. No heat, no sound, and no scent. *How the fuck did they get those? Only a handful exist, and we have three of them.*

Brick had already developed his plan of action and had no time to create another one. There was nothing else to do but go through with it and hope he could improvise and take out the extra soldiers. His remaining hypertime was limited, and he had too many targets in too many places. There was no chance to adapt, no time to do anything but act. So act he did. He remembered Sun Tzu's proverb about the unsuccessful warrior and kicked it to the curb. He was the Ghost's Shadow. People like him didn't exist back then, and like Tish had said, not all proverbs fit all situations.

Brick went hyper. He tossed the first throwing knife at number six. The second knife followed right after towards Smythe. At the same time, he dropped the pistol he'd taken and powered toward Tish. If his plan didn't work, he needed to get her out of the bullet's path and safely under the balcony.

The tendons in Smythe's finger cracked as he pulled the trigger in slow motion. Brick careened towards and over Tish as he prepared his body for the strain he was about to put on it. Tish was right; she wasn't a small woman and was solid, all muscle.

Except in all the right places. Brick's lizard brain interjected the thought at the most inopportune moment.

Bricktay shouted, *REALLY? NOW?*

Brick shuttered the irrelevant thoughts and continued. Tish would be sore in the morning, but she would be alive.

He looked up and saw his first knife drill into number six's eye socket all the way to the end of the taped hilt. The second was the most spectacular. Though he'd missed his target, it was still the throw of a lifetime. The knife reached the barrel of the Glock just as the bullet exited. It shattered the blade, and such was its velocity that the remaining shards flew towards Smythe's face. Brick wanted to watch, but he had to save Tish.

He heard the two tranquilizer guns behind him cough, but he was no longer in their sights as he sailed over Tish. He grabbed her wrists and pulled as hard as he could, focusing all his strength on the effort. To his surprise, Tish was as light as a feather. His mind railed against it because it violated all the laws of physics...until he saw her phase through the couch.

Holy shit! I phased her. I didn't know I could do that. God, please let me not have killed her too.

Then Brick realized that he had planned on Tish's mass to help him slow down, the wall approached, and there wasn't much time left, even for him. He twisted in midair so his back would take the brunt of the collision. He couldn't take the chance that his phase would end as they entered the wall. He pulled the now-solid Tish against him and anchored her with his arms and legs. Brick relaxed his muscles to limit the damage, dropped out of hyper, and waited.

The wall brought them to a sudden stop. The whole house shuddered as a wall stud tried to replace his spine. His head snapped back, and he heard a loud crack. He didn't know if the sound had come from the stud, his skull, his spine, or all of the above. They fell three feet to the floor. His body took the brunt of the force as Tish was still safely wrapped in his arms and legs. Brick's head rang, pain racked his body, he tasted blood, and his vision blurred, but thankfully, he wasn't seriously hurt. His fingers flew to Tish's neck, pulled the dart out, and felt for a pulse. It was slow and steady. He breathed a sigh of relief.

Then the clapper gonging the inside of his skull slowed and screams assaulted him from the balcony above. He hoped that Smythe wallowed in his death throes from the knife shrapnel. The only two mercies left ran toward him and Tish as they slapped syringes into their trank guns.

Brick tried to go hyper, but nothing happened. Phasing Tish had drained him. He was exhausted and ran on just adrenaline. The Dark Seed remained dormant when he needed it most. Trying to rise, he found that his legs wouldn't function. His new plan was to save Tish no matter the cost.

God no. Not again. I can't lose her too. I won't lose her too.

WHUMP, whump!

Rage consumed Brick. They would not harm her. He would save her this time. It won't happen again. He would not lose her. The all-consuming anger filled him until something in the fabric of his mind ripped, and something dark escaped.

Ripped or released?

WHUMP, whump!

The seed within him thrummed, and its dark, primal power flooded his body. The rage remained, fueled by the shadow, but it mixed with a mysterious, golden energy and mutated into a sensation he'd never experienced nor could he name. He was... connected... to EVERYTHING.

WHUMP, whump

He shouted, emphasizing each syllable as his fists pummelled the carpet. "NOT!" Shockwaves turned the rug into dust, exposing the foundation. "A!" Cracks radiated through the concrete, widening with each strike. "GAIN!"

On the third syllable, Brick's downward thrusts rocketed him to his feet, and he stared at the two mercies, but what he saw stopped him cold. An infinity of lights in motion surrounded him. They were everywhere except for the shadows cast by his two adversaries. The darkness inside him now pulled away and enveloped the two mercies, deepening the dark that consumed them.

That was far less important to Brick than the lights. There were billions, maybe trillions, of infinitesimally small lights that danced in constant motion. They were inside the walls, on the floor, and encompassed the air itself. They were everywhere and in everything. He lifted his hand. The lights were part of him too. He looked at Tish, but, like his enemies, she was a shadow within the sea of light.

"Shoot him, you idiots! Shoot him now!"

Fucking Smythe is still alive.

Brick cracked a bloody smile at the inadvertent rhyme. It reminded him of the movie Short Circuit with the sentient robot. Number Five is alive, he said. *Or is Number Five they/them since they didn't identify as a specific gender?*

The newly-named mini-him shouted, *Asshole, focus!*

Bricktay was right. He had a job to do, and he'd better get to it. Tish's life lay in the balance, and he obsessed over the pronouns for a freaking fictional robot from a 1980s movie, even if said movie starred Ally-freaking-Sheedy.

Entranced by Brick's murderous grin, the urgent shout from their leader snatched the mercenaries from their stupor, and they fired. The darts slammed into what remained of the wall behind him. No way they could have missed at that range, but they had passed right through Brick, though he hadn't phased. The shadows reloaded against a background of billions of nanite-sized stars dancing in a complex but recognizable rhythm. The rhythm, there was something about the motion of those lights that bothered him. Then, comprehension struck.

The patterns, dear God, I'm seeing subatomic particles. I'm in the Akashic Field!

He wanted to say something profound, like, *It's full of stars,* but decided it would be blasphemous to use such a sterling comment from a classic.

That connected feeling made sense to him now. The power within him had a time limit, though. Brick could feel it drain from him like grains of sand in an hourglass. He had to take care of the two enemies immediately. That would leave the injured Smythe if still alive, but would he have the time?

He wasn't connected to the two mercies, but the floor beneath them and the air around them were fair game. He gestured. Shadow flowed from him, and the lights under the mercenaries moved away. He wasn't sure if he phased the floor or erased it. It didn't matter because the result was the same. They dropped, and Brick pulled back the darkness, waving the lights back into place when the two mercies had fallen halfway through the opening. Their shadows filled with light, and suddenly, he was connected to them or what was left of them. When the floor rematerialized, or unphased, or whatever, the mercies had become a part of it, converted to the same material as the floor. They weren't a threat anymore.

He had to save Tish before those grains of sand fell, stealing his remaining power. Smythe was undoubtedly on the way, and Brick had few options left. He reached out to Tish's shadow and touched her arm. She lit up like a Christmas Tree. He needed her to be safe; that thought consumed his mind, body, and soul.

She must always be safe, always. I will not lose her, too.

Golden power flowed from him into her. The creature of light that was now Tish grew brighter, flashed once then returned to her normal brilliance. *That's a good sign*, he thought, though he had no clue what it meant. Next, he partially phased, then lifted her; also good.

In Quantum physics, a property called superposition existed: the ability for one particle to occupy two different places simultaneously, and neither time nor space were factors. Metaphysically, psychics called it bilocation.

He and Mara had this freaky psychic twin connection, but Mara usually sensed him in trouble, never the other way. It was worth a try, especially now. He reached out in the direction of his house. Suddenly, he stood in her bedroom and the Owusu house simultaneously. He wasn't sure if she could see him. He wasn't sure if he was even physically there. Mara was also a being of light. He wondered if it was because of her mutation.

Mara. Mara, I need you. Wake up.

His voice sounded strange to him. It was like hearing a ghost speak, like a whisper floating on the wind. It had a slight reverb to it as well.

"Brick? I can barely hear you. How are you doing this? Where are you?"

I'm in the Field, Mara. I'm sending you a friend.

"What? How? Who?"

No time. My power is waning, and I need to keep her safe. Keep her safe for me.

Before Mara could respond, Brick willed Tish to his sister's room. She stretched, existing momentarily in both places at once, then materialized on the end of Mara's bed.

"What the fuck! She's here, Brick. How?" Mara asked.

It worked, thank the Gods. I was able to save her this time, Mara. I couldn't save her before, but now she'll live. So many years passed, so many times I ran it through my mind. She drove away, and I didn't stop her. She crashed the car, and I wasn't with her. I am finally able to save her. I can rest now.

"Gods, Brick. I had no idea you still hurt so much over Kaylen's death. I'm so sorry I didn't see."

I never told you, Mara. We don't talk about things like that in our family. Always the head, never the heart, but I love you, Mara. I want you to know that. I'm almost finished now.

A part of him glowed at his proper use of the word finish. His Lit. professor would have been proud.

"Brick, no. You're fading. Don't leave me, Brick, please. I love you, Lil bro. You're all I've got left. Please don't go."

It's okay, sis. So tired. She's alive. I finally saved her. I'm all good now, but my power's—all—gone.

Brick pulled himself back and closed the connection with Mara. He didn't have the energy to move himself. He was unsure what would happen, but his sister didn't need to see him die if that was his destiny. Only a few grains of sand remained. Brick didn't fear death. He'd cheated it enough times in his short life. He always expected the Reaper to come calling any time.

He was able to save Tish, and if the price was his life, so be it. The lights around him faded as his energy dissipated and darkness rushed in to fill the void. It tugged at him greedily as though it wanted a piece of his soul before Death took him. Or did Death's minions wait in the void, ready to take their pound of flesh as a reward for serving the Grim Reaper?

Then Smythe's shadow stumbled toward him. The closer he got, the more he congealed into a disfigured, bloody, night-vision-distorted wraith that stank of garlic and piss.

"She's gone, dickhead, and you got nothin'. Better hurry. Help's on the way."

"Not close enough to help you, arsehole, and someday, when Zindriya's done with you, I'm gonna make you pay for what you did to me and the seven friends you chilled."

Brick gurgled. It was supposed to be a chuckle, but his mouth wasn't quite working anymore. His mind drifted. He was exhausted. Saliva flowed freely over his chin and pooled on the floor between his feet. Red saliva? That was strange.

He tried to say something about the number seven and how it matched the old Grimm's fairy tale. How they didn't name the dwarves in the story. Like his nameless victims, shadows in the night, but it came out as a jumbled mumble. That thought made Brick gurgle-giggle more. The thought of Smythe as Snow White almost made him choke on his own spit. His red spit. He remembered fake choking with Tish long ago. Smythe still spoke, but his voice faded into echoes as he cascaded into a never-ending tunnel.

The lights were gone. Brick was at peace. He was finally able to save his love after so many years. A part of him knew that Tish wasn't the one who had died, but maybe her salvation would be his. Nothing else mattered. He was light as a feather, like Tish. The darkness no longer gnawed at his soul as it enveloped him, and settled into the Dark Seed for a long winter's nap.

He thought that maybe asshole really was his name, and Mara would put it on his headstone. Or his urn if they cremated him. That might be better because of his genetic mutations. Brick was so tired. He had no clue how he was still standing or why when the concrete floor would be so much comfier. Was that even a word?

Concrete was a lot like brick, and Tish had said he was comfy, so why not the floor? She was safe and alive. He had saved her. The car crash would never happen now. Maybe she could forgive him. Maybe, at last, he could forgive himself.

The darkness was complete, yet he was not alone. That other dark, primal presence accompanied Brick as he sank to the floor and slid into the shapeless, formless abyss of oblivion.

CHAPTER 13: WARRIOR PRINCESS

Tish and Brick guided the spaceship they designed and built into orbit around Jupiter. The vessel's maiden voyage began their honeymoon, and they would spend the rest of it on the base they had established on Europa a few months before.

Finally, they would have the peace they craved for so long. The newlyweds had named the ship The Ghost's Shadow. Tish piloted, and Brick navigated, but at the moment, he just stared at the screen as though he were looking right through it.

"You're safe now, Tish." His voice sounded far away. "Nothing can ever hurt you again. You'll be fine without me."

"What are you talking about, Brick? We're about to orbit Jupiter, for God's sake."

Brick swiveled his head toward her as though it turned on a gimble, and she gasped. His eyes were gone, replaced by orbs of bright, golden light. He smiled at her, and the light shone through his teeth.

"It's time for me to move on into the Field, Tish. I'll always love you. I promise you. We shall meet again, beloved."

Brick burst into a cloud of billions of microscopic orbs of light. Tish yelled at him to come back, but a loud boom and the hiss of escaping atmosphere dragged her back to the controls.

Something struck the ship, breached the hull, and damaged the gravitic drive. The craft was about to collapse, and Europa was still on the far side of Jupiter. Tish fumbled for the switch on her suit collar to activate her helmet. It wrapped around her head but didn't seal properly. Every redundant failsafe had malfunctioned, and the cabin filled with partially frozen ammonia crystals as Shadow's Ghost skirted Jupiter's upper atmosphere.

Brick had left her behind, vanishing into some damned Field. Alone in the ship, Tish realized her lungs would first sear from the ammonia, then freeze in an instant. Doomed to be trapped in Jupiter's toxic, corrosive gasses, the planet's massive atmospheric pressure and immense gravity would compress her body until it was no bigger than a marble. Tish let out a harrowing scream.

◆ ◆ ◆

"Damn girl, you got a set of lungs on you."

The voice sounded familiar, but Tish couldn't place it. At first, she didn't open her eyes, trying to follow Brick's advice.

"You can open your eyes, Tish. You're not in danger anymore. My brother saw to that."

Her eyes remained closed but she recognized the voice. "Mara?"

"Yep, it's me. You okay?"

She finally opened her eyes. "Why are you here?" Tish looked around. "Wait. Where am I? Where's Brick?"

She tried to stand up, but entangled bedsheets restricted her legs.

"How did I get here? Where's Brick?" Tish called out Brick's name, but he didn't answer. She unwrapped the sheets from her legs because she had to find Brick.

"Easy, Tish. Brick's not here. I-I don't know where he is."

Pain flared in Mara's voice. Sadness. Despair. This was not the Mara she knew. Though Tish teetered on the ragged edge of fatigue and panic, somehow, she remained calm—well, calm-ish. She closed her eyes again and practiced breathing as Brick had taught her. In a few seconds, she felt more under control but needed answers.

"How did I get here if Brick didn't bring me?"

"He," Mara paused, "*sent* you."

"Sent me? What the hell are you talking about?"

Mara explained what she had experienced over the last few hours. Tish found it hard to believe, but there she was, on Mara's bed, still in the chemise she'd worn to seduce Brick. What other explanation was there? Then there was her dream, in which Brick had mentioned the Field. The ammonia smell in the dream must have come from the bottle of smelling salts still in Mara's hand.

Tish touched her neck and wiped a droplet of blood that had leaked from the dart that asshole shot her with. She told Mara what she remembered, which wasn't much. She had opened her eyes after Brick had flown from the couch. The first four went down as though a blurred wraith's shadow had passed before them. Tish had been on the verge of retching at the sight of all the blood when she saw the man on the balcony and then felt a sting in her neck. In what might have been a minute or an hour, she woke up in Mara's bed.

"They used ketamine. It has hallucinogenic effects, among other things. Probably why you had the dream."

Mara stood up, grabbed some clothes from the top of her dresser, and tossed them to her.

"These aren't mine." Tish's mind was still a little foggy. She took a few more deep breaths to try and clear it. The disheveled room finally came into focus.

"I didn't have anything that would fit you, so I borrowed them from my dad."

Tish held them up. Olive wasn't her favorite color, but at least they were clean. Still, she hesitated.

"Hey, I'm fine if you want to walk around bare-assed. Shit. My brother has the same good taste in thick women as I do."

Tish watched Mara's smirk morph into a lascivious smile as her eyes tracked up and down. Determined not to be cowed by the older woman, Tish stood up, dropped her chemise on the floor, and pulled the clothing on as Mara watched.

"Your eyes may water, your teeth may grit, but none of my body will you ever get."

"Nice verse, Princess. Let's go," Mara turned to leave.

"I'm not your frigging princess, you frigging hag."

"Maybe not, but you are definitely my brother's girlfriend," Mara stated as she left the room.

Tish opened her mouth to deny what she had said but realized it would have been a lie. She wanted to be Brick's girlfriend. Even if he didn't know it yet, he was her boyfriend, but she thought he did understand on some level. Something clicked in her mind.

The way Mara had said she didn't know where he was implied that she wasn't even sure he was still alive. What if he'd used all his life energy to get her to safety? What if he was dead? What if she never got a chance to tell him that she loved him? Her choice to hide her feelings from Brick felt so stupid. Now she might never get the chance.

I have to find him. I will find him. Tish followed Mara through the door.

Brick's dad, Flint, met them in the kitchen. Several large bags were lined up on the floor.

"Alright, ladies. Grab a bag or two, and let's get to the Hummer. It's a bit of a drive back to the Owusu's, and every minute passed is time lost from finding Brick."

Tish picked up one of the bags. She expected it to be heavy, but it wasn't, so she picked up a second and proceeded to the front door. As she passed the locked door to the basement, she paused and stared at it for a moment as an instance of recognition blossomed, then faded.

Mara and her dad gaped at her, at the bags she carried, then at each other, but she brushed aside the stares and urged them to get going.

They filled the forty-minute drive to Tish's house by questioning her on as many details as possible regarding all aspects of the previous night, including Brantley's intrusion. Based on the things Bran had been saying, Flint and Mara deduced that the goon squad that attacked had been using Bran as a catalyst. The plan worked, or they wouldn't have proceeded with the abduction.

The whole setup indicated a detailed and ongoing campaign to capture Brick. It seemed as though her boyfriend had thrown an enormous monkey wrench into their plan and had, they hoped, forced them into leaving some clues.

When they pulled into the long, sweeping drive, the Owusu estate appeared serene as the sun peered just above the horizon, but the instant they walked through the front door, the sight they were met with utterly destroyed any sense of normalcy.

Blood was splattered everywhere. Brick's initial victims remained where they had fallen. Tish dashed up the stairs to check on her parents before Flint or Mara could stop her. She kept her senses alert, expecting enemies to pop out from every nook and cranny.

The only things Tish found were a puddle of drying blood at the edge of the balcony overlooking the family room and the dead body of another intruder in a lake of scarlet with the hilt of a knife protruding from his eye socket. Sudden, violent death had stolen his bowels and bladder control.

The sight and the smell stopped her, and she vomited for what seemed like hours until nothing but bile burned her throat. A hand on her shoulder shocked her back to the present, and she reacted instantly. As quick as she was, Mara was much faster and effortlessly countered her attempt at a wrist lock.

"Easy, Princess. I'm not the enemy."

Tish shoved Mara away. "I told you, I'm not your fucking princess. Call me that again, and it's on." She stalked off toward her parents' bedroom, stepping over the body of the fallen mercie. Tish breathed a sigh of relief at the forms huddled under the blanket as their chests rose and fell rhythmically.

"You got the smelling salts, right?" Tish asked, sensing that Mara was close behind her. She caught a whiff of cinnamon and turned earth but ignored it as remnants of the ketamine.

Mara placed the vial in her hand and then went back downstairs. She used it on her mother first, and after a quick explanation, she had Hiral use the vial on her father. She thought it would be better if his wife woke him up.

Several minutes later, with her parents up to speed, Tish joined Flint and Mara to check their progress. Tish was about to ask what was happening, but Flint silenced her with a finger to his lips and pointed at his daughter. Mara walked around the family room, arms out at shoulder-width, eyes closed. She reminded Tish of a psychic or a medium in a trance as they traipsed about a room searching for spirits.

Tish had not walked into the family room before running upstairs, so when she saw what was left of the two intruders melted into the floor, bile rose yet again, threatening to decorate what remained of the carpet, but she held it back this time.

Mara withdrew from her trance. She staggered a bit but leaned on a nearby wall for support.

"My Lil' bro is a fucking badass. You won't believe what I saw, Dad. There were eight. He took out seven and severely injured the last one. Trained, well-armed soldiers spread out over far too much real estate. Impossible, even for us, but he did it. Also, the two... um... melted into the floor wore biometric attenuators."

"Yeah, but the one left was enough, wasn't it? My contact is still checking out the leak on the tech. Did you get anything useful?"

Mara glared at her dad for a second, then walked to a section of the wall that had caved in underneath the balcony. Written on the inner wall, in blood, was 'V. Smythe' and 'Zindr…'.' The rest of the second word was unreadable.

"Shit. Zindriya's got him," a look of concern clouded Flint's face.

"Who's V. Smythe?" Tish asked.

"Gun for hire. Venton Smythe, British mercenary. He's moderately capable and specializes in snatch and grabs."

"You two know where to find them?" Tish chimed in.

"Stay out of it, Princess. This is grown-up work."

Tish had had enough of Mara's condescending attitude. She ran up to the taller woman, grabbed her by the shirt, and slammed her against the wall. Mara's feet dangled a couple of inches above the floor.

"Call me princess one more time, you dried-up old heifer, and I'll kick your ass!"

Mara grinned, but her eyes spoke a different story. Tish sensed a change in Mara's scent, knew something was coming, and acted.

She leaned back, dragged Mara into a backward roll, planted her feet in the taller woman's center of gravity, and propelled her ten feet away. This gave Tish time to rise, face her adversary, and prepare for battle. Flint jumped between them.

"Stop this now! This ain't gettin' us nowhere. Time's wastin', and Brick's gettin' farther away."

Tish maintained her fighting stance as Mara picked herself up.

"Not bad, Tish. I guess you ain't such a princess after all. Well, maybe a warrior princess." Mara stuck her hand out as if to shake. "Peace. I pushed you, and I shouldn't have."

Tish took the hand warily, waiting for the hammer to fall. It didn't, but that didn't mean it wouldn't later.

Hiral and Amaye walked onto the balcony and scanned the carnage below.

"Oh, my God. You told us but…seeing…." Hiral wept and buried her head in Amaye's chest, protected by his embrace.

"Brick… did all this?" Amaye asked.

"He did, Dad, to protect us."

"Where is he?" Amaye asked.

"They took him, Mr. Owusu," Mara answered.

"Because of what he is?" Amaye asked.

"We think so. Wait. You know?" Mara asked.

Amaye ignored the question.

"What next?" Amaye asked.

"We go get him, Dad, and make the fuckers pay for taking him." Tish's lips pulled back from her teeth at that moment. That proclamation jarred Hiral out of her state of shock, and she reacted to Mara's exclamation.

"Latisha, language!"

"Like hell you are!" Mara said.

"Sorry, Mom," she turned to Mara, "And I'd like to see you stop me, you cow."

"Oh, it's on now, bitch."

Mara, at five-foot-nine, squared off with the five-five Tish, who didn't back down one inch.

"STOP!" Flint said, "I see the two of you are determined to have it out. Fine, just not in the middle of all this evidence."

Eyes locked with Mara's, Tish told them about the gym. Despite her parents' warnings, Tish took off with Flint and Mara in tow.

She wasn't sure if her parents would come and watch, and she didn't care. Tish needed to put a stop to Mara's assholery. Even if she lost to the older, more experienced woman, Mara would know she'd been in a fight.

The clash between Mara and Tish was monumental. Both were artists, but Tish had a clear advantage in speed and skill. She pressed it and drove Mara back at every encounter. At one point, Mara had gotten in a lucky shot that had snapped Tish's head back and dazed her. She tried to press her advantage, but Tish flew into a back somersault, lashing out with a vicious kick under Mara's chin, who staggered back several steps.

Tish finished the maneuver, landed perfectly, crouched into a fighting stance, and then shook her head to clear it. Rage flashed in Mara's eyes. Brick's sister was now desperate. Every atom in Tish's body screamed that she was about to go hyper. Brick's words filled her mind. It was almost as though he was there with her, urging her on.

You are the most incredible, intuitive, instinctive fighter I have ever known. Have faith in yourself. Trust that instinct, and you will become a true artist with the potential to beat anyone.

Tish stood ready.

She closed her eyes and relaxed her body. She smelled that cinnamon and turned earth scent again as it wafted from Mara's direction, then it changed, as it had back in the house. A part of her wondered when her senses had become so enhanced. She shoved that thought down. It wasn't the time for speculation.

An acrid scent, like rancid vinegar, overlaid the smell. Mara's hyper-mode attack commenced. Tish balanced on the balls of her feet and spread her arms out, prepared for the assault.

Eyes still closed; she felt a rush of air from the leading edge of Mara's charge. It had been the same with Brick. Tish stepped to the side as Mara's bulk brushed her outstretched arms.

She used a Jiu-Jitsu move that Brick taught her, turning Mara's mass and momentum against her. The larger woman flew to the other side of the gym, where she slammed against the padding on the wall, backward and upside-down. Tish opened her eyes in time to see her opponent fall to the ground, dazed.

Flint had been sitting down, seemingly bored with the fight, but he leaped to his feet when Tish finished it.

"What the hell just happened?" He hypered to Tish's side in an instant. "How did you do that? It's not possible."

"What? That I beat Mara in hyper? I beat Brick once too."

"How?"

Tish ignored him as she frowned. "I'm gonna go check on your daughter, then I'll explain." Irony dripped from her comment. Flint wasn't concerned at all with his daughter's well-being.

Once she made sure that Mara was okay and helped her stand, Tish explained the encounter with Brick, minus the intimate details. She recounted what he had told her the previous night.

"She's a natural, Dad, and Brick trained her. Back the fuck off."

Surprisingly, Flint held up his hands as though he were apologizing, dropped them, and trundled off in the direction of the main house. Based on what she'd learned from Brick, that was not normal.

Mara turned to Tish. "Alright, Lil sis. You're in, but you may regret it."

"Lil sis?"

"Yeah. Anyone who can toss me around like a frigging rag doll deserves to be part of the family."

Mara's acceptance made Tish smile.

"What do you mean about regret?"

"To get Brick back, you'll have to do things you never dreamed of in your worst nightmares," Mara said.

"Like what Brick did last night?"

Mara blew a quick raspberry.

"Huh. Probably worse. Shit's about to get real, Tish. One of the most malevolent bitches in the universe has him and will be ready for us. And she'll have countermeasures to deal with our abilities because she's probably working for the organization that created us. Knowing her, though, she's likely working her own angle."

"I don't care. I love Brick, and I never told him. I will get him back."

Mara snorted. "This ain't a movie, Lil' sis. Zindriya makes Pinhead from *Hellraiser* seem like a candy-coated tale about a fairy godmother's fluffy pet mouse."

"I'm not scared," Tish said, locking her eyes on the older woman's.

"Not now, but you will be. This game has a time limit, and you best not expect any happily-ever-afters. The longer it takes, the less of our Brick we get back from that malicious, sadistic bitch. He won't be the same person we know and love, and when this is all done, you won't be either."

CHAPTER 14: TORTURED

Zindriya's opinion of Smythe hadn't improved. In fact, his recent failure had lowered it significantly. The fool had severely underestimated Brick's abilities and lost his entire crew. To top it off, he'd left mountains of evidence, some of which could lead back to her.

After his visit to the infirmary, she had Bruno haul him into her office where she demanded an explanation for his incompetence. He sat across from her now as blood still flowed from the severe shrapnel wounds that marred his ever-unpleasant face.

At least the smell of garlic no longer wafted from Smythe, though the miasma of piss still surrounded him like the cloud of dust from that one character in the Charlie Brown cartoons.

"So Venton, you managed to snatch a catastrophic failure from the victory of Brick's abduction; explain yourself."

"I captured him alive as you asked. I didn't hurt the family as you wanted."

Zindriya bolted out of her chair, slammed her fists on the desk, and loomed over Smythe.

"You bungled the whole thing, you idiot! You left a trail of clues any moron could follow. A trail that will lead back to me."

When she eased back into her chair, Zindriya carefully placed her right foot next to the emergency switch near her desk's leg. As predicted, the enraged Smythe rose to the full height of his measly 170 centimeters in a futile effort at intimidation. Bruno stepped forward and stood next to Smythe, but Zindriya gave him a slight nod, and after a moment, he backed away.

Zindriya barely caught what he had done. Bruno was very good with his hands.

"You sent me there knowing what he could do, and you didn't warn me. I lost seven of my best because of it. I was lucky to get out with my life."

"I did warn you, you toad. You didn't listen, and your people got careless. Still, you did bring him to me. I suppose that's worth something. How about I add ten percent to compensate you for your trouble? Be happy with that. Your blunder will cost me much more in extra security for the attack I know will come."

"Ten percent. Ten percent? Have you lost your fucking mind? I lost seven people. You'll double my fee, or I'll...."

"You'll what, Venton?"

Zindriya never raised her voice, yet Smythe backed down and darted his eyes to and fro. She remained calm on the surface, but underneath, she seethed. *This ingrate dares threaten me?*

"Nothing, mistress. I'll take the ten percent."

"Five."

"What? You're a real bitch, Zindriya," Smythe said as he slapped an empty holster. To him, she imagined it sounded as hollow as the pit that had just opened in his stomach.

Zindriya's smile turned cold and remorseless.

"Until later, Venton. Thank you for saving me the Euros."

Because of Bruno's deft fingers, she hadn't needed to use the switch. No one ever noticed the small hole in the rear wall of her desk. It housed a mega-joule laser capable of drilling through a human body in less than a second.

"And thank you for volunteering to be my muse. I hope you will be at least half as entertaining as Babel was. Try not to bleed on my floor on the way out. Cheers."

Bruno grabbed Smythe and dragged him out of Zindriya's office. His screams followed him down the hall.

Her mood brightened after the somewhat stimulating confrontation with Smythe. She had another muse now, her sister was in her syndicate, and she had her cash cow and future concubinus, Brick. All she had to do was break him, then bend him to her will. He was young and strong.

Once she trained him, he would fill her every need. It didn't hurt that he was also moderately good-looking. She wanted to visit him. Bruno had spent the last three days conditioning the young man, getting him ready for her to 'rescue' him from the mean, old torturer. She would satisfy her needs while offering Brick pleasure to ease his pain.

As she approached the room where Brick was imprisoned, she heard his screams over the underlying hum of a transformer. When she reached the metal door, she slid open the eye-level portal to watch. One of Bruno's assistants operated the transformer switch in cycles. Five seconds of power to ten seconds of peace for twelve hours straight, then the boy could rest and eat, only to begin again the following day.

As she watched him, Brick looked up and stared directly into her eyes as though he knew she was there. His eyes snapped shut, and he screamed as the transformer hummed again. Something wasn't right. Zindriya entered the room.

"You can turn off the power, Hugo. He's faking."

Hugo wasn't his real name, of course. As with Bruno, she had chosen a name she could easily remember. She paid her employees well, so they would answer to whatever name she gave them.

Zindriya approached Brick.

"You're using biofeedback to create a galvanic skin response to minimize the effect of the electricity, using your sweat to complete the circuit. Impressive, Brick. I'm getting all squishy just thinking about it and what other skills you might have."

Brick's eyes grew wide when she entered, but she had already anticipated the puzzled look on his face. She knew part of it was the brew of medications the organization had provided to block his abilities. Also, she presumed he was trying to process the fact that while her face was familiar, the rest of her was alien.

Zindriya wore a black, skin-tight, leather catsuit in classic villain fashion, minus the high-heeled boots. She detested those torture devices, preferring black moccasins instead. Her body was in top fighting condition, and toned muscles stood out on her bare arms, in stark contrast to the sibling he was used to seeing.

"No, I'm not your precious Sandra, or should I use your pet name for her?"

Brick didn't speak as his narrowed eyes glared at her. Although he needn't have, for Zindriya could see the burning anger, his tensed muscles, and his chest's rapid rise and fall. His heart rate had quickened. He had been faking before. *Who is this boy?* She thought. The label 'boy' was ill-fitting now. He was a man, more so than most she had met.

He had killed seven trained mercenaries, two of whom he had melted into the floor. Venton had mentioned a flash of light as he'd rounded the corner, and the girl had been nowhere to be found. She couldn't comprehend how he had managed to whisk her away, but she would find out. Sandra may have been right about him. Her dear sister might be helpful in discovering Brick's true capabilities after all.

"Twins. Definitely didn't see that coming. I should have known there was a reason she was interested in me. How stupid can a guy be?"

"Don't beat yourself up too much, Brick. Your Andra actually has feelings for you, though mostly those feelings are between her legs. I even think she wants to bear your children."

"Who are you, and why am I here?"

"Tsk, tsk, Brick. I expected more intelligent questions from you."

"Sorry. I can't keep up with all the psychopaths roaming the Earth."

Zindriya remained near the door as she inspected her captive. He was wearing the same jeans and blue, no-logo T-shirt from the night they had kidnapped him, and he was getting a bit whiff. His wrists and ankles were restrained with titanium shackles through rings on a chair crafted out of the same and manacled to a titanium plate molecularly bonded with the metal floor.

Brick was much stronger than the average man. Still, with the potent drug cocktail the organization had given her and the titanium restraints, he wouldn't be able to escape or use his powers. So far, the precautions had held, but it had only been three days. What would happen if, or more likely, when, his body overcame the drugs? Bruno entered the room and acknowledged that he had secured Smythe.

"Turned on Smythe, did you? Hear that, bub? When I escape, if I don't kill you first, you'll end up like him. Doesn't pay to work for a psychopath. Or is it sociopath? I get them confused, especially when they're all wrapped up in the same twisted mind."

Zindriya ignored Brick's tirade, "I'm Zindriya, as if you didn't already know, and you are here because I want something from you."

"Not children, I hope, or are you more like your sister than you think?"

"Now that's more like it, Brick. Now I'm getting really hot for you. Tell me all about what you can do."

Brick snorted, "Well, that's a fucking waste of time. I'm giving you nothing. You got no leverage. How now, scarred cow?"

Zindriya turned to Bruno, "Take Hugo with you, then return alone with the paddles."

"At once, Zindriya," Bruno said.

"Nice boy toy there, Zindy. Fuck you much?" Brick said

"He does an adequate job, but I'm looking forward to having you, Brick. My sister tells me you are quite the enthusiastic lover, even virtually."

She inserted just the right amount of seduction into her voice. She wouldn't make any progress with Brick at the moment. However, the interaction planted an idea in his mind, giving him time to mull it over.

"Here's something else to consider, Brick." Zindriya approached him, leaned over, revealed one perfect breast tipped by an engorged nipple, then straddled and grinded on him as she pressed her nipple against his lips.

Brick closed his eyes. He struggled to hold back, but it had been a long time despite the torture, and Zindriya's pheromones filled his senses. Nature could not be denied, and he responded to her.

"I am a very, very willing partner, unlike my sister and your girlfriend. I know many, many ways to please a lover. Think about it for the next few days."

She stood and covered up just before Bruno arrived with the paddles. Brick opened his eyes wide, and his shoulders slumped.

"Ah, you recognize the paddles, don't you, love? You copied and adapted their design to create the neural stimulation module for your AR devices. Well, I acquired them in their original form." Zindriya chuckled. "Oh, the connections you create when you properly cultivate."

"Of course, you know about my device." Brick glowered at the woman.

"Oh, Sandra didn't betray you, Brick. I bugged her device."

She took the paddles from Bruno and held them up so Brick could get a good look.

"Remember what these are called?" She smirked as she pointed at the device.

"Neurovex. I thought you wanted me alive. They were mothballed for good reason, Zindy."

"I know, but we'll be sure to keep the field saturation well below maximum. You can't fake this time, Brick. The paddles will stimulate your nerves to tell your brain that you're in excruciating pain," she said, laughing, "with absolutely no physical damage." Gleefully, she continued. "How's that for leverage, Brick? Ready to talk?"

He sat stone-faced, unresponsive, eyes closed and breathing deeply.

"Not so sure now, are you, love? Well, I'll leave you to Bruno's tender ministrations. He'll supply the pain, and I'll be back to ease it with some pleasure for both of us. Cheers, love."

Zindriya left the room but waited outside the door. When Brick screamed again, she could tell it was for real because his heart rate had increased exponentially.

◆ ◆ ◆

When Brick saw the paddles, he knew he was fucked. How Zindriya had gotten a hold of them remained a mystery, but it pointed to leaks in the government, just like in Myanmar. Leaks could be traced if he could escape. The organization's connections throughout the military-industrial complex must have played a role in acquiring the paddles, underscoring President Eisenhower's warning a century ago. It would also explain how the mercies had acquired the biometric attenuators.

He thought it ironic that he'd helped DARPA with an engineering problem their scientists couldn't figure out, and that very act of assisting would, later, cause him a significant amount of pain. At best, the Neurovex would kill him. At worst, he'd go insane. *No good deed goes unpunished*, Brick mused, as a sour mood gripped him. The three Fates interwove their threads throughout his life, depositing irony here and treachery there. May the Gods help them if he ever caught up with them.

Brick refocused on the immediate danger of the damned Neurovex. Not even he could deflect the illusion of pain they caused. Direct neural stimulation was no joke. The only way to beat it was to compartmentalize his mind and section off a portion of it to use as a buffer to minimize the pain's effects on him.

Still, he didn't know if he could do it. Proficiency in brain compartmentalization was the most ardent task presented at Nil Parity. He'd almost failed their test back then and hadn't done the exercises necessary to maintain the skill since. Stupid, but that's the way it was.

Brick could try and escape using his abilities, but he didn't know where he was or how much phasing the effort would require, if he could phase at all. It would suck if his stamina ran out as he passed through the last three feet of the wall to freedom. Whatever had come undone in Brick when Smythe captured him had vanished, and the dark seed remained dormant; sated after feeding on his rage.

He could feel the breach in his mind, but it was shut tighter than a well digger's, you know what, and nothing he tried would coax it open again. So, there was no Akashic Field, which meant no superposition transition. If he got out of wherever he was, he had to figure out a better name for whatever he'd done to Tish.

Brick missed her so much. After almost three months with her in his life every day, he had come closer to heaven than he'd ever been. He must get back to her.

How long had he been their prisoner? Days? Weeks? Months? Not months, but it was hard to tell with no point of reference.

They controlled the light and the dark and the damned drugs they gave him dulled his senses, so he could not depend on his inner clock. The drugs had affected his abilities somewhat, but he'd retained some of them. He couldn't phase yet, but he had his speed and strength, which he exercised during his downtime after the shock treatments.

Damn you, Brick. Focus. If you can't compartmentalize your mind, Zindriya will eventually break you, then you're finished, and you'll never be with Tish. Focus!

There was also their family's Final Option. The Redstones had decided that, if captured, the prisoner would wait for an opening to escape. Every captor got sloppy, especially if one feigned compliance. When the opportunity arose, the prisoner would take it and kill as many enemies as possible. Afterward, they would try to find the communications room, squawk the location, and, in the end, give the captors no other choice but to kill them. The act would keep the others safe and free.

Brick couldn't do it, though. He knew how Tish would take it. She would blame herself for allowing him to be abducted right under her nose. It would fester in her mind and soul until it destroyed her. That was her personality, and he would not let regret gnaw away at her heart.

No matter what he had to do, Brick would find a way out, even if it meant losing her in the end because of his actions. She'd at least be able to move on without him, and wouldn't have to shoulder the guilt surrounding his death. And, above all, she would be alive.

Brick had the makings of a plan, but could he accomplish

it? Could he turn the tables on Zindriya and do to her what she was trying to do to him? Was he capable of that level of deception? Who would he be afterward? Would Tish be able to trust him again? Would he be able to trust himself? Would Mara? Pops? Hiral?

Thinking how his surrogate mother might possibly end up despising him filled Brick with grief. He didn't want to lose her or Tish, but if he pulled off his impossible, insane plan, at least the loss would be under his control and not Zindriya's. As he considered his options, few choices remained, and all of them were bad.

Brick would have to resolve those issues before he proceeded. He would choose the victorious warrior's path this time because he had ended up as a prisoner the last time. Tish had been right and wrong when she'd told him that sometimes the old proverbs didn't apply. The statement immediately validated that the reverse must also be true, and most times, they did.

He closed his eyes and took deep breaths, recalling the lessons his teacher had drilled into him at Nil Parity. Brick delved into his memory and buried his perception so far into his subconscious that when his body responded to the application of the Neurovex, the screams, and the pain seemed muffled and distant.

It didn't take long to find the information he needed to compartmentalize his mind and split his psyche. The process was not simple, and he could not accomplish it from within the depths of his mind. Being out of practice with this part of his training, he remained unsure how long he could hide.

Hopefully, it would endure until Bruno finished with the Neurovex, but then he would have to contend with Zindriya. Vowing never again to ignore his mental and metaphysical training if he survived this, he eased himself into a Delta state to further minimize the pain level.

For a moment, Brick feared he wouldn't be able to claw back from the depths of his subconscious. Then, with horror, he realized that all he had to do was follow the sound of his screams.

CHAPTER 15: INVULNERABLE

In the span of a few months, Tish had changed. The light-hearted, acerbic college senior had vanished, and a dour, stone-faced hunter had emerged. While the trail had been hot, she and Mara knocked down doors and busted heads to find out what had happened and who had taken Brick.

The investigation had fallen to Tish and Mara because Flint had checked out, citing some secretive project he needed to complete. They hadn't seen or heard from him in two months, except for the occasional inquiry regarding progress or to forward information from their cyber team.

They enlisted associates from several international intelligence agencies through Flint and Mara's security firm to track Smythe's and Zindriya's movements. She had come to the Colorado Springs area and then went underground. No one had seen hide nor hair of her since. Smythe had followed shortly after, and he had been much easier to pursue. He frequented a bar in Peyton, to the east of Colorado Springs. That was the second place they visited after dropping in on Sandra Bennet. During the visit, Tish discovered the full extent of the gift Brick had given her.

Mara acquired an extremely grainy profile image of Zindriya through one of the agency contacts. Despite the picture's poor condition, Tish instantly recognized the scarred woman's striking resemblance to Professor Sandra Bennett. The grainy photograph coalesced all the clues bouncing around in her mind.

The smile the professor had shot to Brick as they left class, the secret girlfriend he'd broken up with, the late-night rendezvous that, on occasion, ended their project work, and Bennett's impromptu meetings with only him for updates on their project all made sense now. Professor Bennet had been the woman Brick had broken up with and the go-between for Zindriya, setting the landscape for the abduction. It was time to pay her a not-so-pleasant visit.

When Tish and Mara checked the good Professor Bennett's house, not only was she already gone, she had left a booby trap. Tish spotted the mass of wires, high explosives, and fertilizer in the professor's second-floor bedroom and reacted with near ghost-like speed. A moment before the firebomb ignited, Tish tossed Mara through the upstairs window and almost ten meters from the house, ensuring her escape from serious injury. Tish knew she was dead, closed her eyes, and spoke a silent goodbye to Brick as the burning house disintegrated around her.

However, no flames burned her flesh, no pain racked her body, and the concussive wave had no direct effect. When Tish finally opened her eyes, she remained unharmed and surrounded by a golden light, like a shield. Mara screamed out her name and wept.

Mara cried for me. Mara, sobbing? She thought.

When Tish exited the house, the older woman ran up to her but stopped short. The heat from the inferno still cascaded from the shield, and the ring of burned grass around her confirmed the theory. She remembered what Brick had told her in her dream: Nothing would ever hurt her again. He'd meant it literally. Somehow, he had changed her. It also explained her enhanced speed, strength, and senses.

Since that day, she tested the theory repeatedly in their

futile search for Venton Smythe, who also seemed to have disappeared. Tish's invulnerability activated when she was in danger and didn't seem to draw on her stamina as the Ghost abilities did for Brick and his family. She didn't know how it worked, how long it would last, or how Brick had done it. While she had this invulnerability, she would use it to find him.

Tish tore through all of Smythe's known associates at the bar, but no one knew where he was or where he lived until she found a man named Krieger more than two months into their search.

He confessed to befriending Smythe until his fear of the crazy woman with the scar made him cut all ties with the man. He wouldn't buckle under physical pressure from either Tish or Mara. He was willing to be bribed, but not with money. He wanted his payment in flesh from Tish, and then he would give them information on where Zindraya's base of operations was.

Tish weighed her decisions. She didn't want to betray Brick, but time was of the essence, and if the man had information that would cut the time shorter, she had to do what was necessary.

She agreed to his terms. She would meet him at the bar in Peyton, dressed in a catsuit incapable of hiding a weapon, and then he would drive them to wherever they would complete the transaction. That part went smoothly.

She stripped when they arrived at the motel room so Krieger could search her for tracking devices. She kept still, closed her eyes, and shut off her mind while he conducted his very personal and thorough inspection. Satisfied she was unarmed, he let Tish call Mara with his burner phone while he first sniffed, then licked his moist fingers.

Once he revealed Zindraya's whereabouts, Tish passed the information to Mara, who drove to the location immediately. It had been one of the recent home purchases her team had been looking at as the most likely prospect. The site was prime, and the purchase had been in cash shortly after the entire family's demise. Mara agreed it was probably the lair. Tish hung up the phone and turned to face Krieger. She would go through with her end of the bargain. Krieger, however, had other plans. He liked it rough and had brought along friends.

Five more men emerged from the closet and the bathroom encircling her. As the men grabbed Tish and held her down, spread-eagled on the bed, she remained strangely calm. That scared her more than what the men had planned.

"It doesn't have to be like this, Krieger."

"Oh yeah, it does, bitch!" He said, his sick laughter sounding almost like a hyena. Then he slapped her. She barely felt it. Mara hit harder than this guy. She nearly laughed, remembering how Brick used to say the same thing. What would he think of her disgracing herself to find him? Would he even want her after this? What will she think of herself?

If he's still al..., no, I can't go there. I have to believe he's alive. When they got him back, at least he'd have the choice of staying or leaving. Right now, he had no choice. Krieger struggled with the zipper on his pants.

Tish looked him in the eyes and spoke calmly, almost soothingly, "Send the others away, and I'll honor our deal. I'll do whatever you want me to."

"You're gonna do what we all want you to anyway, fucking slut," he looked at one of his buddies, "Whip it out, son and fill her mouth up so she won't talk so much." Hyena-Krieger cackled at his stupid joke.

"Last chance, Krieger. Send them away, and you can have me any way you like."

He'd finally gotten his zipper opened, and he pulled out his limp phallus.

"This is your fault with all your jabber, bitch. I'm gonna have to beat it out of you now."

"So be it," said Tish in a voice that echoed off the walls, frightening even herself. Her skin flashed golden, and the men began to scream.

Once it was over, Tish stumbled to the bathroom, vomited whatever remained in her stomach, washed the blood and gore from her body, then dressed. She took Krieger's phone and the keys to his car, then turned the temperature on the air conditioner down to its lowest setting and closed the door behind her. She stopped by the office to pay for another week and told the attendant they wouldn't need any services for the room during their remaining time.

Tish had unplugged the poorly placed camera as she walked into the office, and no others were in view. She or Mara could return later and degauss the cheap security system to wipe any local recordings clean, an easy fix since there was no wifi or cloud connection.

Tish walked to Krieger's car and doubled over, dry-heaving behind it. After she finished, she leaned on the trunk to gather her strength. Then the tears flowed as the grief and disgust at what she'd done finally hit her.

She never believed she was capable of such violence. She had no idea a human body could hold so much blood. Technically, she knew the body contained five liters on average, and there had been six of them. However, the facts paled in comparison to reality. She'd had to use the blankets and bedsheets to mop up enough of it to get from the shower to the door without leaving a bloody trail from the room to the stairs.

Tish didn't even remember everything that had happened. It was as though she had partially blacked out and let a demon take over her body. Every ounce of rage at every injustice she had suffered at the hands of men gushed from her in a tsunami of fury and dark shadows. Frustration and helplessness at Brick's abduction burned within her, and her attackers had been in the wrong place at the wrong time.

Tish recalled scattered flashbacks of scenes and emotions, like watching damaged, incomplete frames from an old reel-to-reel movie. They used to call it venting one's spleen or something like that. It had been more like Tish had vented all of their spleens. The thought nearly brought on another round of dry heaves.

When she finished, she felt something inside her, buried within the flesh behind her solar plexus. She didn't know what it was or from where it had come. Perhaps it resulted from Brick's transformation. For the moment, she let it go. Other things occupied her mind.

Not only am I a whore, but also a serial killer. She thought.

She wasn't strictly a whore because she hadn't had sex with them unless you count Krieger's inspection. Tish was sure he got off on it, but it had done nothing for her.

Maybe not, but they all got fucked, though, didn't they? Tish thought.

The tears threatened to flow again, but Tish clamped down on them, got in the car, and began the long drive west, back to the Redstone home. She called Mara on the way and told her what had happened. She had expected Mara to be ecstatic about her slaughter of the not-so-innocents, but the first thing out of her mouth had been, 'Are you okay?' The empathy initiated a crying fit so strong Tish had to pull over. She hadn't expected compassion from Mara. She had expected a suck-it-up speech or something along those lines.

"Where are you, Lil sis? I'll come to you. We need to ditch the car anyway."

Tish stopped at the convenience store on the corner of Willamette and Union, across from the Olympic Training Center. Mara arrived ten minutes later. She surprised Tish by pulling her from the car and into a tight, warm, and wonderful embrace, then whispered in her ear that everything would be okay. She was family, like the sister she'd always wanted, just with one hell of an edge.

"You were right, Mara. I am scared. I'm scared of what I've become. I just found a man to love, and now I don't even know if he'll ever want me again or if he'll be the man I fell in love with anymore. What if this is too much for us, Mara? What if we've changed too much to be together?"

"Let's get him back first, Lil sis. I don't have any answers, and speculation will just drive you crazy. Shove it in a dark corner in the deepest recesses of your mind until we rescue him."

"You're right. I'll tr..." Tish remembered how Brick pushed Yoda's philosophy on trying and corrected herself.

"I'll do it for him. We'll get him back, kill that bitch Zindriya, and then I'll work on him until we find a way to stay together."

"With life, there's hope, Tish."

Was the Redstone family full of philosophers and not assassins? Or did they become philosophers to justify their place in the universe? Or did they want to find a way to fit in with all the ordinary people and find solace in a world of chaos?

After what felt like an hour, Tish felt better. They drove both vehicles almost a mile down Willamette until they found two auto repair shops across the street from each other. Business must have been good because cars lined the road and the cross streets. They left Krieger's Caddy among the vehicles parked along the street, knowing it would remain undiscovered for a while.

Once they got home, Tish took a long, cleansing bath and fell into a fitful slumber on Brick's bed. She'd slept there since they began the search because of his scent. The smell of the beach, with a hint of sandalwood, was deeply embedded in his mattress. Her enhanced senses were both a blessing and a curse. However, they led her to understand Brick a bit better. She missed him so much.

After a time, his essence eventually soothed her enough to relax. Tish fell asleep soon after. She dreamed of the two of them on a picnic in the middle of a closely cropped lawn of violet blades of grass that stretched for miles. Brick leaned in and kissed her under a lavender sky with a bright, blue sun shining down on them.

◆ ◆ ◆

"Zindriya's had Brick for three months, Mara, and we know where he is. Why aren't we hitting the damned house?"

Autumn was beautiful in Colorado, especially in the rolling hills east of Colorado Springs. Wildflowers bloomed under the partly cloudy sky, and temperatures were mildly pleasant as the summer heat begrudgingly relinquished its hold on the land.

A soft breeze caressed the landscape and carried the roars of lions from the nearby wildlife rescue preserve. It was almost as if they were in the middle of an African veldt. Tish and Mara lay belly down on an aromatic mixture of sage and buffalo grass, one ridge from the canyon where Zindriya's hideout rested.

"The house, as you call it, is a frigging fortress, Lil sis. You may be invincible, but I'm not, and we need more intel before we hit the place. The first rule is to survive. If we die, who will rescue Brick? Don't be like those idiot movie heroes who charge in mindlessly. We don't have stunt doubles."

"But Brick has been in that bitch's clutches all this time. He needs us to rescue him, and here we are lounging on the top of a canyon wall, just doing nothing."

"We're tracking their comings and goings, looking for a weakness in their security to exploit. The house is built into the canyon wall, Tish."

They had no idea how far into the bedrock it went or how many changes Zindriya had made. They still didn't know the enemy's numbers, weaponry, or security countermeasures. Mara's people had scoured the plans of the original home and any upgrades so they could somewhat accurately assess any structural complications, but guessing was a damned long way from knowing. They couldn't use modern scanning methods because the psychopath would undoubtedly have devices to both detect and block the scans. That would raise an alarm, and they would lock down the mountain. The lack of intel could very well be the difference between living and dying for all of them.

"Have you found any EM signals to monitor or hack?" The older woman shifted from one foot to the other.

"Not yet, Mara."

"That means whatever they're using is hard-wired. Old-school, incapable of being hacked, unless... Come on, let's go. I got an idea."

They returned to their hotel room for some equipment. Mara had power sensing devices and an old-fashioned metal detector. If the fortress ran hard-wired countermeasures, there had to be a network hub somewhere. If they could find it or them, they could disable the entire network with a simple pair of bolt cutters. Old-school may not be hackable, but it was easy to subvert with the right tools. Mara had learned the information from a more senior operative she had pity-screwed. She confessed to Tish that while it had begun as a pity screw, the old-timer nearly blew the top of her head off with his mad sexual skills.

Tish's head hung low, and her shoulders drooped as she leaned on the fender of their Subaru. She and Mara loitered about a small park on the east end of Calhan, across the highway from the El Paso County Fairgrounds, as their Bulldog Burgers and fries grew cold. She wasn't hungry.

The uneaten burger in front of Mara confirmed the same. Ever since Brick's abduction, all food tasted like sawdust. Still, she forced herself to eat, if only to keep her strength up. She and Mara sparred to keep their skills honed for when they either rescued Brick or avenged his death.

Tish and Mara returned to the canyon house just after dark, wearing what Mara called biometric attenuators. They masked the life signs of the wearer, making them undetectable by every sense except sight. Mara passed an EM field detector across the ground, tracing buried cables.

It didn't take long to find the first cable on the canyon floor and trace it back to a subsidiary junction box. From there, they followed it back to another box, then another. As they passed each box, the signal grew stronger, indicating that the cabling had increased or grown more prominent as they climbed up the walls to the top of the canyon. They would soon find the primary network box and the trunk line into the house. Once they discovered it, they could subvert the system.

Tish had to wear starlight goggles so she could see. Her new abilities didn't include night vision, as Brick and Mara did. She guessed Brick hadn't deemed such a skill necessary. She caught herself in that cynical thought and admonished herself for it. The man had given everything he had to ensure no one could ever hurt her, and she was whining about not having night vision? Talk about ingratitude.

After an hour, they located the primary junction box, the central hub, and what had to be the main trunk line as it trailed off beyond. Tish and Mara were on top of the canyon wall into which the house had been built.

There was a hatch nearby that granted them access to the main house. Fortunately, it was part of the original design and had been in the cyber team's hacked plans. Mara stood guard while Tish unearthed the box and the trunk line to see what they were dealing with.

So far, they had escaped detection, but the attenuators' power cells were low on fuel after four hours. It took a lot of energy to mask a human body, and they needed to change their fuel cells or call it a night.

Tish was ready to refuel and return. She wanted Brick back as soon as possible, but Mara disagreed. They had the beginning of a plan, but they needed more intel on what awaited them inside the house. It was likely a maze, and they needed to know how many troops they were up against to assemble a large enough rescue team. If they went in with guns blazing without knowing Brick's exact location and current condition, the enemy might kill him before they could rescue him.

Or we might even have to fight Brick. Tish thought. An imaginary vise threatened to crush her heart. She took a deep breath and willed it to stop. What she couldn't change, she would either accept or adapt.

Mara had been right all those months ago. Tish was scared of what they would find when they rescued Brick. He had been in Zindriya's clutches for a long time. She might have brainwashed him into helping her. Maybe she had messed with his mind and made him fall in love with her in some fucked up Stockholm Syndrome bullshit.

Perhaps he had renewed his relationship with Sandra Bennett, the slut professor. Tish worried about it. She lost sleep over it, but there was nothing she could do but get him back and go from there.

She covered up the box and joined Mara. They were about to leave when the sound of retracting lock bars and creaking hinges from the hatch heralded their worst nightmare.

CHAPTER 16: CYCLES

Afraid of failure without the screams to guide him, Brick emerged from the depths of his mind earlier than he'd planned. When submerged, he heard the cries of agony escaping his throat, but they seemed almost detached, at least at first. Once he resumed control of his body, he experienced the soul-wrenching pain first-hand, unlike anything he'd known or imagined.

No stranger to suffering, Brick had encountered torture before, but this went far beyond. It was as though fire scorched his flesh and seared every neuron. No level of mental control would help, and nothing else existed beyond his world of excruciating agony. When the suffering finally ended what seemed like an eternity later, Brick felt drained and on the edge of panic. He had a hard time thinking. He didn't know if he could handle more, but what choice did he have?

The ability to phase still eluded him, and hyper wouldn't help. Or would it? Even titanium had a breaking point, but using hyper to vibrate them would make too much noise. It might take too long, and he'd have to hope all four shackles would break simultaneously. Additionally, the attempt would alert his captors to his only ace in the hole should an opportunity arise. It wasn't quite time yet. All thoughts of compartmentalization had dimmed to the ghost of a memory, and the dark seed remained quiescent, leaving Brick with no viable options but to persevere.

Bruno left the room, and Zindriya entered, and he was grateful. At least the pain would end for the day. For a second, he thought it was Sandra, but the skirt and blouse she had worn when they began their affair couldn't conceal her psycho sister's scarred face or sinewy legs and arms. She leaned forward, braced her hands on his knees, and kissed him lightly.

She whispered into his ear in a calm, soothing, almost loving tone. "I'm so sorry Bruno caused you so much pain, Brick. I told him no more than fifteen minutes. Don't worry, my love. I will take care of you now."

She kissed his neck where he was most sensitive, and, in his weakened mental state, he responded. Zindriya was there now, and the aches had ceased. Maybe she wasn't so bad after all. She unzipped his pants and slid her lips around him, tickling him with her tongue. She said she was very talented, and she had not exaggerated. When Brick was ready, she lowered herself onto him. She hadn't been wearing underwear under Sandra's skirt, either. Brick had gone a long time without physical sex, and with endorphins coursing through him, the pain seemed quite far away.

In the subsequent cycles, days, or whatever, the process repeated itself. The intensity of the pain had driven away almost all of his will to resist. Brick's plan to split his mind was still there but had shrunken beneath the overwhelming layers of agony from the accursed Neurovex. Zindriya appeared at the end of each session to replace the pain with pleasure. Brick's captors controlled his day and night, but at least he had a repetitive cycle to refer to, some framework onto which his logic could grasp.

Brick still had no idea how long he'd been Zindriya's prisoner, but at least he could count the cycles of pain and pleasure. With it came a better grasp of his artificial, forced reality. He'd clung to fragments of his sanity by his cracked and bleeding fingernails, and the reassertion of logic and some sense of the passage of time helped significantly. He assumed more control over his mind as each cycle passed despite the wrenching, soul-crushing agony. The memory of Tish helped Brick through the morning half of the cycle, and the reality with Zindriya got him through what passed for the night. Ten cycles in, he rediscovered what he was supposed to do but couldn't remember how to initiate the compartmentalization.

He didn't resist his captors, and they finally allowed him to shower with a bodyguard instead of hosing him down like a wild animal. After twenty cycles, Brick remembered how to initiate his plan and began compartmentalizing his mind, leaving the part falling for Zindriya on the surface while the rest of his psyche plunged deep into his subconscious.

Something dark and powerful waited for him in the depths of his mind and body. He'd forgotten about the seed, or perhaps it had prevented him from remembering. Maybe it also sought to escape the pain and resented his intrusion into its domain. As Brick approached, waves of energy radiated from the thing inside him, but he sensed neither good nor evil, positive nor negative. Sentience existed within the seed, but neither intelligence nor purpose. It was as though it were a blank slate, waiting for input, akin to a newborn child.

He remembered an excerpt from a book he'd read and now understood its meaning. Power was neutral, and its intent depended on how its user wielded it.

Darkness did not always equate to evil. The color black was, in reality, the complete absence of any hue or pigment, while white was the blending of all colors. Therefore, black represented a blank slate; you could use it for any purpose, good, evil, or otherwise, making it infinitely more flexible.

Before Brick could reach out and connect with the seed, it rushed through the pathway his psyche carved during his escape and touched, then merged with the piece of Brick left on the surface. Tendrils of the being remained connected to where it had lain concealed within his mind. He reached out and connected with the tendrils and found that, by using them, he retained control of the part of him in the real world that was in love with Zindriya. In reality, it was more Stockholm Syndrome than love, but as long as it served its purpose, it was a distinction he could ignore.

A significant portion of his mind had remained intact, and he was thankful for it, though it was severely damaged, maybe broken. Pain had that effect. His first instinct was to use rage to bolster his fractured mind. However, his teachers at Nil Parity taught him the path of wrath and vengeance only ever led to death, not of the body but of the soul. He might continue to walk the Earth, living each day, breathing the air, but he would be little more than an empty vessel.

Therefore, Brick latched on to Tish's memory, the promise of her lips, and her love. He held on to Mara. He was as much her world as she was his. Then there was the inexplicable twin-like psychic bond they shared, so there was hope it would lead her to him.

They were powerful anchors for Brick. It meant that there was more to family than just vengeance. Mara loved him. Tish loved him. So did Hiral and maybe even Amaye. Love could heal him. It could bind the submerged pieces of his psyche until he could merge them again. It would be enough for the moment.

At first, Brick and Zindriya's sexual sessions were entirely controlled by her. They never made love. It was more like rutting, raw and animalistic, and always with a bit of pain mixed in, in order to enhance the pleasure. It was like screwing a bobcat, with all the bites and scratches to show for it. On cycle twenty-five, though, she had spent the night in his prison chamber with shackles only on his ankles. Brick urged his alter ego to take more control during Zindriya's pleasure cycles, giving as much as he received.

Thirty cycles brought back his ability to phase. At last, his metabolism had fought off the drugs they had given him, but he still couldn't access the Field, and the seed, while maintaining the connection, remained dormant. However, he was getting through to Zindriya. He could sense the change in her, first through her scent and then through her treatment of him. They gradually evolved to a give-and-take, but still with her in charge.

It was time to make his big move, the one that would end the pain for good. Even though most of his mind remained partially detached, the pain still affected the submerged psyche, but it was a pain he could manage because his plans were beginning to bear fruit. He felt sorry for what his alter ego was going through and could understand how he could see Zindriya as his savior. However, the part that lay hidden within his subconscious, his core psyche, despised her for the psychotic human she was and longed to be with Tish again.

When Bruno departed after the pain part of cycle thirty, Brick smiled at Zindriya, then stood up, phasing free from the chains. Zindriya's eyes flared wide with panic, and she opened her mouth to scream for help. Brick went hyper, crossed the short distance instantly, and placed a hand over her mouth, whispering that he had no intention of harming her because he was in love with her.

Since she was still alive, she relaxed a bit. "How long have you been able to phase?"

"About a week now." Brick felt no guilt for lying. Some people didn't deserve the truth. "I wanted to prove how much I love you."

"So, you don't want me dead?"

"No, Zee, I want us to be together as equals."

Brick had only seen Zindriya smile once; the previous night, his alter had given her multiple orgasms. She displayed that smile again, then guided him to her quarters as Bruno glared at him. Psionic daggers from the big man's eyes flashed through the ether of his imagination but fell harmlessly to Brick's returned gaze of triumph. The left side of Brick's mouth tilted up, and the wink he shot at Bruno turned the other man's face violet.

That night was like sex with a bobcat while riding a rollercoaster. Brick re-considered it. It had been more like intercourse with a Klingon woman; porn, WWE, and UFC all wrapped up in the same bundle. From cycle thirty to thirty-nine, Zindriya had brought others into the bedchamber to supposedly enhance pleasure for both of them. However, on cycle forty, everything changed for the better since it was the last cycle he had to suffer the Neurovex.

When they entered her chambers, she closed and locked the door, then turned to him. She crossed the short distance between them with a look Brick had never seen. Zindriya exuded tenderness and desire instead of lust. When she embraced him, she said something he'd never thought he'd hear her say.

"Brick, all I've ever known is violence and control, as either the controller or the controlled. I know there's another way, but no one has ever offered it to me. I only know how to fuck, but I want, no, I *need* more than just that. Please make love to me, Brick. I want to know what that's like. Teach me how to make love softly, slowly, and gently. Show me another way."

She kissed him as a lover would, not a dominatrix. Alter-Brick, or A.B., made love to her that night and every night after because she preferred it more than the other way. She was falling in love with him, and the part of his mind living on the surface was already deeply in love with her. His core, however, was still repulsed by the very thought of what was going on, so he closed his inner mind to it and let A.B. do what needed to be done.

Eventually, if his plans worked, he would also have to face Tish and try to explain everything he'd done to get back to her. She'd likely walk out on him, and rightfully so, but at least she would have the choice. She wouldn't have to live with the guilt of his death weighing down her soul. It would be a victory for him, a bitter one, yes, but a triumph nonetheless. A phrase he'd heard off and on over the years surfaced. Sometimes, when you win, you lose. The Fates were whimsical and almost always required their quota of blood.

Sixty cycles passed, and Zindriya gave Brick access to the vast underground complex but not the upper levels. Bruno was nearly apoplectic, but he wouldn't betray Zindriya. Brick submerged his alter ego during the day, allowing him to emerge at night to deal with Zindriya and her incessant demands. He slowly but surely worked on her to take down the organization before they discovered her betrayal. She agreed to consider it if Brick began work on Zero-Point Energy technology, and he immediately volunteered.

Earlier, Sandra informed him that Zindriya would be interested in ZPE and she would help. She had fully integrated with her sister's syndicate and slowly worked her way up, gaining the support of a portion of the staff. Brick knew something was going to happen soon between the twins. He also knew Sandra wasn't even close to being prepared to overthrow Zindriya. The scarred twin was too sadistically cunning for that to happen. He wasn't going to say anything to her, though, because, in his mind, she would get what was coming to her, being, in part, responsible for his capture.

Brick understood the thought was uncharacteristic of him, at least for the person he used to be. He'd grown much harder and wasn't sure he liked who he'd become. He still had that core of decency within, but he no longer worried about the methods he would use to achieve it. Someday, he'd have to ask himself some difficult questions, but now was not the time, and he did not know what he still had to do. He would need a tough shell to get through it all.

He wondered what was going on in the outside world and what

was happening with Tish and Mara, and his dad. He figured his father and sister were looking for him, and maybe they'd already discovered where he was incarcerated. He couldn't do anything to help, though. Zindriya may have let go of the collar, but Bruno and his close-knit crew still held the leash. Brick couldn't make a move without one of them watching, and they were really good. Most of the time, he could only detect them by scent. So, he remained a good boy as long as Zindriya remained in compliance. He would use her to do it and clean up the mess later. Brick had convinced himself that he was fine with it. Occasionally, he even believed it.

Seventy cycles in, Zindriya allowed him access to the outside world via the internet, though he remained confined within the complex. With the additional access, Brick found that nearly three months had passed since his capture. Though his mind had assumed as much, the reality of it still astounded him. Was anyone still looking for him, or had they given him up for dead? What was going on with his sister and his dad? What was going on with Tish? Mom and Pops? Brick wanted to make a move. He could escape now since he knew where he was, but it would accomplish nothing. He would lose the advantage of being an insider, and Zindriya would move her operation or strike back at all of them. He would also lose all of the information she had on the organization. So, as much as he loathed it, he would continue.

After a week of sixteen-hour days, Brick and Sandra made a breakthrough with the Zero-Point project. It wasn't easy working so many hours with her, especially when she would lean against him as he slaved over a circuit board or a casing. The feel of her body pressed against him, combined with her scent, was intoxicating, reminding him of their tutoring sessions and AR encounters. But what they had was over. She had betrayed him, and he needed Zindriya's resources for his own purposes.

They were close to completion. Some of their tests had been

successful, and some not as much. In their most promising failure, the module they fashioned lasted only a few hours, but while it functioned, the laptop-sized generator created enough power to light a city block.

That same day, Sandra prepared her forces to move against Zindriya. She tried to enlist Brick in her coup attempt, and he convinced her he was on her side.

He had no choice but to betray Sandra. It was the only way to prevent a civil war within the syndicate. Before she could initiate her coup attempt, Brick handed her to Zee. Though Brick argued for her immediate execution, Zindriya ordered her twin to the lower dungeon. Smythe had finally died, and she needed a new muse. The look of betrayal in Sandra's eyes devastated him, and that kernel of good left within him could not let it happen. He took a chance on blowing his cover and did something out of character. He offered to participate in the systematic physical and psychological destruction of Professor Sandra Bennett.

Zindriya was ecstatic that Brick wanted to take part. She confessed to concern that Sandra's infatuation with him might win him over to her side. However, his willingness to help with her new muse cemented her feelings for him. She felt they had become true partners.

She was a master in the art of torture, and though Sandra's screams tore at Brick's soul, Zindriya went about her business with a clinical detachment bordering on the insane. All the while, she described everything she did as though she were recording her ministrations into an official report for posterity.

After two hours of endless screams from the woman on the table, Zindriya turned Sandra over to Brick and explained what she wanted him to do. Brick submerged most of his psyche behind the protective wall, and, under his control via the dark seed, A.B. took over. When Zindriya turned her back on him to grab another tool from the stainless-steel table containing the torture devices, Brick stuck his heel out just enough to catch Zindriya's toe. As she turned back around, she lost her balance, then whipped her hand out to steady herself and, in the process, shoved Brick. His scalpel *slipped* and opened the artery in Sandra's armpit. She bled out in minutes despite Zindriya's attempts to save her. Brick apologized for his carelessness, and to his surprise, she was okay. Zee had confessed to having second thoughts about torturing her sister and that he had saved her the trouble of dealing with the conundrum.

After they left Sandra's body for Bruno to deal with, Brick excused himself to go to the bathroom. Hunched across the porcelain basin, he threw up everything in his stomach. No more sympathy remained for what he was doing to do to Zindriya. Despite her recent changes, she deserved every bit of it.

Later that night, Zindriya revealed things about the organization that wanted him, its structure, and the members of the hierarchy. It functioned as a cooperative whose sole objective was world domination, using genetically altered soldiers. They would have their Eugenics War one way or another. That's why they wanted Brick. They surmised that his DNA would be the key to their ultimate army. Did any of these people watch Star Trek? Did they know who Khan Noonien Singh was and what he almost did? Sure, it had been fiction, but as society had seen so many times before, art did imitate life and sometimes even predestined future.

The organization was a collection of individual cells that kept in touch virtually. No one was ever in the same place at the same time, and they used algorithm-spawned hexadecimal codes to rotate the virtual sites where they communicated. They occasionally collaborated on large projects, like the lab they used to convert the Redstones into Ghosts, but it didn't happen often.

Brick's family had always worked under the assumption that the organization they hunted used a central governing body and existed as one single entity. With everything he'd learned, there was no way his family could ever have taken down the organization that had ruined their lives. He needed Zindriya and her collection of misfits if he was ever going to make any headway against their mutual enemy. The sad part was that they might never completely eradicate the organization.

Maybe not, but we can damn sure put a major hurt on them, especially with what I know now.

He would have to keep his barriers up and A.B. in place. His core wasn't in any danger of falling for the psychotic woman. But what was the A.B. persona doing to him? He had to stand by and let her continue brutalizing people whenever she felt the desire or need. At first, he silently railed against her brutality but slowly became almost numb to it. That scared him the most.

A few hours later, he lay in bed, his hands locked behind his head, pondering his dilemma. Zindriya's warm, naked back pressed against him as she snored softly and mumbled something incoherent. His alter ego also dozed, which left him in a rare and welcome state of solitude where he could think and plan. However, his mind didn't grant him peace to ease into sleep. No, it couldn't allow him a moment's respite. It had to air out his ego's grievances as it attempted to mediate between his Id and his Superego.

Was Brick losing himself in an obsession? Was he becoming Captain Ahab, or worse, his dad? Was the obsession more important than life itself? More important than Tish? Or Mara? This was one dark frigging rabbit hole he'd fallen into. He just hoped he could crawl out someday and find that at least a little of who he had once been waiting for him, arms outstretched, to welcome him back from the path of evil. But back to what? To a past that no longer existed or a future as uncertain as the transient whims of the Fates? The only way to endure it was to move forward, cross the last hurdle, and forge a new future from the tattered remnants of the past, hopefully with Tish.

If she'll have me, he thought.

Brick knew for sure that was the crux of it all.

Was his redemption only a fantasy seen through rose-tinted glasses? Was the glass tinted, or smeared with dried blood thinned by the tears their loved ones shed for the lost souls who had unwillingly bequeathed it? Blood that would be washed away by the cold, cleansing rains of the future but would fail to retreat from Brick's hands. Would it be Tish who cringed from those stains or him, head lowered in disgrace for what he had done, doomed to a lifetime of pain, regret, and self-imposed exile?

Who would he be after all was over? Could he find his way back to some semblance of normalcy? Something close to the man he used to be? Or would he have to live with what he had become? The questions weighed heavily on Brick's mind, and the fact that he couldn't begin to answer them made him feel as though he teetered on the edge of the Grand Canyon as the ground crumbled beneath his feet.

CHAPTER 17: DAY FOUR

Part 1

Brick collected information from Zindriya's cyber team about the current whereabouts of the nearest cell. The organization his family chased for years called themselves Cleddyf, Welsh for sword. Sword of what? Damocles? Judgment? Vengeance? Insanity? Murder? It seemed that some idiot plucked a random name from the lexicon and slapped it onto the syndicate's logo for no reason other than sounding cool and enigmatic. In his opinion, it fell far short of both. Regardless, Brick was thankful he finally had a name for the group that had destroyed his family.

I know your name now, fuckers. Soon I'll be coming for all of you. Brick thought.

Historically, knowing someone's true name gave you power over them. Occultists believed using an entity's true name summoned it and gave you control over it. In ancient Egyptian mythology, Isis tricked Ra into revealing his true name and used it to keep him from killing her son Horus, ensuring he would one day possess Ra's power. One of the most well-known cases of a true name equaling dominance over the owner was the Grimm's fairy tale of Rumpelstiltskin.

Brick felt renewed because having a name meant he had a bullseye to aim for instead of some nebulous, nondescript, amorphous mass.

As he walked back to the office he shared with Zindriya, he felt a feathery yet familiar touch on the surface of his mind. Brick stopped and rotated in place until he found his bearings. Afterward, he circled the area in an attempt to locate it. He followed this signal to one of the fortress's outer walls, and the touch transformed into a caress. It was Mara, and she was close. They had found him! He could hardly contain his excitement, followed by abject terror.

Brick could phase through the wall and be with his father and sister right then, but it would mean losing Zindriya's help in destroying Cleddyf. It would turn her and her 'not-insubstantial' resources into instant adversaries. Colorado Springs would become a war zone.

If Mara and his dad were close, they were either about to attack or were surveying the complex, trying to find its weaknesses and deactivate its security countermeasures. What they likely had found were cleverly disguised decoys. The actual defenses were integrated into the front of the house, hidden behind fascia designed to conceal them from even the most skilled observers.

Brick frowned, wishing he had retained the skill to contact Mara as he had the night Smythe kidnapped him. The problem was that he didn't know if it was the drug cocktail they continued to feed him or if the two-way connection had been a unique occurrence. Accessing the Akashic Field also remained beyond his ability, and the damned dark seed continued to sleep.

If he didn't stop them, his family would walk into a trap. He had to do something without revealing his cards to Zindriya. He had only one choice. It was a long shot and depended on Zindriya's ignorance of the details of his capture. Smythe had likely been sketchy on the specifics to hide the blatant errors he and his team had made when abducting him. At least, Brick hoped it was so.

Once again, he had no option but to foil an ally's plans. However, this time, he did it to save the lives of the only family he had left. In addition, he had to play his cards right, or his ploy would get them killed or worse, inmates in Zindriya's lower dungeon. Before that happened, he would use the family's final option and eliminate as many of them as possible, beginning with their psychotic leader.

Let's not forget the irrepressible Bruno. The canny bastard would definitely be at the top of his list as the wielder of the Neurovex.

Brick returned to Zindriya's office and told her what he suspected. She moved to call out all her troops to surround the canyon wall and encase Mara and his dad in, but Brick had a different plan. The two of them would go through the hatch and confront Mara and Flint while they sent a small rearguard around the perimeter to approach from behind, cut off an escape, and make sure their presence wasn't the vanguard of an all-out assault.

If it was a full attack, sending all the troops out would leave the base exposed and defenseless. Zindriya agreed it was a good plan and followed him to the upper hatch. A simple double-slide bolt connected to a ring in the center secured the hatch, similar to those seen in submarines. Maintenance technicians regularly oiled the mechanism and the hinges to ensure they would work as smoothly and silently as possible. Based on what happened next, the tech crew chief would be Zee's next muse.

Brick spun the ring, which drew the bolts back, eliciting a grating screech, like an ogre's fingernails dragging across the world's most enormous chalkboard. Shoving the hatch open, the hinges groaned with almost the same enthusiasm as the bolt mechanism. Yep, the crew chief was toast, especially since Zindriya was right behind him, and when he peered down, her eyes had shrunk to slits, her nostrils flared, and she'd drawn her lips into thin lines. When he stuck his head out, two people a couple of meters away stood ready for combat.

Part 2

When the hatch opened, Mara found nowhere to hide. Their biometric attenuators were useless while in plain sight, so she prepared for battle. A quick glance at Tish confirmed she was on the same page.

Mara was about to go hyper and take down the first person to exit the hatch when Brick popped his head out and flashed a broad grin across his face. He placed one hand on the lip of the hatch as the other braced the lid open.

"Well, hello ladies, fancy seeing you here."

"Brick!" Tish lurched forward.

She was about to run to him when Mara stopped her with a firm grip on her forearm and whispered, "No, Tish. Look at the hand on the lip."

"What about it?" Tish whispered back.

"It's one of our family hand signals. His thumb is sticking out between the index and middle fingers. He's undercover."

Brick moved his middle finger to cover his thumb.

"Hey, Lil bro." Mara stared as her brother in an effort to peer into his soul.

"What's going on, lover? Who's there?" Zindriya's voice echoed from beneath Brick.

He told Zindriya who it was and slowly exited the hatch. Mara took a moment to warn Tish of what was to come.

"Covering the thumb with the middle finger means deep cover, Lil' sis. You're gonna see and hear some things you won't like, but you have to react to what Brick says and does. If you don't, we're all dead, including him. There'll be troops coming up behind us."

"Things? Like what?" Tish squinted her eyes.

"No time to explain. Just go with it, Tish. Don't fuck it up. This shit is for real now."

Once Brick cleared the hatch, he turned and helped another woman who was, with some glaring exceptions, the spitting image of Sandra Bennett. She had short bronze-colored hair, an athletic build, and a scar beginning at her left ear lobe, traveling under her chin, and ending at the outer corner of her right eye.

"Zindriya!" Tish said in a low, raspy voice as she tried to move forward. Mara's grip held her back for the moment. Brick stepped in front of Zindriya and thrust his arms forward, palms out.

"Whoa, Tish. It's all good. We're friends here for the moment."

"Friends? Are you cra...." Tish started.

"TISH!" Mara was thankful her shout stopped the younger woman. This whole thing could go south really fast. She had to find out Brick's angle before her new Lil' sis went nuclear on everyone.

"So, Lil bro, the chick who kidnapped you is now our friend? How so?"

"Because I can help you bring down Cleddyf," Zindriya said.

"Who the fuck is Claydeef, Brick?" Tish ignored Zindriya.

He spoke softly to Zindriya, then she took a half-step back and interlaced her fingers with his. Mara felt Tish bristle. She squeezed her forearm.

"Cleddyf is the name of the organization we've been chasing forever. It's Welsh for..."

"Sword. Yeah, I got it. Why do we need her?" Mara thrust her chin in Zindriya's direction.

"Zee has detailed intel on Cleddyf. It isn't a single entity as we thought. It's a collection of cells that can operate independently or collectively."

"Zee, huh? How do you know she's not lying to you, Lil bro?"

"Because I'm in love with Brick, and he with me," Zindriya said. "I have no secrets from him. He's essentially been running our syndicate for almost a month now."

"Zat true, Lil bro?"

"You heard what she said, Mara. Why would she lie?"

He evaded the question. I wonder if Tish caught it? Mara thought.

She had her answer when the tension in Tish's arm diminished slightly. At first, she thought it was safe to release her but decided against it. Instead, she dropped her hand to Tish's and grasped it firmly.

"So you're with that bitch now," Tish said.

Brick held Zindriya back, "No, Zindriya. Leave her be."

"Do you still have feelings for that child, Brick?"

"A part of me will always have feelings for Tish. That part may be buried deep inside me," he made a point of glaring at Mara, "but it's still there, Zee." His eyes turned back to Zindriya, "Out here, where it counts, I'm with you."

"Then why can't I....?"

"Because I don't know how I'd feel if you killed her. That's why."

Damn, Lil bro. You actually did it, didn't you? You split your mind and buried your true self. And you made that cow fall in love with you. Fuck. It's gonna be hell pulling you back from this one.

"Fine. I'll let it go for you, love, but only just."

"Thank you."

"Don't thank me yet. The night is still young."

Brick turned and kissed her lightly on the lips. Zindriya clamped her hand behind his neck and kissed him back... hard.

Her open eyes flung daggers at Tish the whole time. Mara hoped she would keep it together. The kiss ended, and Brick faced them again.

"Here's the deal."

They would combine their forces and go after Cleddyf. Zindriya had located three cells, while the Redstones had located two cells they thought were only shell companies posing as cross docks for merchandise. Mara revealed their discovery of a third facility since Brick's capture. Zindriya's more extensive intelligence network had determined that there were likely no more than twenty cells of various sizes and functions. Destroying six of them would be a massive blow to their cooperative, but it had to be done simultaneously.

Cleddyf was so well coordinated that the rest of the cells would mobilize and go to ground within minutes of the first attack. While Zindriya had superiority in numbers, the Redstones had the advantage in surveillance technology. She would need access to the tech to track large personnel movements, energy signatures, and cyber and radio chatter for clues. Her cyber unit had algorithms for it, just not access to the satellite tech necessary to deploy them. Mara agreed to allow two of Zindriya's cyber warriors access to their network in the Redstone facility under heavy guard and supervised by their own cyber team.

They couldn't complete specific details of the attack until they gathered more information, so they arranged a future meeting in a secure area to work out the final plans. The discussions wound down, but a sideshow began with an argument between Brick and Zindriya in hushed voices. Mara heard him tell her that he had to close that chapter of his life once and for all. Brick stalked toward Tish with furrowed eyebrows and his lips drew a thin line across his face.

"Hey, Tish. Been a long three days, ain't it?"

"Yeah, so it has."

"After you begged me to screw you on the couch, you turned on me, saying you wanted a piece of my ass over that Brantley shit."

Mara didn't know what was happening, but it didn't fit the version Tish told her. Brick was using code of some kind. Hopefully, Tish would catch on and follow through.

"That was your fault. You knew how I felt about him."

Hell yeah, Tish. Way to go, Lil' sis. Mara thought.

"Yeah, but you still let me, though, didn't you? Then you got all butt-hurt over it!" Brick fired back.

"You took advantage of me, you fucking asshole. You knew, and you did it anyway."

"Yeah. And you liked it."

"You're a dick."

Both of their faces contorted into masks of rage. Mara couldn't tell if the two were Oscar-class actors or if the confrontation was real. She was worried.

"I'm the asshole? You used me to make yourself feel better but blamed me for accepting what you offered. Then all you could think of was getting back at me. You wanted a piece of my ass and challenged me. Remember that, Tish?"

"Yeah, dickhead, and you bitched out and got kidnapped. Bet you set it all up so you wouldn't have to face me. You ran off to get with that haggard old sow over there. Can't handle my young shit, huh? Scared of what I'd do to you?"

"Oh no, princess. We can reschedule day four for sometime after we take down Cleddyf. Then you can try all you want to take a piece of my ass."

"I promise you. I'm gonna collect what you owe me, for damn sure. When I'm done with you, you'll regret every minute, every second. I'm not the weak little girl I once was."

"Won't make any difference, princess."

"I'm not your fucking princess, asshole."

Brick glared at Tish's and Mara's clasped hands.

"And you, dear sister. Didn't take you long to move in, did it?"

"Somebody had to fill the void you left, Brick, and you obviously weren't up to it, little punk-ass negro."

"Frigging hag. So much for trust. So much for family."

Brick turned away from them and stomped back to Zindriya.

"O-o-o-o. Trouble in paradise, lover? Problems with your ex and your sister? Guess you know where they stand, don't you?"

"Don't matter. I got you now. My ex-sister and ex-whatever can go screw themselves and each other."

Brick turned his head to look at Tish.

"Guess we have a deal?"

"Got that right, asshole. Until day four."

Zindriya piped up, "You won't be kissing to seal this one, lover."

"No need to, Zee. I'm pretty sure we both know exactly how we feel about each other. Don't we, Tish?"

"Damn straight."

Zindriya hurled one final insult at Tish. "Just so you know, Brick is oh so very good at filling all of my voids. I suggest the problem lay more with you than with him."

Though Zindriya was the last person who needed it, Brick helped her climb back into the hatch, followed her in, and closed it behind them.

"Let's go, Tish. Too many insects around here."

The two of them traced their way down the canyon wall, past the retreating soldiers, and approached the car, preparing to leave for the Redstone house in The Springs. Before they left, Mara passed a detector over the vehicle, Tish, and then handed it over for her inspection. All of them were clean. Once inside the car, Mara activated a white noise device to block distance surveillance, just in case, and drove away.

"Oh God, Mara. He still loves me!" Tish gushed through sobs. "He totally still loves me."

"How do you know, Tish? That sounded like a straight-up word brawl."

"The reference he used was one only Brick and I knew about."

She had already told Mara about Brantley but had not mentioned what had happened later that night, so she filled in the blanks for her.

"Yep, that's my Lil' bro. A noble bastard through and through, at least with women he cares for."

"Also, he knows I hate it when people call me a princess as much as he hates being called an asshole. He used those references to tell me how he really felt, and so did I. He knows I love him now."

"Even with what he's had to do with Zindriya? Doesn't that bother you?"

"Yah, of course, it does, but if I can get him back, we'll work it out. I'm not saying it'll be easy, but I'm not letting him go without a fight."

"Yeah, and the fight will probably be with him. Brick will feel guilty about what he's doing with that feral bitch and what he'll do later when he dumps her. He's gonna doubt everything about himself and wonder how he was capable of doing it. If he can't trust himself, he won't believe anyone else can trust him either. The frigging noble bastard's gonna want to spare you the trouble."

"I won't let him. Mara, we've both gone through too much shit to let it all go down the toilet. We can accomplish anything when we're together. I mean, look at our invention. He probably doesn't know about it since it hasn't gone public yet. We did that together, and we're set for life, hell, for several lifetimes. I'm getting him back, Mara, no matter what it takes."

"I believe you, Lil sis. Let's go home and get some rest. We need to be prepared for tomorrow. We've got a lot of long days ahead getting ready for this blitz. If we can even pull it off."

"You think we can?"

"With Zindriya's help, maybe..." Mara paused briefly, "there's just one thing I think you need to know, Tish."

Mara was concerned about Brick. She was sure he had compartmentalized his mind, but being sure was a long way from certainty. Mara never discussed it with Tish, wanting to spare her any more grief. Through their pseudo-psychic link, she sensed that Zindriya had tortured Brick mercilessly. Under such severe trauma for so long, an average person's mind could spontaneously fracture just to escape the pain.

Her little brother was by no means average, but she wanted to prepare Tish for that possibility. He might not be faking. Brick might suffer from 'Dissociative Identity Disorder', the new psycho-babble for what used to be called multiple personalities. Mara thought of the John Cusack character in the 2003 movie *Identity* and shivered. She shared her thoughts with Tish, who responded in kind.

What was done was done, and there was no going back. Mara just wanted to get home, talk to her dad about what was happening, and then get some rest. It might be the last time any of them would get a full night's rest for a long time. At least the end appeared to be in sight. They had a name and were gathering intel to construct a plan. Either Cleddyf would go down, or they would. Either way, in a matter of weeks, everything would change.

CHAPTER 18: SPILLED WORDS/ FLINT'S SECRET

Part 1

A week had passed since the meeting atop the canyon wall. Brick kept in touch with Mara, with Zindriya's blessing, and supervision, of course. Her trust went only so far. Once Zindriya's cyber team was in place at the family's lair, the intel-gathering progressed quickly. After three days, they collected all the information necessary to proceed.

Mara's team busted their guests before they planted backdoors, data bombs, and worms in their servers. Zee was lucky to get her team back alive after that. Still, it would take weeks, if not months, for their hands to heal enough to be useful to the scarred mercenary.

Despite the attempted sabotage, their detailed planning session two days ago had gone very well. They negotiated many details, including the distribution of forces and the date of the coordinated attack. That would be in another seven days.

Brick used the time to collect as much information about Cleddyf from Zindriya as possible, citing Sun Tzu and the need to thoroughly know one's enemy. She happily agreed, especially after A.B. applied some very friendly pressure.

He'd spent a lot of his free time in the gym, building up his stamina in both phasing and hyper. He would soon need them for the battles with Cleddyf and then with Zindriya.

Brick's abduction taught him a hard lesson regarding his weapon of choice. Firearms were far too slow when he was in hyper, but throwing knives worked at his speed, and their velocity translated into a devastating amount of kinetic energy. So, he began practicing with an assortment of throwing knives in various shapes and sizes. Since he had regained some semblance of freedom within the complex, he advanced his skill to the point where he rarely missed his target.

His hunch had been correct. When he was hyper, knives were much faster and more effective than firearms. He kept at least fifty leaf and needle-bladed daggers on his person almost all the time. For a total weight of a bit over a kilogram and a half, they were quite the bargain for hypersonic attacks.

Brick developed a rigorous training regime beginning with warm-ups and an hour of knife-throwing in hyper mode, both stationary and mobile. Then he pounded on a 50-kilo heavy bag, tossing it around as though it were a paperweight. He advanced his skills to a level far beyond his pre-abduction ability.

One day, Bruno sauntered in, used one of the other bags for a bit, then confronted him. "You don't run this place, you know, I do."

"Not trying to take your job, Bruno. I wouldn't want to muck out the stables, bag man." Brick's adrenaline ran high, and he had long since lost patience with the pack of vultures who hounded his every step.

Bruno furrowed his brow. "What do you mean by that?"

"What? Not sure if I mean that either you'll need a bag to clean up the mountain of shit after this is over or whether everyone will leave you holding the stinking, shit-filled bag when we're finished?"

Brick had a hard time hanging on to his cover after his close brush with Tish. Professional deep-cover operatives suppressed everything to maintain their chosen persona, but the longer they were in, the harder it became. Any reminder of the past they left behind made it much more challenging to maintain that cover.

His mind was still split, but he'd assumed more control over A.B. when Alter-Brick wasn't screwing Zindriya. He happily relinquished control at those times and let the other guy have at it, blocking as much of the goings-on as he could. It became increasingly difficult as the weeks passed.

At the time, Brick was not in a good mood. Requiring something on which to vent his frustration, he decided that Bruno would do just fine.

He pasted a smirk on his face. "You think you're smart, but I got your number, asshole. When this is over, I'm gonna take Zindriya back from you and put a fucking bullet in your head."

Again with the asshole? Is there some kind of competition? Brick imagined a carnival barker announcing a contest. *Call Brick an asshole five times, and win five dollars. Ten times will win you a hundred! Getcher raffle tickets right here at this booth for the low, low price of free-ninety-nine.*

He sometimes wondered why his mind went on those mental rollercoaster rides in times of conflict. Brick figured it was a way to channel his anxiety into a more productive state. Perhaps productive wasn't the right word, but whatever.

"Bruno, if you're trying to insult me into throwing down, you don't have to. I will gladly stomp your bald ass into the dirt anytime."

He lifted a corner of his upper lip. "Right now good for you? Or do you need an audience?"

"Let's do it, cupcake. You want to puss out and wear gloves, or do we go mano-a-mano, you fucking skidmark?"

"Bare knuckles are fine by me. You don't use your ghost shit on me, yeah?"

"I don't need ghost shit for a dipshit like you, shithead."

He revealed the fact that his teeth hadn't seen a toothbrush for a long time. "I'm gonna enjoy this."

You keep thinking that, jackass. Overconfidence only helps me put you down faster. Brick thought.

Cushioned mats covered a large area on one side of the gym. They met in the middle and, without any fanfare, began the fight.

Brick was true to his word and kept his speed and strength down to average human level. Bruno wasn't a match for him at all. Brick hadn't truly been angry at the larger man. He had simply been an unfortunate victim of his pent-up frustrations.

Brick was calm, cool, and calculating. He predicted every move, every strike, and every hold. He had already planned on annihilating Bruno but grew rather bored with how easy it was, even without his Ghost abilities.

As time passed, however, Bruno's demeanor devolved. It was clear he'd become enraged at the casual way Brick blocked and countered every attack. The fight felt like the final scene in The Matrix, where Neo finally realized he was The One and destroyed Agent Smith.

Bruno charged, so Brick used the large man's momentum and tossed him halfway across the room and into a rack full of blade weapons. The resulting tremor dislodged a sword mounted on the wall.

The weapons were scattered in all directions. Bruno grabbed the sword that had fallen from its wall mount. When he unsheathed it, the antique emanated a power that felt as old as time. It was elegant in its simplicity, and an inscription on the blade written in Spanish flashed with an inner white light.

'No me saque sin razón. No me envaines sin honor.' It's English translation: Do not draw me without reason. Do not sheathe me without honor.

Bruno tossed the sheath across the room and advanced as the inscription turned crimson. Waves of anger pummelled Brick, but Bruno was not their point of origin. They came from the sword. Brick's eyes went wide but with astonishment, not fear. The blade possessed a soul, and they were pissed.

When Zindriya had taken him on his first tour of the facility, she had pointed out the sword, claiming it as one of her most prized possessions. She'd found it while on a mission in Mexico to steal an artifact from the collection of some rich man for the collection of a richer man. She claimed the sword had called to her. At least, that's what Zindriya confessed to him.

"That's the Espada Encantada, the Enchanted Sword, Bruno. You have dishonored the blade, and now, it seeks blood to reclaim its honor." Brick didn't need a weapon to counter.

The big man revealed a secret. "It'll be blooded straight away after I finish splittin' your 'ead down the middle."

Brick hadn't known Bruno was British, but the fight had drawn the accent from him for the first time. "I'm out. This fight is over. You deal with the sword's consequences."

Bruno prevented him from leaving, or at least he thought he did. Brick could have easily gotten around the larger man, but his adversary made one final, fatal mistake.

"Your used-to-be bitch, Tish, will be on my team. Be a bloody shame if somefin' went wrong, yeah?"

Cold fire filled Brick's body. His face went blank as his eyes narrowed to slits. He pulled himself up to his full height and strode toward his prey. Bruno's eyes flared round and wide, and sweat gushed from his pores as Brick slowly advanced. Bruno pulled his lips away from his teeth as he shouted at Brick to stop and tried to back away, bumping into the door frame. The man took several swings at him, but Brick just phased, allowing the sword to pass through his body.

As the Espada whisked through him, he touched the presence he'd only sensed before. They connected with the dark seed and awakened it from its slumber. The Espada had chosen him as its new wielder and urged Brick to obey.

Though he could easily override the compulsion, he decided against it because of the implications the dark seed's awakening offered. The seed and the sword may have some kind of connection, and the gamer in him would not let it go. The blade had a soul and, with the seed's help, he may be able to bind with them.

It may be the real world, but Shakespeare said it best when Hamlet revealed to Horatio how many things beyond our imagination might exist.

The corners of Brick's lips curled a little. His eyes narrowed as he tilted his head forward, then continued to advance on Bruno.

"H-hey. I-I was just j-jokin'."

"Spilled words can never be recalled, Bruno. They've poisoned the sea of eternity, and only your blood can cleanse it. The Espada demands retribution."

Brick's voice sounded flat and emotionless as he pressed forward like a force of nature.

"I promise I w-won't h-hurt her."

"Much too late for that, Bruno. You threatened someone I love, and that alone is enough, but you also dishonored the blade's soul. They have chosen me to renew their honor on this day."

Bruno took one final, desperate slash, but Brick stepped inside the arc of the swing and broke the big man's wrist with one strike. Though he was not in hyper mode, Brick snagged the sword before it fell to the floor. It vibrated as though angry at being treated in such a disgraceful fashion. He drew it across Bruno's forearm so the Espada could taste the blood of the person who had defamed it. The sword drank in the smear of blood along its edge.

After the Espada devoured its bounty, it pulsed once, its pride restored. Brick pricked his right index finger, then gripped the sword's pommel, feeding the soul a drop of his blood. The inscription flashed blue, sent a shock of energy up his arm and into his body, and then the sword spoke one word into his mind.

Bonded.

The sword's soul, which was feminine, was bound to him, meaning no one but Brick could wield the Espada without severe physical consequences, if at all. He didn't know how he knew; he just did. She had a name, Joyeuse, but would allow Brick to christen her with a new one to honor her new bond mate.

Brick slid the sword into his belt, grabbed Bruno's broken wrist, and squeezed. Pain drove the larger man to his knees.

"Please... I don't want to die," Bruno whimpered, grimacing at the pain.

After delivering a monumental amount of pain on Brick for weeks, Bruno disintegrated into a pile of blubbering mush over a broken wrist. The revelation brought him no pleasure, though, and his anger evaporated. This was simply a chore that needed doing, like crushing a Black Widow spider that had set up shop in a child's room.

"The Reaper comes for us all, Bruno. My time will come soon enough, but today is your chance to explore life's greatest mystery. I'll make it quick. Tell me your true name so that I may properly honor your passing." Brick's flat, apathetic voice had given way to a more normal tone.

"Harold Gentry. My name's Harold Gentry." Bruno recovered at least a modicum of control.

"May you follow a more noble path in your next life, Harold Gentry. May you find the peace you never knew in this one."

Tears streamed from Harold's closed eyes, and he babbled something, perhaps a prayer, but Brick ignored him. The stench of piss and shit flooded his nostrils, but it didn't matter. Whatever fear or shame Harold might have felt would be short-lived.

Brick phased his hand into the man's chest, wrapped his fingers around the pulsing heart muscle, and then phased it. In a little over a minute, Harold slumped and fell to the floor. Brick released the wrist and withdrew his hand, leaving the stilled heart in place.

He looked at his appendage and saw pristine skin where he expected blood and gore. Either the phasing had cleansed it, or like the sword, perhaps he had reclaimed his personal honor by absorbing the blood. Harold spasmed as his brain and body failed to cope with the diminishing levels of oxygen in his blood. After another minute, he lay still.

Brick sheathed the Espada Encantada once more, found a proper belt, then buckled it across his back, the pommel extending over his right shoulder. The enchanted sword pulsed twice, then settled into a light but persistent hum. Brick sensed the blade was content. The Joyeuse's soul had chosen him, and he would keep it despite its unknown origins. It held powers he would need to uncover someday, but for the moment, he would add swordcraft to his training regime.

He sensed Zindriya knew more about the sword and would attempt to draw more information out of her if he had the time. If he lived through the raid, he would also search for answers about the Espada Encantada afterward. Brick exited the gym, leaving the body on the mat. He needed to tell Zee she'd have to find a new captain for one of the strike teams. Brick eased the door shut.

Part 2

"What do you think he's doing now, Mara?"

"It's the middle of the night, two days before the attack, and Brick's with a psychotic, feral bitch, Tish. Do you really want me to answer that question?"

"I know, I just..." Tish ran out of words.

"We'll get him back. I don't know what shape he'll be in, but we will get my brother back."

"I was so stupid before, Mara. I should have told him how I felt."

"Yeah, you should have, but it's all water under the bridge. Brick knows you love him now. If I know my Lil' bro, once this is over, he'll stop at nothing to get back to you. He might leave again, but the noble bastard will, at least, face you first."

"I miss him."

"Me too, Lil' sis. Face facts, though. The person we get back won't be the same one we once knew. Just like you've changed, he will have changed a lot. He's gonna be damaged beyond belief after what he's done to survive."

"I know."

"I don't think you do, Tish."

Mara reminded Tish about Zindriya's arduous campaign of torture and the danger it represented. She was sure Brick had split his mind into at least two parts. One part lived on the surface, endured the brunt of the torture, and succumbed to Zindriya's pain and pleasure operation, while the actual Brick remained buried, only taking a peek when it was safe. That would be the only way he could stay sane.

A woman like Zindriya, who trusted no one, would sniff out a pretender. If he flinched even slightly at a kiss or touch, Brick would have to fight his way out of an unknown situation with a deadly enemy at his heels. Zindriya knew what he was, and she would have some countermeasures to prevent him from harming her or escaping.

The only other possibility was that Zindriya had broken Brick, and they were walking into one big trap that he'd set for them. Mara doubted that, though, because she had faith in her brother. He had a strong mind and an unyielding determination, and he deeply loved Tish. She was positive that he remained, somewhere locked inside his own mind. Still, there was a chance that he wasn't.

When they freed Brick, he would have to make a choice. He would need to eliminate his alter ego or merge with it. If he chose the latter, Tish would be dealing with not one ghost but three; his first girlfriend, who died in the car crash; his ex-lover, killed in combat; and Zindriya.

Mara didn't remind Tish, but if the split psyche had resulted from the torture, they might never get their Brick back again.

"Sorry to bust your bubble, Lil sis, but you gotta face reality. He did this to get back to you, but he's fully expecting you to reject him because of what he had to do to stay alive. He won't believe himself worthy of your love or anyone else's."

Tish's mood darkened, and she slumped on the couch in the living room of the Redstone house. The majority of Tish's world had been focused on getting him back. She barely cared enough to eat and had done so only because she needed to stay strong in case that one chance came to rescue him.

The only other thing she was engrossed in was their project. She had finished the device and submitted it to the substitute professor who had taken Sandra's place. Tish also put it on the auction block to the highest bidder and accepted an insane amount of cash for the manufacturing rights and profit-sharing for future sales, though she and Brick retained the patent and ownership rights.

Now here she was, seething over an uncontrollable situation

while the man she loved gave the high, hard one to someone else. Someone whose head she'd rather slowly push into a blender set on puree.

Damn. I have changed. A few months ago, I wouldn't have thought of anything like that. So much blood on my hands, and it's not over yet. If it ever will be. Was this what it was like for Dad after returning from the war? Maybe.

Tish trusted that Brick's feelings for her hadn't changed. Her love for him remained steadfast, even as she adapted to the situation. Two days from this moment, they would likely be knee-deep in death, rooting out the festering boils of the Cleddyf cells.

The old Tish would have shivered in her boots at the thought of such violence. However, the one that existed now wished it would come sooner so she could be in his arms again. So they both had changed, but if they stuck together, they could get through it. She knew they could. She had to find a way to convince him that she was right.

Figures I'd fall for the noblest man on the planet. Brick's almost a carbon copy of the old comic book hero trope. Almost. He's already proven he's no paragon of virtue. But like them, chivalry oozed from his pores. He would shove his happiness aside to protect those around him. Not this time, you knightly bastard. I'm gonna find some way to make you stay.

The idea began as a tiny spark but snowballed into a raging inferno. That thing in her body thrummed, infusing her with energy. Tish had to be sure Brick couldn't get away from her, and there was only one way that could happen. She needed to talk to Flint. She must become a Ghost.

Tish stood before the locked door to Flint's private, underground laboratory. Her knocks boomed like cannon fire. The day after Brick was abducted, she paused and stared at that door, ignorant of what lay behind it, but she felt something then. Since that time, neither she nor Mara had been down there for more than a minute before Flint ushered them out. What they had seen during those brief times was indecipherable.

According to Mara, the lab resembled one in which the Redstones had been subjugated to testing after Cleddyf forcibly mutated them. There were also other people in white lab coats milling about like ants. Tish could only think of one reason why. They were trying to recreate, repair, or restructure what had happened to them.

She believed Brick would be proud of her for using three consecutive words with the same first letter. He used to do that fairly often, which irritated her at the time. Tish would give anything to hear him do it again. She missed him so much.

Time's up, Flint. I'm coming down.

Once she put all her strength into it, the door offered little resistance. Too bad about the locking mechanism. It served Flint right for not answering her knocks and texts.

Tish walked into bedlam. The door had been thick and soundproofed because as soon as it stood open, half off its hinges from her kick, a klaxon shriek blew a wall of sound at her.

Though her view from upstairs was limited, she could see something dark oozing across the floor and a couple of broken light fittings dangled from the ceiling.

On alert, Tish descended into the chaos one step at a time, knowing that the narrow staircase offered nothing short of a prison if an enemy stood at the bottom with a projectile weapon. Tish depended on her invulnerability, but in cases like the present, doubt crept into her mind that it could be the one time her ability failed.

Because of that, she always had a backup plan ready. It was a risky strategy, but it was the only one available for a narrow stairway with no way out but up or down. She slid the nine-inch stiletto dagger from its sheath in the small of her back.

Tish reached the bottom of the stairs with no problem, but sweat poured down her forehead and dripped from her chin into the dark liquid that now flowed when before it had only oozed. She figured it could have been an optical illusion from the flickering lights, but she wasn't sure. The coppery sensation that assailed the back of her throat reminded her of the motel room. It reminded her of blood.

Now at the bottom, Tish could see the wreckage of the lab stretching out before her and to her left and right. Not a single table stood in place. Not one pane of glass remained intact, and bodies lay strewn across the floor. She peered around the corner to her right and saw more destruction and bodies. She sensed danger from her left, darted to her right, rolled, and came up in a fighting crouch, blade in front, point up, a classic knife fighting stance.

The figure in front of her resembled Mara, just older. The woman gestured, and the knife flew from Tish's hand. Without hesitating, Tish charged at the woman, leaped into a flying kick, and struck her opponent in the chest. It should have crushed the woman's breastbone, but it didn't.

The lady staggered back a few paces, gesturing again in her direction. Tish's invulnerability activated. Surrounded by her golden shield, she launched herself at the woman, ramming her at a full sprint. The collision sent her adversary flying across the room and into a nearby wall, cracking the concrete.

Shockingly, her opponent was conscious. The older woman flexed her elbows, disengaged herself from the debris, then held up her hands in surrender. "Sorry. You're not one of them. I shouldn't have assaulted you. Please wait a minute."

"Why should I?"

"Because I'm Ruby Redstone, Mason, and Marble's mother."

CHAPTER: 19 PAWN

Zindriya awoke at 7 AM but didn't open her eyes because she wanted to remain in the afterglow for just a few more moments. She had honed her ability to arise at any time she chose, and on this day she felt wonderful. Brick had been incredibly attentive the night before and had soothed her every worry with his loving touch. She had never dreamed relationships could be like this. All she had ever known was treachery and violence.

Zindriya reached out to Brick, but he wasn't in bed. He was likely in the gym. She didn't blame him for his dedication. It was just that she had been in the mood for a bit of morning delight before her shower.

She pulled herself out of bed, stood, and stretched, admiring her toned body in the wall-sized mirror at the head of the bed. Zindriya looked around the room at the white walls, bed frame, and workstation and decided she would have Bruno bring some color into her living space.

Where is Bruno?

She studied the clock on the wall by the front door.

I would typically have heard from him by now. Ah, well, no matter.

Zindriya's mind drifted back to her new color scheme. The first color that came to mind was seafoam. It seemed a good start for someone who only desired clean, pristine, and contrasting tints. Before she began the project, she needed a shower. Brick stank her up last night, without a doubt. Zee chuckled to herself about how her vocabulary had expanded to include pop culture idioms while being with him.

After a quick shower, Zindriya hoped to find Brick in their chambers once she had finished, but he still hadn't returned. She dressed in her typical black leather. As she clicked the last snap together, the hairs on the back of her neck stood on end. The muscles around her ears tightened as though they attempted to pull themselves back so she could hear something behind her.

Zindriya snatched the pistol from her holster on the bed and whipped it around in one swift movement in time to see a Black woman emerge from a golden cloud around two meters away. "Who the fuck are you, and why are you here?"

Zindriya cocked the hammer centered over the lower barrel of her modernized LeMat cavalry pistol.

The LeMat was a dual-barreled, Civil War-era revolver originally designed with an upper-rifled barrel for nine .36 caliber cap and ball rounds and a lower 20-gauge smoothbore barrel for shot. Hers had been customized to use modern .38 caliber center-fire cartridges and specialized .410-gauge shotgun shells.

The woman wasn't afraid in the slightest, which puzzled her. Then Zindriya took a good look at her face and noted the facial features of Brick and his sister, Mara.

"I'm Ruby Redstone, Mason's mother. I'm here to help you."

"I don't need your help. How did you get in here? What was the gold glow you just appeared from?"

"You need my help, especially if you want to hold on to Mason. In return, I require your assistance to escape from a prison of my husband's design."

"What do you mean?"

Ruby explained how Flint had revived her from a self-imposed healing stasis and held her prisoner in a secret lab. She needed Zindriya's aid to escape because the countermeasures used against her were too efficient to override, but they wouldn't stop someone without her specific DNA pattern.

"How will I get there? I'm sure their security is insane, and I can't spare the time or the effort to overcome it right now. And why should I trust you anyway?"

"Because you will lose Mason to the Latisha girl and his sister, Marble. I can help you keep him."

"How?"

"By eliminating the threat they pose."

"You'd kill your own daughter?"

"If she's part of the plot to keep me prisoner, then she's no daughter of mine."

"Still, if I agree, how do I get to a secret lab?"

"Your agreement is irrelevant."

Ruby stepped forward, and Zindriya fired a shot towards her face at point-blank range, but it passed through Ruby, sending golden sparks flying in all directions. Ruby touched her. Zindriya felt a tug at her abdomen, a moment of disorientation and nausea, then a feeling of motion. Suddenly, she was in another place, by the smell of it, as golden sparks fell from her body and disappeared before they struck the floor.

The scarred twin's head still spun, and her vision remained blurred, but she tried to react when someone snatched the LeMat from her hand.

"Sit down before you fall, Zindriya. You're with me in my prison now."

A hand shoved her backward, her legs struck something that felt like a bed, and she toppled onto it.

"I am going to kill you!" Zindriya bared her teeth.

Ruby snorted. "Right. I just instantaneously transported you against your will, and *you* are going to kill *me*? That sounds like one of those stupid movies where humans take down a race capable of crossing interstellar space using baling wire and a homemade bomb. Laughable, to say the least."

Her voice lowered and turned guttural. "This isn't one of those movies, little girl. You can't lay a finger on me, but I can snap my fingers and end your existence."

To say Zindriya was scared would have been an understatement. The woman's voice sent chills up and down her spine. Ruby was indeed speaking the truth. Zee closed her eyes and fought to control the terror gripping her. A few seconds later, the dread still held sway, but as her vision cleared, she gained enough control to respond.

"What do you want from me?"

"That's better. All I need is for you to walk through the energy barrier surrounding my cell and turn off the switch just over there."

Ruby pointed to a wall to their right, which housed a pad with a biometric security system.

"You will need a full handprint, DNA, and a retina scan. I'm sure you can figure that part out on your own."

Zindriya's vision had cleared, and she assessed the difficulty of her task. "Will anyone do, or do I have a limited group from which to choose?"

According to Ruby, anyone would do. She had chosen that time of day because there were fewer people around, and security would be too involved with the shift change to bother with watching her. Still, time was of the essence, and she would have to move quickly.

Zindriya approached the energy barrier and extended her index finger. The closer it got to the wall of energy, the more the hairs on her arms stood on end. She expected a blast to numb her finger, but it passed right through, and the wall shimmered where her digit breached it. She looked back at Ruby.

"I told you it would be fine. Now hurry. Time's wasting, and that's something I can't yet control."

Zindriya moved towards a door on her right, glanced carefully down both ends of the corridor beyond, and then slipped into it, choosing to go left. Ruby's remark about not yet possessing the ability to control time took root in the back of her mind, but she would deal with it later. For now, Zindriya's only goal was to find someone and use them to free Ruby. After that, she would see how things progressed.

The next door was ten meters down the hall to her right. No alarms rang, and she had seen no cameras once she exited Ruby's cell, but it didn't mean they weren't there. Zindriya peeked around the doorframe, spying one woman in the room with her back to the door. Swift and silent, she all but glided across the room and then delivered a sharp blow to the base of the woman's head, who slumped forward.

Fortunately, the unlucky scientist had been short and slight, so Zindriya had very little trouble carrying her back to Ruby's prison. She freed Ruby, then laid the woman gently on the ground. There was no need to kill her since she remained unconscious. However, Ruby had other ideas.

"Dr. Geisman. She's the one who created the energy barrier for my cell."

Before Zindriya could move, Ruby lashed out and slapped the prone woman, who disappeared in a flash of golden sparkles.

"Wha-what in the bloody hell just happened?"

"The first of many deaths, but not yet. We have a week to give you complete control over Cleddyf. The task will be difficult even with my help. Come."

Ruby shifted them back to Zindriya's bedroom. The move didn't affect her too much the second time. "How do you know about them? Or me? Or what's going on outside this lab?"

Ruby stared at her for a few seconds. Zindriya could almost

hear the wheels of her mind turning, likely determining her fate. She let out a breath she hadn't remembered holding when Ruby began to speak.

"The barrier that bitch created held my physical body in place but not my non-physical form, like the one you saw in your bedroom." Through her access to the Akashic Field, she had kept tabs on everyone in her family and others, such as Zindriya.

Once she had determined that taking down Cleddyf was possible, Ruby decided to side with Zee and would give her control of the shadow organization to do with it as she pleased with two codicils. The first required Zindriya to remain with Brick and never stray. Ruby refused to reveal the second condition until the appropriate time arrived but hinted she would.

"Be ready to accompany me whenever I appear. I will ensure that you are alone. What we do must remain secret. Not a soul can know. Understood?"

Zindriya nodded her agreement, but Ruby didn't seem to listen. She had turned her head to the side like you do when you strained to hear a faint sound.

"Well, I won't have to worry about you telling a certain person, anyway. Brick has seen to it all on his own."

"Who are you talking about?"

"You'll find out soon enough. Well, lots to do and I'm short on time. Must run along. Ta!" Ruby turned away briefly and then faced her again. "One last thing, do not tell Brick what little you know about the Espada Encantada. He must earn the knowledge to access the sword's full capabilities. He will need them in the future. Well, once again, ta. Much to do and many places to go."

Before Zindriya could ask more questions, Ruby disappeared in a shower of golden sparkles. A rush of air ruffled her hair, rapidly filling the vacuum the mysterious woman left. Ruby hadn't been gone for two minutes before Brick casually walked into the room with the enchanted sword strapped to his back to tell her he had killed Bruno.

Confusion filled Zindriya. How could Ruby know about Brick having the Espada? Or about Bruno? The only other person she could have confided in? She prided herself on always maintaining control over her surroundings, but now her reality had been shaken by a stranger with absurd powers. A person who called herself Ruby Redstone. Brick was her son, so what kind of powers did he have beyond the ones she already knew? It left her feeling vulnerable for the first time in years.

In a rare moment of weakness, Zindriya fell into Brick's arms. She was trembling. At first, it seemed as though he didn't know how to handle her. No one had ever seen her in such a condition, much less Brick. After a few seconds, he squeezed her tightly and whispered soft nothings in her ear. His warm embrace and soothing voice drove the tremors away.

He asked her what had happened. Zindriya lied to Brick. She told him she had experienced a flashback of the night her mother killed her father. Then she spoke the truth when she confessed that the trembles consumed her on rare occasions, but she'd never known anyone to make them go away until he arrived. Caught up in the moment, Zindriya realized she was in love with Brick and told him so. Usually, she would have taken him to bed but was content to stand there and bask in the flood of unfamiliar but welcome emotions coursing through her. She relished in the warmth of his body and the way his comforting embrace chased away her worst nightmares.

Safe in Brick's arms, she realized what the second codicil Ruby required of her would be. It was the only way to keep Brick from leaving her, not that she thought he would. Still, as with her twin sister, a little leverage went a long way. Zindriya smiled, nestled her lips against Brick's neck, and squeezed him even more tightly.

The next four days passed in a whirlwind of activity, fighting, and secrecy. Between preparations for the coming battle and working with Ruby to take over Cleddyf, Zindriya barely had time to sleep. To be honest, the sleeping part always took a backseat to making love with Brick. She wouldn't miss it for anything, not even Ruby's crusade. They had been successful, though. It had been easier than either of them could imagine.

Once several of the cells observed Ruby's raw power combined with Zindriya's ruthlessness and command ability, the rest caved quickly. In most cases, the troops took out the resistant hierarchy before the dangerous duo ever set foot within their hideouts. They all recognized Zindriya as their new leader and Ruby as the strong right arm leading them out of the shadows and into a bright future of world dominion.

Once they had tamed Cleddyf, Zindriya, and Ruby finalized their plans for the coming attack. They still needed the attack as a smokescreen for the second codicil Ruby had demanded in return for her help. She hadn't been surprised that Zindriya had already pieced it together. Her cunning was the reason Ruby had chosen her.

Finally released from her pact, Ruby left to finish what she had started with her escape from the cell in her husband's secret lab. She bade her goodbyes and vanished in a shower of golden sparks. Zindriya smiled and collapsed into the chair at her workstation, glad the Cleddyf part of it was over.

Brick had been suspicious of her frequent, unexplained disappearances, but now she could focus on their relationship. She needed to bring him closer than ever to weather the coming storm. It was still relatively early, but Zindriya sent word across the fortress communications system for Brick to meet her in their quarters. She had an urgent need for his loving touch.

Brick arrived, satisfied her every desire, and then Zindriya fell asleep in his arms.

An annoying alarm dragged her from a pleasant, deep slumber, her head foggy. Having been asleep only a few hours, she reached for Brick, but he wasn't in bed. At last, the confusion passed, and she remembered what that particular alarm signified, then cursed under her breath. She tapped the monitor next to the bed just in time to see Brick walk out of a glowing, golden cloud in the gym.

CHAPTER 20: QUANTUMLY ENTANGLED

Part 1

Tish's mind reeled at the possibilities. "But you're dead!"

She was wary of the older woman who claimed to be Brick and Mara's mother.

Ruby gazed into the distance as he voice took on a wistful tone. "What was Mark Twain's infamous misquote? Oh yes. Ahem. Tales of my demise have been greatly exaggerated."

She spoke with a flourish, adding flamboyant hand gestures. Tish stood firm, ready to react to any aggression.

"Dear, you really must loosen up a bit. I was dead, sort of, but now I'm not. To be honest, it was more of therapeutic hibernation." Ruby spoke as though it were the most natural thing in the world. She was far too relaxed for the situation. Tish had just thrown her into a concrete wall, and she stood there as if she'd taken a sip of tea.

Tish's brow furrowed. At least the alarm finally stopped blaring. "But how?"

"Above your pay grade, dear. Where are Marble and Mason?"

"Why don't you ask your husband?"

This was starting to sound like a conversation with her mother. Tish guessed moms were the same everywhere except for those who came back from the dead and could move objects with the wave of a hand.

"Because I killed him." Ruby took a step towards Tish. "And you're next if you don't tell me where my children are," she said through gritted teeth.

The muscles in Tish's neck and shoulders tensed. Every sense told her there was far more to this woman before her than she'd already seen—something primal, something deadly, and despite her invulnerability, she needed help. She yelled for Mara.

Ruby folded her arms across her chest. "And by the way, who are you, young lady?"

Tish yelled for Mara a little louder, but she didn't think her voice would make it upstairs despite the open door.

"I'm Brick's girlfriend."

"Who's Brick?"

"It's... it's Mason's nickname. Everyone calls him Brick."

"Hmmm. His girlfriend, eh? Did he do that to you?" Ruby waved a finger at her, drawing a distorted figure eight in the air. "Can he control the Field?"

"Do what? And what field?"

"I can't affect you. It's like you're protected, and I mean the Akashic Field, of course."

"He was able to access it once, and that was when I changed. How can you tell?"

"Your glow is different from everyone else's. I can't hurt you directly. Pity for you because this way will be much more painful."

Ruby closed her eyes for a second, and when she opened them, they glowed golden. Tish began to feel heavier, like every part of her body was sluggish, slowly pressing her to the floor. She tried to turn and run up the stairs but could barely move. She yelled for Mara again, and once more, she didn't come.

Tish tried to focus on Brick, but she wasn't able to. As each second passed, she found breathing harder, her strength failing. She had enough air for one last cry for help, but saved it. Tish concentrated everything she had left on contacting Brick. What happened next was not what she expected.

Part 2

Brick couldn't sleep. A.B. had been especially active with the insatiable Zindriya and had problems blocking it out. His mental compartmentalization had weakened over the last few weeks. He wasn't sure how much longer he could keep his mind split. Watching A.B. use his body to pleasure Zindriya troubled him more each day. Brick turned his head to look at her. She snored softly, and as she slept, her face appeared so innocent.

He reminded himself how brutal, sadistic, psychopathic, and spiteful she was. She was about as far from sinless as you could get. Refusing to remain naked next to her, he got out of bed, pulled on a pair of lounge pants and a t-shirt, then sat on the end of the mattress. Somehow, his feet found their way into his Crocs. He sat there with his head in his hands and eyes closed, trying to block the past few hours from his mind.

Brick felt a tingle snake up his neck. Then, it turned into a rush of warmth spreading throughout his body. He sprang to his feet when he heard Tish singing in his mind. He didn't know she could sing. But it wasn't singing. It was more like a siren's song. He felt like Jason lashed to the mast of the Argo because it compelled him to go to her immediately.

Brick opened his eyes into a universe of light. He was in the Field again. He searched his mind, and the rift he'd been trying to breach was wide open. Tish's voice flowed from it, and he somehow knew she was in trouble. It was she who had given him access to the Akashic Field.

He stood up, zoomed in his vision towards his house, and saw Tish face off with a woman who looked vaguely familiar. The memory was like sand that slipped through the fingers, or a dream that faded with the dawn. It didn't matter. Tish needed him. As with the night he transported her, Brick stood in both places at once. All he had to do was step forward, so he did.

Brick didn't know that a lab was concealed beneath his house, but the place looked like a tornado had just passed through, leaving bodies strewn across the floor. Always secrets in his family. Blood flowed freely down a nearby drain, staining his shoes as it passed. Crocs may not have been the best footgear for the lake of blood he'd shifted into.

Shifted, he thought, *that's a good name for this skill.*

An older woman stood a few feet from him, and Tish was to his left on all fours at the base of a set of stairs, her face contorted in pain. The woman glowed like a Christmas tree on steroids, and power emanated from her in waves, directed at Tish. She was the one causing her agony.

"Release Tish, now!" Brick readied himself for action.

He wanted to wipe the smirk from her face. "And if I don't?"

"Then I'll have to make you." The grin spreading across his face did not quite reach his eyes.

"Brick." Tish barely squeaked out the one word. "Careful... Field..."

"I said, let her go, last warning." A low, menacing voice warned the woman.

"You're Mason. You don't recognize me, do you?"

"Should I?"

"I died, sort of, when you were three, but you must have seen images of me."

"Last warning. Let her go."

"Fine. I have released her. Whatever you did to change your girlfriend would have rendered my actions null and void anyway. My power would have been ineffectual in a matter of minutes."

Tish was finally able to stand. Keeping an eye on his adversary, Brick was prepared to pounce if the woman made a wrong move. Tish limped to his side and slid her hand into his.

"So you're saying you're my dead mother?"

"She is, Brick." Mara agreed from the stairs. "You should recognize her from the images I showed you."

Brick finally took a good long look at the woman. She appeared to be an older version of Mara but with his nose and ears.

"Hello, Marble. So glad to see you again."

"How are you alive, Mom? You died almost nineteen years ago."

"I don't know what or who this thing is, Mara, but they're not our mother, not exactly."

"But it is her, Brick. You were just a baby when she died."

"I may not know what she looked like, but I remember how she smelled. It's the only thing I know of her, sis. Remember that, Mara?"

"Right. She smelled of…"

The two of them responded simultaneously with the word, the emotion, and the sensation: raspberries. Their mother had smelled of raspberries; it had been emotionally soothing and felt like home. The being standing before them did have the scent of raspberries, but it was so dim it was like the afterthought of a forgotten memory. The dominant smell seeping from her was dank, musty, and very old.

"You're right, Lil bro. They smell like moldy mushrooms in a root cellar."

"Whatever this thing is, they may have once been our mother, but not any longer."

"While all of this is fascinating, you do realize I am still standing here. And what's this 'they' stuff all about?"

Tish finally had a reason to chime in. "It's a collective pronoun we use now when it's unclear what a person's, or in your case, entity's, gender identification is. We try not to use 'it' anymore. It's a bit degrading."

Brick focused his attention back to the being that was once his mother. Tish's presence at his side filled him with hope, courage, and dread. He cherished her touch even though it reminded him of the possibility of losing her.

Brick leaned forward. "Who or what are you, Ruby?"

"And here I was, hoping for a family reunion."

Tish added more information. "Don't trust her, either of you. She killed all of these people, including your father."

A flicker of regret gripped Brick's heart, but the man who had been his father had checked out long ago. At least now he knew why. Secret lab. Secret project. Always secrets with him. When he glanced at Mara, he sensed she experienced similar emotions. It was the freaky connection they had. Brick repeated his question to Ruby.

She sighed, and a look of disappointment flashed across her pinched face. At least, that was the look Brick thought she was going for.

"You need to know the truth about who and what we are. Unfortunately, Flint kept that from you and would have continued if I hadn't intervened."

Tish's snark intruded. "Is that the new euphemism for murder?"

"What are you talking about, Ruby? What truth was worth all the lives you took?" Brick glowered at her.

"The universe is far more dangerous than any of us ever imagined. If we do nothing, we risk our existence, Mason."

Brick squinted his eyes. "Why should we believe you?"

Ruby's shoulders fell. "You have no reason to, but I ask you to at least hear me out."

Brick locked eyes with Mara, who nodded.

"Alright, Ruby. Let's hear it."

Back in Antarctica, what everyone called a virus wasn't. The organisms looked and behaved much like viruses do, but, in truth, they were individual cells belonging to a much larger entity. Ruby had discovered the fact shortly after they found them in the ice core. She tried to tell the other scientists what she had identified and showed them her evidence, but they dismissed her.

Even a third of the way into the twenty-first century, the men degraded her with phrases such as: 'You're just being overreactive; I don't know why you persist in such outlandish theories; You're doing your woman thing again; Is it your time of the month?' Despite the mountains of evidence she presented, they would not budge. When the lab director dismissed her from duty, Ruby gave up and began working on her own as the geneticists attempted to discover what the 'virus' did and develop a vaccine to counteract it.

Ruby had not been party to the hierarchy's decision to infect members of their community but had figured it out pretty quickly when people began to die of old age. In secret, she had predicted that the geneticists, acting on the idea the cells were viruses instead of pieces of a larger organism, would fail at their attempts to eradicate the aging effects.

Viruses were independent organisms whose sole goal was to multiply and mimic the living cells of other creatures. They accomplished this by inserting their DNA into the nuclei of those cells. When enough of them were infected, the virus took over the entire creature.

The organism they had found acted in much the same way, but being parts of a larger whole, they communicated on a quantum level, each cell having a base memory core. This ability to exchange information also allowed them to resist any attempts at genetic alterations and bestowed them with the capacity to download their original DNA patterns from the normal cells if something did change.

Ruby discovered that aspect during her analysis as well. It was why she had been able to create a vaccine to slow down the aging process for herself. Her serum disrupted each cell's ability to communicate with any other, but only temporarily. Unfortunately, with each subsequent injection, the serum became less effective.

Furthermore, Ruby found out the reason for the aging. The cells multiplied and devoured the body's life energy to replicate themselves. The ultimate goal was to convert every cell in the body into new cells.

The original host personality would be incorporated while the new cells reorganized into a new physical and psychological construct. In the end, the host and the organism merged into a new being. The process for a human would take nearly a century, while the body remained in a recuperative stasis.

After her supposed death, Flint found her notes and devised a method of speeding up the conversion process. He immersed Ruby's body in a nutrient-rich liquid he created to give the organism all the nourishment needed to rejuvenate his wife without consuming her completely.

That was why she still smelled of raspberries; part of her was still Ruby. What remained a mystery was who controlled the entity they faced. Ruby or the larger creature from which the cells originated?

"And you killed him for it." Brick pulled no punches.

"Well, they tried to hold me hostage with some ridiculous excuse about keeping me safe. Preposterous. They just wanted to use me as a guinea pig."

Mara chimed in. "You needn't have killed them, Mom, I mean, you have access to the Akashic Field, so you could have just left. They couldn't have stopped you, right?"

Ruby hesitated ever so slightly before answering. Squinting at the pause, Brick glanced at Mara, who responded with an almost imperceptible nod.

"Of course not, but I couldn't have them chasing me all across the planet. I have things to do, and I don't need distractions."

Mara frowned at the thing that was once their mother. "Things like what?"

Ruby ignored the question and spoke to Brick and Tish. They had something special. Tish had used a siren song to summon Brick to her side. She had also activated his access to the Akashic Field, which he had failed to accomplish on his own. Whatever Brick had done to change her had linked them. Brick probably established a subatomic bond with Tish, a quantum entanglement of sorts. She was now the key to his accessing the Field.

Ruby cracked a joke, referencing a movie from the '80s about trapping ghosts. In that movie, the man was the Keymaster, and the woman was the Gatekeeper, in a classic, misogynistic fashion. With Tish and Brick, the roles were reversed.

Brick pressed forward, backing his sister up. "All fine and dandy, Ruby, but answer the question. What things do you have to do?"

"So much for a sense of humor, Mason dear, but fine. That's for me to know and you to find out, and I'm sure you will once you get over your anger and think. Mull this over. What is the purpose of a virus? Well, lots to do and time's a-wasting. So nice to see you two again. Rest assured. This won't be the last time. Ta!"

Ruby vanished in a shower of golden sparkles, and a rush of air filled the vacancy.

Mara drove a fist into the wall. "That was some fucked up shit!"

Brick nodded in agreement. "You got that right, sis."

A moment later, his sister pounced, wrapping a shocked Brick in her arms and squeezing. Tish had been trapped in the hug as well. His shoulder felt damp where Mara's head lay. "God, Brick, I missed you so much! I was so worried we'd lost you."

"Mara? You okay?"

"I'm fine, Lil bro. I've just been spending way too much time with your hyper-emo girlfriend. She's starting to rub off on me. I love you, Brick."

Surprised but happy, Brick hugged Mara back with one arm. He wasn't letting go of Tish's hand for anything.

"I love you too, big sis."

Mara released him, rubbing her eyes. "How long can you stay?"

"Not long. Zee is still asleep and doesn't know I'm gone. I need to get back."

He told them about his encounter with Bruno. He couldn't afford to shake her confidence in him as the hour to strike Cleddyf drew so close. What would happen later was a different story altogether. Mara and Tish understood. They talked about Flint briefly. Mara would take care of the arrangements.

Brick wanted them to preserve the lab in its present state so he could go over it later with a fine-toothed comb. Ruby's hesitation at Mara's question made him wonder if Flint had found some way to restrain Ruby despite the Field. Obviously, Tish caught her before she'd finished whatever she'd been doing.

Brick shook his head at his idiocy. Tish and Mara could go

through the lab. What made him think he had to do it?

Still shaking off the last vestiges of misogyny, old chap? You, of all people, should know better. Brick thought.

Brick prompted Mara. "Did you catch the hesitation after your question?"

"I did, Lil bro. I think that's why the lab is shredded. Tish got here before Ruby found what she was looking for."

"You guys need to find it before she comes back. Tish, can you hack my dad's computer?"

"No problem. I'll get on it as soon as you leave."

Mara hugged them both again and then climbed the stairs so he and Tish could say their goodbyes. Brick thought it odd she hadn't found it strange that he was there and not at the fortress, but figured she had some vague idea that the Field had something to do with it. The impossible had become commonplace in their lives.

Before he knew it, Tish was in his arms, and her lips pressed against his. The kiss was short but intense.

"I love you, Brick."

"I know. Our tête-à-tête on the mount told me. You were brilliant, by the way, but what else can I expect from the woman I love?"

"I won't pretend what's going on with Zindriya doesn't bother me, but I know it can't be easy for you, either. I can smell her on you. Am I talking to my Brick or hers?"

"You know about that? Good, Mara told you. A.B.'s asleep right now. He thinks he's still next to Zee."

"A.B.?"

He explained who his alter ego was and how it had become more challenging to filter out his associations with Zindriya.

"I just have to hold out a few more days until the strike."

"Then what?" Tish's eyebrows raised.

"Then we figure out where to go from there."

"Don't go all frigging noble bastard on me, Brick."

"You've obviously been hanging out with my sister." The right side of Brick's mouth pulled up slightly.

Tish cocked one hip and folded her arms across her chest. "At least I didn't call you an asshole. Don't evade my question. We don't have time for bullshit."

"I don't think it would work if I tried. You summoned me here, Tish. I'm sure you can do it again."

She kissed him once more.

"You still owe me my two days, Brick, and I aim to collect. It'll take that long just to get the stink of that feral bitch off you and begin replacing it with mine. After those two days, if you still feel the need to leave, I won't stop you. Deal?"

"Deal."

They sealed the deal. The two of them didn't need an excuse to kiss anymore, but this was one of those habits Tish refused to relinquish, and Brick was happy to oblige. The kiss was sweet and tender yet tinged with a hint of desperation and sadness.

She pulled herself from his arms.

"Tish, I—"

"We both have done terrible things to get back to each other, Brick. Remember that. Neither one of us has been an angel through this. Honor be damned, and nobility can go fuck itself. This is a fight for our future. *Our* future Brick, yours and mine. This is no fluffy, neat, and clean superhero movie. It's ugly and dirty and raw and bloody. This is real life."

"You're right, Tish. We got a lot to talk about. We both have changed so much."

"Too much, you think? Am I too different?"

"No, but maybe I am. You're still my dream, Tish, and always will be."

"I want you back more than you can imagine. I never knew I could love someone so much. I never understood what love was before you. I don't know what love or life would be like without you."

"I guess we still have a lot in common." Brick nodded his head.

"We do, and we'll figure it out if you listen to your heart and not your head. It's helped me cope with everything we've had to do over the last few months, Brick. Remember sci-fi night in the kitchen when you kissed me on the forehead? Well, that and what happened later, on the couch..." Tish's face reddened ever so slightly as her eyes searched his. "We can accomplish anything when we're together. You heard what Ruby said about us. We're quantumly entangled. You know what that means, math-boy."

The right side of Brick's mouth curled upward. "Not exactly proper terminology, but close enough. I suppose we are two particles with identical quantum characteristics connected by a strange, inexplicable attraction."

Tish wasn't finished. "Those with access to the Akashic Field can affect subatomic particles. We have the potential to do whatever we choose. When you changed me, perhaps you changed us both into something new, something more than human."

"It's possible. Been studying up, have we?"

"Ever since you changed me, I've developed an affinity for math and physics. If it's true, Brick, and I believe it is, you're no longer alone. Neither of us will ever be alone again. Two entangled particles experience the same events no matter how far apart they are."

Tish kissed him deeply. The thought of no longer being the only one of his kind gave Brick new hope for the future, including Tish, should he ever manage to overcome his guilt.

"But for now, get your head back in the game so we can take down Cleddyf. Go back to her before I change my mind." The wrinkle over Tish's nose appeared.

She took one step back, just out of his reach. Though the move caused some emotional distress, Brick knew she had done it not out of spite but out of necessity. He didn't think he deserved such a strong, magnificent woman like Tish, but she loved him. Now he had to earn the right to her love.

Brick gazed towards the direction of the fortress. He would return to the gym so he wouldn't wake Zindriya. He could still see her asleep on the bed. Brick needed time to wash the blood off his Crocs and his feet. He turned to Tish and watched their impending separation draw wrinkles across her face.

Definitely not a pristine, everything-will-be-all-right, happy-ending fairytale. This will be a pile of shit we'll have to muck out for years. Can I seriously put Tish through all that?

Brick realized the last question was stupid. He should have asked himself if she'd even let him walk away. Why would he even want to? Would his guilt and self-loathing at what he would do to Zindriya be so intense? Add that to the regret over his two dead lovers. He honestly didn't know.

An old saying surfaced in his mind. It was from Fulton Oursler. Something about not allowing regret from the past and the fear of the future destroy you.

And I can't forget Corrie Ten Boom, who talked about how worry wouldn't change tomorrow but would ruin today. Finally, I must remember Tish's wisdom. Follow my heart. I lost Kaylen and Fritz because I didn't. I can't make the same mistake a third time.

"I won't fail you as I failed them, Tish. I will do anything to keep you safe."

"You have kept me safe, Brick. You made sure nothing could physically harm me. The only person on this planet who can hurt me is you by not giving us a chance. Go. Get back into character and complete this quest so we can get down to what truly matters: Love and Us."

Tish was right. He needed to knuckle up and end this.

He stepped away and then shifted before either of them changed their minds. Brick imagined what she would see. He would vanish in a puff of golden, glittering lights while a slight breeze would ruffle her hair and caress her lovely face as the air rushed in to fill the vacuum left by his departure.

CHAPTER 21: CODE KEY/ ESPADA UNLEASHED

Part 1

Two more days remained before the assault on Cledyyf. Brick showered after his workout, relishing the warmth of the water. He placed both hands on the wall beneath the shower, leaned his head forward and allowed it to ease the tension from his neck and shoulders.

He went over everything that had taken place the night before with his moth... with Ruby. He couldn't bring himself to call them his mother. Part of them still retained her personality, but the rest was an alien infestation that had set itself up in that body.

Ruby mentioned he would know what to do when he figured out what viruses did best. They hid and multiplied until there were too many of them for an organism to fight without outside assistance. Now Brick had the foundations for a strategy, but he couldn't solve it without Tish's help. It would have to wait until after the attack on Cleddyf. He wished he could contact her.

Why can't I? He thought, and turned the water off. He stepped out of the shower, dried himself off and hung the towel on the nearby rack.

If his prior actions had interwoven the two of them quantumly, as Tish had put it, then perhaps he could give it a shot, fully expecting to fail, of course. Brick focused on the rift in his mind. It remained shut tight as usual, but he didn't try to force it open this time. Instead, he centered his mind on contacting Tish.

As thoughts of her filled him, a crevice formed within the rift, so he projected his psyche through it. Surprised by his presence, she fully activated the Field. Brick turned a shade of golden and partially shifted, finding himself in both places at the same time. Tish was in his old bedroom, wearing one of his shirts and filling it nicely. His instantaneous physical reaction surprised him.

"Brick! Oh wow! Baby you came prepared! I'm down for a quick booty call!"

Tish yanked her shirt off before scanning him up and down. It was the first time they had seen each other completely nude.

"Oh. Heh, heh. Sorry. I didn't think it would work," Brick said.

"Shit, I'm not. You are one fine ass man, Brick, and I'm talking damn fine," she said, eyes focused just below his waist.

"My dreams can't even compare to the reality before me." *Yeah, I'm still a nerd.* He thought.

His eyes traced every wonderful curve of her body, etching them into his mind forever. How in the world could his physical response to her intensify? How much blood could that thing hold?

The grin spreading across her face was the smile he'd always desired to see. Her eyes were bright, and her heart rate increased, emanating the vanilla aroma from every pore of her body. His heart raced at the same pace as Tish's, but as much as he wanted to pursue this, time was against them.

Brick grabbed the towel and wrapped it around his waist. Tish raised her eyes to his, but the smile didn't change, filling him with hope and joy. He ignored the urge to pick up the shirt so that Tish could put it on again. He remembered movie-night when he had found the error in coding. She had told him then only to cover her up when she told him to. Brick was happy to oblige.

"Oh, yah. You are definitely giving me those two days. I'm not letting you out of that deal, lover."

Tish reached out to grab Brick's hand, but hers passed through his body. He wasn't physically in either place. Instead, he remained in transition, hovering between the time and space separating them.

"How did you contact me, Brick? I thought my siren call was one way."

"Siren is good, but Banshee sounds cooler, but you're right. You control my access to the Field. I could only crack the rift inside my head because I focused all my thoughts on you. You heard and fully breached the rift so I could visit."

"I wish we had known. Maybe we could have, well, you know…"

"I do, but it wouldn't have been a good idea. Zindriya would have smelled you on me. Either that or what's left of my control would have long since evaporated."

"Then what?"

"All hell would've broken loose in the bedroom, and only one of us would've left the place alive. Then all the plans to take down Cleddyf would turn into so much shit," Brick said.

"You don't sound like you would have minded," Tish said.

"Not for a guy who would tear down the illusion called civilization just to be with you. Still, I can't do a damn thing without you. I'm completely under your control."

Tish seemed pleased at that, but Brick never found out if it was because she could control him or because she had infiltrated his mind enough to push everything else out. It didn't matter which. Brick relayed his clue about Ruby, what he thought it might mean, and the need to collaborate after taking down Cleddyf. Tish responded with pleasure because he was so optimistic they all would succeed and survive.

She wanted him to super-position to her location so they could, in her words, get busy. But as much as he wanted to, he couldn't take the chance. Zindriya's actions of late had been bizarre.

She was up to something, and he didn't know what. It wouldn't do to have Tish's scent all over him. It would destroy all of their work, setting them back for years in their goal.

"I don't call it super-positioning anymore. I settled on shifting."

"I like it. So, what are you really worried about? Are you here for me or because you think Ruby is more dangerous than Zindriya?"

Tish's crossed her arms, cocked an eyebrow, and the upturned corner of her mouth greeted Brick's widened eyes and dropped jaw. "How the hell did you know?"

"Practice, lover."

"Huh?"

"After spending so much time together during our project, I know you almost as well as I know myself. Cliché, I know, but there it is."

"Still in the dark." Brick was confused.

"The only reason you would break cover would be to talk about Ruby. I hoped it was because you wanted to get with me, but when you didn't, she was the only other logical reason."

Tish moved closer to Brick.

"I know you want to be with me." Her voice was soft and sultry. Her eyes glanced down and then back up. "Something that, um, obvious is hard to miss. But you wouldn't break cover for that.

Not when we're so close to finishing our mission."

"*Our* mission?"

"If it's your mission, it's mine too because we're a couple. A couple, Brick, remember that. I can't even begin to imagine what you went through, but you did it to save me. I will get you back, Brick, and when I'm done with you, it will take decades to remove my stink from your body."

"I seriously need to listen to my heart more, don't I?"

"You're getting there, math-boy. It takes a minute to get past a lifetime of propaganda, and you've made amazing progress, enough to earn my love. Now, what about Ruby?"

Brick seemed to think Ruby's whole scenario was staged. She could access the Field but didn't use it to challenge them. Sure, she had tried to harm Tish but had given up far too easily. Brick sensed she had been manipulating them. To what end, however, he was not sure. Tish placed a hand on her chin, and the cutest wrinkle budded between her eyebrows. After a few seconds, she agreed with him.

Towards the end of the attack, Tish realized her invulnerability had begun to overcome the effects of Ruby's gravity attack. Regardless, she also felt that Ruby had given up way too quickly. She had too much command over the Akashic Field to press the attack with a single tactic. Ruby wanted Brick there to see how far he would go. It was as though she had assessed his abilities and had found them, at the very least, adequate. Brick came to the same conclusion and took it one step further.

"I think she planned the whole thing with Dad, his lab, her resurrection, all of it. I just don't know her motivations. We need to know what those are, to fathom her goals." Brick said.

"Sticking with she/her instead of they/them?"

"Our lives are complicated enough," Brick said.

"Fair. So, how do we find out her true motivations?"

"I wish I knew, but it has to do with her riddle at the end."

"The one about viruses, yah?"

"Right. I figured out the clue, but I need your help to discover the endgame. We need to delay Ruby long enough to get some answers."

"I might have a way. I found what Ruby was looking for," Tish said.

"Really? What was it?"

Tish had hacked into Flint's computer and discovered a plethora of information, including how they could imprison Ruby's physical form with a DNA-tuned energy barrier. She pressed a button on the console in her, his, their... whatever nightstand.

It projected a holographic image of a three-inch by four-inch rectangular object about a quarter of an inch thick to eye level. Black and gold circuitry covered the exterior. Tish rotated it so Brick could get a good look. A slot was embedded in one of the short edges as though it fitted into something.

"This is an electronic key, but the weirdest one I've ever seen. According to Flint's notes, the whitecoats biometrically coded it with Ruby's digitized DNA. That's next-level tech, Brick. Have you heard of it through your connections?"

Tish referred to his work with DARPA and the OSRD.

"Not at all. I would've jumped all over this. I mainly resurrected old, abandoned projects."

"Well, they used it to adapt a standard energy barrier to trap Ruby using resonance field harmonics." Tish pointed at the device. "This is what pissed her off, the thing she was hell-bent on finding. It's the only thing that can hold her."

"And we can use it to draw her into a trap," Brick said.

"My thoughts exactly."

"I'm thinking I should hold on to it."

Tish tilted her head to the side. "And if she comes back for it?"

"Tell her I have it. Let her try to come and take it."

"I have to be there with you. Why don't I keep it? She can't hurt me. She tried before, remember?"

"But she can hurt Mara, and she'll get you to turn it over to her. If I have it, Ruby will have to face me directly."

Tish's logic shone through. "She could do the same if you had it."

"Maybe. But you'll be there to keep her from harming Mara. She won't go after your parents until she does a number on you and Mara. You'd warn me by then, and I'd move heaven and earth to save Mom and Pops."

"And you'll call me for help if she came after you, right?"

Brick hesitated.

"Right?" Raising her voice, Tish glared at him.

He knew he had no choice but to agree. This new Tish was awesome and a bit intimidating as well. She wasn't someone to cross.

"I will. Damn. I love the new you as much as I did the old." Brick said.

"Did?"

"I misspoke. I meant to say as much as I do the old you."

"Better." Her voice softened. "I don't want to lose you, Brick, just as much as you don't want to let go of me."

"I can't lose you, Tish. If I do..." Brick didn't want to finish the sentence, but Tish did it for him, proving, yet again, how much they truly belonged together.

"If you do, you will tear down the fabric of all creation and cast it into the abyss."

"Something like that."

"Kinda how I feel too. Scary, to know we're actually capable of doing it. I can see how supervillains can be seduced by power and how important Peter Parker's uncle's saying was," Tish said.

"Now I'm really impressed. You are, officially, the wimpy, pacifist nerd-freak's girlfriend."

Tish chuckled at his statement."How do I give this thing to you? You're not here." She opened his secret compartment in their nightstand and withdrew that actual key card. He was not surprised she'd found the hiding place, or was able to open it. She was his quantum companion after all.

Brick reached out his hand. "Let me make contact with it. I'll try to absorb it into the shift."

Tish did as he asked, and it worked. Brick was able to grasp the code key. It was a good indication that his control over the Field was improving with usage. Such a skill might be useful in certain situations. In this case, however, it proved to be irrelevant. Tish's face relaxed into a half-smile; her eyes softened as the next question validated his deduction. He was getting to know her much better.

"I want one kiss before you go, Brick. Just one kiss, okay?"

Brick put the code key in the small of his back under the edge of the towel, then shifted into Tish's arms. Their kiss was brief but intense as she took the liberty of wrapping her hands around his manhood.

"You touched mine way back when on the couch. It's only fair I get to touch yours." A devilish grin spread across her face. "I love you, Brick."

"I love you too, Tish." Brick reluctantly extracted himself from her embrace and shifted back to the washroom before he changed his mind. He checked to confirm that the code key was still in the small of his back, just in case. It was.

Part 2

Ruby's hand rested on the back of Mara's neck as they stood beside the door to what was now Tish's bedroom, listening. She gently caressed her daughter's tense neck muscles while golden sparkles dripped from her fingers and across Mara's shoulders. After Brick shifted away, Ruby led her daughter back to her bedroom.

"I need that key, my darling daughter. I want you to retrieve it at your first opportunity."

"Yes, Mother." Mara's voice sounded hoarse and mechanical, far from the commanding tone Ruby heard her use. "But why? It's safe with Brick."

The sparkles increased in intensity, and so did Ruby's voice. "He is not to be trusted with the key, Marble. It belongs to me, and Mason has no right to it, understand?"

"Yes, Mother. I will do my best to retrieve it for you."

"Good."

"But what do you need it for? You're free from its influence now."

Ruby's frustration increased. Zindriya had been so much easier to manipulate. Marble should not have been able to put up so much resistance against her power. Her bond with her brother was much stronger than she had predicted, perhaps too strong. She didn't want to destroy her daughter's mind to get the code key, but she might, if necessary. All of this was for humanity's future, and her own.

"It is much safer in my hands, my darling daughter. It is of great danger to your brother. The longer it remains in his possession, the more likely the key will harm him. Neither of us wants that, do we?"

"No, Mother, we don't. I will do as you ask."

"Thank you, Marble. Just wait until after the battle with Cleddyf. His guard will be down then."

"Understood, Mother."

"Good. Sleep well, dearest Marble. Mother loves you."

Ruby removed her hand from Mara's neck and watched as she shuffled down the hallway and into her room. She shifted to a nearby Cleddyf hideout, where she'd set up a temporary living space, and lay on the plush bedding, fingers interlaced behind her head.

Phase one of my plan is nearly complete. After the battle, I will retrieve the card and begin phase two.

Ruby didn't truly need to sleep any longer, but she relished the oblivion it offered. She closed her eyes and willed her mind to rest while a broad smile crossed her face.

Part 3

"You're going to pay for what you did, asshole!" One of the men from Bruno's posse said as Brick returned to the shower.

There we go with the asshole again. I gotta get these guys a thesaurus. Then again, asshole sounded cooler than rectum-face or colon-man. Brick thought.

He waited for Bricktay to add in his two cents, but all he got was silence. He hadn't heard from that part of his mutation for quite a long time. He had to wonder if they had retreated into A.B.

Nope, still here. You're busy now. Besides, if you die, so do I. Carry on, donkey-butt.

Well, at least he cares. Brick thought.

Don't flatter yourself. I've been enjoying watching you squirm while your other personality screws Zee. That's entertainment enough.

Or not. Later, Bricktay.

Brick phased just in time to save himself from the onslaught of rounds fired from the MP5s aimed at him. Bruno's posse had been waiting for him to return. It was stupid of him to think they would just give up after he killed their leader. As four of them depleted their magazines, a fifth pointed a device in Brick's direction.

He snorted at this ridiculous gesture until an energy beam from the device struck him while phased, immobilizing him. He'd known Zindriya had been too confident in her power over him. He suspected that Cleddyf had given her an ace in the hole. He'd been right.

He should have found a better place to shift than the damned community shower, especially with Bruno's crew ready to avenge their leader's death. Stupid and reckless, much like Bran and Korolev. And like him with Kaylen—spilled milk.

Let's find a way out of this, or Bricktay will hound me all the way to Hell.

Brick closed his eyes and filled his mind with thoughts of Tish, but the rift did not open this time. He could feel his phase diminish as the four replaced their depleted magazines. If he didn't think of something soon, he was dead. Phasing didn't work, nor did hyper or his strength. Resonance. The thought invaded Brick's mind. They had figured out his quantum resonance frequency and the signal that interrupted it as his dad had done with Ruby. It would only work for a short time without rotating the frequency, but it would likely be long enough for them to mow him down with a hail of 9mm rounds from those MP5s.

He felt a familiar presence in his mind. Brick recognized it from the day he killed Bruno. It was the Espada Encantada calling to him. Ever since the incident with the big man, he had gone nowhere without the sword. It was in the gym's shower but on the opposite side of his enemies. The feeling grew stronger, and an idea sprang to him.

Venga. Brick psychically projected the Spanish command for 'come'. The sword flew to his hand, removing the arm holding the resonance device as it whisked by. Brick was free from its influence and his abilities returned. The Espada had saved him and required its due as it flamed with white fire outlining the words engraved onto its blade. The dark seed awoke and lined the blade's edge with shadow.

Brick entered hyper and waded through the troop of six fighters. The Espada cleaved through weapons as efficiently as it did flesh and bone, and in a matter of seconds, all of them were dead without one additional shot fired.

The scene lingered for a moment. Brick stood stock-still, his right arm extended. The blade felt like an extension of his arm. The six of them stood motionless. Round, dead eyes hovered over gaping mouths, each one frozen as though trapped in stasis. Brick turned as the blade consumed the blood along its edge. When he resumed his normal speed, their severed bodies tumbled to the floor with wet, heavy, thunks.

The sword drew in more blood from its victims, then settled into a steady hum as the shadow retreated. Brick smiled, sharing the strange sensation emanating from his two new weapons. The Espada contained a sort of sapience that was strong, ancient, and, without doubt, unearthly.

Part of it existed in at least one other world, or will, in the far-flung future. With no clue how he knew that fact about the sword, Brick dropped the subject for the moment. The seed was sentient, though not sapient, because it acted or reacted on instinct. It was possible that it might evolve into sapience.

As with the Quantum Universe, the existence of both did not conform to the same principles as the known universe. Brick would have to explore the origins of the sword later. As for the dark seed, it seemed to be a product of his Field access, maybe some power regulator or something. Maybe. Perhaps he would figure it out someday, but it seemed to work with both the Espada and the Field but not against either.

They would attack Cleddyf in two days, and this incident might jeopardize that. He needed to remove the soldiers and repair the damage to the shower. He didn't know if he could do it all, but he would need Tish to try. Brick opened his mind and filled it with thoughts of his beloved. She answered, and together, they got to work. They took care of the bodies, or what was left of them rather quickly. The code key had been destroyed by the resonance device. Brick gave Tish the weapon. She and Mara could reverse engineer it, and attune it to Ruby using a copy of her DNA pattern on Flint's computer. The device might come in handy once they were done with the Cleddyf operation.

CHAPTER 22: BETRAYED

Brick meditated on the floor beside the bed as Zindriya snored softly. It wasn't easy to sleep after watching her and A.B. go at it for hours. Apparently, the night before an operation, she got incredibly horny, more so than usual. He'd been surprised when she hadn't reverted to her feral ways. She seemed to have genuinely changed because of him and A.B. She hadn't had any more of her muses in the dungeon, and she'd even been less cruel to the Cleddyf prisoners her minions had captured during their reconnaissance missions.

Sitting in a full lotus position usually relaxed him, but this time, it was less than helpful. Still, it was better than sleeping next to Zindriya. He tried to empty his mind, but none of the techniques he'd learned at Nil Parity worked. Managing more than one psyche for so long wore down his mental abilities. He'd already decided to erase A.B. instead of merging with him. He had enough memories of the depravity he'd endured before Zindriya had changed. She'd invited others to their room on several occasions, men and women. He had complied with her wishes, though it had gone against his proclivities.

Brick had only been attracted to a man once, in his freshman year in high school before Kaylen. He and Fritz had a brief and torrid relationship that ended with the school year when his parents moved to New Zealand for work.

For a time, Brick wondered if he might be bisexual or bi-curious, but he'd never been attracted to another man since. He also thought he might participate in what used to be called the Down-Low culture, where straight Black men secretly sought out gay men for sex.

Brick had never acted on it because he saw it as a betrayal of his ex-lover's memory. Truth be told, he'd never been attracted to men, in general. Until his time with Zindriya, that had been the only time he'd had sex with another man. However, he put his foot down when she wanted to bring animals into their bedroom.

Brick sighed. *Who am I kidding? I'm never gonna get any sleep. I gotta walk this off.*

As he walked through the fortress, he wished the rift in his mind had stayed open so he could leave. And go where? Perhaps to Sunlight Peak in the mountains near Durango, Colorado. It had one of the most breathtaking views in the state, and he'd always felt at peace there. Or Organ Mountain, a natural formation in the western San Juan Range. It looked like a massive, god-sized pipe organ.

As he continued walking the expansive base's empty, sterile, whitewashed halls, another thing gnawing at him rose to the front of his mind. It had to do with phasing Tish through the couch and again when he used the technique to lift her. Phasing should have only re-aligned her quantum structure so it would pass through another object. Widening the spaces between subatomic particles should not have affected her mass. It didn't make sense that she had been lighter. Then there was what Ruby had done to Tish. Then, it hit him.

In an episode of one of his favorite sci-fi shows, a nearly all-powerful being had explained how he would stop a black hole from destroying an inhabited planet. The being would change the gravitational constant of the universe, which would alter the black hole's mass, allowing the crew simply to push it out of the way with a repulsion beam.

He and his mother could affect the gravitational constant in a limited area. That was why Tish had been so light and why he could lift her so easily. It was also how Ruby crushed Tish to the floor. She had not attacked Tish, but the area immediately surrounding her by multiplying the force of gravity.

Brick's theory also explained why her ability had slowly overcome his mother's attack because Tish had acquired her power from him through the Akashic Field and drew energy from it. One would cancel the other out over time.

His hypothesis explained everything, but it was near unbelievable. If it were true, he and Tish could accomplish anything. That scared him... *really* scared him. So much power in the hands of two people? Still, power itself was neither good nor evil. The use of that power determined its moral position. Ultimately, the ability to determine its true alignment must lie not with those who wielded it but with those affected by it. Only then could the powerful genuinely serve those around them so that everyone may flourish, but that rarely happened in real life.

Was it a good idea for the two of them to be together? Would it corrupt them as it had Ruby? Too many questions, not enough answers, and no time to figure it all out. Or maybe he wanted another excuse to walk away after they completed their mission.

Since Brick's dream woman and the woman of his dreams were now one and the same, why in the nine hells would he walk away? Because they might collapse the Multiverse? Hadn't he been the one who swore to destroy the thin, fragile fabric of civilization to save Tish?

A few more hours before I can kill off A.B. for good and try to heal my psyche. Or maybe it's my soul that has been damaged by this whole scenario? Brick thought. *Maybe that's why I'm having these random thoughts.*

What about insanity? Should he even go down that road?

Maintaining two personalities in one head would be enough to drive anyone mad. But Brick wasn't just anyone. He was the Ghost's Shadow, the most dangerous creature on Earth. What did that make Tish?

She wasn't the same as him. Being the catalyst, she was more like the light creating his shadow. After changing her, he was no longer the only danger to Creation because he needed her to give him access to the ability. Does it make them a blessing or a curse, or both? Comprehension teetered at the edge of his mind but refused to resolve into a roadmap for their future.

During his meanderings, Brick stopped by the lab to check on the status of the latest version of the Zero Point Module he'd crafted. It had been running continuously for three days, and none of the imbalances that had driven the other models literally into dust had manifested.

He ran an ultrasound to check for microscopic stress fractures in the casing but found nothing. An analysis of the power flow showed none of the fluctuations of the previous models, and there was no degradation of the containment field. The upgrade from a magnetic containment to a gravitic one had made all the difference.

He had gotten the idea of a gravity-based containment field from a strange dream he'd had the night Zindriya's now deceased goon, Venton Smythe, had kidnapped him. In the fantasy, he and Tish orbited Jupiter in a ship they had designed. The vessel had utilized a gravitic drive they'd built.

The dream also provided Brick with specific designs for circuitry and modules that directly translated into functional devices in the real world. It was like those explorers from films in the 1980s, where extraterrestrials sent designs for building a spacecraft to a group of kids through their dreams.

He remembered a snippet of free verse he'd read somewhere, written by a woman named Mirna Maldonado fifty years ago. It was in Spanish and was titled "Si Lo Sueñas," which loosely translated to "If You Dream It":

If you dream it, believe it,
Work for it, achieve it.
For what are dreams
If not realities
Your waking mind
Has yet to discover.

Knowing that he and Ruby could affect gravity changed his thinking about a great many things. The possibilities were infinite. He'd decided that if his dreaming mind could invent a gravity drive for a spacecraft, his waking mind could at least create a gravity field to contain the necessary components for Zero Point energy generation.

It took weeks, but he did it. Since then, Brick's mind began analyzing the technology for possible conversion to propulsion for all types of vehicles, including spacecraft. He'd need a master coder to further his inventions, though. He'd need Tish. A stab of pain pierced his heart at the thought. He missed her so much, but now was not the time for such musings. He shoved the discomfort deep within his mind.

With any luck, they would have struck a severely damaging blow to Cleddyf in a few hours, sending the rest of the cells into hiding. Then, they would hunt each of them down one by one until the entire organization was only a rumor of a vague recollection in the scattered remnants of the few who would remain.

After the main attack, Brick would take Zindriya to the Redstone headquarters, debrief her, extract as much information they could, and then... what? He struggled to find the answer. She'd had the same thing planned for him. She would have seduced him, used him, and then passed him off to Sandra. At least, that had been the plan before her sister's coup attempt. Sometimes, Zindriya's idea of pillow talk was unnervingly enlightening. For the most part, though, it was disturbing. He didn't have to decide on the precise form of punishment at that moment, so he let it go.

After Brick dealt with Zindriya, he would have to face Tish while carrying all his baggage, only to lay it on her shoulders. Add to it the gravity-affecting thing, and God knew what other abilities he had yet to discover. She shouldn't have to carry that burden. This was his mess. Yeah, he'd agreed to give her two days, but some deals needed to be broken. At least, that's what he told himself. Deep down, Brick didn't believe it, but his guilt made him think it was a plausible excuse. In his heart, he knew it was a lie, and he'd burn for it.

Tish's words still rang in his mind: "… we'll figure it out if you listen to your heart and not your head… We're connected at a quantum level." Maybe it was time Brick listened to her and stopped burying himself in his ludicrous, esoteric notion of nobility. Perhaps the thing he once considered a shield had become a crutch.

His wanderings had taken him to the top floor of the house, in front of a window that faced the southern canyon wall. Dawn was nearly upon them, and he could see figures below preparing for the attack. Cleddyf had a cell in one of the abandoned mines near Leadville, Colorado, in the mountains west of Denver at a lung-bursting 10,000-plus feet. It would take five hours to get there, and then they would have to ready themselves for the attack planned for midnight. They also found an additional cell, bringing their total to seven. The other six teams were already in place all across the globe. Tish and Mara were together and commanding one team composed of their own people, ready to attack a cell in the northwestern part of Wyoming.

Brick returned to Zindriya's quarters. She woke up when he

walked in.

"Hello, love. Couldn't sleep?" She sat up, supporting her weight on her arms.

"No. I always get butterflies before a big operation. If I force myself to sleep, I end up more tired than if I just stayed awake."

She got out of bed, hugged, and kissed him.

"I'm sorry. You know, you could have awakened me. I would have found some way to work out your anxieties."

Zindriya had changed. She was kind and comforting, whereas she would have been cruel and unyielding before. If not for the history branded on his brain, he might have even thought about staying with her. However, something told him the beast still prowled underneath the surface, biding its time for the right catalyst.

She took him by the hand and led him to the shower. Brick brought A.B. to the surface for what would likely be the last time.

◆ ◆ ◆

It was nearing go time. In late, fall, the crisp cold air at 10,000 feet bit deeply with its accompanied wind. The Cleddyf cell nearest Brick and Zindriya turned out to be a central hub. Taking it out would hurt the organization and put them on notice that they were no longer operating in a shroud of anonymity. Someone knew who they were and was coming after them. The hunters would become the prey.

Any more euphemisms you can think of?

Shut up, Bricktay.

At first, Brick had been concerned with the increased appearances of his annoying inner voice since the shower attack until he realized what it was. Balance. There had to be consequences for splitting your mind into pieces. It took an unimaginable amount of willpower and energy. All that raw power had to come from somewhere, and the excess had to be accounted for somehow.

The multiverse was balanced, or so said the Laws of the Conservation of Energy and Matter. It contained a finite amount of both. Nothing was ever created or destroyed, only converted from one form to another. Bricktay was the counterweight that sat on the opposite end of the scales of his mental stability.

He existed to keep Brick precariously balanced on the razor's edge between sanity and insanity. He'd been silent before because Brick remained strong. His increasing appearances indicated his waning strength. So far, it had worked, but for how much longer?

Brick ended the brief exchange with his second, far more annoying, alter ego. It was thirty minutes before midnight, and their units were in place all across the world. The coalition forces synchronized their attacks to midnight, Mountain Standard Time because all but one of the cells hid in locations that would be dark at the time of the attack.

Brick, Zindriya, and their shock troops of twenty of their best fighters were on top of a hill, directly across a shallow creek from the entrance to the cell's hideout. The area was densely forested, and you would miss the opening if you didn't know exactly where it was. He would take one of the soldiers with him, phase into the facility, deactivate whatever countermeasures they could, and open the entrance. Two days before, he'd infiltrated the base and located everything he would need to render the facility accessible. It was time.

Brick and his partner, a soldier named Naomi in her mid-thirties, pressed the buttons on their biometric attenuators and then stood to leave. Zindriya stopped them and kissed Brick. It was an urgent, passionate kiss and stimulated him despite his inner feelings. Something of Andra existed in the kiss, and residual emotions stirred within him.

She whispered, "Please come back to me. Everything I've done is because I love you, Brick. After tonight, no one will be left to take you away from me."

Brick thought her confession was odd but pushed it aside and forced himself to lie to her. Guilt threatened to invade his mind, but he crushed it. There was time enough for that after everything was done.

When Brick and his partner reached the rock wall about forty meters to the left of the mine entrance, he grabbed Naomi by the forearm, phased them both, and walked through the wall. It only took a few seconds to cross the ten feet to the storage room Brick had scouted the day before. No one waited in the roughly hewn rock walls of the small chamber. The first stage of their plan was a success. The security room was fifty meters to the left, down the mine-like corridor outside the door. It was ten minutes to midnight.

Naomi remained in the storage room as he made his way to the security office. Something had been nagging at him ever since they had entered the facility. He shoved it to the side, thinking it was a case of the jitters, but it exploded in his mind when his hand touched the security office door. There were no noises in the facility other than the soft whispers of the air circulating system. There was no radio chatter, no banter between soldiers, no coughs or sneezes, and none of the noises a large group of people would make. Guards should have occupied the security room, but he could hear no heartbeats, none at all. Midnight fell amidst the deafening silence of the hollow hideout.

Brick opened the door to the security room to confirm it was empty. It was. He returned to the storage room, where Naomi still awaited him. Apparently, she wasn't a part of whatever mischief was afoot. What was going on? Why was the room empty? A chill threatened to grip Brick's abdomen, and Zindriya's words exploded in his mind. *There will be no one left to take you away from me.*

Brick had expected a trap. Perhaps there had been a leak in Zindriya's organization, and Cleddyf had gotten word of their attack. It was a trap, alright, and there was also a leak. Zindriya was the leak, but the noose wasn't for him.

He left Naomi in the storage room without saying a word and strode confidently to the facility's front door, activating the opening sequence for the massive blast doors. He went hyper and sped toward Zindriya, who remained, predictably, in the same place he'd left her along with the rest of her troops.

"What have you done, Zee?"

"What I needed to do, Brick. I've decimated most of Cleddyf's hierarchy, and now, almost all the remaining soldiers work for me."

"Then why are we here?"

"The only way to ever be safe is to never have any more enemies, love."

"But we both still have adversaries, Zee."

"None alive. Not after tonight."

"Wha…"

Brick never finished his sentence. A massive sound wave pummeled his mind and drove him to his knees. It was all he could do to keep himself from screaming. The pain was mind numbing. He found himself on all fours when it began to subside. It was Tish's siren song. Zee had set a trap for her and Mara. Zindriya's words, *There will be no one to take you away from me*, rang in his head once again.

The rift in his mind snapped open, flooding him with power and eradicating the initial effects of the siren song. Brick stood and faced Zindriya.

"This is your idea of love, Zindriya?"

"You're not going to her again."

"So, you did know."

"I have cameras everywhere, Brick." With the speed of a ghost, she drew her Browning High Power 9mm, "You're not going anywhere, lover. You're staying with me."

"You're a Ghost. How?"

"Connections, lover. Power down."

"You first."

Brick whisked the Espada Encantada from the sheath strapped to his back so fast that it appeared to teleport into his hand. The blade glowed green as it sheared the barrel from the pistol.

"I'll be back to deal with you later, Zee."

He turned toward the siren's song, summoned forth the golden light, and saw Tish and Mara pinned down by enemy fire behind a hastily made barricade but safe for the moment. The glow enveloped Brick as he began to shift but stopped and looked back at Zindriya.

"Those two are the only ones keeping me tethered to this world, Zee. Pray they survive because if they don't, you will become *my* muse, and I promise you this. I'll use my abilities to make you last for years."

He nicked his forearm to sate the blade, turned, tucked the Espada Encantada back into its sheath, and entered the fray on the plains of Wyoming. He ignored Zindriya's screams for him to return.

CHAPTER 23: DESTROYER

In the Ghost's Shadow lay the truth of its passing.
In the Ghost's Shadow lay the path it has trod.
Could the Ghost's Shadow hide the lie everlasting?
Could the Ghost's Shadow hide the power of a god?

-FROM THE CHARRED REMAINS OF A JOURNAL FLINT RECOVERED FROM A SECRET LAB

Part 1

Tish teased as a golden cloud congealed into Brick. "It's about time you got here."

"Next time, try and tone down the banshee call, babe. You nearly blew my brain out of my skull."

Tish was in his arms in an instant, kissing him despite the imminent danger of the approaching enemy horde. He heard Mara say something about waiting until later, but both ignored her. There might not be a later, and they had waited long enough.

"You done with her now?"

"No. We have some unfinished business after we scatter these clowns."

Mara chuckled at his comment. "Lil' bro, there's more than two hundred of your *clowns* out there, and they aren't carrying guns that shoot large flags that say *Bang* on them."

Those 'clowns' had killed or captured their entire team, and she and Tish had escaped only because of Lil' sis' invulnerability. Brick loved that Mara considered Tish family now and wondered what she had done to earn such an honor, but there was no time to dwell on it. They were in trouble.

Tish and Mara had their backs against a rock wall and had built a makeshift fort using a few burned-out armored vehicles and scraps of thick metal shrapnel that had detached from some other craft. It was adequate to hold off the approaching throng until they moved some troops to the top of their shield rock. Then, it would be all over.

Fortunately, they did not appear to have gravity-surfing vessels, or they all would have been in a pickle. Mara's periodic hyper-mode forays into the enemy's frontlines kept them at bay, but Brick could see that the effort exhausted her.

Tish carried the German Heckler & Koch G11, an odd-looking, rectangular-shaped assault rifle supposedly retired in the 1990s. It fired a 5.56mm caseless round, which meant no hot brass casings to trip over, and was very light. Likewise, Mara wielded the Belgian-made FN P90, a submachine gun that fired both caseless and classic brass rounds from a top-loaded, horizontal-feed cartridge. Both weapons were highly effective, reliable, and extremely deadly.

A plan began to take root in Brick's mind. "I have an idea, but you're not going to like it."

"You know, baby, I've heard that line in too many movies. You should think up your own material." Tish didn't waste any time subjecting him to her snark.

Brick cocked an eyebrow. "When did you get to be such a comedian?"

"Since I got my boyfriend back. You are back, right? For good?"

"Not going anywhere, Tish. First, we gotta get out of this mess, then deal with the psycho behind them, but we'll do that together."

"Gladly." Her voice lowered to a near growl. "So, what's your plan?"

The army had regained some of its composure from the last time Mara put the fear of the Ghost in them, so Brick took the liberty of reminding them why they were afraid. They needed to keep the enemy at bay for a few more minutes. He returned several seconds later and inspected his blade before returning it to its scabbard.

"Where did you get the sword, Lil bro? I've seen images of something similar before."

"She's the Espada Encantada, and I got her from Zindriya's armory."

Her brows raised in apparent shock. "Dude, it's for real? Not a myth? Is it Joyeuse?"

"Yeah, sis, she's the real deal, blood, honor, and much more."

"You figured it out yet?"

"She's soulbound to me, and it's a growth weapon. But I haven't named her yet." To keep things simple, Brick used gaming terms.

"Of course, you'd get a soulbound growth weapon. Ancient or Epic quality by the looks of it. You are such an asshole, lil punkass negro." Mara grinned.

"Bite me, you frigging hag."

Not being a gamer, Tish was feeling left out. "Somebody want to clue me in on what you two are talking about,"

"Sorry, Tish. My sword isn't supposed to exist outside of myth and legend. For lack of a better word, it's got magical properties I don't completely understand yet."

"Yeah, lover, we know what Arthur C. Clarke said about magic. You've heard of the sword before?"

"Just through rumors and innuendos. I didn't truly believe them until the Espada chose me after Bruno disgraced it. It's a long story, and we ain't got the time right now."

"*It* chose *you*, Lil bro?"

"Yeah. Like I said, it's a long story. Look, we gotta deal with the horde out there. Here's my plan."

Brick outlined his idea.

Mara pursed her lips. "Lil bro, you lost your damned mind? How do you think it'll work?"

Tish didn't doubt its validity. "You saw what happened to the two at my house, Mara. Why wouldn't it work here?"

"Cuz that's one hell of a lot of real estate with a couple hundred soldiers, not two within a couple meters." Mara shook her head. "You on board with this, Lil sis?"

"You got a better idea? Some secret cavalry we don't know about ready to ride over the hill to rescue us? We're it, Mara. The rest of our troops are spread across the world, raiding empty bases because Cleddyf sent all those soldiers here to take us out."

Brick chimed in. "It was Zindriya. She did it to keep the two of you from taking me away from her."

"I am so going to kill that bitch!" Tish's voice went low and gravelly.

"No. This is my fault, and when the time comes, I'll fix it."

"Brick, we're partners in all of this. We do things together from now on. No more cowboy shit, got it?" Tish smiled, took his hand, squeezed it, and Brick nodded in agreement.

The women inspected their weapons and checked their ammo. He used this time to exorcise A.B. from his mind. He'd already enclosed the aspect inside a mental cage, so it was much easier to excise him that he thought it would be. Once he finished the deed, he searched his mind for any remnants he might have missed.

Bricktay, could you help me out, please?

Yeah, your alter's gone. Just don't expect me to do the same. I'm with you forever.

Figured as much. Kinda used to you, though. You might be a dick, but you keep me on track.

Yeah, yeah. Fuck off, asshole.

Brick sighed and returned to the outside world as the ladies completed their inspections.

When they assured him that they were ready, he phased.

Brick hypered across the plain and into the middle of the army, passing through everyone between him and his goal. It felt indescribably weird phasing through all those living bodies, but he gritted his teeth and persevered. After four seconds, he arrived as close to the center of the military as he could deduce. He stopped and then jumped. The one leap carried him almost a hundred meters straight up, then he unphased. Part one of the plan was a success.

Initiating part two, he shifted into the place between the physical world and the Akashic Field and absorbed shadow from the seed as golden light surrounded him.

As his ascent slowed, he gazed down at a universe of gold covered by the mass of shadow that was the army. The only break in the shadow was his path from their makeshift fort to the midst of the army. Everyone he had phased through glowed, looking like a river crashing through a black canyon. As he had done in Tish's house, he used the dark energy to push the lights beneath the shadows away. The area he covered was far greater than he'd calculated. It appeared as though more than half of the soldiers below had vanished into the abyss before he waved the lights back into place. Most of the remaining attackers panicked and began to retreat, but several warriors charged forth.

Dear God, what have I done? What have I become? Brick thought. He knew the attack would be destructive, but he never imagined such devastation.

It was time for part three of the plan, and that belonged to Tish and Mara, who dashed from the fort, guns blazing. Still in the space between the Field and the Real, his near-zero mass allowed Brick to drift back to the ground as he recalled the dark seed energy. There was more than he had expelled, but before Brick could ascertain why...

WHUMP, whump!

A sharp pain racked his body as the seed pounded once.

WHUMP, whump, WHUMP!

The pain increased as it pulsed twice...

WHUMP, whump, WHUMP, whump, WHUMP!

Then thrice, as a wave of agony coursed through him.

Though close, it was not quite equivalent to the Neurovex, so he was able to manage it. He realized whence the extra energy had come. The seed grew into a shard the size of a fist, fed by some of the life force, or perhaps souls of those he had cast into oblivion, then went quiet. On all fours, Brick's stomach retched.

After taking a short moment to recover, he remembered he was behind enemy lines and had more to do to help the ladies on the ground, so he plucked one grenade after another from his belt and lobbed them at the rear of the advancing line of soldiers, ignoring those who retreated. The palm-sized explosives demolished the soldiers from behind as the two women mowed them down from the front. The massacre lasted less than a minute before the final enemy combatant fell.

Brick had experienced fear in nearly all its forms, but what he felt at that moment was stark, raving terror at the raw power he'd displayed. He thought he had it all figured out before, but it turned out he knew nothing. He thought the mark he left when he phased was what made him the Ghost's Shadow, but it wasn't. The last two lines of the verse his father had found in the lab said it all, and he'd finally pieced it together. What he'd done was what made him what he was. He stood at the center of the black, blighted land, dotted with the remains of partially transmuted soldiers looking like miniature Easter Island statues merged with the darkness. Their souls screamed his name.

Despair dropped him to his knees again. Nothing within the zone lived, not a blade of grass, not an insect, and definitely nothing human, including him. He couldn't even call himself human again—not now.

What remained of the enemy force dropped their weapons and ran as fast as their legs could carry them away from the circle of desolation. At best, maybe fifty survived. On his knees in the lifeless black dust, Brick wept. When he reached a hand out to one of the half-sunken soldiers, she crumbled at his touch as Tish and Mara made their way to him.

"Brick, baby, what's wrong? We won." Tish leaned over him, hand on his back, stroking him gently.

"It's too much, Tish—too much power. I didn't know, not until it was too late. It's too much for one person. No one should be capable of such wanton death and destruction."

"But it's not just you, Brick. You're not alone in this. I called you, and I opened the Field for you. Remember, I'm the Keymaster, and you're the Gatekeeper."

"I know, but still…" Brick pulled himself together, sort of, and stood while wiping the tears from his eyes, smearing black lines from the dead soldier's remains across his face.

He told them about the inference he had drawn on the way back down.

"Remember the last two lines of that verse Dad found, Mara? They were:

Could the Ghost's Shadow hide the lie everlasting?

Could the Ghost's Shadow hide the power of a god?"

"Yeah, I remember, Lil bro. What's it mean?"

The *'lie everlasting'* spoke of a difference between matter and energy. There was none; they were the same. It's one's perception that distinguishes one from the other.

"Schrödinger's cat, Heisenberg's Uncertainty Principle, it's all fucking true, guys, don't you see?" Tears threatened to spill once again as he fought them back.

"No, we don't, baby. Calm down and explain it in English." Brick heard the concern in Tish's voice.

She moved closer and wrapped her arms around him, which helped Brick a little. A phrase from John Carpenter's movie Prince of Darkness had stuck with him ever since he'd heard it. He paraphrased it for Tish and Mara.

We assume everything is linear, that cause leads to effect, and that the beginning comes before the end. But everything we understand about logic, time, physics, and causality fades into ghosts and shadows in the quantum verse.

"Ghosts and shadows, Mara. I think the whitecoats named us from what the physics professor said in the movie. He used Quantum Theory to give credence to the supernatural. The scriptwriter was a freaking clairvoyant."

"Keep going; we're getting there." Tish urged him on.

Brick took a breath and continued. He felt slightly calmer. Perhaps if he shared the burden, he could live with who he had become. Who? Or what? Was he a natural-born humanoid or a construct, a genetically engineered, non-human, biological entity? He shook his head to clear it. At the moment, he had no time for semantics.

"Okay. Okay. This is an extreme oversimplification, but I'll fill you in on the bottom line. Heisenberg suggested that you can't predict a particle's movement because it is too fluid. You can never pin a vector down because its state depends on your observation. When you take your eyes off it, it changes to something different or disappears altogether, suggesting it's only real while subjected to one's perception alone. With me so far?"

"Yah. Keep going." Tish glanced at Mara briefly.

"The Schrodinger's Cat thought experiment supposes that you can't know the actual state of a particle, or the cat, until you see it, and until you do, it exists in all states. That's why the cat is presumed to be both alive and dead until it collapses to one state when you open the box and look at it."

Brick paused. Both women urged him to continue. He nodded and proceeded.

"Following that stream of thought, matter and energy exist in both states until someone observes them as one or the other. If you look away and then back, it could be something else, the same or non-existent. Perception eliminates uncertainty, but only if you never look away."

"Sorry, but that's as simple as I can break it down." Taking a breath, Brick found himself calming down.

Talking helped, Brick felt more in control again, and Tish's embrace strengthened him.

"I think I understand. Isn't it somewhat like solipsism, where you can't trust the reality of anything outside your own mind?" Tish seemed to have a grasp on the subject.

"Close enough. Quite literally, your perception becomes, or maybe, in our case, creates your reality."

"Kind of like in Heinlein's *Number of the Beast* novel, right?" Again, she came up with an adequate correlation.

"Correct again, Tish. Whatever the mind imagines could be

real on some plane in the Multiverse. Heinlein was a freaking prophet."

Mara needed more information. "What's the 'power of a god' thing?"

"Access to the Akashic Field allows us to manipulate subatomic particles, which means the ability to create or destroy anything and everything. It gives us control over the forces of Creation and Chaos, Life or Death." The more he talked, the better he felt.

"Holy shit, lil bro. Does that mean what I think it does?"

"Yeah. It means that someday I..." Brick looked Tish in the eyes. "Or rather, we, might be able to change reality. We could make Multipersonal Pantheistic Solipsism a real thing and visit the lands of Oz, Lilliput, and Blefuscu as the travelers did in *Number of the Beast*. Only we won't need a machine to do it. We can just will ourselves there."

The sound of one person clapping echoed around them. As they listened, it gathered to a point on their left. When they focused on that point, it crystallized into a familiar yet unwelcome form. Ruby.

"Well done, Mason. I knew you'd figure it out sooner or later. By the way, nicely done with the army. Don't think I could've done better. Well, maybe I could have, though I didn't recognize that energy you used. What was that?"

Brick faced Ruby Redstone, what was left of his birth mother, as she materialized another figure from a golden cloud. Zindriya. The look on Zee's face contained a mixture of shock, horror, and rage but softened as she looked at Brick.

Ruby continued speaking, oblivious to the tension that coalesced around her guest's appearance.

Brick kept an eye on the treacherous, psychotic kidnapper. "That energy is unique, but you should know that since you engineered me, right, Ruby?"

"It wasn't my doing, but anyway..." Ruby didn't get to finish.

"Shut up! So, you're the final piece of the puzzle." Brick interrupted her. "You planned all of this from the jump, Ruby, didn't you? What do you want, and why did you bring her?" Brick pointed at his former captor.

Though angry, he now understood that Ruby didn't know of the dark seed or its origin. So where had it come from? Yet another question for some other time.

"Still won't call me mother? Ah well. About Zindriya, well, the two of you have some unfinished business, yes?"

"Your plan could have killed your daughter. Did that occur to you?"

"Yes, it did, Mason. Though you have much to learn about the Field, my son."

"I'm not your fucking son, Ruby."

Knowing it was more accurate than not, Brick felt better saying it.

"As I was about to say, I knew you would figure this out. Remember the non-linear aspect of time at the quantum level, Mason. Once you master the Field, you can access many things beyond your present knowledge. You will figure it out, though. I can see your neural pathways expanding already."

"Brick, what's all this?" Zindriya interrupted.

"I'll leave you to it. Make me proud, Mason."

"Kiss my Black ass, Ruby."

"Brick?" Zindriya pressed him.

"You tried to kill my family, and we stopped you, that's what!" Brick's brows knitted.

Zindriya's face contorted in pain and anger. "What has that little bitch done for you, Brick? I betrayed my employer just for you. I destroyed Cleddyf's leadership and took over for you. I rescued your mother for you. For the first time in my life, I fell in love; pure, unadulterated. This is how you repay me?"

"Um, I must interject that without my help, Zindriya, you couldn't have taken over Cleddyf." Ruby held a finger up to press her point.

Brick glared at her, then returned his blistering gaze to Zindriya, whose look had softened. Her eyebrows peaked over the bridge of her nose, and a half-smile graced her lips.

She actually looks hopeful. Brick thought, shaking his head.

"You tried to kill the two people on this godforsaken planet I love the most, Zee. Is that what you call love?"

Zindriya responded in a soft, almost pleading voice. "They were the only ones standing in the way of our happiness, Brick. Without them, you would stay with me and love me."

He replied through clenched teeth, and it was nothing if not explosive. "I never loved you and never could love a vile, despicable, selfish creature like you. Ever."

Zindriya's eyes narrowed, her nostrils flared, and she bared her teeth.

There she is, Brick thought. Still, a part of him wondered if he hadn't exacerbated this whole situation just to justify his actions. Guilt was a powerful and often silent motivator.

He readied himself for what was coming. He was still in the Field, and Zindriya blazed like a Christmas tree. Ruby had done something to her, but he didn't know what.

"Then I'll take a love for a love, asshole."

Zindriya went hyper, snatched a knife from a bandolero on her thigh, and flung it in their direction. Brick and Tish were ahead of her. One of Brick's throwing knives already hurtled towards Zindriya before her hand touched the hilt of her blade. Tish had previously drawn her .50cal Desert Eagle and had fired less than a tenth-of-a-second after Brick unleashed his deadly missile.

After releasing the knife, Brick hurled himself towards Tish to protect her. Ignoring the projectiles flying in her direction, Zindriya directed her blade... at Mara.

Realizing his mistake, Brick hypered toward Mara, knowing he'd be too late. He didn't trust his ability to disintegrate the moving projectile since he'd only get one shot, but he tried anyway and missed. The throw caught Mara off guard, she tried to dodge, but the knife flew too fast.

No time, Brick thought. *Time? You're in the Akashic Field, you idiot! Moving from point A to point B in the real world is instantaneous.*

Brick shifted himself within the Field, but he'd wasted too much time. The knife plunged into Mara's heart just as he unphased, and tackled her to the ground.

"No, no, no, no! Please, God, no!" Brick screamed as the woman who had been everything to him lay in his arms, limp and lifeless. Tish flashed to his side and held him and the woman who had become her sister.

"Well done, Mason! I knew you could do it."

Wrath flared in him, and the dark shard thrummed, but this time, Brick controlled it and took its power to boost his own. A cloud of shadows burst from him, pushing Tish out of harm's way as he lay his sister on the ground. Chaotic, powerful energy surged within him as he drew power from the Akashic Field. He braided them together, forming a new, more powerful strand, impossibly unifying chaos and creation. He focused his gaze on Ruby.

Brick's voice resonated as he spoke. "Because you were once my mother, I will give you this one chance to leave. If you do not, I will add your energy to my own, and you will cease to exist."

For the first time, Ruby stared in open-mouthed shock. "Wh-what are you... How?"

"I'm your son, Ruby. Come. Embrace your creation." His words trembled the ground.

"No. You're something else," Ruby backed away. Brick thought he saw fear in her eyes.

"Then leave, NOW!" Brick's shout shook the ground hard enough to buck Tish and Ruby off their feet.

Ruby vanished in a shower of golden sparks. He turned to his sister's body.

His voice rippled the air around everyone. "No. Not today."

"Are you sure this is the right thing to do, Brick?" Tish wasn't questioning him, but wanted him to consider the consequences.

"I'm sure it's not, but I don't care. The shar... my Shadow Core and the Espada have shown me the way." He pulled the golden essence of the Field around himself, mixing in more of the shadow. He gazed at Tish. "Will you stop me?"

"Not this time, but we will talk after. Now, do what you can to save our sister."

Unsurprised that Tish understood what he intended to do, Brick closed his eyes and entered the space between the physical world and the Akashic Field. He pulled more dark energy from the Core and light from the Field and shrouded himself in their embrace, adding the braided strand into the mix. The level of energy coursing through him ripped his flesh, but he ignored the pain and pressed forward as blood drew crimson tracks through the black dust that clung to him.

The Espada Encantada hummed in anticipation, and when he drew it, the braid infused it. White light shone from the blade while the dark energy lined the edge. A sense of sharpness emanated from the Espada. He held the sword aloft, then brought it down, slicing through the fabric of Reality. Brick plunged his mind into the void beyond in search of the Time-Space Continuum.

Everything in the present, the past, and the future happened at the same time, and much like Schrodinger's cat, it only coalesced into reality when mortals perceived it. As a result, they experienced the present linearly as time passed from moment to moment.

With enough power and access to the Akashic Field, you could glimpse into whatever moment you wished and influence events to a certain extent. Of course, he didn't know how, leaving him with but one option, work it out one step at a time and hope he didn't crash Creation or die in the attempt. Though it would be beyond extreme, he could wipe himself out of existence.

Other, more ephemeral influences such as karma, causality, and paradoxes might create problems for Brick, but he cared little. He would save his sister and pay the price later.

Part 2

With no idea what else to do, Tish removed her vest, tore it into shreds, and applied bandages to the worst wounds on Brick's body as he stood over Mara, eyes closed. The contortions ravaging his face concerned her because they alluded to the possibility that he may not be able to do what he wanted, what they wanted. In less than a minute, Brick called out to her, then extended a blood-soaked hand towards her.

"Tish." Though excruciating pain racked his body, Brick asked for help. "I need you."

Despite the waves of energy cascading from him and the danger it represented, Tish took his hand. "I'm here love. I'm with you to the very end."

Darkness enveloped her, but because she trusted Brick, fear did not.

Part 3

When Brick entered the void and located the Continuum, he knew he was way out of his league. He understood what he saw on an intellectual level, but the scope was far beyond everything he could imagine. One experience from his past allowed his mind to comprehend the cacophony of images before him.

The summer before he began college, he attended a Wiccan summer solstice festival. It was during a phase in his life when he searched for a belief system that aligned with his view of the universe. A silversmith exhibited her craft, creating a tree of life by twisting together over a hundred strands of silver. She'd begun at the roots, moving on to the trunk, which she'd fashioned into a woman's body, and finally, her arms shot off to form the many branches and encompassing leaves. It was one of the most intricate designs Brick had ever seen.

As he witnessed the Continuum, he could see striking similarities between the tree the Wiccan artisan created and the construct before and around him. If you multiplied the strands by about one billion and could imagine all of the branches and leaves they would make, you might come close to one-hundredth of one percent of what lay before him. Now change the silver into a bright white glow with every color you can imagine shooting through each strand, and you have an inkling of the majesty of the Continuum in its full glory.

Finding the one strand that represented Mara's demise was far beyond daunting, but Brick tried it. With so much power coursing through him, his mind worked faster than a Quantum computer, but it still wasn't enough. Linear time did not exist in the void, so he had no reference to calculate how long he would need to search. Still, he made no progress and realized he required assistance. It didn't take much energy to project his consciousness through the rift the Espada Encantada created, so he asked Tish for help.

"What is this place, Brick, and what in the hell is that?" She pointed at the Continuum. "Are we in danger?"

"We are in the void between one second and the next." Brick explained the construct and what they needed to do.

"How will we find a single strand in all this? It's impossible!"

"Alice believed in at least six impossible things, and we only need one. You told me to listen more to my heart than my head, and since you are my heart, I need your help."

"How can I say no to that?" Tish touched Brick's arm, not caring about the blood covering it. "How can I help?"

"Just hold me and think of Mara. Your instinct and intuition far surpass mine. Together, we can accomplish anything."

"Oh, I can definitely hold you in my arms." Her arms enveloped him, He felt real even though their physical bodies remained on Earth.

The two of them embraced and pressed foreheads together, their noses touching. Brick reached out with his mind and touched hers. She resisted for a moment, then dropped her barriers, merging their minds into one. Energy from the shard and the Field wove together, then enveloped them and began spinning. The braids increased in speed until they merged into a white glow that matched the color of the Continuum as the couple remained suspended in the eye of the vortex. Their merged minds focused on one person, one period of time, and the love each shared with Mara, sister to both.

Once the energies around them changed color, they morphed into a funnel, arrowed towards one section of the Continuum, then zoomed in on the moment that mattered. Brick needed to make one infinitesimal change. He nudged their sister a few centimeters to the side. The knife would still strike her but would not instantly kill her.

Tish's influence returned at least a portion of his humanity. As much as he loved Mara, for one life, he would not risk creating a paradox that would, at least, branch their reality into an altered timeline or, at worst, destroy it entirely. Perhaps their action pushed the ephemeral influences to the limit, but he deduced that allowing for at least a chance she could die might reduce the karmic and causal kickback.

When they finished their task, the Espada led them back to and through the tear into their Reality. Brick sheathed the sword. They needed to seal the rift. Parting from their embrace, they held hands while extending their other towards the breach in space-time. Golden energy emerged from the sheathed sword, flowed to Tish, and encircled her extended hand. Dark energy from his Core did the same for Brick. They moved their hands downward, their interlaced fingers closing the fissure like a zipper.

Once done, the Shadow Core re-absorbed the dark energy, and the Field reclaimed its golden light.

The physical world filled Brick's vision, and he looked around. The knife Zindriya threw impaled the right side of Mara's chest instead of her heart. Zindriya had fallen into a pool of her own bodily fluids. Looking down at his own body, rivers of blood gushed from the many ruptures in his skin and pooled at his feet. Acting as a conduit for so much power had been too much for his already-stressed mind and body, and his knees buckled. Tish caught him, then lowered his flaccid body to the ground.

"Our sister lives, Tish." His voice diminished in volume with each word. Still, a smile creased his face as his mind descended into darkness.

CHAPTER 24: THE WAY FORWARD

Part 1

Pain devastated Brick's body, making him think he was still in Zindriya's clutches as Bruno applied the Neurovex. Opening his mouth to scream caused more pain as he realized his face and lungs ached. The only thing he could manage was a gurgling sound.

Two voices from afar called his name, they sounded familiar, but as his brain attempted to reconstitute their identities, agony coursed through it. That was impossible, though, because the brain had no pain receptors.

The voices sounded less distant but remained an echo resounding in his ears, hurting his eardrums. Why did everything throb so much?

Because that's what happens when you alter reality, asshole.

Bricktay. Great. Just what he needed as he...

The memory flooded his mind, driving a little of the agony away. Energy rushed through him as adrenaline coursed through his body, overriding the pain. His eyes snapped open, and he sat up as hands failed to hold him down.

"Just take it easy, Brick. You're safe." Tish's soothing tone lifted his spirits. "Backup's on the way along with our medics."

Relaxing slightly, Brick heard shuffling, first from his left, then from behind, as hands lowered him onto what felt like someone's legs. Tish's upside-down face entered his field of vision from above.

"I'll hold off with the million questions for now, Brick, but we did it. We saved Mara's life, though it damned near killed you."

Struggling to speak, Brick voiced a request. "Zindriya?"

"She's dead," Tish smiled.

"L-lift...G-gotta s-see."

Tish lifted and leaned him against her chest so he could see Zindriya. She lay dead in a sea of her own blood. Brick started wheezing but had to stop because of the pain wreaking havoc in his chest.

"Don't make me laugh!" He choked out.

"What's so funny? I thought you wanted her dead!"

Brick shot Tish a quizzical look over his shoulder and laughed, cringing in agony at the same time.

"Oh shit. Sorry, I didn't mean it the way it sounded."

Brick took her hands in one of his own. "I know." Lifting the other to her face, he cupped her cheek. "I love you." His fingers left crimson streaks.

Tish kissed the palm of his blood-soaked hand, "I love you, too. Now, what's so funny?"

Brick revealed the prophecy of Zindriya's death made by one of her muses she'd named Babel:

'When the lover becomes the liar, the eagle will strike, and your silver tongue will drown you in the Red Sea.'

He was the lover who had become the liar; his knife had wedged itself in the roof of her mouth, giving her a silver tongue. Blood streamed down her throat, drowning her. The round from Tish's pistol was the eagle's strike and had torn through Zee's femoral artery, spilling almost all of her bodily fluids on the ground in seconds. She had died in the red sea of her own blood.

In a matter of minutes, two of their gravity-surfing crafts landed in a silent battlefield disrupted only by the hum of their power units. A security unit dispersed and then cordoned off the combat zone before a legion of medics and soldiers flooded the area to care for Mara and Brick, who demanded to see his sister before they carted her off to their private hospital.

The knife remained lodged in her chest, the silver handle protruding from her dark skin as splatters of red sprayed from the wound covering most of her upper body and the right side of her face. Bleary eyes rotated toward Brick as Mara gave him a thumbs up. "I don't know what you did, lil punk-ass negro, but thank you."

"Moving heaven and earth was a small price to pay for the woman who shaped my entire world, you frigging hag."

Each smiled at the other, which assured Brick that his big sister would be fine. What price he would have to pay for their actions remained uncertain. He had no doubt the Three Fates or the Universe would exact some form of retribution for disturbing their balance.

Knowing Mara would survive, Brick's eyes refused to remain open. The events of the last few hours had drained him, and he could feel his control of the Field slipping. In addition, the Shadow Core returned to its slumber. This time, when darkness took him, he welcomed it with open arms. Tish's voice eased him into his well-deserved rest.

"It's my turn to protect you now, love. Sleep easy, knowing I will never leave your side."

Part 2

A golden glow drew Brick from his slumber. At least he thought he was awake, but perhaps not. Tish sat in a chair to the left of his hospital bed, chin on her chest and a book in her hands, but she did not move. No sound assailed his ears despite various tubes and wires puncturing his skin or adhering to his body. The machines neither blinked nor beeped. The only thing moving was the figure who stood at the foot of his bed.

"Ru-by!" Brick struggled through a parched throat and dry lips. Forcing himself to sit up, he gathered his energy to remove the threat the creature before him represented, but she smiled and raised a hand.

"I'm not here to fight, Mason..." but she didn't get to finish whatever she was going to say.

A flood of power rushed into him. Golden sparkles surrounded both him and Tish, who now stood behind Ruby, holding a knife to her throat. His wounds began to heal visibly.

"That's a shame because I'd like to finish you right here and now," Tish displayed more glee than Brick wanted to hear.

Fear did not cloud Ruby's gaze as she looked at Brick.

"How did you... Ah, you shared your power with her. The thought never occurred to me with Flint."

"Well, narcissistic megalomania has that effect on the clinically unbalanced, Ruby." Brick glanced at Tish, who nodded back at him. A fleeting thought made Brick wonder how much his girlfriend had changed for the look of steely calculation and cold determination to have manifested in her. She would kill Ruby and not think twice about it. Some part of him was proud, but another knew the loss of innocence would hit her one day and devastate her. It had done the same to him, and Mara had guided him through his grieving process.

"Is that any way to talk to your mother?"

"No. It's not, *Ruby!*" Brick spat the name. "What do you want?"

"Does your girlfriend know what you did?"

"That is filed under none of your fucking business, Ruby. State yours, and leave, or we end you." He sat upright, prepared to access the Shadow Core.

Ruby focused on his eyes for a moment, then nodded.

"Fine. I came here to warn you about what's coming."

Ruby revealed the actual truth of their existence, and in many ways, it was cataclysmal. She had been Cleddyf's chief virologist stationed in one of the most remote areas of Antarctica. They had found a microscopic organism that defied all biological norms in a melted ice shelf. As the other scientists argued about its origins, Ruby conducted tests to determine its roots.

During one of her experiments, she placed it in a Petri dish of nutrient-rich agar, which unbelievably brought it back to life. She'd been so sure it would not work that she had not conformed to proper isolation protocols. When the organism resurrected, it grew to the size of a Boba in seconds, flew from the dish into her nostril, and took over her body in less than a minute.

Though the organism invaded her, Ruby remained in control of her mind, for a while at least. But she had chosen to infect her husband and daughter. Once they acquired their abilities, she crafted the story that led them to slaughter the remaining occupants. Despite what his father had told him, Brick's birth was not due to an accidental pregnancy. Ruby had meticulously engineered his DNA and his conception but met with significant difficulties during his birth. She'd fought off the consequences for three years, but it eventually rendered her unconscious, leading to an auto-imposed regeneration stasis.

Brick's suspicions were now confirmed. He wasn't human, but a crafted entity. The only one of his kind. Oddly, it didn't affect him as much as he thought it might. The gauntlet of lies his life had been disturbed him more than his origin. In the last year, he'd discovered, what, four different versions of the past?

Well, fuck it. He thought. *I'll write my own past and forge my own future.*

He gazed into Tish's eyes, afraid of what he would see. She stared back at him with nothing but love in those beautiful light brown orbs. He would be just fine.

At last, Ruby came to the gist of the matter. The organism that had infected them was of extraterrestrial origin and had remained dormant, frozen in the Antarctic since before the Ice Age. Climate change had melted the glacier within which it had lain trapped for millennia. These were not offspring, but cells from a much larger entity with a purpose. Designed to travel the cosmos until it found a suitable biosphere with life advanced enough to birth another of the larger entities, it found a home on Earth.

Because of Ruby, the entity knew of Earth and would come to claim its prize and absorb every living organism to procreate. The planet's only hope was Brick because his birth represented an evolutionary leap for humankind. Due to his ability to control and manipulate the Akashic Field, he alone would be able to find a solution to their dilemma, and since he had shared his power with Tish, the planet now had two saviors instead of one.

Because she was patient zero, Ruby could not help with the upcoming war because the closer the entity came to Earth, the less control she would have over her own mind. Until then, she would do what she could to shape what was left of Cleddyf into a force that might give Earth another option.

"How long do we have?" Brick's mind struggled to comprehend the tale Ruby had woven. Could he believe her?

"I cannot give you an exact time frame, but we have, at minimum, a decade before the entity arrives."

Now for the question of the century. Brick steeled himself for an answer he could not come close to predicting.

"Why was I born, and what did you do to me?"

"I used the abilities I gained from the organism and manipulated your DNA to fashion a human version of the extraterrestrial entity. Or as close to it as I could get. The creature has limited control of the Field but nowhere near as strong as your current abilities or what they will become in the future."

"Why?" Brick felt no better upon hearing confirmation of what he'd already deduced. Being called a freak most of his life did nothing to prepare him for the reality of being an actual freak of nature.

"Because, though sentient, it isn't sapient. It is driven only by an instinct to expand its race. Controlling the Field is as natural to it as breathing is to us, but that is its only advantage. In terms of strength and adaptability, you have the edge, Mason."

As he absorbed the information, Brick's mind threatened to overload. There had been too much going on in too short a time, and his brain wanted to shut down.

Despite the accelerated healing, or perhaps because of it, he was fell back, exhausted again. He surmised that since he didn't have anything akin to a mana pool or a patron deity, the restorative energy had to come directly from him. A soft voice cut through the haze, enveloping him. A flicker of movement at his side failed to capture his attention, but on some level, it did register.

"Brick." Tish caressed his arm. "Stay with me. Whatever the future holds, we'll conquer it together."

When had she moved away from Ruby? How long had he been out of it? After refocusing his eyes, he saw Ruby standing at the bed's end.

"The two of you have done better and have come much farther than I could have ever imagined in so short a time. I'm proud of you both."

"Fuck you, Ruby. You almost killed my boyfriend!" Tish's tone spoke of dangerous consequences.

"The moot point is 'almost,' yes?" Ruby took a step back and raised her palm in supplication. Fire flashed in Tish's irises as she lifted the blade she'd held to the older woman's throat.

"I'm leaving. Look, there will be times ahead when we will be at odds, but trust me when I say we are working towards the same goal. The two of you armed with the Espada Encantada may be the only ones who can make the difference between the beings on this planet surviving in their original forms or mutating and being devoured. The being that birthed us is coming to collect, and we must be prepared. You must discover the secrets of the sword, Mas... I mean Brick."

"What chance do we have, Ruby?"

"Have you read the Bhagavad Gita?"

"Yes," Brick had a hard time keeping his eyes open. He was so tired. He wondered where Mara was and how she was doing. Tish was on the bed with him, now. She was so soft. He paused for a moment, waiting for Bricktay's backlash. When nothing seemed forthcoming, he refocused on Ruby.

"Don't be like Prince Arjuna. Don't make a god convince you to do your duty."

"What duty?"

Prince Arjuna balked at war against those who were family and friends, but if he refused, everything his predecessors had done to improve the lives of their people would have been destroyed. Krishna morphed into his true form as the god Vishnu to convince Prince Arjuna to do his duty and go to war for the good of all.

"You and your girl may face the same decision, and the fate of everyone on Earth may rest in your hands. When you come down to it, humans belong to this planet, and that is all that matters over love, life, and family. You may have rebuked the

Fates for now, but they have long memories. When the time comes, you must be willing to make whatever sacrifice is necessary to save Earth and her people. I can only hope that this new energy you've added can give you an edge in the coming war."

Ruby departed in a flash of golden light. Brick passed out.

◆ ◆ ◆

The next time he woke up, Mara, looking much worse for wear as the green hospital gown hung from one shoulder, grasped his hand and stared at him.

"Hey, sis!" Brick mumbled.

"It's about time!" She pounced on him, wrapping him in a one-armed bear hug.

He groaned in a combination of pain and joy.

"Sis." Brick managed to grunt. "I'm happy to see you too, but I can't breathe, you frigging hag. Get your boobs off me and pull up your gown."

"Oh, sorry, I didn't even think. You okay, Lil punk-ass negro?"

"Yeah, I'll live." Brick swallowed hard. His throat was dry, "About that, how long?"

"Three days, lazy butt." She paused and handed him the cup of ice chips next to his bed. "I guess altering space-time is hard stuff, huh? Man, Tish is gonna be pissed. I forced her to shower and grab a bite to eat half an hour ago. She was getting a bit ripe if you know what I mean."

"Hand me my clothes, please." Brick sat up, and the pain rattled him.

"Before I do, you need to know something."

"Don't preach, sis. I hurt too much."

"Brick, that woman loves you. I mean, really, really loves you.

I've never seen anyone do the things she did to find you, lil bro. We found Zindriya's fortress because of her. When we were ambushed in Wyoming, she slaughtered over a hundred soldiers so she could get back to you. She put my death toll to shame. She deserves a chance before you go all noble on her. She's the strongest person I know, and she's family. Think about it, okay?"

Tish, wearing jeans and one of his Star Wars shirts, walked into the room carrying a book but tossed it on the bed and flew to his side.

"Brick! You're awake! Thank God, I was so worried!"

"Me too. Somebody hand me my clothes. I need to get outta here." Brick looked at the book, noticing it was the Mahabharata, the longest epic ever written, and within it was the Bhagavad Gita.

"Uh-uh. You're not going anywhere until the Doc releases you." Tish's voice brooked no argument.

Mara stood up to leave, refusing to get sucked into a lover's spat in a hospital. She exited the room and closed the door behind her.

"So, you plan on going all noble bastard on me?"

"I just don't know, Tish."

"Don't I get a say? I mean, I am involved and all. And the mind-sharing thing? We know everything about each other, and I'm still here."

"The things I did... how can you still love me?"

"You mean, how can you love yourself? As Mom once said, 'the issue doesn't lie with us.'"

"I know," Brick said, looking down at his hands folded in his lap on top of the scratchy, white hospital blanket.

"Then stay. After what we've shared, neither of us has any doubts about our feelings for each other. You know how rare that is?"

Tish reached into her bag on the floor at the foot of the bed. She pulled out fresh clothes and tossed them to Brick, who stumbled his way out of bed on trembling legs. While he dressed, Tish told him their invention for the science project had gone global. She sold the manufacturing rights, though they still owned the patent and the rights to all upgrades.

They had enough money for several lifetimes, and the residual income would add to it. And that wasn't counting the Zero-Point generator he'd invented. They had taken down the most dangerous person on the planet together, and if Ruby was right, they would save the world together someday.

He understood that she'd have to work through his escapades with Zindriya, but she was willing because he'd done it to get back to her. They both had performed vile acts that had changed them forever. Throwing their relationship away would make all their sacrifices meaningless. In her eyes, the only way they would ever get through it, the only way to justify their sins, was to stay together.

"Otherwise, the bitch wins from the grave. We can get through this if we just stay together, Brick. I told you before. I won't leave your side. I'm willing to tough this out."

He gazed into Tish's eyes. They were strong and steady, though unshed tears glistened yet. How could he think of leaving this woman? Hadn't he screamed and yelled at all those movie heroes who left their love interests all alone to deal with the trail of destruction they left in their wake? How fair was that? They took off to handle or hide their own emotions. They left the women behind, to clean up the mess, deal with their own issues, and fend for themselves.

Despite all they had to do, the women served as the glue holding everything and everyone together. Women were the true heroes, while the supposed protagonists were all cowards in his book, and while he was a lot of things, Brick was no gutless wonder. He was an idiot even to consider leaving her, not that she'd let him. It was time for him to follow his heart.

"I'm not gonna beg, Brick, but you made a deal, and I'm calling you on it." Tears lingered in her eyes, held at bay by her unwavering will.

"I suppose you'll just Banshee me back anyway."

"Got it in one, math boy. We made a deal, and I damn well earned those two days."

"That you did," He said, nodding his head and pressing his lips into a straight line.

"So?" She asked, crossing her arms.

Brick sighed. "What if you can't stand the sight of me after two days?"

"Then we try two more, then two after that, and so on until you can stand the sight of yourself again. The only person who can ever drive me away is you. I'm not the problem, but I can be the solution if you let me. So, do we have a deal?"

Everything that happened while he was in Zindriya's clutches weighed on him. He would never be the same. The darkness he'd cultivated to survive his ordeal would remain within. The way he used the Shadow Core and the Field to bend the universe to his will scared the crap out of him. Though he'd done it to save Mara, in that moment, he knew power had corrupted him.

Still, despite the dark seed evolving into a shard and now a Core, it remained under his control. With Tish's added strength and the Espada Encantada, it would stay that way. She was his anchor. Her fortitude would prevent him from transforming into a monster.

Why choose a lonely sunset when the whole Multiverse and more waited for him in her heart? A half-smile crept across his face. He still wasn't sure they would work, but fighting for a life with Tish, no matter how difficult, would be light years better than just existing without her.

Brick gazed into those warm brown eyes and admired the cute crinkle that formed atop the bridge of her nose. Hope blossomed in his chest and spread through him as she threaded her fingers through his. Who was he kidding?

At last, Brick shrugged off the last vestige of his father's ironclad rule. He smiled and answered Tish.

"Deal."

They sealed the deal.

AFTERWORD

Thanks for reading my work. I hope you enjoyed the tale and are looking forward to the next book in the Shadow Core Saga.

If you'd like to view my other works and sign up for my mailing list, check out my website at:

https://authorcliftonbrown.com/

You can also follow me on my FB page:
https://www.facebook.com/profile.php?id=61558564643773

It would be awesome if you could leave
a review on Amazon here:
https://www.amazon.com/dp/B0DJF3YJ1R/

Unfortunately, my publisher, Wicked Shadow Press is closing its doors. Unless I find another, I'll be submitting my future books as an Indy. While I was excited when they accepted my novel, I'm equally excited at the future. Now that I know for sure there are those that value my work, I'll keep at it.

My next book will be a nonfiction focusing on the non-Eqyptian African Gods. After that, I'll publish a collection of the short stories Wicked Shadow Press offered in their Anthologies. By then, I'll have finished book 2 of the Shadow Core Saga.

I have three complete manuscripts that I have to dredge up from the ethereal heap of my computer storage. All of them need complete re-writes during my next editing phase, so they will take a while. Still, stay tuned. I'm just getting started.

ABOUT THE AUTHOR

Clifton Brown

Clifton Brown is an author who draws deeply from his experiences in the U.S. Navy, weaving them into dark, evocative stories that explore the boundaries between light and shadow. With ten published short stories and a debut novel, Clifton has found writing to be a powerful way to navigate his past, honoring his service while exploring the catharsis of storytelling. His fiction often deals with the struggle for hope amid darkness, guiding characters through love and loss in unpredictable ways. As he crafts tales of demons, extraterrestrial forces, and the supernatural, Clifton brings to life flawed, yet resilient characters, pushing them toward growth even when the path is painful. His stories delve into dark fantasy, horror, and romance, creating a space where the mysterious and the mundane collide. Clifton's latest works include his debut novel, In The Ghost's Shadow, a dark fantasy romance about a young man with extraordinary abilities fighting alongside his love to protect Earth from a powerful, enigmatic threat. He is also the author of short stories like Dark Pink Carnations, The Z-Word, and All Hallows Snipe Hunt, each blending elements of the uncanny with human struggle and desire. These works, published by Wicked Shadow Press, continue to showcase his penchant for dark fiction—stories where heroes must confront monstrous forces, both within and without, to emerge into whatever light they can find. With an affinity for the weird and the wondrous, Clifton enjoys creating worlds where danger is ever-present, but love and resilience still shine through, however unexpectedly.

Made in United States
Troutdale, OR
12/26/2024